HIGH PRAISE FOR RAY GARTON!

"*Live Girls* is gripping, original, and sly. I finished it in one bite."

—Dean Koontz

"The most nightmarish vampire story I have ever read."
—Ramsey Campbell on *Live Girls*

"It's scary, it's involving, and it's also mature and thoughtful."
—Stephen King on *Dark Channel*

"Garton never fails to go for the throat!"
—Richard Laymon, Author of *Cuts*

"Garton has a flair for taking veteran horror themes and twisting them to evocative or entertaining effect."
—*Publishers Weekly*

"Ray Garton has consistently created some of the best horror ever set to print."
—*Cemetery Dance*

"Ray Garton writes horror fiction at its most frightening best."
—*Midwest Book Review*

"Garton is, simply put, one of the masters."
—James Moore, Author of *Blood Red*

"A real storyteller."
—S⋯⋯⋯⋯⋯⋯⋯⋯⋯⋯⋯⋯⋯ne

D0681030

PRAISE FOR *RAVENOUS*:

"*Ravenous* is Ray Garton's most disturbing, affecting, and ferocious novel since *Crucifax Autumn*—which is to say, he's going to cost you a lot of sleep with this one. There are images and sequences in this book that only a frontal lobotomy will make you forget."

—Gary A. Braunbeck, Bram Stoker
Award–winning Author of *Mr. Hands*

"Witty, warped, and steeped in blood, this novel of hungry horror tumbles toward a delicious finale that will only leave you wanting to read more and more of Garton's ferocious fiction."

—Douglas E. Winter, Author of *Run*

"*Ravenous* grabs you by the throat in Chapter 1 and never lets go. Ray Garton, master frightener, is at his best in this one. Read it alone at your peril."

—Gary Brandner, Author of *The Howling*

"Ray Garton is one of the true kings of old school horror. *Ravenous* is fierce, fearsome, blood-soaked fare, a werewolf novel that's bound to snap its jaws together on your throat."

—Tom Piccirilli, Author of *The Midnight Road*

NOTHING HUMAN

Hurley heard the door push open and turned to see George come out of the morgue in a long white smock stained in blood. He wiped his hands on a strip of paper towel as he smiled down at Hurley.

"Well, that's done," George said.

Hurley stood. "So, what's the story?"

"It's a *strange* story, Sheriff," George said. "Very strange."

"Well, let's hear it."

"From what I found, Sheriff, you shouldn't be looking for a man. You should be looking for an animal."

"An *animal*?"

George took in a deep breath as he nodded. With the wadded paper towel in his right hand, he put his fists on his hips, elbows out at his sides. "Your deputy was partially *eaten*, Sheriff. His insides and his throat were torn by fangs, and his intestines and other organs were partially eaten. By something."

Other *Leisure* books by Ray Garton:

NIGHT LIFE
LIVE GIRLS
THE LOVELIEST DEAD

RAY GARTON

RAVENOUS

LEISURE BOOKS NEW YORK CITY

A LEISURE BOOK®

April 2008

Published by

Dorchester Publishing Co., Inc.
200 Madison Avenue
New York, NY 10016

ISBN 10: 0-8439-5820-0
ISBN 13: 978-0-8439-5820-1

Printed in the United States of America.

10 9 8 7 6 5 4 3

Visit us on the web at www.dorchesterpub.com.

This book is for
my friend, Dr. Evan K. Reasor
who saved my life
and for
my wife, Dawn
who is my life.

ACKNOWLEDGMENTS

I would like to extend my sincere gratitude to the follow-ing, who aided in the writing of this novel: My wife Dawn, who makes my work possible, and who, for more than eight years, was my rock and carried on with everything when I could not—I will spend the rest of my life saying thank you, and it still won't be enough; Scott Sandin, my best friend and always my first editor, whose never end-ing friendship, support, and contributions to my work are invaluable; Brian Hodges, dearest and oldest of friends, whose quiet strength and support I cherish; Derek San-din, a fountain of knowledge and information, and a great guy; Steven Spruill, a brilliant writer, and my long-lost brother with whom I grew up in the smothering, frighten-ing world of Sister White and silent Friday nights—but in different places and times; my parents Ray and Pat Gar-ton, whose love and support mean everything; the fun and fabulous Sarah Wood, a priceless friend; Randy Adams, whom I've known longer than anyone outside my family, and with whom I've had countless long, enjoyable, laugh-filled telephone conversations; Barbara Youngblood, who's come to mean so much to me; Jen Orosel, Bill Lindblad,

Tom Piccirilli, Dave Yeske, Cathy Kortzeborn, Teresa Anderson, Stephanie Terrazas, the great Peter Straub, the 2006 World Horror Convention, the people at the Red Light District message board, and everyone I may be missing (please forgive me) whose support, patience, and friendship helped get me through the last several years; my dear, late friends, Paul Meredith and Francis Feighan, whom I think of and miss every day; Steve Ericsson, a devoted lover of the genre; James Newman, a talented writer and a good guy; the televised school where I received the beginning of my horror education, and where I saw my first werewolf—*Creature Features* on KTVU Channel 2, gone now but far from forgotten, first hosted by Bob Wilkins, the man with the cigar, then by John Stanley, the master of horror films; my agent Richard Curtis, a great man from whom I've learned so much; my wonderful editor at Leisure, Don D'Auria, whose love and respect for the genre has done so much for all of us who share it; most of all, I would like to thank my precious readers, who keep my fingers typing.

Los Angeles—eighteen months ago

It was a dump on Western Boulevard called the Vanguard Hotel. Daniel Fargo could tell by the entrance that it was barely a notch above a Depression-era flophouse. He pushed through the single-door entrance—a brown door with a porthole—and stepped inside.

Everything was a shitty brown and tan. It was as if the walls of the hotel's lobby had been painted with depression and despair themselves. Two tones of misery. Numerous tiles were missing from the tan floor. Fargo decided that spending much time at all in the lobby would put one in need of a Prozac. The place smelled of Lysol—no attempt was made to disguise it with a pine scent; it was plain old stinging Lysol, and the lobby reeked of it.

Ahead and to the right was an open area with a large kidney-shaped table in the center. There were magazines and paperbacks on the table. Along the walls were couches and chairs, none of which matched, a couple of lamp tables, a coffee table with more magazines. At this end of the room stood an old television set with a pair of aluminum-foil-wrapped rabbit ears on top. The furniture had been arranged so that no matter where you were seated, you were pointed at the television.

To the left was a cage with a counter across the bottom of the front, and on the counter, an open registry book. Fargo went to the counter and looked into the cage.

An enormously fat man sat leaning back in a chair, watching a game show on his cell phone, and reading a newspaper. He took up a lot of room in his small, cluttered cubicle—he was so big, he made the space seem much smaller than it actually was. He wore a filthy, once-white T-shirt that was too small for him and clung to his rolls like a second skin. The bottom of his enormous belly, a half-moon of white, pasty flesh, stuck out from under the bottom of the shirt. His breasts rested in opposite directions and settled against his massive, cottage-cheesy upper arms as he leaned back. His skin resembled mashed potatoes, and his dark curly hair looked like it had not been washed in ages. Beneath his chin was a bulge of fat so large, it looked like a growth—it was simply excess fat around his face. A few stray hairs grew here and there on the otherwise hairless bulge beneath his face. It went from earlobe to earlobe. It was impossible to tell his age. He did not look up when Fargo approached the counter.

"Excuse me," Fargo said.

The man didn't do or say anything for a long moment. "I *said, excuse* me."

The man took in a deep breath, then let it out in a long, put-upon sigh as he lowered the newspaper, closed it, and set it aside. The chair he was sitting on had squeaky wheels, and he scooted forward with difficulty, until he was at the counter. He had to tilt his head back to see Fargo's face.

Fargo was a tall man—six feet, four inches—and had a striking face, a face that shocked people, made them look twice, then look away. It was covered with horrible scars. His nose was crooked, having been broken. He had a jutting chin, with high cheekbones beneath scarred flesh, cheekbones that rose up beneath piercing violet eyes that leaped out from his face. He had a well-trimmed mustache and shaggy hair that fell from beneath his charcoal fedora. Strands of shimmering steel were strung all through his black hair, which he did nothing to conceal. He wore a long, heavy black coat over a black suit, with black leather boots. The shadow of his fedora fell over his eyes, but it did not conceal them.

"You wanna room?" the man said. Something white had gathered in the corners of his mouth.

"I do not," Fargo said. "You have a man staying here named Arnold Lutz. What room is he in?"

"Look, man, I don't know if there's anybody here by that name. This look like the kinda place where people use their real names, huh?"

Ignoring him, Fargo spun the registry around and ran his finger down the list of names. Arnold Lutz was not listed, but Fargo recognized his handwriting. Lutz had written the name "Burl Ives" instead of his real name, but there was no mistaking that handwriting. Back at Yale, Fargo had been an English professor, and he'd had some students with lazy, almost childish handwriting like Lutz's, the kind of handwriting that Fargo believed revealed an inner laziness, a certain lack of pride in oneself, and usually a lack of curiosity and imagination.

"Burl Ives," Fargo said, pointing at the name in the book. He turned it around so the fat man could see it. "He came here—" He looked at the upside-down book, found the date and time. "—last night. Apparently with two other men—Hoss Cartwright and Rod Serling."

"Them names're fake," the man said.

"You think?"

Something bubbled up from inside the morbidly obese man. Fargo realized it was a single laugh. "Yeah, I reckanize all them names."

"What room is Ives in?"

A lazy smile rested on the man's wet lips.

"Tell me now," Fargo said, leaning close to the cage, "or I will reach through this opening, pluck your eyeball from its socket, and stick it into your mouth before you have time to scream in pain."

The fat man rolled his eyes, and that lazy smile grew a little at first. Then his rolling eyes found Fargo, and their gazes locked together. The smile fell away slowly when the fat man got a good look at Fargo's piercing eyes. They were eyes weary from seeing things that no one should ever have to see, but there was a glow of rage in them as well. The fat man looked at Fargo's hands on the counter, just on the other side of the long opening about eight inches high. They were big, strong hands with long fingers and tiny tufts of black hair growing above the two rows of knobby knuckles. The fat man looked up at Fargo's eyes again, and in that clear, gripping gaze, he saw that the man would do what he threatened to do—looking into those eyes, he could imagine the big man reaching through that opening and plucking out his eyeball.

The fat man reached beneath the counter and produced a clipboard. He ran his finger down the clipboard, stopped, then said, "Room 204."

"Thank you."

Fargo turned away from the counter and his coat whipped around his legs.

"Elevator's broken," the fat man said as Fargo walked briskly away.

The stairs were next to the elevator. Fargo yanked the door open and headed up to the second floor. The stairwell was dark and filthy and smelled of urine and vomit and semen. The gritty floor crunched under his black boots.

The second floor corridor was narrow, dark, and gloomy—lots of brown, and only pale, yellowish lights

on the ceiling. Running down the center of the hardwood floor was a hideous carpet runner with a once-
colorful jungle pattern. Now the carpet was dark with
grime down the center, littered with cigarette butts, burn
in places, worn to the threads in others.

Fargo went straight to room 204. He stood there a moment, staring at the doorknob and listening.

The entire hotel was strangely silent—no voices, no
music, no television or radio, nothing. This room was no
different.

He put his right hand on the doorknob and tried it. It
would not turn. Fargo straightened his back and reached
under his suit coat, and wrapped his right hand around
the grip of his Desert Eagle .50 caliber semiautomatic. He
removed the gun from the shoulder holster, stepped
back, and aimed the gun at the door. He looked left, then
right. There was no one else in the corridor. He moved
forward and was about to knock on the door when he
heard a door open to his right. He turned his head and
looked down the corridor.

A short, round man in shabby clothes stepped out of
his room, carrying a worn old suitcase that had been
patched in places. He turned, reached in to pull the door
closed; then he saw Fargo. The man froze a moment,
then dropped his arm at his side, stiffened his back, and
gawked at Fargo with a slack jaw. He turned his head
from side to side, then said, "I'm not surprised. He kept
me up *all night*, that son of a bitch. Know what they
started doin' at one point? *Howlin'!* Like a buncha fuckin'
animals. Then they took it outside, heard 'em howlin' out
there. Like a buncha fuckin' animals." Then he turned
and headed down the hall to the stairs.

Fargo turned back to the paint-peeling door in front of
him. He reached out his left hand and rapped his knuckles against the wood, then stepped back and held the
gun in his right hand, which he rested in the palm of his

left. The big gun was heavy, black, and mean looking, and Fargo thought he would not like to open his door to find himself staring into that ominous bore, into that black tunnel of death. He did not plan to give Arnold Lutz the chance to register any fear when he saw the gun.

He knocked again.

"Who is it?" a thick, groggy voice called.

"Special delivery."

"Special . . . for *who*?"

For whom, Fargo thought irritably.

"I don't know who it's for, pal, I'm just delivering it to this room."

He waited.

There were thudding footsteps on the other side of the door. A lock clicked, another snapped. He pulled the door open and stared openmouthed at the gun, but—

—he was not Arnold Lutz.

Fargo lowered the gun. His mouth hung open, too.

The heavy, bald man standing in the door in blue sweatpants and a blue sweatshirt said three words— "What the *fuck*?"—but as he said them, his voice thickened more and more with each syllable, and his eyes suddenly shimmered a bright silver, and two sharp fangs jutted up from behind his lower lip like miniature tusks.

Fargo did not hesitate, because he had no time to hesitate. He lifted the gun and aimed at the man's chest and squeezed the trigger.

The gun's explosion of sound slammed against the walls of the corridor.

There was a blossom of red on his chest, and a much bigger splash of it behind him, caused by the bullet's gory exit.

The man was knocked over. He fell on his back on the floor and lay there for a moment. Then he laughed as he sat up. He was smiling, but it was barely recognizable as a smile because of the crackling, popping changes in his face.

The smile disappeared.

A hairy hand went to the man's chest. Then he made a horrible retching sound as his eyes widened with horrified realization. Red blisters began to rise all over his face. He screamed in pain as he fell over on his side and curled into the fetal position. His scream was something other than a scream, though, because of the changes in his voice. The blisters popped and fluid ran from them as more blisters rose in their place. He opened his mouth and vomited blood.

He was dying a horrible death.

With one of them out of commission, Fargo hurried into the room to find the other two, especially Arnold Lutz. It was a dark, dingy room with a bed against the wall to the left, a lamp shining beside it, a sink straight ahead, and an open door to the right. Fargo assumed that would lead to a bathroom, but instead, it led into the next hotel room, 206.

He was tackled from the right and taken down, but he held tightly to the gun. As he scrambled to get up, all he saw were claws and fangs. He was clawed badly in the face and on the throat again and again, then head-butted in the solar plexus, which knocked the wind from him and sent him falling over onto his back.

There was a moment of utter silence and calm, like being in the eye of a hurricane. Fargo was half-blinded by the blood that ran into his eyes. Two things happened at once—first, the creature dove into the air, up and over Fargo, about to land on him, and second, Fargo remembered he was holding the gun.

The dark figure seemed suspended in midair for just an instant, and Fargo took advantage of it. He lifted the gun, elbow locked, and fired.

The bullet went into the creature's flat belly.

Then the creature landed on top of Fargo.

During the time it took for the creature to begin to die, it tore and bit at Fargo. Its claws slashed across his face and he lost the sight in his right eye as searing pain exploded in his eye socket. He did not know it, but his right eye dangled out of its socket on his scarred cheek.

Sharp claws sunk into the right side of his neck, into his rib cage, then, worst of all, it closed its jaws high up on Fargo's right thigh, in the area of the hip. The teeth ground into him mercilessly and Fargo cried out in pain. The creature tore a large chunk of flesh and muscle from Fargo's hip and he felt it rip away, and the pain was overwhelming.

Fargo passed out.

While he was unconscious, the creature used its last moments to further maul him. But it did not have long . . . not long at all. . . .

1

ATTACK

Tuesday

Emily Crane had lost another four pounds, bringing her total weight loss to sixteen pounds, and she felt good about it. Of course, she still had a long way to go—her goal was to lose eighty-five pounds—but she tried not to think that way. It was a day-to-day process, a one-day-at-a-time endeavor. As soon as she started thinking about how much she had left to lose, it became overwhelming and she became discouraged, and when she became discouraged, she wanted to eat.

She was returning home from her T.O.P.S. meeting. T.O.P.S.—Take Off Pounds Sensibly—was a weight loss support group she met with every Tuesday night. On that particular Tuesday night, she had left the meeting early, right after the weigh-in, because she had a splitting headache. All she wanted to do was go home, take some aspirin, and sink into a hot bubble bath.

That was not entirely true; that was not really *all* she wanted to do. What Emily *really* wanted to do was stop at the Carl's Jr. on the way home and get a Double Western Bacon Cheeseburger.

T.O.P.S. met in the neighboring town of Seaside, and

Emily lived sixteen miles south in Big Rock. It was an inconvenience to drive over to Seaside every Tuesday, but it was worth it to her. She needed desperately to lose weight, and she could not do it on her own. She needed the kind of support she couldn't get from anyone but other women struggling with their weight. Hugh tried to help, but she knew his heart was not in it. Hugh's heart was not in much of anything lately—that was why she wanted so badly to lose a total of eighty-five pounds.

They had not made love in over a year—close to a year and a half now. It made Emily sad to think about it, made a knot form in her chest, a soggy, thick knot, and her throat burned with gathering tears. They used to have so much fun together in bed. They'd been married for twelve years, and for most of those years everything had been perfect, especially in the bedroom. But three kids and a lot of afternoon snacking later, Emily had packed on the pounds, and the incidents of lovemaking had grown further and further apart. She gave Hugh credit for one thing—not once had he ever mentioned her weight gain. He did not criticize her for it, or make snide remarks about it, not even when they fought. Emily knew other women at T.O.P.S. whose husbands were cruel about their weight, husbands who publicly ridiculed their wives, humiliating them and hurting them so badly that they only wanted to eat more—a vicious circle. But not Hugh. Instead, he'd simply become less and less affectionate. Hugs and kisses became more scarce, and it had been a long time since he'd playfully grabbed her ass or tickled her or squeezed her breasts. She missed those little things, and she was determined to get them back.

Overall, it had been a good marriage, even though much of the life had gone out of it in recent years, mostly due to her laziness and her weight gain. She spent her days at home with Jeannie, their youngest, at three. Donald, six, and Annie, eight, got home from school in the afternoon.

Emily spent most of that time on the couch, eating while she watched old movies on television, and while Jeannie puttered and played around the room with her. There were days when she did not lift a finger to do any housework, and as a result, her once immaculate home looked dusty, cluttered, and a little *too* lived-in. Sometimes, Emily missed the early years of their marriage, when it had been just the two of them, herself and Hugh. Back when she was still a slender one hundred and nine pounds. She'd had a great body back then: petite and compact; full chestnut hair that cascaded past her shoulders; clear, large brown eyes. Now her eyes seemed to have shrunk—her round fleshy cheeks had given them a piggy look that she hated. She had no illusions; she knew she would never be that svelte one hundred and nine again. But she planned to slim down to some semblance of her former self, for Hugh if for no other reason. Of course, she sometimes wondered what she would do if she met her weight-loss goal, and Hugh still had no interest in her. Had he fallen out of love with her? He was still considerate and treated her well—he left little notes for her on the fridge, and every once in awhile, he brought her flowers for no reason at all. Emily took comfort in that, and clung to the hope that, once she'd slimmed down, things would go back to normal and they would have a sex life again.

Clouds obscured the moon, and the night was dark and misty. It had been raining since Christmas—about three weeks straight—with no end in sight. Emily drove along Seaside Trail, a two-lane road flanked by lush woods on both sides. Fat-trunked redwoods towered overhead, and to her right, it was possible to catch glimpses of the ocean during the day in the occasional gaps in the strip of woods. Mixed in with the occasional patches of towering redwoods were scattered Douglas firs, bay laurels, and a few spruce trees along the edge of the road. Below them, thick green ferns and other foliage carpeted the mossy woods. But none of that was visible in the dark of the misty night—it was, instead, sensed. She could feel the thick woods around her.

Emily reached up and rubbed her right temple with two stiff fingers, traced small circles over it, pushing hard. The headache was only on the right side of her head, behind her eye.

She was in the middle of a yawn when a *ding* from the dashboard made her look down at the lights. The "check engine" light was blinking.

The engine died.

Her power steering died with it, and she had to struggle with the wheel to pull her metallic green Volkswagen Jetta onto the shoulder to the right. Gravel crunched under her tires as she brought the car to a stop.

"Shit," she said.

She turned the key in the ignition to start the car again, but nothing happened—the engine did not make a sound.

"Oh, *shit*," she said, her voice higher, more shrill. On the verge of tears, she took in a deep breath to steady herself, let it out slowly. She pounded a fist on the steering wheel once, then reached over to the passenger seat for her purse. She reached up and turned on the light above the rearview mirror, then unzipped her purse and plunged her hand in, groped around for a moment, then found her cell phone. She flipped it open, pushed the button with her thumb to turn it on, then put it to her ear. The phone beeped three times, and she heard no dial tone.

"Oh, no!" she shouted.

The cell phone's battery was dead.

"I *knew* that, dammit!" she said. She'd been meaning to recharge the phone, but she used it so seldom that it had slipped her mind. With a lugubrious sigh, she threw the phone into her purse, then sat there for a long moment, staring out the windshield at the beams of her headlights, which melted into the misty, murky darkness up ahead. She killed the lights.

A car drove by going the same direction she'd been going, and a couple of minutes later, another came the opposite way. She turned on her emergency blinkers.

Tears stung Emily's eyes. She sniffled, but tried to hold back the crying. She took in a deep breath and said, "I'm screwed."

She was getting out of the car when she heard it, and it made her freeze where she stood, in the open door of the car, made gooseflesh crawl over her shoulders. It had come from the woods to her right and had been very distinct—a howl. She frowned. It had to be a dog, that was the only explanation—but it had not sounded like the howl of a dog. Not really. Not at *all*. It was a full sound, but piercing, a resonant cry. A chill trickled down her back like ice water.

Emily got the long, heavy Maglite from the backseat. She leaned in, popped the hood, then closed the door. She went to the front of the car and shone the light onto the engine. Gravel on the shoulder crunched beneath her feet, and the Jetta's emergency lights blinked on and off with a soft clicking sound.

She laughed coldly and muttered, "What am I doing?" She knew nothing about cars and had absolutely no idea what might be wrong with the Jetta. Even Hugh's knowledge of cars was limited. They relied on Phil at the Volkswagen dealership in Eureka when something went wrong with the Jetta.

Facing the front of the car, Emily pulled her denim jacket together in front—it was shudderingly cold.

Something moved in the bushes to her left, the same side from which the frightening howl had come, and she took a step back from the car and turned the flashlight on the woods. The bright beam pierced the darkness and passed over some heavy ferns and thick tree trunks. The night smelled of the sea, and, in the overwhelming silence, she could hear the whisper of the surf beyond the strip of woods.

As she lowered the light, he rushed out of the woods, tattered clothes dangling all around him, a shadow that quickly took on features—wide silver eyes that weren't right, somehow, they were *wrong*—

No, that can't be, she thought.

—and then he was on her.

Emily shifted into a murky, dreamlike state as he grabbed her arms and his fingernails dug deeply into her flesh, piercing her denim jacket and her blouse and her skin. He reeked of filth and the stench of him clogged Emily's nostrils.

He spun around, dragging her with him, and threw her into the ditch. She landed on her side and rolled halfway up the ditch's other side. Pain exploded in her ribs as she landed on a large rock. She fell still in a puddle and cold water shocked her through her clothes. She dropped the flashlight, which sent its beam this way and that as it rolled back and forth in the ditch's water. For a moment, he was gone—

—then he was on her again, and she heard him growl as he tore at her clothing, ripping it loudly. She managed to scream as cold air touched the bare, wet parts of her body exposed by her attacker. Emily kicked her legs and flailed her arms, but when she tried to scream again, it caught in her suddenly dry throat like ground glass and remained lodged there.

He continued to make low growling sounds in his throat, and something warm and wet spattered her face. It was spittle—he was slobbering on her as he growled, a sound punctuated by the *clack-clack-clack* of his jaws snapping shut repeatedly.

The flashlight, in its final rolls back and forth just above her head in the ditch, passed its beam over his face, giving her a glimpse, just a glimpse, but it was more than she needed—his face would haunt her dreams for the rest of her life. The face simply was not . . . right. It was wrong in some way she could not yet define, in some way that her brain refused to process.

Long stringy dark hair, with silver eyes—they were eyes that did not look human, like the rest of his long face.

That was it—his face was too long, too narrow, somehow misshapen.

More ripping as her clothes were torn from her body. Then she felt his fingers under her panties, and he tore through the panties with his sharp black claws, ripped them off of her and touched her most private place.

He's going to rape me! she thought.

And then she screamed, a long ragged scream that was swallowed up by the night's silence, a silence that towered over them like some invisible dome, holding her scream down, keeping it from reverberating or carrying, smothering it. She tried to close her legs, but he was already between them.

She was dry and it hurt, but he was soon lubricated by his own fluids, and she continued to scream and fight as he pounded into her again and again.

He panted furiously and continued to slobber on her, releasing a low growl each time he exhaled.

He laughed then as he thrust into her harder, a deep, throaty laugh, nails scratching her and drawing blood. His long hair fell down over her face. His smell enveloped her like a filthy, oily blanket. Something happened to his throaty laughter—it became deeper, rougher.

Emily's hands began to claw the ground, searching desperately for a weapon, for something, anything she might use to stop him, to get him off her.

The thing on top of her screamed. It was a sickening sound, a sound that made her wish she were unconscious so she did not have to hear it. The ragged scream collapsed into a howl.

The howl . . . the one she'd heard earlier . . .

Her right hand found something on the ground beside her. It was hard and cold, made of metal. She closed her hand on it and swung her arm back, then plunged it forward. She drove the metal object home hard, and something crunched beneath it.

The long howl stopped.

Her rapist stopped moving.

He collapsed on her heavily, suddenly still and silent, not even breathing. He was so heavy on top of her, she found it difficult to breathe. But he had stopped. He was still inside her, but he had stopped slamming into her.

Is he dead? she wondered. *What did I do to him?*

She remained there for an endless time, unable to move at first. Then, when she did move, her movements hurt, as if her entire body were raw. Emily tried to crawl backward, out from under him. When that did not work, she put her hands on his shoulders and pushed. She threw her whole body into it, all her weight, and heaved him off her to her left.

When his body hit the ground beside her, it expelled a long, gurgling breath, its final sound.

Then she crawled backward, away from him, until she reached the flashlight. She rolled over and closed her right hand on the flashlight as she struggled to her feet. Her torn clothes dangled from her in wet tatters, and dirt and gravel clung to her exposed skin. She turned around and shone the beam down on him.

The long, dark hair looked unwashed and matted. Dark stubble grew all around his gaping mouth, covering the lower half of his face. He was a man of medium height, pale, arms spread at his sides. His filthy clothes were torn and tattered into strips. His right eye was no longer silver, and there was no longer anything wrong with it. It was open wide, like his mouth, a blue eye, perfectly normal. There was, however, something wrong with his left eye— something protruded from it. She stepped toward him, bent down, and turned the light on it.

It had a fat black handle, caked with damp earth. Emily reached out, closed her hand on it—the black handle was plastic. She pulled on it, not very hard at first, and it did not come out. She put a little more strength into it, and it came out with a wet sound. It lifted his head off the ground for a moment, then his head flopped back down as it was released.

It was a long rusty corkscrew—with the man's left eyeball impaled on the end, something long and wet and jiggly dangling from the back of it.

Emily gasped and dropped the corkscrew as she stumbled backward. Her right heel hit something—a rock embedded in the ground, maybe—and she fell backward, flailing her arms for balance, trying to come out of the fall.

The back of her head struck the edge of the paved road hard, and blackness overcame her.

Hugh Crane closed his hands on Vanessa Peterman's round breasts and his thumbs flicked over her nipples, which stood rigid beneath them. Vanessa straddled his lap in the backseat of her white Chrysler 300 with darkly-tinted windows, which was parked in his driveway. She bounced up and down on him.

The children were planted in front of the television in the living room, enraptured by the Cartoon Network, or the Disney Channel, or Nickelodeon, or whatever it was they'd been watching when he'd left them there. They were avid television watchers, and he knew they would stay right where they were, their attention focused on the screen, until he called them away.

Vanessa made high-pitched sounds behind tightly

closed lips, and her hands closed on his chest, her fingernails clawing him through the cotton of his unbuttoned shirt as she came. Hugh quickly followed her, crying out short, staccato sounds as he thrust his hips upward, driving himself into her.

It was the second time for him—he'd lost count of Vanessa's orgasms. She was wildly orgasmic. It was one of the things about her that drove him crazy.

They both gasped for air afterward, their skin moist with perspiration in spite of the night's biting cold. She fell limp against him and he embraced her with weak arms. Their scents mingled—his cologne, her perfume, their sweat. The air in the cab was heavy and warm, and the tinted windows had fogged up.

Vanessa laughed between gasps. "That was hot," she breathed. "So hot."

"*You're* hot," he said, his voice trembling just a little.

She laughed again. "We sound like Paris Hilton." She put on her goofy Paris Hilton face and spoke in a breathy, brainless voice: "That's hot."

It made him laugh. That was the other thing about her that drove him crazy—she was smart, and she made him laugh a lot. He put his mouth to her ear and whispered, "You do it to me, Vanessa, I'm serious. I've never known a woman who's done to me what you do."

They sat there for a long time, winding down, their breaths steadily coming slower, their heartbeats gradually slowing down.

Hugh lifted his left arm and looked over Vanessa's shoulder at his digital watch. It was eight forty-nine. Emily usually got home from her club by nine fifteen, nine thirty.

"It's late," he said.

He flicked the switch on the door that rolled down the window, but nothing happened.

"What're you doing?" Vanessa said.

"Trying to roll down the window to check on the kids."

"It won't work unless the ignition's on." Vanessa slowly rolled off him to his right, until she was sitting beside him. "What time is it?" she said.

He told her. "We should wrap this up." Hugh sat up and reached down, pulled up his pants. He raised his hips off the seat, pulled them all the way up, and fastened them, zipped up the fly, fastened the belt. Then he slowly buttoned his shirt up.

"I need to shower before she gets back," he said.

"Sure you don't wanna try to go one more time?" Vanessa said.

He laughed. "You kidding? My dick is raw."

She leaned over and kissed him, then started to pull herself together.

Inside the house, the phone sounded its high, shrill, chirping sound.

"Oh, shit," he said.

"What?"

"That's probably for me, and the kids will come looking for me."

"Run in and get it, then. I'll wait."

Hugh opened the door and got out. As he walked to the front door, he checked the windows. The vertical blinds were still closed—no one peered out at him.

The phone continued to trill.

He broke into a jog, went up the front steps, and into the house.

Annie was heading for the phone.

"I'll get it," Hugh said. He picked up the receiver, put it to his ear. "Hello?"

"Is this Hugh Crane?" a woman said. Her voice was pinched and she sounded officious.

"Yes, it is. Who's this?"

"You're married to Emily Crane?"

Hugh frowned. "Yes. Who *is* this?"

"I'm calling from Sisters of Mercy Hospital, Mr. Crane. Your wife is here, in the Emergency Room."

His forehead relaxed and the crooked frown lines disappeared as his face went slack. His eyes widened a little. "Oh, my God, is she all right?" he asked, then realized what a stupid question that was if she was in the Emergency Room.

"Why don't you come down here, Mr. Crane? She's been asking for you."

"I'll be right there."

He dropped the receiver back in its cradle, then stood there a moment. A list of possibilities scrolled through his mind—a car accident, a shooting, a heart attack, a stroke—on and on they raced through his head, bringing with them pangs of guilt that shot through his chest like ice-cold bullets.

Hugh turned around and clapped his hands once. "Okay, kids, get your coats, we're going out."

They whined in response, annoyed to be dragged away from the television.

"Come on, get your coats on, let's go," he said. Then he remembered Vanessa in the car outside. "Oh, shit," he muttered. He hurried out of the house, went to the car, and opened the door. "You've gotta get out of here," he said.

"What?"

"Emily's in the hospital, I've got to go to her."

"What's wrong?"

"I don't know."

"I'm sorry, I—"

"Thanks, but you should just go, okay?"

She scooted across the backseat toward him, and he stepped back so she could get out. Vanessa stood taller than Hugh. Auburn hair cascaded over her shoulders and part of the way down her back. She bent down to kiss him.

Hugh pulled back and hissed, "Not out here, dammit!"

She frowned as she stood up straight, then turned and got back in the car, behind the wheel. "Okay, I'm going."

"I'm sorry, I'm a little, you know, I'm—I don't know what's wrong with Emily, and I'm upset."

Vanessa pulled the door closed, started the car. She lowered the window and he bent forward, gave her a quick peck on the mouth.

"I'll call you, okay?" he said.

"Okay. I hope it's nothing serious."

She raised the window again.

Hugh hurried back into the house to get the kids and his black leather jacket.

Sisters of Mercy was a small hospital on a hilltop overlooking Big Rock. There were a couple broad weeping willows in front of the hospital, a patch of lawn, a huge statue of the Virgin Mary in front of the entrance.

Hugh drove the blue RAV4 around to the Emergency Room entrance in the rear of the building. Back at the house, he'd told the children that Mommy was in the hospital, and they had not stopped grilling him ever since. They wanted to know why she was there, what was wrong, what had happened, and he kept telling them he didn't know, until finally he'd snapped at them and told them to be quiet for the rest of the ride or they all were gonna get it. They fell silent. He could hear Donald and Annie whispering in the backseat, while Jeannie sniffled quietly in her safety seat.

Inside, he went to the front desk, carrying Jeannie, with the other two trailing along, and told the woman there who he was and why he was there. She told him to come into the back. Hugh herded the children through swinging double doors in the Emergency Room, where a tall doctor with dark hair and a mustache approached him.

"You're Mr. Crane?" the doctor said.

"Yes."

"I'm Dr. Lattimer. Look, your wife has been—"

"What's wrong with her? What happened?"

"Calm down, Mr. Crane, please. She needs you to be calm right now, okay?"

"Okay, okay. What happened?"

"It seems your wife's car broke down on Seaside Trail. She was attacked there. By a man. She was not too badly beaten. But—" He took a step closer to Hugh and lowered his voice to a murmur. "—she's been raped, Mr. Crane."

"Oh, my God. Is she—what was—do you know who attacked her?"

"Well, she managed to defend herself quite well. She killed him."

"She *what*?"

"Her attacker is dead."

Hugh clenched his teeth as he felt rising up in his chest a warm swelling of pride for his Emily; then he said in a hoarse whisper, "*Good.*"

"It might be a good idea to put the children in the waiting room for now."

Hugh took them out to the waiting room and told them to sit still and wait for him. There was a television playing the news suspended high in a corner. He went to the front desk and asked the woman behind the frosted glass window if it would be possible to change the TV to cartoons, or something else the kids might be interested in. She came out with a remote and switched channels until she found *Scooby Doo.* She told Hugh not to worry, that she would keep an eye on them from her window. He went back through the swinging double doors.

Emily was lying on a gurney, dressed in one of the flimsy white, blue-speckled gowns they make patients wear in hospitals, the kind that ties in the back. A thin white blanket was drawn up to her chest. Her beefy right forearm was resting across her forehead. A pale green curtain had been drawn around her to give her privacy.

The moment she saw him, she dropped her arm and sat up, her mouth and eyes open to their limit.

"Oh, Hugh, oh, *God*, Hugh!" she said, and her face screwed up as she began to cry. Her arms reached out to him and he bent forward and embraced her, held her close. His hands moved over her back, over the rolls of fat she'd been trying so hard to lose. She pushed away from him and looked up into his eyes. As she spoke, her voice gradually grew louder and louder. "Oh, Hugh, he-he, his face was—he didn't have—his eyes, Hugh, his *eyes*!" She stopped talking long enough to sob a couple of times. She gripped his upper arms, squeezed them hard. "He growled at me and, and he made this sound, this high screaming sound, luh-like he was trying to, I don't know, trying to *howl*, like some kind of *animal*, and his eyes, my God, his *eyes*, they weren't *right*, Hugh, something was very wrong with his eyes and his face because it changed, his face, it *changed*!"

"Calm down, honey, please."

Tears rolled down her already moist round cheeks. "And his eyes, there was something wrong with his eyes, they were—"

"*Please*, Emily—"

"—silver, his eyes were silver—"

"—calm down, now, okay?"

"—silver, Hugh, oh, *Jesus*, his eyes were *silver*!"

The curtain pulled aside and Dr. Lattimer peered around its edge.

Hugh turned to him. "Doctor, do you have something to calm her down?"

He nodded, then disappeared.

Emily continued to babble and cry, her sobs fracturing her words. She went on about hair and eyes and teeth and nails, and Hugh wondered if she'd been attacked by a man or an animal. But she'd been raped—how could an animal rape her?

The curtain pulled aside again a few minutes later, and a nurse came in with a syringe.

"This is just some Valium, Mrs. Crane," she said, "to calm you down."

"No," Emily said, "you've got to *listen* to me, this man, he *wasn't* a man, he was something *else*, he was, wait, *listen* to me!"

"Calm down, honey, and let her give you the shot, okay?" Hugh said.

The needle went into her inner elbow; the plunger was depressed.

A moment later, Emily slowly laid back on the gurney, her head on the pillow. Her chest rose and fell with frantic breaths, but those calmed, and she put her right forearm across her forehead again.

"Hugh," she whispered, "he was . . . he wasn't *right*, he . . . he wasn't *human*." She closed her eyes then, and her breaths came evenly, slowly.

"Don't be alarmed," the nurse whispered. "She's been through a lot."

Hugh nodded as the nurse left.

He looked down at his wife and wondered what had happened to make her say such crazy things.

2

THE NAKED CORPSE

The television was on, but Sheriff Arlin Hurley wasn't watching it—he was reading a collection of essays by Mark Twain. His wife Ella crocheted as she watched a rerun of *Law & Order*. It was a quarter after ten—almost bedtime.

At fifty-one, his rust-colored hair was graying and thinning on top. He stood six feet, three inches tall, with a bit of a belly on him. His face was squarish with blue eyes that he'd always thought were a tad too deep set. Fine lines networked over the surfaces of the half-moon pockets of flesh beneath his eyes, and crows' feet sprouted from their corners. Smile lines extended downward from the sides of his nose to his jaw, cutting off the corners of his mouth. His nose was straight and unremarkable, he had a strong, square jaw, with a small roll of excess flesh beneath it, and dimples in his cheeks when he smiled.

He looked up from his book for a long moment to gaze at his wife, at her exquisite profile. She had the same strawberry blond hair he'd found so appealing twenty-eight years ago, although age had lightened it. The same angular face with those big blue eyes and that smile that sometimes turned into a provocative smirk that could improve his mood in a heartbeat. Still slender and shapely, with small breasts and long legs. There were a few telling lines in her face, of course—she had not escaped age entirely, but she'd apparently made a deal with it, a deal in her favor, because she still looked damned good.

She looked over at him without turning her head, cocked an eyebrow, and smiled. He returned the smile, then continued reading.

Their fat black-and-white cat, Izzie, was curled up and sleeping on top of the television. Hurley thought it was one of Izz's favorite spots because it made him feel as if he were the center of attention. He was an affectionate cat—when he wasn't on top of the television, he was in Hurley's lap, or Ella's, purring contentedly.

To Hurley, having Izzie in his lap was very satisfying. He liked dogs, too, but dogs were always affectionate toward everyone—to dogs, affection came naturally and unconditionally. But you had to earn a cat's respect. He knew that, when a cat came over and sat in his lap, it was because the cat really wanted to be there, and no other reason. Cats loved you unconditionally, too, but they only showed it when they wanted to, when they really meant it. And unlike dogs, they did not love everybody.

The phone chirped and Izzie lifted his head, looked at Hurley with sleepy eyes, and flicked his tail once, then lowered his head again.

Ella reached over and picked up the cordless receiver from its base on the lamp table between their chairs. "Hello?" she said. After a moment, Ella said, "Just a second," and held the phone out to Hurley. He took it, removed his reading glasses, put it to his ear.

"Yes?" Hurley said.

"Hey, Sheriff, it's Garrett." Billy Garrett was one of his deputies. "I'm at Sisters of Mercy."

"What's up?"

"An ambulance just brought Emily in. She was attacked and raped tonight."

"*Our* Emily?"

"Yep."

"Oh, God."

"I thought you'd want to know. Thought you might want to come down and get in on this yourself."

Emily Crane was the receptionist at the Sheriff's Office. She had been working there for eight years, and she almost felt like a member of Hurley's family. They'd invited Emily and Hugh and the kids to barbecues, had taken them on a picnic once. Emily had become more than an employee; she had become a friend.

"I'll get up there right away," Hurley said. "See ya." He turned and put the receiver back on its base, then put the book and his glasses on the table beside the phone.

"Something wrong?" Ella said.

"It's Emily. She's in the hospital. She was raped."

Ella gasped and her crocheting hands dropped into her lap. "Oh, Lord, no."

" 'Fraid so." He stood. "I've got to go." He went upstairs and put his uniform back on.

As he drove up to the hospital, Hurley thought about his two daughters. Mandy was twenty-six, Jennifer was twenty-four. He imagined how he would feel if what had happened to Emily happened to either of them. The very thought of it created an ache in his chest. He clenched his teeth and his hands clutched hard the wheel of the white Ford Explorer with the green seal of the Sheriff's Office on both sides.

Mandy—named after the song because Ella was such a Barry Manilow fan—lived in Crescent City with her husband, Will, a contractor, and their little three-year-old boy, Mark, who was Hurley's pride and joy. Jennifer was still single and not interested in getting married yet—she had a successful young career as a commercial artist in San Francisco, into which she poured her all. The big old Victorian house in which Hurley and Ella lived had seemed huge and empty ever since the girls had moved out, but they just couldn't bring themselves to sell it and move into something smaller. Hurley and Ella had lived in that house ever since they'd gotten back from their honeymoon, and it had become a part of them.

He did not know the details yet, but he had little doubt it was their serial rapist—the Pine County Rapist, as the *Big Rock Herald* called him. If that were the case, Hurley would be even more sickened by the attack, because the Pine County Rapist was his responsibility, and in spite of the considerable efforts of his department, he hadn't been able to catch the bastard yet.

The shortest route to the hospital took him by the old Laramie place. It was just off an undeveloped strip of Perryman Road, standing alone, with no other houses around it. Across the street was a stand of Sitka spruce trees, and beyond that, thick woods. More woods grew wild on either side of and behind the old two-story house. At night, the house was difficult to see—it blended in with its wild surroundings, a greater darkness against the dark woods. As he looked at it going by, a familiar knot tightened in his stomach. All these years later, and the house still made him tense up. He had not been inside it since he was a boy, but the memory was still quite vivid, still powerful, and it still haunted him, still inhabited his nightmares. A simple glance at its vague shape there in the darkness took him back to that Halloween night when he'd gone in on a dare, by himself, helpless and unprotected.

The story was that it was haunted, of course. That old man Laramie still roamed its halls, an angry, insane spirit that hated children. He'd killed his own children, then his wife, then himself ages ago, and the story lingered and grew before Hurley ever came along. Then it was enhanced by Hurley's childhood buddies, told again and again. Hurley wondered if the children of today talked about the place, if they were as afraid of it as he and his friends had been.

How old had he been? Nine or ten, he couldn't remember. But he still remembered, all too vividly, what he had found in there—the dusty, cobweb-caked, maggot-eaten man sitting on the rotten old couch, empty eye sockets staring at nothing from a face that was little more than a skull wearing a few traces of leathery, long-dead skin. The mouth hung open, several teeth missing, and small insects crawled over the dangling jaw.

He'd gone nowhere near the house ever since. He was amazed it still stood after all these decades. Refusing to crumble and collapse, it stood there, defiant, upright, not unlike the rotting, stiff-backed corpse he *thought* he'd seen inside. He remembered how he'd screamed, how he'd been unable to stop screaming as he ran out of the house. Waiting for him outside, his friends had laughed at first—until they'd seen the terror in his face and had heard the sincerity of his screams. Then they'd run screaming after him.

An involuntary shiver passed through him, even though he fought it. He took a big, deep breath, scrubbed a hand down his face.

He'd never told anyone what he'd seen in the Laramie house because, frankly, Hurley was not too sure himself. As soon as he'd gotten a good distance from the place, where he felt safe, he began to wonder if perhaps it hadn't *exactly* been the decayed, rotted body of a person on the couch. It could have been some kind of doll or mannequin, or even something as simple as the play of light and shadow in the dark, dusty house, mixed with his hyperactive imagination. Still, all these years later, he'd told no one, not even Ella. The house had inhabited his dreams ever since he'd run from it, screaming, as a terrified boy. Even now, all these decades later, it made rare but memorable appearances in his sleep, filling him with fear.

It started to rain as he drove up the hill to the hospital. He parked beside Garrett's cruiser in the small lot in front of the Emergency Room entrance, got out, and went inside. There were only a couple other cars in the lot, one of them parked in a space reserved for a doctor. It was obviously a slow night for the Emergency Room.

Hurley saw Emily's husband Hugh and their three children in the waiting room. The kids were seated around their father in a row of chairs, looking worn out and sleepy. Hurley went to Hugh, who stood up and shook his hand. Hugh was frowning and distracted and pale.

"I'm really sorry about this, Hugh."

"Thanks. I'm, uh, I'm . . . I don't know, I'm just beside myself."

"That's perfectly understandable. Sit tight, I'm gonna go back there."

Hugh nodded and sat down again.

"Emily Crane?" he said to the nurse at the front window.

"Go on back, Sheriff, she's back there."

He pushed through the swinging doors and found Deputy Garrett standing just outside a curtain that was pulled around one of the gurneys, writing something in his small notebook.

"What's up?" Hurley said.

"She's been sedated," Garrett said. He was tall and gangly, twenty-nine years old, with his cap on his balding head, his black leather jacket still on. He had a carefully-trimmed mustache which hid the scar left behind by a corrected cleft palate. "They had to give her something to calm her down because she was pretty hysterical for awhile, wasn't making much sense. Now she's very sluggish, but she's talking. They're doing the rape kit right now."

"What about the attacker—was it our guy?"

"If it was, she killed him for us."

"*Killed* him?" Hurley said with a smirk.

"Far as I can make out, she felt around on the ground while he was raping her, found a rusty old corkscrew, and stabbed it into his eye. Went right into his brain."

"On the ground? Where did it happen?"

"Seems she was driving home on Seaside Trail, car broke down, and she got out to look under the hood. Next thing she knows, this guy is on her."

"And she killed him." The smirk became a smile. "I'll be damned. Good for her. I take it he's down in the morgue?"

"Yep, he just got here a couple minutes before you did. But if you ask me, he's not our guy. This guy looks like he's been living on the street for awhile. Stinks like you wouldn't believe."

"He does, huh? Well, maybe he's not. None of the rape victims have reported a smell. But we can hope. How'd she get here?"

"A phone company truck drove by and saw her lying beside the road. She was unconscious. The driver called 911. Ambulance brought her here. Kopechne and Selwyn are still at the scene."

Hurley clenched his teeth and shook his head. "Hm. I may go out there and take a look around when I'm done here. Okay, I'm going down to the morgue. I'll be back in a bit."

Hurley left the Emergency Room through a side door that opened onto a corridor. He turned left and went to the nearest elevator and pushed the button. When it opened, he stepped inside and punched the button marked B. The elevator descended, stopped, and the doors slid open on a basement corridor. Hurley turned right, the *clock-clock-clock* of his shoes on the tile echoing slightly. Overhead, exposed pipes ran along the corridor, painted the same beige as the walls. He turned right down another corridor.

"Hey, George," Hurley said as he approached the morgue.

In an alcove on the left, a desk stood outside and to the left of the double doors that went into the morgue, and at the desk sat George Purdy, the deputy coroner. A small brown paper bag stood on the desk and George was eating half a sandwich as he read an old dog-eared John D. MacDonald paperback. George looked up and smiled as he chewed. "Hey, Sheriff, how goes it?" He was a broad, paunchy man in his mid-forties, with a fleshy face and a thick head of mussed black-and-silver hair. He wore a long white coat with an ID badge on the left breast pocket. He folded a top corner of a page over and closed the book, put it on the desk.

"It goes, George, it goes. You got Emily Crane's attacker down here?"

George nodded, swallowed his food. "Yeah, he just came in. A John Doe."

"No ID on him?"

"Nothin' on him but his torn and filthy clothes. A transient, I think. The victim sure did a number on him. Took his left eyeball right out of the socket." He put his sandwich down on a piece of paper towel and brushed his hands together a few times to rid them of crumbs. "You wanna see him?"

"Yes, please."

George stood and jerked his head toward the doors. "C'mon in. I haven't had time to cut him open yet. I was gonna do that after my break."

George pushed through the door on the left and Hurley followed him in.

Only half the overhead flourescents were on in the morgue. It was dim and cool and shadowy. On the right wall were a few large chrome-fronted drawers. George led Hurley to the left, around a pale green curtain that hung from a track on the ceiling. On the right were two chrome tables with shallow gutters on the edges and a scale hanging above each. To the left were two gurneys with white sheets on them. On the far gurney, the sheet rose up over the fat belly of the body it covered.

Hurley caught a smell in the room—a harsh, stinging body odor.

George froze in place and made an abrupt coughing sound of shock in his throat.

The gurney closest to them was empty. The sheet had been thrown back, and whoever had been lying there was gone.

"Holy shit," George said, his voice suddenly hoarse and breathy. He stared at the empty gurney with his mouth hanging open. "He's gone," he said in an almost-whisper.

"Who?" Hurley said.

"The John Doe." He held out his arms at the gurney, palms up. "He was here, right *here*! Where the hell did he go?"

"Would someone move him?" Hurley asked.

"Who? *Why?* I've been here all along; nobody could get in or out without me seeing them."

Concern wrinkled Hurley's forehead—he'd never seen George Purdy look so upset. "Well, someone *had* to take it, right?" Hurley said. "Because he was dead . . . right? George? He *was* dead."

"Yes, of *course* he was dead. You think they send *living* people down here?"

"Well, he didn't just sit up and walk out, did he? I mean, he was naked, right?"

George nodded as he gawked at the empty table. "I cut his clothes off and threw them away. What there was of them."

"What's the protocol when this happens?" Hurley said.

George shrugged. "I'm not sure. It's never happened before. Every once in a while, somebody gets funny and pulls a hoax—they move a body around, or something. Change the toe tags, maybe, to make my life miserable. But never anything like this."

As George spoke, Hurley heard something. It took him a moment to identify it. He had to shift his attention from what George was saying to focus on the sound—the quiet smack of bare feet on the tile floor. Hurley frowned. While George was still talking, Hurley turned, went to the curtain, and peered around the edge. He was just in time to see the left door swing the last few inches until it was closed. Someone had just quietly sneaked out of the morgue, someone wearing no shoes.

Hurley moved around the curtain and pushed through the door. He looked left, then right, where he caught the briefest glimpse of someone rounding the corner in the corridor—a foot, a flash of long, stringy, dark hair.

He started walking quickly toward the corner. He could hear the bare footfalls—the person was running. Hurley broke into a jog and rounded the corner.

It was a straight stretch down to the end of the corridor—no one was there. He hurried to the elevator and looked up at the numbers above the doors. The elevator was not moving. The barefoot runner had taken the stairs.

Hurley went through the door to the left of the elevators—a rectangular plastic plaque beneath the door's square window read STAIRS. He heard the slapping footsteps up above. Seconds after Hurley started jogging up the stairs, he heard the door open and close on the first floor. He picked up his pace and reached the door in no time, pulled it open so hard it slammed against the wall, and threw himself through it.

He looked both directions in the corridor but saw nothing. He stopped and listened a moment and heard shouting in the Emergency Room waiting area. He ran in that direction and ducked through the open door into the waiting room.

Hugh Crane was standing in there, his youngest girl in his arms, the other two children staring openmouthed at the door that led outside. The door was slowly swinging closed.

"Did somebody just run through here?" Hurley said.

Hugh Crane nodded frantically and said, "Yeah, a naked man! Your deputy saw him and just went running after him out that door."

Getting winded, Hurley ran across the waiting room, nicked his leg on the corner of a chair bolted to a whole row of chairs, and nearly fell on his face. Pain radiated up and down his leg from the point of impact. He pushed through the door and limped outside into the cold, wet night.

The parking lot hissed with falling rain. Off in the distance, in the dark, beyond the glow of the Emergency Room sign overhead, he heard footsteps fading rapidly. Hurley started running again, but instead of following the footsteps, he ran to his SUV and opened the door, reached in for the flashlight. He slammed the door and turned around, clicked the light on.

He swept the beam back and forth slowly, but there was no sign of Garrett or the naked man. He could no longer hear them, either. He saw no sense in running after them himself. For one thing, he didn't know where they'd gone, and he was sure Garrett could take care of himself.

He was rapidly getting wet in the rain. He returned to the truck and put his flashlight back on the passenger seat, closed the door. He was walking back to the Emergency Room at a good clip when he heard something that made his scrotum shrivel up—from somewhere nearby came a high, piercing howl that sharply cut through the night. He froze a moment, then spun around and looked in the direction of the sound, into the darkness.

It had been close, and it definitely had been a *howl*.

A coyote, he thought. *It's got to be a coyote. Hell, we don't have wolves around Big Rock. Do we?*

Coyotes were common around the area. But Hurley rejected that theory almost as quickly as it had occurred to him. Coyotes did not howl so much as they yipped. And the sound they made was not as strong, not as throaty and full, not as sustained.

A dog, he thought. *Maybe it was a dog. Dogs howl, too.*

He stood there in the rain, getting soaked, and waited for it to sound again. But it did not. All he heard was the rain. There was a white blink of lightning a good distance away. A low growl of distant thunder rolled through the clouds, like God clearing His throat.

Finally, Hurley turned and went back inside, dripping wet.

Hugh Crane was seated now, still holding his little girl, who appeared to be asleep. The other two children were across the room rummaging through some magazines. There were some storybooks on the table as well, and the little boy was looking them over.

Hurley lowered himself into the chair across from Hugh and leaned forward, put his elbows on his spread knees and dangled his hands between them.

"How's Emily?" he said.

Hugh shrugged. "They took her over to radiology for some X-rays. Her ribs, she hurt them, and they want to see if any are broken. I'm just waiting for her to get back."

"Can you tell me what the man looked like?" Hurley said. "The man who ran through here?"

"Well, like I said, he was naked as a jaybird, of all things. He had long hair and a kind of stubbly beard. And boy, did he smell bad."

"Anything else?"

"Well, he ran through here pretty fast. Your deputy took a dive for him and almost knocked him over, but he missed by an inch or so and he fell on the floor. But he got right up and ran after him."

Hurley shook his head. A naked man. And he'd run out of the morgue, where a naked corpse was missing.

"One thing," Hugh said. "There was something wrong with his left eye. Looked all bloody."

Hurley frowned.

Took his left eyeball right out of the socket, George had said.

"Thanks, Hugh." Hurley stood and left the waiting room, went back down to the morgue.

He found George back at the desk, putting his dinner back in its bag. "I can't finish my dinner," he said, frowning. "I've never lost a body before, man, I mean . . . a whole body, just *gone*. You're wet."

"What did your John Doe look like, George?" Hurley said.

George leaned back in his chair, frowning thoughtfully. "Well, he was gangly, medium height, long hair, unshaved." He shook his head. "I'm *flummoxed*. I got a missing corpse, and I'm supposed to—"

"He stank?"

"Yeah, he was pretty ripe. And like I said, his left eye was gone."

"The man who left your morgue ran upstairs and through the ER waiting room. My deputy chased him outside. A man in the waiting room—the husband of the victim of your missing John Doe—told me he had long hair and beard stubble, that he smelled bad, and that there was something wrong with his left eye. And did I mention he was naked?"

George stared at Hurley for a long time, lips parted, forehead creased. Finally, he said, "Then that had to be the guy."

"*Your* guy, you mean?"

"Yeah. He wasn't dead. That's the only explanation. But why the hell did he run out of here like that? Naked, for crying out loud."

"He woke up in a morgue. What would *you* do? Did you check for a pulse when you got him?"

"Hell, no. I figure if they bring 'em down here, they're pretty damned sure they're dead. All I did was remove and dispose of his filthy clothes." He ran a hand back through his hair and sighed. "I'm gonna talk to the big boss when he comes in tomorrow morning. I don't know what I'm going to say—One of our bodies got up and ran out? Sir?—but I'm gonna talk to him." George's entire face darkened. Almost whispering, he said, "Jesus . . . thank God he got up and ran out before I cut him open."

"You don't even want to think about the lawsuit *that* would've brought down on the hospital," Hurley said with a smirk.

"I'll have nightmares about it."

Hurley pushed away from the desk. "Okay. I'm going back upstairs to see if my deputy caught the naked corpse."

"Good luck."

Back in the waiting room, Garrett had not yet returned.

Hugh had not moved from his seat and still held his little girl. He stared up at the television, but his eyes did not seem to be focused on it—he seemed lost in thought. The other two children had returned to their seats—the girl was reading a *Highlights* magazine, while the boy read a storybook.

"My deputy come back through here yet?" Hurley asked.

Hugh blinked a few times and looked at Hurley. "Uh, no, not yet. At least, I didn't see him. I haven't been paying much attention to anything."

Hurley went back outside. The rain had receded to a light sprinkle. He went to his truck and got the flashlight again. There was a small umbrella on the floor, but he saw no point in using it now—he was already soaked, his khaki uniform dark with water.

He turned on the flashlight and walked toward the entrance to the parking lot. The road to the hospital forked, with one side coming to the Emergency Room parking lot, the other going to the parking lot in front of the building. He walked all the way to that fork, his shoes crunching over grit on the wet pavement.

A blue Ford Focus came up the hill and took the left side of the fork. Hurley stepped out of its way as it drove into the Emergency Room parking lot.

Hurley saw no sign of Garrett. He called his name once, twice, then turned and went back to the parking lot. He turned left and went to the lot's edge. The pavement ended and rocky earth took over. It sloped down steeply into bushes and a few pines. On the other side of that patch of sloping woods was the road that led up to the hospital.

He heard something. It was so quiet that, had it been raining any harder, he never would have heard it. It was a distinct, wet, slurping and smacking, accompanied by an occasional low, quiet growl.

"Garrett?" Hurley called. *"Garrett!"* he shouted, louder this time.

The sound stopped. It was replaced by a frantic rustling in the bushes, a sound that faded quickly down the slope.

Hurley started down the slope, stepping carefully, but trying to hurry. The ground was wet and muddy, slippery under his feet. Once, the mud gave way beneath him and he started sliding down, out of control. He took another quick two steps and came out of the slide, continued down. He zigzagged around bushes, ferns, stood

against the trunk of a pine tree for a moment, then went
farther down.

He tripped over Garrett and fell flat on his face in the
mud. He clutched the flashlight hard as he rolled, until
his back slammed against the trunk of a pine tree, sending sharp pain up and down his spine.

Leaning heavily on the tree, Hurley climbed to his feet,
covered with mud. He turned and shone the flashlight
back up the slope. It fell on Garrett. Hurley trudged back
up the muddy slope and stopped at the prone figure of
his deputy.

Garrett's leather jacket had been pulled half off, his
spread arms almost completely out of the sleeves. The
shirt of his uniform had been torn open. The undershirt
beneath it had been ripped to shreds. So had Garrett's
abdomen. Ropes of intestines hung out of the great hole
that was his torso. Hurley moved the flashlight's beam up
to Garrett's face and saw that his throat had been torn
out. His eyes and mouth were open wide.

"Oh, sweet Jesus, Garrett," Hurley said, his voice broken. His stomach turned over inside and, for a moment,
he thought he was going to vomit. But he swallowed frantically and held it down.

Then he stopped moving, stopped breathing, and listened.

No more rustling bushes, no sounds of movement.
Only the gentle whisper of the drizzling rain, the dripping
of rainwater from the branches of trees.

Hurley was alone in the patch of woods with his
eviscerated deputy.

3

AN ANIMAL

An hour later, three Sheriff's Department cruisers were parked in the Emergency Room parking lot, and four deputies were spread out, looking for the naked man. Sharp flashlight beams cut through the rainy night in the strip of woods on the slope that ran down to Finch Road—the road that led up to the hospital—as well as across the road in another patch of woods. So far, no sign of the man had been found—except for Deputy Garrett's eviscerated corpse.

Hurley sat at the desk outside the morgue, listening to his deputies communicate on his portable radio, waiting for word that the man had been found, and waiting for George Purdy to finish the autopsy on Garrett. George had invited Hurley to observe the autopsy, but he wasn't up to it—finding Garrett as he had was enough for one night.

He heard the door push open and turned to see George come out of the morgue in a long white smock stained with blood. He wiped his hands on a strip of paper towel as he smiled down at Hurley.

"Well, that's done," George said.

Hurley stood. "So, what's the story?"

"It's a *strange* story, Sheriff," George said. "Very strange."

"Well, let's hear it."

"From what I found, Sheriff, you shouldn't be looking for a man. You should be looking for an animal."

"An *animal*?"

George took in a deep breath as he nodded. With the wadded paper towel in his right hand, he put his fists on his hips, elbows out at his sides. "Your deputy was partially *eaten*, Sheriff. His insides and his throat were torn by fangs, and his intestines and other organs were partially eaten. By something."

Hurley frowned as he looked at the deputy coroner, tilted his head to one side. Before he could speak, George continued: "There's no way my John Doe could have done what was done to your deputy, Sheriff. It was an animal, most likely a large animal."

"Like what? A . . . a bear, maybe?"

"Possibly. A bear, a mountain lion, something big and strong, with claws and fangs."

"We don't have bears around here."

George shrugged. "You've got *something* out there, Sheriff—something big and hungry, now with a taste for people. You hear stories all the time these days about wild animals showing up in all kinds of places. Civilization spreads and drives animals out of their natural homes and into towns and cities. Surely there are bears up in these mountains, right? It wouldn't be impossible for one to make its way down here."

Hurley remembered the howling he'd heard earlier that night. He was just as certain that there were no wolves around Big Rock as he was that there were no bears, so he decided not to mention it. It probably was, after all, a dog. But he filed it away in the back of his mind.

"You're sure it couldn't have been done by your John Doe?" Hurley asked.

"My John Doe was unarmed—he was naked, remember—and he didn't have fangs. It took fangs to tear your deputy open like that, Sheriff; fangs made the bites on that body. It wasn't done with a knife, or any other weapon. There are bite marks around the edges of the openings in both the throat and the abdomen and on the arms, bite marks made by large jaws—marks no human could make."

Hurley nodded as he slowly stood. "So I'm looking for an animal."

"That's right. You might want to tell your deputies who are out there searching tonight. They could be in danger."

"Thank you, George. I appreciate it."

"No problem, Sheriff."

"I'll see you later."

"Not too soon, I hope. It's never anything good that brings us together."

They shook hands and George went back through the swinging double doors.

As Hurley started down the corridor, he took the microphone clipped to his shoulder. Its curly black cord was attached to the radio on his belt. He depressed the button with his thumb and said, "This is Hurley. Come on in, all of you. I'll meet you at my rig in the parking lot."

Another woman raped, but probably not by the serial rapist who had already attacked four women in town . . . a missing corpse that apparently was not a corpse after all . . . and . . . an *animal*. Hurley released a heavy sigh as he walked down the corridor.

The Pine County Rapist, Hurley thought as he pushed the button to summon the elevator. It would be nice if Emily had killed the rapist for them. But Hurley had his doubts. For one thing, nobody had reported that the rapist had such a bad odor. Emily said her attacker reeked, and everyone who'd come into contact with the John Doe confirmed it. And so far, the Pine County Rapist had killed no one, while Emily's attacker had, according to her, been trying to kill her. The Pine County Rapist wore a mask, Hurley knew that much, a cheap Halloween mask, and Emily had said nothing about a mask. It certainly didn't sound—or smell—like the Pine County Rapist, who was described by two of his five victims as smelling of some kind of cologne or aftershave, although they'd been unable to identify it.

Hugh Crane pulled the RAV4 into his driveway, waited for the automatic garage door to open, then pulled into the garage. Before going home, he'd stopped at the all-night Walgreens to fill the prescription for Valium that the doctor had given Emily.

She slept beside him, her head leaning against the window at her right as she snored purringly. The kids were sound asleep in back. He reached over and put his hand on Emily's shoulder, nudged her gently.

"Em? Em, honey? We're home."

She did not stir at first. Hugh hoped she'd wake up, because there was no way he could carry her into the house—she was simply too heavy.

"Emily? Honey?" He shook her carefully, not wanting to startle her.

"Mmmm?"

"We're home. Come on, let's go inside."

Finally, she lifted her head and looked at him with heavy-lidded eyes. She smacked her lips as she sat up, then opened her door.

Once inside the house, he put his arm around her and said, "Come on, let's get you into bed."

She did not argue. They went up the stairs slowly, then down the hall and into the bedroom. She went to the bed, sat down on the edge, turned on the lamp on her side. She just sat there for a long moment, then started to unbutton her torn and dirty blouse. She stood and Hugh helped her undress.

"I want to take a bath," she said.

"Of course, of course. I'll start it for you." He went into the attached bathroom and ran the bath. When he came out again, she was wearing her blue robe. He put an arm around her and led her into the bathroom.

"I'm fine now," she said. "I can . . . y'know . . . take it from here."

"Okay. Just call me if you need anything. I'm gonna get the kids and put them to bed."

She nodded.

Hugh left the bathroom and closed the door. He went out to the garage and woke the kids in the backseat, brought them inside and put them to bed, carrying Jeannie. That done, he went back to the master bedroom and into the bathroom. "Everything okay?" he said.

"Yeah, fine," she said. The bath was thick with sudsy bubbles. Her eyes were puffy, as if she'd been crying.

"Okay. I'll be right outside."

He closed the door, went to his side of the bed, and turned on the bedside lamp.

Before they left the hospital, a rape counselor had come to talk to Emily. She was a thin, pale woman with mousy brown hair in a bun, wearing a long blue coat and carrying a large leather bag slung over her shoulder. She wore large glasses, spoke in a high, tremulous voice, and had a pinched, thin-lipped smile. She'd gone behind the curtain and she and Emily had spoken in quiet voices for awhile. She'd left a card with Emily and told her to give her a call when she was feeling better physically and wanted to talk. Emily had given the card to Hugh, and he'd put it in his pocket. He took it out now and looked at it. It read, simply, DIANE CONNIVER, with a phone number below that. He put the card on the nightstand, along with the bottle of Valium.

Hugh took off his clothes and put on his plush dark-green robe. He stretched out on the bed with his back against the headboard. He used the remote to turn on the television so Emily wouldn't hear him talking in the bathroom, then he picked up the phone and punched in Vanessa's number.

She sounded sleepy when she answered. " 'Lo?"

"Hi. It's me."

"Hey. What's up?"

He sighed. "I got her home. She's in the tub."

"What happened?"

He gave her a brief version of the night's events.

"God, that's awful."

"But you know what?" he whispered.

"Hm?"

"I wish I was with you."

"Aw, that's sweet," Vanessa said. "But she needs you now."

He was silent for a long moment. Then: "I have an empty house I'm showing. Can you meet me during your lunch hour tomorrow?"

"You're going to work tomorrow? Don't you think you should stay home with her?"

"Yeah, I'm going to call in, say I can't work tomorrow. But I can get away for your lunch hour. The house is on Clauson."

"Sorry, I can't tomorrow."

"You can't? Why?"

"I have plans."

"Plans?"

"Yes."

"Well . . . what kind of plans?"

She was silent for a long moment. Finally, she took in a breath and said, "Hugh, you know, you don't have any exclusive claim over me."

He opened his mouth, but nothing came out.

"You realize that, don't you?" Vanessa said.

"What do you mean? Are you saying . . . are you seeing someone *else*?"

"You're married, Hugh. There's no real future for us,

right? On the other hand, I'm single and free, and . . . well, I'm taking advantage of that."

Hugh felt a knot tighten in his stomach. "Then you're seeing someone else."

"I'm not saying if I'm seeing someone else or not, I'm just saying that I'm *free* to see someone else if I want. Understand?"

"Are you . . . am I . . . am I losing you?"

"Of course not. I'm just saying that for me to devote myself exclusively to you would be a waste of my time, because our relationship isn't going any further than it's gone already. Understand?"

He said nothing for awhile—he didn't like it, but he could not think of a good way to argue against it. Then: "Uh, yeah. Yeah, I guess so."

"Good. Now, maybe I can see you the next day. Will that house still be available?"

"Sure."

"Good. It's a date. My lunch hour on Thursday, then."

After he hung up, Hugh sat on the edge of the bed and stared at the phone, frowning. He imagined Vanessa with another man and felt a pang of jealousy. He rubbed his eyes with the heels of his hands, then stood. He set his alarm, took off his robe, and got into bed.

They'd met in the parking lot of the Safeway grocery store at the northern end of town. She'd hit the back fender of the RAV4 when she backed out of her parking space without looking. They'd both gotten out of their vehicles, exchanged insurance information, and Hugh had found himself, quite surprisingly, flirting with her. She was very attractive—tall and voluptuous, with that beautiful auburn hair, milky skin, big dark-brown eyes and luscious, rosy, kissable lips. The flirting had been innocent at first, and she'd played along, laughing with him, reaching out and touching his arm a couple of times. Then he'd said it, surprising himself even more: "How would you like to have lunch with me today?" He'd already bought his lunch in Safeway, intending to eat his pastrami sandwich in the car. He had almost two hours on his hands until he had to meet with a couple who were interested in seeing a house on Rampart just outside of town. But when he'd asked her to lunch, that sandwich in the paper bag on the passenger seat was immediately forgotten.

"Lunch, huh?" She'd looked at his wedding ring quite obviously, then into his eyes. There had been a challenge in those brown eyes then, a question: *Are you sure you know what you're doing?*

"Yes, lunch," he'd said. "We could go right over there." He pointed to the Perko's in the front part of the Safeway parking lot.

"Sure," she said. "Lunch sounds good."

That was how it had started. The lunch had been slightly uncomfortable for Hugh because he was so attracted to her, he'd found it difficult to concentrate on their conversation.

He had never been unfaithful to Emily before, but things had changed between them. Emily had gained a lot of weight since having Jeannie three years ago. She'd become lazy, sometimes going for days without doing a bit of housework. She seemed to have lost interest in sex, and when they did make love, she was sluggish and tired easily. More often than not, she turned him down with one excuse or another—usually, "I'm too tired right now." Hugh had begun to feel neglected without even realizing it. And his eyes had begun to wander. The excess fat on Emily's body was a turnoff to him. The jiggling, hanging flesh, the long jagged stretch marks, the patches of lumpy cellulite, the rolls of fat that went around the middle of her body like gelatinous belts. He found himself noticing other women more than ever before, fantasizing about them. Vanessa had come along at precisely the right time, and he did not waste any time in getting the relationship moving.

Ever since then, they had been getting together in empty houses. They had gone to a hotel over in Seaside a couple of times, but mostly they used the houses.

The bathroom door opened and Emily stood in the doorway a moment, clutching the robe together in front. Her hair was wet, her face clean, although her left eye was swollen and bruised. She came into the bedroom and went to her dresser, opened a drawer, and pulled something out. She took off the robe, tossed it onto a chair, and quickly put on a pair of flannel pajamas she hadn't worn in ages—they covered her from neck to ankle. Then she came over and got into bed.

Usually, Emily slept in the nude, like Hugh.

He reached over and touched her shoulder and said, "How are you feel—"

She jerked her shoulder away and her entire body stiffened under the covers.

"Okay, okay," he said, pulling his hand back, "I'm sorry."

After saying nothing for a long moment, she said, "Where are the Valium the doctor prescribed?"

Hugh said, "On your nightstand." He got out of bed and went to the bathroom and returned a moment later with a glass of water, which he handed to her. She took one of the pills and drank it down. She thought about it a moment, then drank down a second pill.

"Look, I'll call into work tomorrow and tell them I can't come in. I can get the kids off to school in the morning. Okay? You can stay in bed as long as you want."

She stared at the television and said nothing for awhile. Then she nodded jerkily and said, "Okay. Thank you."

"Maybe tomorrow you'd like to call the counselor who came in to see you tonight, Diane Conniver."

She nodded once and whispered, "Maybe."

He offered her the television remote and said, "Here, you can watch whatever you want."

She shook her head. "No, I don't care. Really."

He nodded, turned off the TV. "Well, maybe we should both get some sleep, huh? It's late."

She reached over and turned off the lamp on her side of the bed, punched her pillow once, and lay down on her left side, with her back to Hugh. She usually went to sleep on her back.

Hugh reached over and turned off his lamp, plunging the room into darkness. He yawned as he lay back and shifted around in the bed, trying to get comfortable. He wondered what this was going to do to Emily. Would she need therapy? Would she never let him touch her again? Would she gain *more* weight? As he thought about that possibility, he sighed and tried to think about something else, because he realized he did not really care anymore.

4

Morning in Big Rock

Wednesday

The coastal town of Big Rock, California, was named after the enormous boulder around which it was built. The boulder jutted from the earth in a conical shape, standing a full twenty-five feet high and about sixty feet across at the base, a mottled gray, speckled with bird droppings and spotted with dark-green moss. It stood in the middle of Hallwell Park, which was in the center of town. The park was named after Nathaniel Hallwell, founder of Big Rock. A bronze statue of Hallwell stood at the entrance to the park, but it was not nearly as impressive as the big rock.

Big Rock was the Pine County seat. It was the smallest county in the state of California, encompassing Big Rock, Seaside, and a few little villages including Borden and Raven's Port. None of these towns and villages had their own police department and all were served by the County Sheriff's Department.

On that Wednesday morning in January—the morning after the rape of Emily Crane and the evisceration of Deputy Billy Garrett—the rain stopped, a fog rolled in before dawn, and blanketed the town in a color very similar to that of the big rock itself. The sun rose over the mountains in the east, but no one saw it through the soupy mist. The low fog would dissipate later in the morning, leaving behind a steel-gray sky thick with clouds. The weatherman on the radio predicted more rain for the rest of the week, with no sunshine in sight.

Hugh Crane's digital clock radio turned on and a newscaster began to talk loudly about more troops in Iraq killed by a car bomb, and the most recent drug binge by a young, rich, airhead celebrity. Without lifting his head from the pillow, Hugh reached over and slapped the clock radio a few times before hitting the right button and turning it off. He sat up and yawned and rubbed his eyes, smacked his lips a few times.

He looked down at Emily, and the previous night came back to him in a rush. She'd said the man reeked, that he was filthy. Something about him being like an animal. Hugh shuddered at the thought. He felt a sudden urge to reach out and touch her comfortingly, but he did not want to wake her.

He got out of bed, took a shower, and got dressed. He shuffled down the hall, stopping at the kids' rooms to wake them. He went downstairs to the kitchen.

The automatic coffeemaker was already brewing coffee. He called his boss at Champion Realty at home, a chipper woman named Natalie Rayburn, and explained what had happened the night before. He told her he wouldn't be in for the next couple of days because he wanted to give Emily time to get back on her feet. She expressed concern, and told him to give Emily her best.

The kids shuffled into the kitchen one at a time as Hugh cooked a breakfast of scrambled eggs and bacon.

"Where's Mommy?" Jeannie said.

"Mommy's not feeling well," Hugh said. "She's going to stay in bed for awhile."

"Is she gonna be okay?" Donald said.

"I think so. But maybe not for awhile. Listen. Remember last night, when I told you Mom was attacked by a strange man?"

The children fell silent and stared at him with big eyes. They slowly nodded, one after another.

"Well, to save herself," Hugh went on, "she had to . . . to hurt the man who was attacking her, hurt him very badly. It's a terrible thing to have to do that to someone, no matter what the reason. But he beat her up pretty bad, and he would've hurt her a lot worse if she hadn't. So we're all going to have to be very understanding with Mom, okay? That means we might all have to pitch in and do some housework. Can you do that for Mom?"

Again, they all nodded, their eyes wide.

They ate quietly after that.

When breakfast was over, he got the kids dressed. He drove Donald and Annie to school. On the way home, he sang songs with Jeannie.

Back at the house, he went upstairs to the bedroom and checked on Emily. She snored gently as she slept.

On his way back downstairs, he thought of Vanessa and wished he could see her that day. He was bothered that she was doing something else, with *someone* else. And he was bothered that it bothered him so much.

5

ANDREA AND JIMMY

Andrea Norton made breakfast for her husband as the baby, Marnie, sat in her high chair and flapped her arms, slapping the tray before her, smiling at nothing in particular. Andrea looked over at Marnie and she smiled, too. She was hit hard with an overwhelming feeling of love for the baby. It happened every time she smiled like that. Or winked at Andrea, or giggled or . . . *anything*, really; it would just hit her so hard all of a sudden, an almost physical punch in the stomach, only it didn't hurt, it felt *so good*—to be able to feel such love about something that hardly had begun to form yet. She was such a happy baby, so well behaved. Andrea had never before seen a baby smile so much, and each time, that sudden gut-punch of enormous affection hit her.

Jenny, Andrea's four-year-old, sat at the table on a couple of phone books and ate a bowl of cereal. The footstool she used to mount the phone books stood beside the chair. She was a tiny girl, but Andrea had been tiny at first, too; then she'd sprouted at puberty—Andrea expected the same thing to happen to Jenny.

"How do you like the cereal, sweetheart?" Andrea asked. It was a new cereal they'd never tried before—

Jenny had loved the television commercial that advertised it, and had insisted on trying it.

Jenny looked at her mother and screwed her face up tightly. "It's too *fwooty!*"

"Too fruity, huh? Well, you knew it was going to be fruity. It's called Fruit Sparkles. Right?"

Jenny looked very deep in thought as she scooped another spoonful into her mouth. She chewed slowly, then turned to Andrea again. "But . . . this is *too* fwooty!"

Andrea laughed quietly as Marnie suddenly released a happy squeal, high and shrill and long. The baby's cry made Andrea cringe, and she looked over her shoulder to see if Jimmy had come into the kitchen yet.

"Shhh, honey," Andrea said, "be quiet now." As a couple of pancakes cooked, Andrea took a bottle of baby food and a little spoon from the counter and went to the high chair. She pulled a chair away from the table, sat down, and fed Marnie some Gerber's mashed peaches. She whispered, "You know how Daddy likes it quiet in the morning, baby, right? Right, sweetie?" She smiled at Marnie, and the baby smiled back as she chewed her food, letting some of the mashed peaches dribble down onto her chin. Her chubby cheeks were as rosy as if they'd been rouged. She had Andrea's gold-streaked dirty-blond hair, and Jimmy's big blue eyes, but the smile was all her own.

Andrea gasped when she remembered the pancakes. She stood and stepped over to the stove, flipped the pancakes with a spatula. "Oh, damn," she whispered. One pancake was a little darker than Jimmy preferred. Maybe if she put it in the middle of the stack, he wouldn't notice.

She wore gray sweatpants and a black T-shirt. She was slender, five feet, six inches tall. She had gained only a little weight both times she was pregnant, and she'd lost even that little bit quickly, because Jimmy hated overweight women. He hated overweight people, period. He said it was a sign of laziness and lack of self-control. Her blond hair fell to her shoulders and framed a face that was pretty, even without makeup, but that appeared strained and tired.

Jimmy came into the kitchen, dressed in jeans and a long-sleeved plaid shirt and carrying the newspaper, which he'd gotten from the porch. He silently hung his down jacket on the back of the chair, sat down at the table. Jimmy worked at Marx's Brickyard, where he operated the heavy equipment used to move piles of rocks and gravel and stacks of bricks. He was five-eight, with a mop of black hair and a mustache, a narrow face and a wiry, taut body.

Andrea served him his breakfast, then went back to feeding Marnie. She cooed at the baby and made her smile as she ate. Marnie suddenly sprayed a mouthful of mashed peaches all over Andrea's hand, and Andrea laughed in spite of the mess. She got up and went to the counter, tore off a couple of paper towels and wiped up the baby food, then continued feeding the baby.

From the corner of her eye, she saw Jimmy stand up at the table, and she wondered if he'd finished his breakfast so soon.

An explosion of breaking glass nearly knocked Andrea out of her chair, and she dropped the spoon with which she'd been feeding Marnie—it clattered onto the high chair's tray—and shot to her feet. Jimmy had thrown his breakfast across the kitchen. The plate had shattered against the cupboards over the counter. One of the syrupy pancakes stuck to the cupboard, while the rest of Jimmy's breakfast fell to the countertop and floor, and shards of the shattered plate scattered everywhere. Andrea's mouth and eyes were open wide in shock, but that passed quickly. She closed her eyes and bowed her head a moment before turning to face Jimmy.

"How many goddamned times do I have to *tell* you?" he shouted as he came around the table toward her.

Andrea tensed, anticipating the blow.

He slapped her face hard once and she made a high, sharp sound of shock mingled with pain. Then his arm swung back and he backhanded her, his knuckles slamming against her cheekbone. He kept slapping her as he went on shouting, his arm sweeping back and forth, back and forth.

"I told you, I don't like my fucking pancakes burnt!" he shouted. "One of 'em's too fucking dark, goddammit! Is it just that you're so fucking stupid or do you do it on *purpose*?"

Marnie screamed, and her scream dissolved into wracking baby sobs.

"Shut that fucking little rat up!" Jimmy shouted. He snatched his jacket off the chair, put it on, and said, "I'll have to stop somewhere and *buy* my fucking breakfast, because it seems—" He picked up his glass of orange juice and threw it at the cupboards. The glass shattered with an explosion of liquid orange. "—you don't know how to fucking cook!"

Marnie wailed as Jimmy left the kitchen.

Andrea tasted blood. The inside of her lower lip had been cut against her teeth. Her face burned as if her cheeks were in flames, and it felt like the right one was beginning to swell a little under her eye, where his knuckles had hit her repeatedly.

Jimmy slammed the front door on his way out.

It did not matter how many times it happened—it was always as shocking as the first time. Andrea never knew what would cause it, and she was never prepared for it.

Jimmy Norton ordered a hearty breakfast at the counter of Tess's Diner on Beakman Street. He liked a big breakfast.

He seldom ate much for lunch, so he was hungry when he got home at the end of the day, and Andrea always had a hot dinner waiting for him when he arrived, which was as it should be as far as Jimmy was concerned. She knew what would happen if she didn't, or was late.

When Jimmy and Andrea had married, she'd wanted to remove the words "to honor and obey" from the vows. Jimmy's father had predicted this would happen back when Jimmy was thirteen. His father had given him a long lecture about how to "handle" women as he got older, and he'd said that when Jimmy married, his bride probably would want to remove those words, and he'd told Jimmy to resist it. That, Dad had said, was how it was supposed to be—the wife was *supposed* to "honor and obey" her husband.

Jimmy remembered how his mother had obeyed his father, and how, on the rare times that she had not, Dad had punished her with a beating, sometimes with the belt. He'd punished Jimmy and his brother Neil the same way, of course. Punishment had been a big part of life when Jimmy was growing up.

Jimmy and Andrea had been married four years, and there were times when he could not stand the sight of her, days when he wanted to pick up that baby—a baby he sometimes suspected was not his—and beat Andrea to death with it. Times when he wanted to go through the house and just lay waste to the place, devastate it. When that happened, he had to get out of the house. He would come home from work, have his dinner, then go out and get into the truck and just drive and look around. Sometimes he would come across a woman who appealed to him. He would watch her house, or follow her around town, sometimes for a few nights in a row. Then, he would introduce himself to her in his own special way, show her what a real man was like.

After that, he always felt better.

Those times came more often these days—the feeling he was about to explode with tension, anger, that desire to destroy his own house, his own family. He'd had to go out at night more often and give himself air to breathe. And more often, he had to find a woman. So he could introduce himself to her . . . in his own special way.

As he waited for his breakfast, Jimmy watched the waitress pass back and forth before him. She was just a little plump—not fat, he could not tolerate fat people— nicely voluptuous, with honey-blond hair, big pouty lips. She caught him watching her, but he did not stop, did not avert his eyes. Instead, he smiled. She looked at him briefly and returned the smile. As she smiled, Jimmy winked at her. Her smile grew and she ducked her head bashfully as she turned away from him to take a plate from the order window. He watched as she took the plate to a table.

Andrea was skinny. Her breasts were small and flattish, her knees knobby. She had a nice ass, he gave her that much. But Jimmy was more of a breast man. The fact was, he never would've married her if she hadn't been pregnant with Jenny. Hell, he hadn't wanted to marry her even then, but after beating the crap out of Jimmy in his bedroom, his dad gave him a lecture on how stupid you had to be to get a woman pregnant these days, and about doing the right thing. Then he'd kicked Jimmy around some more. He'd been drunk at the time, of course. So they'd married, and Jimmy found himself where he was today—restless, trapped, with a growing rage inside him.

The curvaceous waitress placed his breakfast before him, gave him a smirk and a silent wink, then walked away.

Jimmy chuckled a little as he began to eat.

6

JASON

The Northgate Mall opened at nine, and early shoppers came in as soon as the doors were unlocked. The Donut Hole was the only vendor in the food court that opened that early, and a short line formed right away. Most of the stores opened at nine, though the higher-end boutiques and art galleries did not open until ten.

The two-story mall stood at the eastern edge of Big Rock, right on the border of the city limits. It was patronized by shoppers from neighboring Seaside, Borden, Raven's Port, and even Crescent City to the north and Eureka to the south.

In the back room of the B. Dalton Bookseller where he worked, Jason Sutherland pinned his rectangular name tag to the pocket of his long-sleeved green plaid shirt, and went to the front of the store. The manager had opened the doors just a few minutes earlier and there were already three shoppers browsing the aisles—two middle-aged women and a man in his sixties. Jason smiled at them as he passed on his way to the register in front.

Jason's light brown hair was short and wavy—he'd just gotten a trim the day before at Northgate Hair Design across the way. He had brown eyes with long lashes beneath heavy brows that tilted slightly downward on the outer ends. He had a straight nose, and a strong jaw. It was a fine face, but sad, even when he smiled. His body was soft and tended to be overweight. Jason had fought his weight all his life. He was not athletic—he preferred reading and writing to just about anything. He had no brothers or sisters and had grown up around more adults than children. He'd been a precocious child with an impressive vocabulary, which he had not used much because he was so very shy. His weight had been the cause of a lot of pain for him growing up—the other kids never let him forget he was overweight. His weight was also, he'd decided, the primary reason why, at the age of twenty-one, he was still a virgin. His weight, and his painful shyness. He'd made attempts to lose the weight. He did not eat any more than anyone else he knew—he didn't binge eat or use food as comfort. He didn't get as much exercise as he should, he admitted that. But he was so deathly afraid of embarrassment and humiliation—and that was what he felt every time he tried to exercise.

The manager of the bookstore was a petite woman in her forties named Georgia Williams. She was a chilly person, stiff, abrupt, even when she wore her empty smile, which always looked forced. That morning, she was unhappy because another worker, Cynthia Newell, was late yet again.

Jason worried that when Cynthia arrived, Miss Williams would fire her. She had been warned a couple of times about her tardiness. He did not want Cynthia to be fired. Cynthia was, of course, barely aware of his existence, even though they often worked side-by-side at the register when it got busy, but Jason enjoyed working with her, being near her.

Cynthia arrived at precisely nine eighteen. Jason smiled and said, "Hello, Cynthia," but he said it so quietly that she did not hear him as she hurried toward the back.

He closed his eyes as he breathed in the perfume left in her wake. She wore a long gray coat with a black fur collar, and her red purse was slung over her shoulder. She was about the same age as Jason, with short, curly blond hair and a beautiful oval face. Her shiny curls bounced slightly as she walked.

"Cynthia," Miss Williams said. She was standing in the humor section, tidying up the shelves, when Cynthia came in. She'd stepped out into the center aisle, blocking Cynthia's path.

Jason watched as the young woman stopped, her small hands closing into fists, her back stiffening.

Miss Williams said, "I'm not going to warn you again, understand? The next time you're late, you might as well not come in, because you'll be dismissed. Is that clear?"

"I'm really sorry," Cynthia said. "Really, I mean, I would've been on time, but there was a wreck on Westphal Street, and I had to wait, along with everybody else. Really. I mean, it was, like, this really *bad* wreck, there were three cars all scrunched up so bad that you—"

"At this point, Cynthia, your reason for being late is hardly relevant. It's happened much too often. Do you understand what I'm saying? Once more, and you'll have to look for work elsewhere."

Cynthia nodded. Miss Williams returned to what she was doing, and Cynthia went through the door at the back of the store.

Jason knew she would come back out in no time at all, and they would spend another day working together. He had to admit to himself that he had a bit of a crush on Cynthia. But she was not the woman he thought about the most, the woman for whom he reserved his true affections. That would be his next-door neighbor, Andrea Norton.

He'd heard shouting over there again that morning as

he ate breakfast. His mother had heard it, too, and had shaken her head as she stood at the stove cooking.

Jason lived in an apartment over his parents' garage. From a side window in his apartment, he could see the Nortons' front yard. His heart broke for Andrea. He had elaborate fantasies in which he saved her from her terrible marriage and they went away together with her baby and little girl, married, and lived far away in another town. He had other fantasies about her, too, which were not quite as elaborate, but no less exciting. He dreamed of burying his fingers in her long, thick blond hair as he kissed her on the mouth, then the throat, then her breasts, kissing and smiling.

Andrea came into the bookstore now and then. She told him she usually bought her books at the used bookstore, but she had a favorite mystery writer and she always bought his books as soon as they were released in paperback because she hated to wait for them to show up at the Paperback Trader. Jason sometimes visited her in the afternoon while her husband was at work, and even mowed her lawn sometimes during the summer, so she wouldn't have to do it. Her husband never did any yard work.

It did not seem fair that Jason was alone and had no one, and yet a prick like Jimmy Norton had a wonderful wife whom he mistreated and abused.

Cynthia was Sunday afternoon shopping sprees and sexy clothes and bubblegum pop music. Andrea, on the other hand, was something more ... she was a *real* woman—thoughtful, intelligent, mature. Jason had a schoolboy crush on Cynthia, but his feelings for Andrea were deeper, stronger.

Andrea's favorite writer had a new novel in hardcover. Miss Williams had opened the box in back that morning, and Jason would be putting the books out on the front shelves a little later. He'd already decided he would buy one for Andrea—it would give him an excuse to go over and see her that afternoon when he got off work at three.

The two middle-aged women came to the register with their purchases and Jason smiled.

7

FISH AND GAME

Sheriff Arlin Hurley awoke at seven, as usual. He did not even have to set an alarm anymore—he'd been doing it so long, he now automatically woke at seven every morning, whether he needed to or not. Upon waking, he went to his home office and got on the treadmill for awhile. As he walked, he tried to read more of the book of essays by Twain, his favorite writer. After showering, he usually made breakfast for Ella and himself. That Wednesday morning, he felt edgy, nervous. He hadn't even been able to read while walking on the treadmill—he kept reading the same paragraph over and over again before finally giving up. He made a breakfast of waffles and strawberries, but he repeatedly dropped things or tripped over his own feet going from one counter to another. He turned on the radio on top of the refrigerator and he and Ella listened to the morning news as they ate. When the female newscaster came to the report of Deputy Garrett's death, Hurley stood and turned off the radio, then returned to his breakfast. They usually talked over breakfast, but on that morning, Hurley was silent, and so was Ella. He hadn't caught her yet, but he had the feeling Ella was watching him when he wasn't looking. Was his jitteriness that obvious?

He could not rid his memory of the face of Deputy Garrett's wife when he'd told her what had happened the night before.

Fran Garrett was a thirty-year-old office manager in a large insurance office. She had short rust-colored hair and a fair-complexioned face with a mouth that was just a tad too wide and smiling all the time—*all* the time. She was tall—five-nine, or so—and curvy, animated when she talked, a little loud, with a generous laugh.

When she opened the door late last night, she'd been in a pink terry cloth robe and had looked sleepy eyed. She'd smiled at Hurley at first, then at Deputy Kopechne, but after looking around for her husband, the smile had melted away and the sleepy eyes opened a little wider.

"Hurley?" she said, her voice hoarse. "Is it . . . is it . . . Billy?"

"I'm sorry, honey. I'm really sorry."

That wide mouth became wider as the corners pulled back and the eyes crinkled up and the left hand clutched at the front of her robe while the right slapped over her mouth. "Oh, no," she said into her palm. "Oh, dear Jesus, no." She trembled as tears spilled down her cheeks.

Hurley stepped forward and took her in his arms, and she collapsed against him, seeming to shrink in his hold.

Fran pressed her face to his shoulder; her words were muffled, but he understood them. "What huh-happened?"

"We're not sure yet, Fran. We think it was some kind of animal."

She pulled away from him and searched his face, frowning above wide eyes. "*What*? A *wha*—an *animal*?"

He nodded once. "I'm afraid so. Something big and strong."

"I want to see him."

Hurley closed his eyes as he shook his head. "No, Fran. No, you don't want that. Believe me. I've seen him. You don't want to remember him like that. You can't."

"Thuh-that . . . that bad?"

"Take my word for it, Fran."

She'd fallen against him then, collapsing completely, and sobbed for a long time. Hurley pulled her over to the couch and gently sat her down. She slumped forward and put her face in her hands.

After awhile, a small voice from inside the house said, "Mommy? What'samatter?"

She'd lifted her head from her hands. She'd stood then, and bent down to pick up her little boy as she said, "Oh, baby, oh, baby."

"Can you call someone, Fran?" Hurley had said. "You shouldn't be alone."

She'd nodded as she turned to him again. "I'll call my parents. My whole family will be here within half an hour. Don't worry, Hurley. Really. And thanks."

"Okay. Look, if there's anything Ella or I can do, anything at all, you just let me know, day or night. Okay?"

"I will. Thuh-thanks again, Hurley."

Along with that, Hurley kept remembering Garrett himself. A jagged, blood-blackened hole where his throat had been that revealed his torn trachea. His gut ripped open wide and his insides hanging out—what was left, anyway, what hadn't been—

Eaten, he kept thinking. *He was* eaten, *for God's sake.*

Hurley was unable to finish his breakfast. He sat there and poked at his waffle.

"Not hungry?" Ella said. "The waffles are as good as ever."

Hurley took in a deep breath and let it out slowly as he shook his head. "I was hungry, but my appetite . . . it left earlier this morning."

He kissed Ella good-bye, and he let his lips linger a little while on hers. With a spark of surprise, Ella responded and put a hand to his face. He pulled away and smiled at her, then went out and got into his Explorer and drove to work, getting to the station a few minutes after ten, his usual time. First thing he did when he sat down at his desk was to call the Department of Fish and Game over in the courthouse. He identified himself to the secretary and said he needed to talk to Lenny—that was Leonard Hill.

"Sheriff?" Lenny said. "How are ya?"

"Well, not too good, Lenny, not too good. I lost a deputy last night."

"Damn, Sheriff, I'm real sorry about that. I heard it on the news this morning. What happened?"

Hurley gave him a quick account, slowing down and getting more detailed when he discussed his deputy's remains.

"My God, are you serious?" Lenny said. "An *animal*?"

"That's what the deputy coroner says. He says we've got a big, powerful animal in the area, something like a bear."

"A *bear*?"

"That's what he said. Is that possible?"

Lenny was silent a moment, then: "Well, it's not *im*possible, I suppose. But there hasn't been a bear seen around here since the early seventies. And never have any actually come into town. Not *ever*."

"Can you get your people on this right away?"

"Sure. I'll go over there myself right now and see if I can find any sign of a bear, or maybe a mountain lion."

"I'd sure appreciate it. The idea of finding anyone else like that . . . well, it just makes me sick. Are you planning to do this right away?"

"I'll drive up there as soon as I hang up the phone."

"Ah, that would be great, Lenny. I can't get away to meet you, but I'll send a deputy over there to show you the exact spot. And as soon as you're done up there— don't even wait to get back to your office—just call me on your cell right away and let me know what you find, could you do that?"

"Sure, Sheriff. No problem."

After hanging up, Hurley looked at the messages on his desk, things he had to do. But the office felt very small that morning, and Hurley felt cramped, closed in. All he wanted to do was go out in the steel-gray day, get in the SUV, and drive.

So that was what he did.

8

DORIS'S WINDOW

Doris Whitacker had been at her front window crocheting a little blanket for her seventeen-month-old great-grandson, Noah, since a little while before the sun—what there was to see of it beyond the fog and clouds—had come up. On a TV tray in front of her plush, rotating rocking chair, its red-wine color blending with nothing else in the room, stood a steaming cup of coffee, a paper plate with two raspberry Pop-Tarts on it, and a pair of Swarovski binoculars. On the wall across the room was a large flat screen television. She'd paid a fortune for it—the chair hadn't been cheap, either—because her most recent late husband, a successful retired attorney, had left her a healthy chunk of money when he'd died. It upset her children to see her buy such expensive items. That was why she enjoyed buying them so much. When she'd bought the binoculars, Victoria, her oldest daughter by her first husband, had become apoplectic. Doris had honestly thought she was going to have to perform some kind of CPR on Vicki, because she sat on the couch and stared at the wall with her mouth hanging open, the receipt for the binoculars clutched in her right hand, as Doris called her name again and again. Then, so suddenly that it made Doris flinch, Victoria had blurted angrily, "And you're using those to spy on your neighbors? That's what you do when you sit around here all day? Spy on your *neighbors*? With your ridiculously overpriced binoculars? That's what you spend your *money* on?"

"They're glad I'm here, my neighbors," Doris had said, "ask any one of 'em. I watch this neighborhood like a hawk while they're away at work, or school, or day care. They know that I'll call the police if anything suspicious happens."

"Mother, listen to me," Victoria had said. "The sheriff him*self* took out a restraining order on you, just to keep you from coming down to the station every day."

"I have every right in the world to call them," Doris said. "I pay my taxes."

"You can't call them every time you see a black person. Black people are *around*, Mother, they're *out* there. There are black families living in this very neighborhood, and they have every right to be here. And just because you see a few Asian teenagers does not mean the tongs have come to Big Rock, okay? There are *Asians* around, too, Mom; you've gotta get used to it."

Doris saw everything that happened on Weeping Willow Drive—at least, the part of Weeping Willow Drive that she could see from her front window. She knew almost all her neighbors, knew their schedules, their habits. She spent most of her time watching them through her binoculars, for which she'd paid nine hundred and sixty dollars over the Internet (which her grandson had shown her how to surf after the family had presented her with a computer a couple of Christmases ago—Doris had taken to it surprisingly well, and for that reason, her grandson thought she was pretty cool). They were better than television, her neighbors, although she usually had the television on all day, as well. She managed to divide her attention between her window and her morning game shows and her afternoon stories. And

Oprah, of course. Doris had nothing but admiration for Oprah Winfrey.

Sometimes, weather permitting, Doris would take a stroll along Weeping Willow Drive, and as she walked, she would peer into windows and garages. She knew when her neighbors were home, when they were away— she knew the best times to take a peek. Sometimes, she even lifted the lids on their garbage cans to see what they'd been discarding. One could tell a lot about people's lives by taking a look at their garbage.

Doris was a slight woman—short, reed-thin, with a face covered by an intricate cobweb of wrinkles. Her once blue eyes were now gray, her once full lips now paper-thin. Her white hair was pulled back in a bun. The patch of shriveled skin that dangled beneath her chin jiggled when she spoke or moved her head. She wore a simple blue housedress and a beige sweater she kept buttoned up halfway. The sweater's right pocket bulged with tissues. Her mouth was always dry, so she usually sucked on a peppermint as she sat at her window.

Doris knew the Nortons had marriage problems. She heard shouting from over there a lot. Always from him, never from the wife. She strongly suspected he beat her, because the poor young woman frequently showed up with black eyes and swollen lips. Once, she'd limped for days.

Doris had heard the shouting from over there this very morning. From him, of course. And one sound that had come from her—a high, sharp *yelp*, like a dog being kicked. They frightened Doris, those sounds. She was frightened again when she saw Jimmy Norton come out the front door less than a minute later, putting on his coat. He was whistling something. He was *whistling*—it both frightened and infuriated Doris. She'd phoned the Sheriff's Department immediately.

Doris suspected they didn't take her too seriously down at the Sheriff's Department. She had a tendency to call too often, she realized that. But this was something real, something solid—that girl could be badly hurt; no telling what that bastard had done to her. And there was a baby and a little girl to think about, as well.

She waited for a car to show up. Plenty of cars went by in both directions—people going to work, or taking their children to school. But none of them were the white cars with the green-and-gold decals on the side doors—a gold star with a green pine tree standing in the center of it, the whole thing outlined by a bold green triangle. Beneath that were three lines written in green:

> *To Protect,*
> *To Serve,*
> *To Unite.*

But no one came.

While she waited, she tried to distract her thoughts by taking a look at the other house across the street. The Sutherlands.

The fat Sutherland boy had a job, but it wasn't one he enjoyed—she could tell by his sad, drawn demeanor on his way to and from work. She thought it was rather pathetic that, at his age, he was still living at home, even though he lived in the apartment over the garage. He should be out on his own, making a life for himself.

His parents were alcoholics, no doubt in Doris's mind about that. She saw how much liquor Mrs. Sutherland toted home in those bags with the Liquor Barn emblem on the side. She'd seen the discarded bottles in their garbage. Doris had their number.

Of all her neighbors, Jimmy was the most insufferable. It made Doris furious every time she saw the man. Of course, her sympathy for Andrea Norton could only go so far, because as far as Doris was concerned, women who stuck around for it secretly *liked* it—sometimes it was even a secret to themselves, she suspected. They didn't even know they liked it, because they were too terrified to admit it to themselves.

She was sure Andrea Norton was terrified, scared of every evening when he came home from work, dreading every morning when he woke up. She felt trapped, no doubt. Maybe one day she would kill her husband—but she would never go for help for herself. And for that reason, if she killed him, she would go to prison for the rest of her life. Might even get the death penalty. Because who *knew*? He was such a nice guy, a real generous, stand-up guy, and everybody liked him, right? If he'd been beating her, why hadn't she told someone—before blowing up and stabbing him to death, or shooting him in the head, or poisoning his food? Nobody would believe her then. Off to prison she would go. Or maybe she'd get really fat and hope he stopped finding her attractive and would stop touching her. Because Doris knew one thing Andrea Norton probably did not know yet—her husband was fooling around behind her back. A coworker, or a secretary, or someone. Or maybe it was a different woman each time—maybe he was a prolific adulterer. Doris could not be sure of which, but she knew his type—he'd been wettin' his willie ever since they got married, from before they were married, Doris was sure. Andrea would find out sooner or later, and it would hurt, but maybe that pain would be enough to convince her to finally leave. She might know already. You could never tell with such women.

But Doris knew. She always nodded to herself when she thought about it. Doris believed herself to be a stellar judge of character. She could size people up quickly and accurately. Jimmy was easy. The man *walked* like a predatory womanizer, and he had the face of a wife beater, a face that looked secretly mean, even when it smiled. She worried about Andrea Norton. There was always a chance, of course, that Jimmy would go the O. J. route and end up killing *her* before she could kill *him*.

Doris wasn't sure which was worse. All she knew was that, no matter what happened, those poor little girls would get the worst of it all the way around. They were probably already damaged by all the shouting and screaming their father did.

Oprah had done a number of shows on it over the years, because, of course, Oprah had been abused as a child, and she knew what it was like. She'd risen above it to become one of the richest, most powerful women in the whole world. Doris was as proud of her as she would be if Oprah were her own sister, or her daughter.

Regis Philbin bantered on the television.

Is it after nine already? Doris thought.

And still no one from the Sheriff's Department had shown up.

Doris reached over and picked up the phone to call them again.

9

HURLEY AND DORIS

Hurley had heard the call on the radio.

The dispatcher had said with such reticence, "A call from Doris Whitacker about a possible 273.5, across the street." A possible domestic abuse situation. She gave Doris's Weeping Willow Drive address, then said, "Anyone nearby there?"

"I'll take it," Hurley had said into the microphone.

Hurley had been dealing with Doris so long that he knew how to talk to her, how to cut through all her nonsense.

"It's about time you came," Doris said as she let him into her house. "Do you know how long I've been waiting?"

"I'm very sorry about that, Doris," Hurley said.

"You've got to do something about the shouting across the street at the Norton house."

"What kind of shouting, Doris?"

"He shouts at her. I can tell he's being very abusive to her with his words. And then she shows up with black eyes and fat lips. I heard shouting over there early this morning—he was shouting—and then she *yelped*. Just an abrupt *yelp*. Then he left the house, whistling. I've been worried about her ever since. She could be bleeding to death over there," Doris said, gesturing at her window, "or already dead."

"Does this happen often, Doris?"

"Often? It happens almost every day. Usually in the evening, after he comes home from work. I've called your department about it before, but deputies just come out and go across the street and tell them to hold it down, like I'm complaining about the noise, for God's sake. I'm not complaining about the *noise*, I'm worried that poor girl over there is going to be killed one of these days, that's what I'm worried about."

"Now, you know, Doris, that I've come out here before about this, and I've heard the shouting myself. Remember? I had a talk with Jimmy Norton and told him to get into an anger management class, or something, because his temper was liable to land him in jail. Remember?"

"I might remember that time."

"Well, it wasn't just one time, Doris. You've had us out here a few times about the Nortons. But I've seen nothing I can do anything about. Not yet, anyway."

"Then go over there right now," Doris said, pointing out her window with an arthritic index finger. "She's there now, and her face is all messed up, go and see."

"Is he home now?"

"No, he's at work. But she's home."

Hurley nodded. "Okay, I'll do it right now."

"Hey, Sheriff, tell me—do you still have a restraining order against me?"

"Now, Doris, I told you why I had to do that."

"I was never that bad."

Hurley laughed and shook his head. "Doris, you were coming into the station three and four times a day and interrupting my deputies and my staff while they were working, and interrupting *me* while I was working. You wouldn't stop when you were told, so I got the restraining order. And no, it's no longer in effect. But if you show up down at that station so much as once, Doris, I'll get another one. There's absolutely no reason for you to go down there. All you have to do is call us."

"Oh, all right, all right."

"Now. I'm going across the street to have a word with your neighbor," he said, starting for the door. "I'll come back and let you know what happened when I'm done."

"Thank you, Sheriff. I really appreciate it."

Hurley released a long sigh as he left Doris's house and walked across her front lawn. He went across the street to the Norton house, a small white ranch-style house with pale blue trim. The yard was a mess. Flowers shared their beds with weeds and the shrubs grew wildly up past the top of the white picket fence that bordered the yard.

Rain fell in an unenthusiastic drizzle, and a cold, biting breeze was coming up.

He went up the walk—which had a few cracks in it—up the front steps, across the small covered porch, and rang the bell. Then he waited.

The door opened and the once pretty, blond young woman who stood on the other side of the screen door looked harried.

"Yes?" she said with a smile, but the smile did not last long.

"Mrs. Norton? Andrea Norton?"

"Yes."

He took off his cap. "I'm Sheriff Hurley and I'd like to have a word with you. May I come in?"

"Uh . . . well, I'm doing housework at the moment. I was, um, mopping the kitchen floor and then I was gonna—uh, look." She pushed the screen door open and stepped outside, leaving the front door half-open. "Why don't I just step out here, okay?"

"Sure, that's fine. Boy, that's quite a shiner you've got there, Mrs. Norton."

There was a darkened half-circle under her puffy right eye, and the bruise seemed to dribble partway down her cheek. A small cut was visible on her lower lip.

Staring at the black eye, Hurley thought he'd love to catch the son of a bitch doing that himself sometime, show him what it's like to get beaten on for awhile. Men like Jimmy Norton—who weren't really men at all— brought out the worst in Hurley. They were just one notch above child molesters, and barely that.

Andrea shrugged. "Well, I tripped over the vacuum-cleaner cord and slammed my face right into the, uh, front of the entertainment center." She released a breathy chuckle. "The thing almost fell over on me. It hurt pretty bad, I'll tell you."

Hurley frowned, reached around and slowly rubbed the back of his neck. "Look, Mrs. Norton, your neighbors have been complaining about the shouting."

"The shouting?"

"The shouting your neighbors say your husband does so much. At you."

"Neighbors? Really? Or just one neighbor? Mrs. Whitacker, right?"

"Well, I, uh—"

"Has anyone besides Mrs. Whitacker complained?"

"Uh, no. To be honest, they haven't."

"See? I thought so. That old woman—"

"But wait, Mrs. Norton. I've been out here before, and I've talked to your husband about this. This has been going on awhile. And this is the first time I've seen you actually, uh . . . banged up."

"I *told* you, I tripped over the vacuum-cleaner cord and I—"

"Yeah, I know, that's what you said." He smiled. "But I don't believe you, not for a second, so why don't you drop the story. Use it on your neighbors and the cashier down at the grocery store. I know exactly what's going on here, Mrs. Norton, and I'm here to tell you that every time your husband hits you, he breaks the law. You could have him put in jail. You could do it *right now*—all you have to do is tell me your husband caused those injuries and you want to press charges. I would then go to his place of work and arrest him. Then you'd have to testify against him in court. But it would put him in jail for awhile. And maybe, uh . . . maybe you could use that time to figure out what you want to do with your life. You might ask yourself if you really . . . *really* want to stay here and keep getting beaten up."

She gasped, but then her face, registering first anger, then fear, slowly relaxed.

"I've seen it before, Mrs. Norton," Hurley said, lowering his voice and joining his hands in front of him, one still holding his cap. "I've *seen* it. It just keeps getting worse and worse. And then he kills you."

A baby made loud sounds of delight inside the house, but Hurley ignored it. Then a child called, "Mommy!"

"Just a second, honey, I'll be right there," Andrea said. A tear trickled down the side of her nose, then down past her mouth, to dangle from the edge of her jaw.

"He won't really mean to kill you, of course," Hurley went on, almost without a pause. "He'll be horrified when it happens. He'll go just a little too far, is all. He won't *mean* to kill you. But you'll be dead. And your babies will be without a mother. And they'll be raised by your husband alone. How would that be, Mrs. Norton?"

She said nothing. The teardrop quivering at the line of her jaw finally let go and fell to its death. Andrea Norton's eyes, which had been locked onto Hurley's, now slowly wandered downward, and she turned her head slightly, until she was staring down at the top porch step.

"Mommy!" the child inside the house called impatiently.

"You think about that, Andrea," he said, almost whispering now. "Think about it hard, but not long. Because you never know with these guys, when they're gonna go two or three punches over their usual quota. A couple more punches, a little harder. Or maybe he'll pick up a heavy blunt object and use that instead of his fists. You don't know how much time you might, or might not, have. There are places you can go, people who will help you. Like I said, you can put him in jail today, right now."

The baby squealed and began to cry.

"Mommy, pwease come here!" the child called.

"I'm sorry, but I've, uh, I've gotta go, okay?" Andrea said, but her voice was thick and wet now, and she did not meet his eyes with hers, which glistened. She turned away from him quickly, and clumsily pulled the screen door open and went inside.

"I hope you'll give it some thought, Mrs. Norton," Hurley said as he put his plastic-covered cap back on.

"Thuh-thank you, Sheriff," Andrea said, her back to him. "I've got to go now." She closed the front door. An instant later, the lock clicked.

Hurley went down the front steps, left the yard, and crossed the street back to Doris Whitacker's house.

"Well?" Doris said, her thin arms folded over her flat chest. "Did you see? She's been knocked around, hasn't she?"

Hurley nodded as he once again removed his cap. "Yeah, she has a black eye, Doris, and you were right to call."

"*See?*"

"I had a talk with her," he said. "I let her know she has options. Maybe she'll think about her situation a little differently now."

"Ah, well," Doris said with a flippant shrug of her shoulders, "I think they like it if you ask me."

"What?" Hurley said, blinking beneath a frown.

"The women who stick around for it and never leave," Doris said. "They get something out of it. They need it. They get off on it. That's my theory, anyway."

Hurley sighed. "Look, now, are we square, Doris? Think you could stop calling us every time you see someone walking down the street? Now this, calling about your neighbor beating on his wife—that's a legitimate reason and I'm glad you called. But really, Doris, please ... you've got to stop calling so many times a day."

"You told me to stop dialing nine-one-one, and I did," Doris said.

"Yes, you did, Doris, and for that, I'm very grateful. Now you've got to stop calling the nonemergency number, okay? Unless you've got a real emergency."

Doris frowned and cocked her head. "You only want me to call the nonemergency number when I have an emergency?"

Hurley sighed and rolled his eyes. "You *know* what I mean, Doris. If you keep pressing me on this, I'll just go ahead and put you in jail for it. There's a law against it, you know—I'm not enforcing it, is all. Yet."

"You'd put me in jail?"

"In a second, if I get so much as one more phone call from you, unless it's a legitimate emergency. See, when I find out it's Doris calling, I want to be able to think to myself, well, if *Doris* is calling, something's really *wrong*, because I know she wouldn't call for no reason. Do you think we can get to that point with you, Doris?"

After a moment of thought, Doris sighed and bowed her head. "All right, all right," she said, her voice quivering a little. "I-it's just that, uh ... well, I ... I just need to know that, uh, that you're ... there."

"We'll always be there, Doris. We're not going anywhere. I promise. We're there when you need us."

Back in the SUV, Hurley felt ... sorry. He felt sorry for lonely Doris Whitacker ... for battered Andrea Norton.

He turned on the radio, which played some loud rock and roll—Led Zeppelin. The album-rock station he listened to played nothing but hard driving rock and roll from back when there was such a thing. It made him feel good.

He turned the music down a little when a call came over the other radio. He listened closely, hoping it was close by and he could take the call.

He did not want to go back to the station—he wanted to keep busy.

10

DISTURBED

Hugh held the lunch tray precariously on his left arm while he opened the bedroom door with his right hand. He went to the bed and sat down on the edge beside Emily, put the tray in his lap, and carefully reached out and touched the side of her sleeping face.

She awoke with a jerk and a gasp and immediately pushed down on the mattress with both hands, dragging herself away from him, her eyes wide, lips parted. Then she blinked several times as she looked at him, as she looked around the room, her face shiny with perspiration. Her eyes closed slowly and she sighed. Her left eye was swollen and bruised and there was a small cut on her chin, another gash on her forehead, both covered by small white bandages.

"Hi," she said sleepily.

"Hi. You didn't eat breakfast, so I thought maybe you should have some lunch. I made you a tuna salad sandwich, and there's a little potato salad, I've got an apple here, and a banana, and a Diet Dr Pepper. You can eat all of it, or part of it, but I think you should eat something."

She nodded as she reached back and adjusted her pillows. She sat up with the pillows between her back and the headboard. "Thank you," she said.

Hugh put the tray across her lap. "If you want anything else, just let me know."

"No, this is fine, really. It's great, honey. Thanks."

"No problem."

"How's Jeannie?"

"She's had lunch, and now she's taking a nap."

Emily nodded.

"How are you?" he asked.

She shook her head slowly. "I keep having this nightmare. I wake up from it, then go back to sleep, and I have it again. I keep reliving that . . . horrible thing." She picked up half the sandwich and took a bite. "And something else," she said with a frown. "A house. I keep seeing this house." She chewed slowly. "It hurts to chew," she whispered. "Everything hurts. I even hurt . . . between . . . between my . . ." Her face screwed up and her shoulders began to hitch with quiet sobs.

"Oh, Emily." He reached out to touch her shoulder, but she moved away from him.

"Don't touch me," she said with food still in her mouth. She pushed the tray down her legs and shook her head as she said, "I can't eat. Take it away. Just go away, please. I want to sleep. That's all. Just sleep. I need a couple more of those pills, then I'll sleep. Please."

Emily reached over and took the orange prescription bottle from her nightstand. She popped the lid off and shook two Valium into her palm, swept them into her mouth, then drank them down with the glass of water on the nightstand.

Hugh picked up the tray and stood. "Would you like to call the counselor and—"

"No, just go. Please."

Hugh left the bedroom, frowning. She was still sobbing as he pulled the door closed. He went downstairs to the kitchen, put the tray on the table and went to the counter. He put his hands flat on the countertop and leaned forward, elbows locked, his head bowed between jutting shoulders.

It was not like her not to eat. Hugh was concerned. Of course, the truth was, she could stand to lose a few pounds, but he knew this was not the way to do it. He felt guilty for so much as thinking it. He hoped there was nothing seriously wrong with her. Could her head injury be worse than first thought? Maybe Emily should still be in the hospital. Whom should he call to ask? He knew a lot of people, he knew medical people; maybe someone he knew would have some advice. But who? He couldn't think, couldn't line his thoughts up in a row because . . . because . . .

Because he couldn't stop thinking about Vanessa Peterman.

He could look at his wife in bed upstairs, knowing she'd been through the worst experience imaginable, a horrible rape right beside the street—and at the same time, he would be thinking about Vanessa in some other part of his mind, thinking about what her breasts felt like under his hands, what her neck smelled like when he nibbled it. He might think about the amazingly sexy lingerie she wore for him, or about finding her smooth and shaven when he went down on her one day. She'd done it because he'd mentioned it in passing once, that he thought it might be fun, and she thought he might like it. It drove him insane. He did not want to stop kissing and licking and sucking on that perfectly smooth, soft, plush flesh. Even with his wife in her current condition, Hugh could not get his mind off Vanessa. On the one hand, Vanessa pleased him, preoccupied him—on the other, he felt disgusted with himself for it, and the guilt had gotten into his bones, deep, like arthritis.

He went to the kitchen sink, ran the cold water, splashed some over his face, then rubbed his hands up and down from chin to forehead. He turned off the faucet, tore several paper towels from the roll above the counter, and dabbed his face dry.

I'm going to burn in hell, he thought. *Sure as shittin', I'm going to burn in hell.*

11

FIRST TIME

Andrea was washing loads of laundry and ironing Jimmy's shirts; before that, she'd scrubbed the toilet and tub and damp-mopped the kitchen floor—she was tired. Her right eye was still swollen and dark. She'd held ice against it for awhile that morning, but it hadn't done much good. Her lower lip was slightly swollen, too, around the small cut she'd received that morning.

Andrea had put Marnie and Jenny down for their naps, and the house was quiet. At a quarter after three that afternoon, she poured herself a glass of chilled red wine, went to the living room, sat down in Jimmy's recliner, and put her feet up with a long sigh. Even though she seemed to do nothing but work around the house all day, Andrea enjoyed her time alone—without the kids, and especially without Jimmy. She felt so relaxed when he was gone. The moment he left the house, she could feel the tension flow from her body, but the moment he came back into the house, she tensed back up—her chest and throat felt tight; she would jump at the slightest sound—and she remained that way until she went to bed. Even then, it always took her awhile to get to sleep. She could not sleep until he started snoring, until she knew that *he* was asleep and no longer a threat.

She took a few sips of the wine. It felt warm in her belly and she relaxed even more. She picked up the remote and tried to find something on TV. She settled on an old black-and-white movie that was just starting.

The doorbell rang and she put her wine on the end table. She opened the door to find Jason Sutherland standing on the porch. He wore black pants and a blue jacket over a plaid shirt, and he held a hardcover book in his right hand.

"Hi, Jason," she said, smiling. She enjoyed his company and was always happy to see him. He was a curiously sad young man. She suspected he was lonely—he had no siblings, and as far as she could tell, he didn't seem to have many friends, either. He was always pleasant, and he made her smile, even laugh sometimes. Most of all, he listened to her like no one ever had. She felt like she could tell him anything, and she practically had. She had not known him all that long—a couple of months now—but she already felt with him an intimacy that she'd never achieved with Jimmy, an emotional rapport that existed beneath the surface of their conversations. "Come in."

He came inside and she closed the door.

"How are you, Andruh—oh my *God*!" he said. "Your eye! And your lip!"

"It's nothing, Jason, really, I don't want you to—"

"What do you mean, it's *nothing*? It's a black eye, is what it is. And a cut lip. Did . . . did your husband—"

"Just ignore it, okay? Please? For me? Just pretend it's not there."

Frowning, he slowly nodded his head.

Andrea placed a hand to the side of his face. "Thank you," she said. She nodded at the book in his hand. "What's that?"

"It's for you." He handed her the book.

Her face opened up with a big smile as she took the

book in both hands. "Oh, a *new* one! Thank you, Jason, thank you so much. Let me pay you for it."

"Oh, no, it's a gift."

"A . . . gift?"

"I know how much you enjoy his books, and that one just came in today, so I—"

Andrea could not help herself. Her chest swelled inside, her throat burned, and suddenly, she was sobbing.

"I'm sorry," she said as she turned away quickly. "Come in and sit down."

"Andrea, what's wrong? What did I—did I say something that—"

"I'm sorry, really, just ignore me, it's just *me*, that's all." She fought to get herself back under control. She went to the recliner, picked up her wine, and took three quick gulps, emptying the glass.

Something about Jason's kind gesture tore her up inside. It was the kind of thing she'd once imagined her husband doing for her. But of course, she never got any kind gestures from Jimmy—never any gifts or flowers or even a card now and then. Jason's gift reminded her of that in a vivid way and it just tore her up, made her wonder how she got here, where she stood today, in this marriage, and the thought felt so big, so massive, that it completely filled her head and threatened to make her skull explode. Andrea shook her head back and forth a couple of times and sighed, trying to get rid of that smothering, overwhelming thought.

"Sit down, Jason," she said, her back to him. She sniffled as she wiped her eyes with the heels of her hands, the book tucked under her arm. "Can I get you something?"

"Andrea, what's wrong?" He was standing right behind her. He put a hand on her shoulder.

Andrea turned around and stepped forward, put her hand on his soft chest, her head on his fleshy shoulder, still clutching the book in her right hand.

"I'm sorry," she said. "It was just so nice of you to give me this book. It just . . . it reminded me how . . . I don't know, I'm juh-just . . . I'm sorry." Her body shook with sobs.

Jason slowly lifted his arms and put them around her cautiously. He tried to say something, but only stammered, and finally fell silent.

Andrea took a few deep, steadying breaths. The sobs subsided and she sniffled a few times. After some initial hesitation, Jason squeezed her warmly in his arms. Not unlike his gift, the hug reminded her of affection she never received. Even when they had sex, it was all for him, Jimmy did nothing but take, and it was always a violent experience. The hug reminded her of that, but at the same time, it made her feel good—it made her feel like she was really being *hugged*.

"Oh, boy," she said with a smile, "I can't remember the last time I got such a great hug."

Finally, they pulled apart a little.

"Okay," Jason said. "What happened to your eye?"

"Can't leave it alone, can you?" she said with a humorless chuckle. "I could tell you I ran into a door, but . . . you probably wouldn't believe me. Would you like a glass of wine? I'm having one. I'll get you some." She stepped away from him, took her glass from the end table, and went into the kitchen. She put the book on the table, got a second glass from the cupboard and poured some wine into it, then refilled her own. When she turned around, he was right behind her again, and she handed it to him.

"Thank you," he said. "He hit you, didn't he?"

She nodded, still sniffling. "Again."

"Why do you stay with him?"

"Let's go back into the living room."

She sat down in the recliner. Jason put his wineglass on the end table, but did not sit down. He stood in front of her, his hands closed into loose fists at his sides. His lips worked in and out of his mouth, as if he were trying to get the feeling back in them after a shot of novocaine. He slowly shifted his weight back and forth from foot to foot.

"Why do you stay with him, Andrea?" he said again, finally.

"Where would I go? I don't have any family here anymore. My parents moved to the Bay Area. My brother lives in San Diego. I have a baby, a little girl, and—"

"Where are they?"

"Napping. I've got friends who could put me up, but me *and* the girls? I couldn't ask them to do that. Besides, Jimmy would . . . he'd find me, no matter where I went. And boy, would he be pissed."

"I . . . I heard the shouting this morning. I hate it, Andrea. It kills me to hear . . . well, when I think of you over here being hit, being knocked around . . . well, it makes me *sick*. And angry. I don't like it."

She wiped tears from her eyes again with the backs of her hands. "That's very sweet of you, Jason, really, but . . . well, I have Marnie and Jenny to think of, and they should have a daddy."

"But . . . *him*?"

"If I left Jimmy, I'd be alone. I'd never find anyone again."

"*What?* What are you talking about? You're a beautiful woman, Andrea. You'd have no trouble finding someone. I'd . . . I would . . ."

He stopped, looked at his feet a moment.

"What?" Andrea said, head tilting to one side.

Without lifting his head, he whispered, "I'd marry you in a second."

Andrea felt more tears coming, but fought them back. She was touched by his words, and she put a hand flat to her chest, tucked her lower lip between her teeth. She stood slowly, went to him, put her hands on his shoulders. His head was still bowed, so she hooked a finger under his chin and lifted it.

"That's so sweet, Jason. Thank you." She kissed his cheek, pulled back, and smiled.

Something happened then. The very air between them changed, became suddenly charged with sharp, crackling electricity. Their eyes locked and the tiny pale hairs on Andrea's arms and at the back of her neck stood up straight.

Jason lifted an arm, put a hand to the left side of her face. He opened his mouth as if to speak, but could say nothing. Instead, moving suddenly, clearly determined to do it before he lost his nerve, he leaned forward and put his mouth over hers.

Andrea could not remember how long it had been since Jimmy had kissed her. For a moment, she considered pushing Jason away, but then . . . it was such a nice kiss, so warm, so sweet. She let it continue, and it went on for awhile, became more intense. She lost herself in the kiss, fell over backward into it like a big, fat featherbed into which she sank down and down until she disappeared in all its softness.

Finally, Jason pulled back suddenly, as if he'd just become aware of what he was doing, and said, "Oh, I'm sorry, really, I'm—"

"Don't apologize," she said, her voice hoarse, her heart pounding. Her hands still on his shoulders, she lifted one and buried the fingers in his hair as she pulled him to her, and they kissed again.

It was something she was doing for herself. Jimmy never kissed her, not even a peck on the cheek now and then, not even during or after sex. He used to at least kiss her *before* sex—Jimmy's idea of foreplay used to involve him sticking his tongue down her throat while he stuck his hand between her thighs. But that was back when he made any effort at foreplay whatsoever—that had been before they'd gotten married. After the exchange of vows, sex became little more than an exchange of fluids for her. And kissing had not been a part of it in a long time. Instead of kissing her, when he reached orgasm he liked to spit in her face. He'd just get on top of her, pound away until he came, and as he came, he'd spit in her face, maybe call her a cunt, then roll over and go to sleep. No tenderness, no affection. So this was Andrea taking something she never got from her husband, something she hadn't had in a long, long time—a little warmth, a little affection, some human contact. Was that asking too much? Andrea did not think so, and she refused to feel guilty about it—she just had to make sure she did not get caught.

After standing there in the living room and kissing for awhile, Andrea took Jason's hand and led him to the bedroom. She rushed back and grabbed their still-full wineglasses and took them back to the bedroom with her. For afterward.

12

DORIS SPOTS A ROMANCE

Doris enjoyed watching as many of her neighbors as she could see from her window, but this afternoon, it was the Norton house that intrigued her most.

Oprah was on, and Tom Hanks was her guest. Doris liked Hanks. He seemed like such a nice man, so unlike most of today's movie stars who were sluts and whore-mongers and homosexuals and drug addicts. But even Tom Hanks was having difficulty competing against the Norton house for Doris's attention. Something was up.

On the one hand, Doris could understand the Norton woman straying from her marriage, breaking her vows. After all, the man beat her, and that was never good. Doris often thought that if any of her husbands had beaten her, just once, she would've been gone before the next sunrise. There was also a very good chance she would crush her husband's testicles in his sleep before leaving. For some reason, the Norton woman stayed around for it. She was one of *those*.

Taking a lover would be understandable, but it was un-seemly for the Norton woman to start messing around with the Sutherland boy. She probably wasn't that much older than Sutherland, but the boy seemed so immature—still living with his parents, still carrying around all that

baby fat. What was she doing bedding *him*, of all people?
That was what Doris suspected was going on over there.

That Norton woman had better be careful. If her husband ever found out, he just might kill her, even unin-
tentionally—he might even kill them both. If not, he
would no doubt beat her to within an inch of her life,
and he'd probably do the same to the Sutherland boy.

That was Andrea's problem, of course, not Doris's. That
made it no less interesting to Doris, though. Almost as interesting as Oprah's guest.

She turned her attention back to the television. . . .

13

CHICKEN CASSEROLE

Hurley entered his house with a heavy sigh. Something from the kitchen smelled good. He found Ella loading the dishwasher. He got a glimpse of that beautiful profile in the gray glow of the window. His eyes wandered down her body and he smiled. Hurley loved her no less than the day he'd married her twenty-eight years ago, and found her to be no less beautiful. How he loved coming home to those warm curves that were so pleasing beneath his hands.

"What's cookin', lover?" he said as he wrapped his arms around her from behind.

"Chicken casserole," she said.

"Ah, your chicken casserole, my favorite."

"You're actually home in time to eat it this evening. How was your day?"

"I've had better."

"Any sign of your naked man?"

"No. None at all."

"What about the animal?"

"Lenny from Fish and Game went over to the hospital and looked around through that patch of woods today for prints, droppings, fur, something to tell him what had been there last night, what had killed Garrett." Hurley sighed. "He found nothing."

"Nothing at *all*? Isn't that odd?"

"It's downright strange, is what it is. Lenny said if there'd been something there, there'd be some sign of it. I told him what George had said, that Garrett had been killed by a large animal with fangs and claws. But Lenny found no sign of anything but squirrels and coons. Plenty of human prints, though, especially around where Garrett's body was, footprints everywhere, a totally useless mess—some barefoot, which would be our naked guy, I'm guessing. Anyway, Lenny said as far as he could tell, the biggest thing hanging around in that patch of woods was a fox."

"What are you going to do now?" Ella asked.

"I don't know, honey, I just don't know. As for *right* now, I'm gonna sit down and have some of that chicken casserole."

"It'll be ready soon. Go change and wash up, and I'll make you a drink."

"Aaah, good," Hurley said. He left the kitchen smiling and feeling pleasantly hungry, looking forward to that drink. It was the best he'd felt since leaving the house that morning, and he hoped it would last.

14

THE LARAMIE HOUSE 1

Irving Taggart awoke suddenly, feeling cold. When he'd found this empty, rotting old house early that morning, just before sunrise, he'd gone up the stairs and found a bed and a blanket. His foot had gone through one of the stairs on the way up—he'd nearly broken his leg and badly scratched and scraped his shin and calf. The wounds had healed up within minutes.

Downstairs, he'd found the remains of a body. It was little more than a pile of bones. It had been there so long, it no longer smelled. The odor of death had simply become one of the layers of the whole rotting smell of the house—layers that Irving Taggart could smell individually, vividly. The corpse on the couch had been there a good long time. Patches of blackened, mummified skin covered the bones in places, but not enough to hold them together.

In the bedroom upstairs, Irving Taggart had found some smelly, dusty old clothes in an open suitcase. He poked through them until he found something that looked like it might fit him. As well as being old and smelly, they were as ugly as golf clothes, but they were *clothes*. He also found a pair of broken, mud-caked deck shoes.

Irving put on tan plaid pants, an orange shirt which was a tad snug and missing a button, and the deck shoes. He found a mattress on the floor, and a ratty old blanket. The mattress was a mess—stuffing coming out, covered with stains and rat turds and piss. The blanket was moth-eaten and thin, as smelly as the bed. But he had not cared about that, he'd just wanted, *needed*, to sleep after feeding. He was always tired after feeding, and it had taken him quite some time to find the old house. He'd slept all day long once he'd settled down on the mattress.

He had no idea it was the Laramie house, of course, nor would he have cared had he known. All he wanted was shelter . . . and privacy.

Now, in his new clothes and under the ratty, smelly blanket, on the rotting, stinking old mattress, he shivered with cold. Night had arrived again—the house was dark, all the shadows of the daytime gone, swallowed up by the blackness. The smells of nighttime were seeping into the house. Soon, Irving Taggart would go out into the night to satisfy his pounding desires, his gnawing appetites.

He could not decide which he wanted to do first—fuck or eat. Maybe he would do both at the same time.

15

AFTER DINNER

Jason lay on his bed with the radio on. He'd just finished eating a spaghetti dinner with his parents and his stomach was full, although he had not been able to eat much. He'd been too preoccupied to have an appetite. All he could think about was, of course, Andrea.

He had finally lost his virginity that afternoon.

"I hope you don't mind if I ask this," Andrea had said after the first time, "but was this, um . . . was it your . . . first time?"

Jason had been unable to lie. He never wanted to lie to her. He'd nodded. "It was that obvious? I-I'm sorry if I wasn't any good, I'll—"

"No, and *stop* that—berating yourself like that, it's not good."

"Yes, ma'am."

Her face had opened up into a big smile and she'd said, "I'm so glad I was your first, Jason. You never forget your first. Decades from now, when you're an old man, one of the memories that will comfort you the most will be of your first time with me."

"Oh, I'll never forget you," he'd whispered. "I wouldn't forget you if you were my hundredth, or my thousandth—although by then I suppose I'd be pretty, um, tired. I wouldn't forget you even if we never made love, Andrea. I'll never forget you. Ever."

Lips closed, smiling, she said, "Mmm."

"What?"

"I like the way you say it," she whispered. "Instead of 'having sex,' or 'fucking.' Making love. That's nice."

He couldn't wait till tomorrow, to get off work and come home. He would go see her again, and they would be together again.

He could. Not. Wait.

16

SEX IN THE NIGHT

Hugh got the kids' baths over with and got them all in bed, Donald in his room, the girls in theirs.

Jeannie was worried about monsters in her closet.

"They come out while I'm dreamin', Daddy," she whispered as he pulled the covers up to her chin.

"Honey, there are no monsters, okay?" He sat on the edge of her bed. "They're only in books, or on TV, or in the movies. There are no real monsters, sweetheart."

"You sure? 'Cause I've *seen* 'em."

"I'm positive, baby, there are no monsters, sweetheart. Bad dreams only take place inside our heads."

"Sometimes she wakes up screaming," Annie said quietly in her bed across the room. "She has bad dreams a lot."

Hugh frowned. "She does? Wake up screaming, I mean?"

"Sometimes," Jeannie whispered. "When that happens, Mommy comes in and tells me a story, or sings me a song, so I can go back to sleep."

"Baby, honey, I *promise* there are no monsters," Hugh said, brushing her hair from her face. "Just in your dreams. And you know what?"

"What?"

"Dreams can't hurt us. They can be really scary some-times, and they can seem very real, and we can wake up scared from a bad dream, but there's nothing a dream can ever do to hurt you."

"Promise?"

"Promise." He drew an X over his chest. "Cross my heart."

"Since Mommy's feelin' bad, will *you* come tell me a story if I have a bad dream?"

"You can bet on it. I'll be here." He hoped he would be there—he'd never heard Jeannie screaming in the night before. Apparently, Emily always got to her and quieted her down before Jeannie's screams had a chance to wake him up.

"Okay. G'night, Daddy."

He bent down and kissed her on the lips. "Good night, sweetums." He got up and went over to Annie's bed and kissed her, too. "Good night, honey."

" 'Night, Dad," Annie said.

He left the room and went across the hall to Donald's room. It was dark, but music played quietly on the radio.

"Time to go to sleep, tiger," Hugh said.

"Mom lets me listen to the radio at night," Donald said. "Helps me get to sleep."

"Really?"

"Yeah. It's my clock radio, and I set it to turn off after an hour."

"Okay. Sounds good to me." He went to the bed and sat down on the edge of the mattress. Donald was frowning. "What's the matter?"

The boy said nothing for awhile, then: "It's Mom. Is she gonna be okay?"

Donald was a worrier. Sometimes it concerned Hugh—the boy seemed to take everything so seriously. "She's going to be fine. It's just going to take a little while."

"Oh. Okay." But the frown did not relax.

"You okay?"

"Yeah."

"You're sure?"

As if he sensed his expression's effect on his dad, Donald relaxed his frown and smiled a little. "Yeah, I'm fine."

"Okay." Hugh bent down and kissed him on the forehead.

" 'Night, Dad."

"Good night, tiger."

By the time he went downstairs to enjoy the silence, he was exhausted, ready for bed. He turned on the television and tried to watch, but he could not focus his eyes on the screen. Hugh turned off the television, all the lights, then went upstairs.

The bed was empty and the bathroom door was closed. As far as Hugh knew, it was the first time Emily had left the bed all day. She hadn't eaten, other than a couple bites of the tuna sandwich he'd fixed her for lunch. Hugh was worried about her—but he was too tired to worry right now. All he wanted was to stretch out in the bed. He had a new respect for the work Emily did while he was out showing houses all day.

He took off his clothes and got into bed, sat up against the headboard, and turned the TV on with the remote. He turned on Letterman and locked his hands together behind his head, elbows out.

The toilet flushed in the bathroom; then the faucet turned on. A moment later, Emily came out. He was surprised that she was naked—Emily had become quite modest since her weight gain. She stood in the doorway and looked at him. There was something odd about her eyes, about her whole expression. She pulled her lips back over her teeth and it took him a moment to realize that she was smiling.

"Hugh," she said, her voice breathy. "*Hugh.*" She rushed to the bed and tore the covers off of him. She fell onto the bed and got on top of him.

"Emily, what are you *doing*?" he said.

She breathed heavily as she straddled him. She smelled of an unbathed muskiness. Her breasts jiggled above the rolls of fat that went around her middle.

"What does it *look* like I'm doing?" she whispered raspily.

"But, but today, you didn't even want me to *touch* you."

"That was today. I want you now, Hugh." She clenched her teeth and spoke through them. "I have to have you, I *have* to. I want you inside me, you hear? Right now. Right *now*. Fuck me, Hugh, *fuck* me."

He laughed with wide eyes, his eyebrows high. "Well, what's, what're you—"

She reached down and grabbed his limp penis, then took it in her mouth.

"Oh, God," he said.

Emily hadn't gone down on him in years. She'd done it a lot before they were married, but afterward, it had become more infrequent, until it had stopped altogether. As she sucked on him, he got hard in her mouth and let his head fall back, rolled his eyes up in his head as he closed them and moaned. She hummed with him in her mouth, then made a low, guttural sound in her throat. She climbed back up his body, reached down, inserted him, and bounced up and down on him, laughing like a child.

Hugh closed his eyes and just enjoyed it. It had been a long time since Emily had shown this kind of enthusiasm in bed. He did not understand it—it made no sense under the circumstances, given the fact that she'd just been raped, and had just killed her rapist, for crying out loud—but he did not think about it.

He rolled with it. And it was great, like the old days—if he closed his eyes and forgot about how fat she'd gotten, it was their honeymoon in Mexico all over again. Emily was making the same laughing but desperate sounds, clutching at him in the same way, blindly and tightly, her nails scratching his skin, breath coming in a fast pant. Then she clamped her lips together tightly and started to make high humming sounds through her nose. She was getting close. It was a familiar sound, such a good sound, Hugh couldn't help smiling a little. She embraced him and held him almost smotheringly tight as she came, pounding down on him harder, holding him desperately, crying out repeatedly, "Oh! Oh!" Then she stopped moving and pressed herself down on him hard and ground her hips over him for awhile, moaning softly. She put her mouth over his, sucked on his tongue as she ground on him. Then she slowly started humping him again.

Hugh laughed a little and whispered, "What, are we going again?"

"Fuck, yeah, I want more," she whispered through a beaming smile. "I'm horny, sweetheart, and I just really, really need to fuck until I drop right now, okay?"

He shrugged. "I hope I hold out long enough."

She kept moving slowly up and down on him.

"Don't worry, we'll take breaks if you want." She giggled. "We can fuck all night, right? I mean, you're not going to work in the morning, are you?"

"No," he said, smiling.

"And you're still hard right now, right?"

"Like a rock."

"Then there's no problem, is there?"

He laughed. "None that I can see."

"Okay, then. I'm going to roll over, and I want you to fuck me hard. You hear me? *Hard.*"

Hugh had no problem with that plan at all.

At one point, at the height of their passion, both of them gasping for breath and shiny with sweat as they approached orgasm, Emily made a sound that almost made Hugh stop and sit up on his knees. *She growled.* It was deep, throaty, so uncharacteristic of her, that it was startling, and a little frightening. More than a little. It did not sound like her at all. But he was too close to coming, and he quickly swept the growl from his mind and focused on his imminent ejaculation.

In a few seconds, he felt like growling himself, and he was not entirely certain that he didn't.

17

VANESSA PETERMAN

"You really need to go," she said, still smiling as they stood facing each other beside the bed. Somehow, she could not stop smiling, in spite of her greatest efforts. He was such an enthusiastic young man, her masseur. He always made her feel good, made her smile. His name was Oscar, but everyone called him Ossie. He was quite well hung, and Vanessa enjoyed teasing him about it. He was the only man she'd ever known whom she could tease about his penis. Most men would crumble at a remark about their members. Not Ossie. He was quite secure about his penis.

"Why can't I stay the night?" he asked.

"Because I said no, that's why," she answered. "I have to get up early in the morning and go to work, and I won't have time to see you off then. So you'll have to go now. I mean, of course, I'd love to have you in bed for the night, but . . . no. You have to go."

He was still naked, and he stood before her all bronze and rippling. With his shaggy black hair and impeccably tanned and cut muscles, he looked like he belonged on the cover of a paperback romance novel, or in an underwear ad.

Vanessa was naked as well, and she stepped forward,

pressed her body to his, and embraced him. They kissed. The kiss lasted longer than she'd intended, and she felt his thick penis begin to harden against her thigh.

"No, no," she said, gently pulling away from him. "Time to go."

He finally put on his clothes. She remained naked as she walked him through the apartment to the door, where his folded-up massage table and leather satchel leaned against the wall. They kissed again, promised to see each other soon, and he left.

Vanessa was still smiling when she closed the door. She went to the kitchen. An open bottle half-filled with red wine stood on the counter. She poured some into a glass, sipped it as she leaned back against the edge of the counter, cold on her hips.

Vanessa Peterman liked sex. It was something she got plenty of—she had a number of men with whom she'd developed friendly, casual sexual relationships. Nothing serious, no commitments, no obligations, just occasional dates followed by romps either in their beds or hers. Friends with benefits. Vanessa knew she was attractive, which made the sex easier to get. She saw no reason why she shouldn't get as much as she wanted as long as she was capable, while she was still young, while men still found her appealing, and while she was still emotionally unattached. She had not been raised with any religious beliefs, so she felt no guilt about it. She knew women who were so screwed up by religion that they felt guilty having sex with their own husbands! But not Vanessa— she didn't care *whose* husband he was.

She loved everything about sex equally. She was as fond of kissing as she was of actual intercourse. She was a foreplay junkie. At work, she thought of sex often, and each thought made her warm between her legs. Some- times she wore no underwear and enjoyed the feeling of her clothes rubbing against her naked flesh. She was always eager to try new things, and new men.

As she sipped her wine, she thought about tomorrow. Things she had to do. She remembered that she was seeing Hugh tomorrow during lunch.

Hugh. She wondered if he was going to be a problem. The jealousy he'd expressed when she'd told him she had plans and couldn't see him worried her a little. Jealousy was a sign of possessiveness, and Vanessa did not like possessiveness at all, not in anyone, but especially not in her men. She avoided possessive men the way she avoided religious programming on TV. No one possessed her. They could hold her, have their way with her, if she so desired, but they could not *possess* her.

She decided she would have to see how things went tomorrow. If it became necessary, she would simply let Hugh go.

Vanessa owned a popular music and video store in Big Rock—people came from all directions to the Flaming Disc. Ever since she'd opened the place, she'd made an effort to carry hard-to-find films and recordings, foreign stuff, old stuff. It was a hip place to shop for CDs and DVDs, even vinyl records, and part of the store's charm was that if it did not carry what you were looking for, the employees would find it for you. Another part of the store's charm was Vanessa herself. From the beginning, she was the face and voice of the store. She used to appear in her own late-night TV commercials—for awhile, she'd sponsored a late-night double feature of old movies on a local independent TV station. She'd advertised the sales at Flaming Disc, and scattered in a few comments about the movie that was playing—like the fact that it could be found at Flaming Disc. She'd stopped doing the commercials last year because she didn't need to anymore. The store was so popular, she was about to open another one in Redding.

These days, she didn't work as much as she used to—she had a very loose work schedule that allowed her to pursue . . . other pursuits.

She had proven to herself—the only person who really mattered, as far as she was concerned—that she did not need anyone else. Her business had been successful because of *her*, no one else, because of *her* hard work, no one else's.

She raised her glass in a little toast to herself, tipped it back and finished the wine, then went to the bathroom to brush her teeth before bed.

18

WALKING COSMO

Patrick Hollenbeck opened his front door with one hand, and held Cosmo's leash with the other. His right hand wore a plastic glove with which to pick up and dispose of Cosmo's droppings. The small porch was dark, so he reached in and flicked on the porch light; then he pulled the door closed and checked to make sure it was locked.

It was a cold, misty night, with a light drizzle in the air, not the kind of night Patrick would care to be out in, but Cosmo had his needs before bed. Cosmo was a black-and-rust-colored mutt, a big walking mop with a jaunty step and a tongue-dangling smile for everyone.

Patrick struggled with the latch of the front gate, which had been sticking lately, opened it, and then went out onto the sidewalk. He closed the gate behind him and they turned right—turning left would take them to the intersection of Magnolia and Manzanita, while turning right gave them a whole block to walk. Cosmo trotted happily ahead of him.

Patrick was a thirty-eight-year-old bachelor with a successful mobile home repair business who lived in a two-bedroom house on the corner of Magnolia and Manzanita in a nice neighborhood in Big Rock. He had a lovely girlfriend named Nadine; his parents were healthy; he was close to his younger sister. Patrick was a pretty happy guy—happy with his life, with himself. He was the upbeat guy other people liked to be around; he elevated the mood when he entered any room.

Each block in that neighborhood had two streetlights, and the first one was coming up. Its yellowish light had a halo of mist around it. As Cosmo led him through the pool of light, Patrick looked ahead and saw a dark figure walking toward them. The figure was all the way across Ivy and on the next block, walking rapidly. As the dark figure stepped into a pool of light, Patrick laughed a barking laugh that echoed in the night—the man walking rapidly toward him was completely naked. Although that moment of illumination was brief, Patrick was certain that the man was not wearing any clothes.

The naked man reached the end of the block, crossed Ivy, and stepped up onto Patrick's block. As he passed beneath the streetlight at that end of the block, Patrick flinched. Suddenly, the man was wearing a full suit of dark clothes. Or . . . was that some kind of dark coat? Even his face looked dark. He even seemed . . . *taller*. Patrick frowned and quickly questioned what he had seen earlier. He was *certain* the man had been naked—he'd seen it clearly. Now, he appeared to be wearing something. Where had it come from? What was it? It didn't look quite right for a suit of clothes. As the man continued to walk toward him, Patrick squinted a little. With the other streetlights behind him, Patrick saw only a dark silhouette—what appared to be a rather *shaggy* silhouette.

Cosmo stopped at a crepe myrtle tree, sniffed around, then stopped and lifted his head. The dog looked down the sidewalk and sniffed the air with minute nods of his head. Patrick held the leash, but instead of watching Cosmo, his head remained turned to the right to look down the sidewalk.

Then something strange happened. The man hunched forward and walked that way for a few steps. Then he dropped forward until he was down on all fours.

My God, is that some kind of . . . *monkey?* Patrick thought.

It did not look quite like a monkey—but then, it did not quite look like a man on all fours, either.

It was moving faster. A lot faster.

Cosmo growled, and his growl became more intense as the figure neared.

Patrick felt a shudder of fear of the unknown, because he didn't know what he was seeing. Whatever it was, it was getting closer, and it was bigger than Patrick first had thought. A *lot* bigger.

Cosmo began to bark; then he pulled the leash taut and tugged on Patrick's arm, going back toward the house. Cosmo was afraid and wanted to get out of there. Patrick had never seen the dog so adamant about going back home. He looked over his shoulder. The low figure loped quickly toward him, almost on him.

He saw fangs, a gaping maw of fangs.

Patrick began to run, and Cosmo ran with him.

Something turned Patrick's blood to ice water with the sudden awareness that although he knew the thing behind them was rapidly catching up, he could hear nothing, not a footfall, not a breath.

At the gate, Patrick reached over and found the latch, and tried to jerk it aside, but it stuck. It would rattle, but it would not slide, it would *not*, and Patrick mustered the courage to turn his head to the left. The loping figure was upright now. Patrick saw that nightmare of fangs again, and something heavy and strong slammed into him.

Patrick felt nothing but pain after that. It rose up and slammed down on his fear, overpowering it with agony. He screamed a high and shrill scream, but his cry was abruptly cut off as jagged teeth sank into his throat and tore viciously. Making horrible gargling sounds, he choked on his own blood, which quickly filled up his throat and poured out his mouth.

Patrick's violent death was prolonged. He did not die quickly, or easily. He felt a lifetime of pain and agony in those final minutes.

Meanwhile, once Patrick had released Cosmo's leash, the dog had kept running. He'd already run across Manzanita and was well into the next block, dragging his rattling leash behind him.

Cosmo had been so badly terrified by what he'd smelled that he did not pause to look back, not once.

19

NIGHT CALL

Hurley parked the Explorer at the curb on Magnolia a few minutes before midnight. There were already two cruisers there, as well as the coroner's pewter-colored van. He yawned as he killed the engine. The SUV's heater worked well and it was nice and warm inside. As he sipped coffee from a silver traveling cup, Hurley realized how much he did *not* want to leave the inside of that vehicle. He'd just drifted into a deep sleep when Deputy Kopechne called earlier. His eyes felt puffy and he could not stop yawning—he did it again as he got out of the SUV. He walked over to the body, where three deputies and George Purdy stood talking. The body was covered with a green tarp. They fell silent and turned to Hurley.

"Kopechne . . . Garvin . . . Wiley," Hurley said with a nod. "Hello, George." He sipped coffee from his cup.

George said, "Sheriff, did you talk to Fish and Game about my conclusions regarding your deputy's body?"

"I did. I spoke to Lenny Hill." He told George that Lenny had checked the area and had found no signs of any large animals whatsoever.

George nodded. "Yeah, I don't suppose Lenny would find any signs of large animals around here, either, but

I'll tell ya, that doesn't mean much." George bent down and grabbed the corner of the tarp and peeled it back.

Hurley winced and gasped when he saw the shredded, eviscerated, blood-soaked body. It was impossible, at first glance, to determine the corpse's sex.

"Oh, Christ," Hurley whispered. "Oooh, dear *Christ*," he barked, turning away from the body, hands on his hips. He turned to George then. "What . . . what the hell are we dealing with here?"

"I gotta get him on the table before I can even guess," George said, "but this looks exactly like Deputy Garrett's body. I bet I'll find the same fang marks on this guy."

"You're *sure* they were fangs?" Hurley said.

"They were either fangs or long, slightly curved, sharply-pointed teeth."

Hurley's eyebrows huddled together. "That's . . . the same thing."

"My point exactly." He stepped closer to Hurley and lowered his voice. "Listen, Arlin. It's not like someone put on some artificial fangs and went to work on this guy. I mean, hell, that wouldn't even *work*. The positioning of the teeth, the shape of the jaw—there's no way a human being could fake that, Arlin." George hunkered down beside the corpse and turned his flashlight onto it. "Look at this, the same as before—the throat, the abdomen. It's almost identical to—"

When George said nothing more for a long moment, Hurley said, "What's wrong?"

"Found something."

Hurley hunkered down at George's side.

George took a pen from his pocket and pointed at a small, dark tuft of fur caught on the zipper of the man's jacket. "Anybody got a baggie?"

A moment later, one of the deputies came to him with a small plastic evidence bag. George put away his pen, took a long pair of tweezers from his pocket, then carefully plucked the tuft of fur off the zipper. He dropped the fur in the bag, then stood as he put away the tweezers. He offered the bag to Hurley.

"You think that came off a person?" George said.

"Okay," Hurley said quietly, taking the baggie. "Maybe Lenny doesn't know what he's talking about."

"The lab in Eureka will be able to tell you what kind of animal it is from this fur, or from saliva found on the corpse. I'd take the lab results over anything Lenny says."

Hurley handed the baggie to a passing deputy and said, "Give this to someone in the Eureka Crime Scene Unit when they get here." He turned to Deputy Kopechne. "Any witnesses?"

"The people in the next house made the call when they heard a man screaming," Kopechne said. "I'm sure they weren't the only ones. We haven't canvassed the neighborhood yet."

"That house there?" Hurley said, pointing.

"Yes."

Hurley walked down the sidewalk to the next house. There was no fence around the yard, just a concrete path that cut across the lawn to the small screened-in porch. Hurley tried the screen door, but it was locked. He knocked hard on the door's frame and called, "Hello?"

A moment later, the front door opened and a man in a robe came out and stood at the screen door. "Yes?" he said.

"I'm Sheriff Hurley. You called about someone screaming earlier?"

"Oh, yeah. Come on in."

The man unlocked the screen door and opened it. Hurley crossed the porch and followed the man into the house.

It was dark in the living room, with only one lamp on at the end of the couch glowing a pale yellow, and the television running quietly, spreading its shimmer out over the floor. A woman sat on the couch, also in a robe.

She held a glass of some amber beverage. Her blond hair was mussed, as if she'd already been in bed for awhile.

Hurley turned to the man. "I need to know everything you heard, Mr.—?"

"Arden. David Arden. My wife Maxine."

Hurley smiled. "Why don't we sit down and get comfortable?"

"Yeah, sure," Arden said, gesturing toward a wingback chair. Then he went to the couch and sat down at the other end from his wife.

"Now, what did you hear tonight, Mr. and Mrs. Arden?" Hurley asked.

"Maxine was already asleep, but I was lying awake in bed," Arden said. "I heard this scream. Not a typical scream, because it wasn't a woman. It was clearly the sound of someone in pain. I got up, went out on the porch and looked around."

"See anything?"

"Not at first. I heard something, though. Somewhere out front, it came from the left—" He gestured with one hand. "—over by the corner of Magnolia and Manzanita."

"What kind of sound was it?"

"Well, it's hard to describe. Grunting? Movement? It was a combination of things. When I heard it, I knew something was happening just up the sidewalk. I left the porch and went out to the mailbox, looked up the sidewalk, and I saw this . . . well, it was like . . . somebody on the ground and—"

"It was a person?"

Arden frowned. "Of course. It took me awhile to figure out what I was seeing because it wasn't much more than a silhouette, but I realized it was somebody lying on the sidewalk, and somebody else, somebody big, hunched down over him. Or her."

"And you're sure that what you saw was a *person* hunched over this body?"

He frowned again. "Well, *yes*. I mean, he was huge. Way too big to be an animal. Unless we've got some animals around here that I don't know about."

"Yes, you and me both," Hurley said. "What did you do then?"

"I ran in the house and called you."

Maxine took a couple of swallows of her drink, then shook her head. "I can't believe you went out there. What *possessed* you to actually . . . *do* something for a change?" She was an attractive woman, but as she spoke, her face became ugly with a twisted, bitter expression.

"Why don't you go to bed?" Arden said quietly.

"You woke me up, and I'm awake now," she said. She took another drink.

"Is it possible for you to be awake and *not* drink?" Arden whispered harshly.

"Um, excuse me," Hurley said, "but if I could just ask a few more questions, then I won't bother you anymore."

"I'm sorry, Sheriff," Arden said.

"While you were out there, did you notice any cars parked on the street that aren't normally there?"

"Cars?" Arden said, squinting a little. "Not that I remember. I wasn't really paying any attention to the cars."

"Was there anyone else around, maybe someone standing or walking nearby?"

Arden turned his head back and forth. "No. It was very quiet. This is a quiet neighborhood, especially late at night. It's mostly families, some senior citizens. Not much going on after nine. Tonight was no different."

"Actually, that's the neighborhood my husband would *like* to live in," Maxine said, "not the one we *really* live in. There are a lot of teenagers in this neighborhood, and right here on Magnolia, and they're anything *but* quiet."

"Maxine," Arden said.

She leaned forward. "We've got pregnant teenagers on

this street, we've got a registered sex offender a block over, a *child* molester."

Through clenched teeth, Arden said quietly, "Maxine, will you just shut up and go to bed? Can't we do this later?"

"Plenty of your deputies have been to this street time and again," Maxine said to Hurley. "Mostly because of the teenagers, but once they came because Millie Pruitt, across the street and a few houses down, finally stabbed her abusive husband." She sat back and turned to Arden. "Oh, yes, this is a quiet neighborhood. A *great* place to live." Then she added, with a sneer in her voice, "And the best we can do." She tipped her glass back and emptied it. She got up off the sofa and shuffled out of the room.

Arden's head drooped for several seconds as he leaned forward, elbows on his thighs, hands locked together. Then he sat up and said, "Again, I'm sorry, Sheriff. You came on a bad night."

Hurley hoped to finish the questions before Maxine came back and continued whatever domestic squabble was going on between them. "If we could get back to what you saw. This person who was hunched over the body on the sidewalk—was there anything distinctive about this person, anything at all?"

Arden frowned as he thought about it. Finally, he shook his head, "I can't think of anything, except that it was somebody big. And maybe muscular. Well . . . either muscular or fat, but . . . well, I just didn't get the *sense* that it was a fat person, you know what I mean?"

Hurley nodded.

"It didn't *move* like a fat person."

"How did it move?"

"Well, it didn't move much at all," Arden said with a shrug. "It kept making a . . . well, this jerkinglike motion, but with its head. I *think*. Like I said, it was just a silhou-ette. All I knew was, it didn't look right, which is why I called you. Because it looked somehow . . . violent. Also because that scream sounded like someone was hurt pretty bad."

Hurley nodded, then stared at the floor for a little while. He was disappointed. He'd been hoping for something solid from David Arden. What he'd gotten so far didn't add up to much. But it suggested one thing— George Purdy's wild animal was most likely a person. A serial killer?

That's just what I need, Hurley thought.

He stood and said, "All right, Mr. Arden."

Arden stood, too.

"You'll get a visit from one of my deputies in the next day or so. Tell them what you told me. And if you remember anything else, please tell the deputy, okay? Or—" He reached into his shirt pocket under his jacket and produced his card, which he handed to Arden. "—give me a call."

"Will do," Arden said, taking the card. He went to the front door and opened it.

Out on the porch, Hurley nodded to Arden and said, "My best to your wife." Outside, he went along the sidewalk to the spot where the horribly mutilated body lay. Hurley walked over to George, who stood beside his SUV talking to a deputy.

"Well, our witness doesn't help your animal theory any, George," he said. He told George what Arden had said.

George frowned and said, "Too *big* to be an animal?"

"That's what he said."

"Then how do you explain that bit of fur I found? You wait and see, the lab will tell you what that fur came off of, and *that* will be your killer. It's obvious your witness has his head up his ass."

Hurley sighed as he looked in the direction of the Arden house. What was he to think? A witness told him a *person* had been hunched over the body, and the deputy coroner, and perhaps a tuft of fur, insisited it was the work of a savage animal. Whatever it was, apparently it had killed two people so far.

He hoped—he *prayed*—that it was an animal. Hurley did not want to have to deal with the kind of monstrous person who could do such a thing to a fellow human being.

20

EMPTY HOUSE, EMPTY BED

Thursday

Hugh Crane sat in his car across the street from the house on Clauson shortly before noon on Thursday, waiting. He'd gone into the house as soon as he arrived and spread a blanket he'd bought that day at Wal-Mart over the immaculately made bed. He did not want to leave behind any unseemly stains.

Emily almost had not let him out of the house. He'd mentioned going back to work that day, and she'd practically had a tantrum, so he'd decided to take one more day off. But he told her he wanted to go down to the office to pick up some files he needed to work on, and he promised not to be gone more than an hour.

"An hour?" she'd said as he shaved at the bathroom mirror, her arms wrapped around his waist, chin resting on his shoulder, breasts pressed against his back. She was warm against him. "Why so long? It doesn't take an hour to get there and back."

"Well, I'm sure people will ask about you. I'll want to answer them, won't I? Then I thought I'd stop and pick us up some fish and chips at Blue Cove for lunch."

"Really? I'm not hungry, though."

"You will be when lunchtime rolls around."

"No, I mean, I haven't been hungry. It's like the . . . like it killed my appetite."

"You had a horrible experience, Emily. I really think you ought to call that counselor. Hey, that's a good idea—why don't you call her, have her come over while I'm gone. You two can talk."

"I suppose I could do that." Then, with a smile: "Or . . . you could stay here and we could fuck some more." She laughed.

Hugh smiled at her in the mirror and lowered the razor for a moment. "I must admit," he said, "I'm a little surprised to find you so . . . horny all of a sudden."

"How do you know it's sudden? Maybe I've been feeling this way for a long time and it just finally came out."

"*Have* you?"

She giggled. "No, it *was* sudden. But I think it has something to do with wanting to get that . . . that horrible man, that *creature*, out of my mind, to fill that space with something good, you know? I need you to erase all that."

He nodded. "Okay. I've never heard of such a thing, but I guess it makes sense." He continued shaving.

"But that's not really the reason, either," she said. "I . . . I don't know what brought this on. But it's overpowering, Hugh. Last night, when I came out of that bathroom, I had to have you. It wasn't just an urge, it was an all-consuming *need*. I *had* to have you. I think I would've gone insane if you'd pushed me away. And I need it again." She reached down and grabbed his crotch.

He jumped a little and jerked the razor away from his throat. "Jeez, Emily, you trying to make me open a vein here?"

"But I want it again," she said, squeezing his penis rhythmically until it began to harden.

"But I just got dressed."

"You're turning down *sex*?"

"You've worn me out, Emily. My knees are still shaking. My penis is an exposed nerve." He finished shaving, then bent down and washed off the remaining bits of cream. He turned off the faucet, then took a towel from its rack and scrubbed his face dry. He turned around to face her. "I'm pooped, Emily."

That wasn't very far from the truth. He wasn't entirely sure he'd be any good for Vanessa—Emily had been relentless.

Emily had said good-bye to him with cloying reluctance.

He did not understand her horniness—it made no sense. Everything he'd read and heard about rape victims indicated that they were more likely to have trouble *having* sex after being violated. He'd heard nothing about increased libido after a rape—*right* after a rape. Besides that, Emily acted differently. Even back when they'd been having sex regularly, even before that when they couldn't keep their hands off each other, she'd never been as vocal or as enthusiastic—as *animalistic*—in bed as she had been last night and today. She'd been a beast in bed, and the rest of the time she'd been positively *manic*. It was almost as if the rape had *released* something in her. But that didn't make sense . . . did it?

Hugh was tempted to talk to that counselor himself, just to ask her about it.

He saw movement in his rearview mirror and turned to it. Vanessa had just pulled up behind him. Hugh got out, put on his brightest Realtor smile, went back to her car, and opened the door for her.

"Am I late?" she said as she got out. She aimed her key ring at the white Chrysler 300 and locked it with a beep.

"A little, but that's okay," Hugh said.

They did not touch as they crossed the street and went up the front path to the door of the empty house that was up for sale.

"The owners of this house are in Barbados. They live in Seattle, but they had this place because they frequently made trips down here—for business, I think. Now they no longer need to make those trips, so they're selling the place. They haven't moved their stuff out yet." He unlocked the lockbox on the doorknob, then unlocked the doorknob, and pushed the door in. He stepped back and gestured for her to enter.

Once inside, Hugh kicked the door closed, locked it, and pulled Vanessa to him, wrapped his arms around her and held her tight. They kissed as they began to undress each other there in the small tiled foyer. Once they'd found a rhythm, they began to head down the hall as they kissed and undressed. Hugh freed Vanessa's breasts, put a hand on one, squeezed it, stroked it, then lifted it up as he bent down to put his mouth on it. He sucked the milk-chocolate nipple between his teeth and moved his tongue over it as they waltzed down the hall, sometimes bumping the walls.

He hadn't been sure it would happen after all the sex he'd had with Emily, but sure enough, his penis was so hard it ached, and he moaned. Emily had behaved like an animal for awhile; now it was his turn. She no longer brought the animal out in him, even when she was in such high form as she'd been lately. But Vanessa did—she made his bones tremble with lust.

By the time they got to the master bedroom at the end of the hall, Hugh was in his undershorts and socks, while Vanessa wore nothing. Her curves were all bare, skin like alabaster traced here and there with thin, faint lines of the vaguest blue, some of which branched out into more lines. Her breasts curved gently, and Hugh could not get enough of them. He buried his face between them as they went to the bed.

He pushed her over backward onto the bed and Vanessa laughed. He straddled her closed legs, bent over and propped himself up on his elbow-locked arms. He lowered himself further and kissed her, sucking her tongue into his mouth. He kissed his way down her body, spending some more time with her breasts. Her skin was so smooth and soft against his recently shaved cheeks, like the wings of a butterfly. She smelled of sweet spices and he inhaled her deeply. He got onto his knees beside the bed and stopped at the triangle of hair between her legs, hair that had been growing back ever since she'd shaved it. He opened her legs with his hands and pressed his tongue to her—she was already wet, as always.

They moved all over the bed as they took turns pleasuring each other, changed positions, moaned and cried out each other's names. Hugh lost all track of time.

Finally, he was inside her. They moved together, slick with sweat, working together, building a rhythm, a tempo, that pounded slowly and relentlessly. Words gave way to grunts and hissing breaths and the wet slurp of sex organs engaging. Hugh stared down at Vanessa. His mind flashed pictures of her round hips, her spread legs, and his penis pinning her beneath him.

When Hugh came, it felt like he physically exploded inside her—his shaft torn down the middle and tattered on the end as he blew up. At this moment, Hugh unknowingly sealed her fate. Without realizing it, with one fateful ejaculation, he doomed Vanessa to a horrible nightmare existence that he could not even dream about and would not believe in if he did.

And Vanessa laughed happily, embracing him as he came inside her.

21

THE PINE COUNTY RAPIST

It was going to be one of those nights. Andrea could tell by the way Jimmy came home from work. He was agitated, silent, and he paced around the house. It was dark by the time he got home. Dinner was ready for him on the table—meat loaf. The only ones who made any sound at the table were the girls. Jimmy might as well be sitting there alone for all he noticed Andrea or the children.

He sat there, back stiff, eating his food, looking everywhere else but at her—no word for his wife, no smiles for his daughters.

Jimmy stood five feet, eight inches tall, black hair short and naturally curly. Andrea had thought he was so handsome the first time she'd seen him at a Fourth of July picnic. At the dance that night, he'd asked her to dance. After that, she'd followed him everywhere. She remembered running her fingers through those tight curls for the first time—so soft, like stroking a cloud. She also remembered passing her hands over his firm muscles for the first time. She hadn't feared that strength back then.

When he was done eating, Jimmy got up from the table, went out to the living room, and turned on the TV. He surfed the channels; then he put the remote down and paced the living room for awhile. Then he went out to the garage and tinkered around for a little while. He could not settle on anything, seemed unable to be still, just to sit. That's the way he always was on nights like this—silent, restless, as if a heated argument were going on inside his head.

They used to come every two or three months, these unsettled nights, but now they happened more often. Andrea had tried to suggest that they get him some help once, but he'd angrily changed the subject. She hadn't pursued it.

So Andrea silently endured these long, slow nights of no talking, not even any yelling. She almost would've preferred that he be angry at her and shout at her and even hit her—*almost*. That was the only good thing about these dark nights—he did not hurt her. He was too involved in himself, so far inside himself he couldn't see what was in front of him.

What's he thinking about? Andrea wondered. *Or whom is he thinking about? Maybe it's another woman. Or maybe something is really wrong—something that could affect all of us. Are we broke? Is he sick? In trouble with the law?*

The same things went through her head each time it happened.

Finally, after a an hour of pacing nervously and wandering the house, he put on his jacket, picked up the keys and his wallet from the table by the front door, and left. No good-bye; not a word. Andrea had no idea where he went on nights when he fell under the spell of that heavy, dark mood—or whatever it was. She realized that he was gone at night a lot lately. She'd asked him once where he was going, and the beating she'd gotten for it convinced her never to ask it again.

Andrea heard his Ford pickup start up; then he backed out and drove away. She knew that when he came back, he would drink. After the second or third whiskey, he'd tell her he wanted to go to bed—that meant he wanted her to come with him, whether she wanted to or not. They would have sex. Or, rather, *Jimmy* would have sex. Always the same missionary position. He would take her angrily, aggressively. He'd call her names through clenched teeth, and when he came, he'd spit in her face.

She thought of Jason—such a tender, considerate lover yesterday, then again today, so eager for her to come first. It had been a long time since she'd come at all, so it took a bit of adjusting that first time with him. He'd spoken to her so softly while they moved together, said such sweet things.

Andrea couldn't wait to see him again.

He went to her apartment complex and parked on the street out front. Willow Park Apartments was a pricey, well-lit place with a small security force that drove around in white cars. He couldn't just drive in and park someplace. He'd have to sneak in, hide, wait for her. He'd done it before, gotten in there with no problem, just to watch her. Her apartment was up on the top level of the right side of the two-level U-shaped complex. He'd found her bedroom window, peered through the break between the curtains with the aid of a small, powerful pair of binoculars. He'd watched her from the top of a hillock just behind the building, seen her undress twice. It had been his greatest hope to catch her masturbating sometime, but he never did. Besides, what did it matter? If you've seen one cooze beat off, you've seen 'em all. They were all alike. Sniveling bitches who'd sell you out in a second flat if the price were right.

He'd found the ideal place for their little rendezvous some time ago. There was a cream-painted cinder block structure in one corner of the complex—the laundry room. Eight washers and eight dryers. Top of the line appliances, too, not cheap clunkers. A row of plastic molded baby-blue chairs ran along one wall. A rack of magazines stood next to the detergent vending machine. A large restroom was in the back, and the door locked with a deadbolt. It would be perfect for them. No interruptions. And there was a small window above the toilet in case he needed to make a quick exit. A handful of quarters would ensure enough machine-noise to drown out any screams. As long as he could keep her quieter than half a dozen washers and dryers, he foresaw no other problems.

He fidgeted at the wheel of his pickup.

He reached over and opened the glove compartment, took from it a long hunting knife in a leather sheath. He snapped the sheath to his belt, reached into the compartment, and removed a rubber mask. It was a cheap Halloween mask, but it was hideous—a screaming face covered in what looked like the results of a flesh-eating virus run amok. He closed the glove compartment, stuffed the mask under his jacket, and tucked part of it under the waist of his jeans. It dangled at his left side.

He stayed away from the well-lit gate and kept an eye open for the white security cars. A six-foot wall surrounded Willow Park Apartments, but he knew where there was a large rock embedded in the ground in front of the wall, a perfect step up to hop over. He was good at it by now. He slipped over unseen, and headed straight for the parking lot on the southern side of the complex—there was another parking lot on the other side, as well. Cars were parked in rows of carports. In front of each car was a storage room, about the size of your average walk-in closet—it was there for the tenant to use or not use, as their needs dictated.

Her car was not in its space. There was always the chance she was gone for the night. But he decided to bet that she would return soon. She did not use her storage room, so it had no padlock like most of the others. He stepped inside, closed the door, then opened it an inch or so. The storage room was black inside, but the parking lot was well lit, and its light came through the small opening and cut through the darkness.

If one were to get close enough to the door's opening, one would see that dark inch-wide strip of darkness, until one reached the eye in the middle, the staring eye that peered out of the storage room.

Today had been an employee's birthday at the Flaming Disc, a woman who'd been there since the store opened. She'd been presented with a cake at lunch, and after work, Vanessa had treated them to a party at a bar called Aurora. She also presented the loyal employee with a new laptop computer. They were good people, her employees, and she liked all of them.

After the party, Vanessa drove home through the rain. She pulled into Willow Park Apartments, drove to the left and into the parking lot, where she slipped into her slot. She killed her engine, grabbed her purse, and got out.

She hunched her shoulders against a chill as she walked around the front of her car.

An arm wrapped around her neck and something cold and sharp pressed against her right cheek.

"Make a sound and I'll cut you," a man said calmly and quietly behind her. "You'll never be pretty again. Nod if you understand."

Vanessa was terrified of moving her head because of the sharp point sticking her cheek lightly. She managed a small, single nod against the man's hand.

"Okay, I'm gonna take my hand away, and you're not gonna make a sound, or you're dead." He slowly peeled his hand from her mouth. "Now, we're gonna walk to the laundry room, you and me." He grasped her shoulder and turned her around, getting in her face.

Vanessa gasped and cried out. He was so hideous—his face was eaten away and his mouth hanging open and—

No. No, it was just a rubber mask, she saw with relief.

Adrenaline coursed through Vanessa's body and her ears rang. She was so afraid, she felt as if her shaking were going to tear her apart. She tried to get the shaking under control, but failed.

The masked man took her elbow, and they walked away from the parking lot and over to the low, pale building that was the laundry room.

Once inside, he closed the door, then led her to the restroom in back, slowing to feed quarters into several of the coin-op laundry machines along the way. He opened the door, reached in and turned on the light, then shoved her inside. She stumbled and fell to the floor, her right cheek against the cold tile, which smelled of a sickly-sweet cleanser, mixed with the faint odor of urine.

What's he going to do? Vanessa wondered. She began to shake uncontrollably. A sob tore upward from inside her and made her shudder as it came out. *Is he the one in the news?* she thought. *The Pine County Rapist?* She tried to remember if she'd read that he wore a rubber mask, but her thoughts were jumbled. She knew that, so far, he had not killed any of his victims, only raped and brutalized them. *Raped and brutalized,* she thought. *I'm about to be raped and brutalized.*

He came into the restroom, closed the door, and locked it. The click of the lock seemed so loud to Vanessa, like a blow to the skull with a hammer. Then he stood there and looked down at her through the eyeholes in the hideous mask. He clapped his hands and rubbed them together vigorously as he came toward her.

Get a good look at him! Vanessa shouted at herself in her head. *Remember everything!*

He wore a blue down jacket half-zipped up over a blue chambray shirt, above a pair of blue jeans, and a pair of work boots. *Blue,* she thought, *he's blue up and down. Hands, his hands,* she thought as she noticed he wore a wedding ring on his left hand, a simple gold band. In his other hand he held an evil-looking knife with a serrated edge along the long, silver blade.

He swung his right foot back and then kicked her in the side.

Pain exploded inside Vanessa and she cried out as she rolled against the toilet.

He stepped forward and kicked her again. Then he bent down, grabbed her wrist, and dragged her back to the middle of the floor.

"Get up," he said.

That second kick had knocked the wind out of her, and as she struggled to her feet, she grunted and gasped for breath. He grabbed her hair and pulled her onto her feet. She screamed because of the burning pain that spread over her scalp.

"Take off your clothes," he said. "And do *not* scream again."

She stood there, slightly hunched forward, her arms across her chest. Her entire body quaked with fear. Her arms shook, her knees trembled.

The masked man started walking toward her again, as he said, "You're going to take off your clothes—" He put the tip of the knife against the skin beneath her chin, just the very tip. "—or I will make sure you never talk again. Or worse . . . yeah, worse. I'll make you slobber like a re-tard for the rest of your life."

Is he that surgically proficient? a voice asked in the back of her mind.

He finally took the knife away and stepped back. "Okay. Do it."

She slid her red coat off, tossed it onto the long counter that had two sinks in it and one large mirror above it.

She unbuttoned her tan sweater and dropped it on top of her coat.

It was cold, so cold.

She peeled her jeans down her legs, stepped out of them, put them on top of her other clothes, then added her red panties a moment later. She'd worn no bra that day. She hugged herself in the shuddering cold.

"Arms at your sides," he said.

She lowered her arms, but could not make them stop shaking.

He slowly nodded his head as his eyes traveled down her body, then up again. Standing directly in front of her, he put the knife in his left hand, then used his right to squeeze her breast.

"You could make a lotta money selling these, know that?" he said as he slipped the knife into a leather sheath on his belt. "Might as well. Deep down inside, you're all whores. Alla ya. Buncha money-hungry cunts."

He squeezed her breast harder as he twisted it. She cried out in pain, and he squeezed it harder, twisted it farther. He put his left hand to the back of her head, then punched her in the face with his right fist, three times, four—

Vanessa lost consciousness.

When she woke up, she was lying on her back, and her entire body was shifting up and down repeatedly; she felt a burning pain between her legs. Her head hurt, and it only hurt worse when she moved it, but in spite of that, she lifted it up and looked down her prone body. Everything was blurry at first. She lowered her head and blinked her eyes several times, tried to focus. Then she lifted her head again.

Ah, yes. Of course. He was fucking her. She was dry, and each hard thrust sent fire rising upward into her belly. It felt as if he were shredding the tender tissue.

He's not wearing a condom, she thought. *Oh, God, please don't let him have anything, please, God.*

Vanessa flinched when he lifted the bottom part of the mask with one hand and spit at her. A thick glob slapped onto her cheek. She lifted her hand to wipe it away, but her arm shook so hard, she could not manage it, and it dropped back to the floor.

She had no idea how long it lasted. She slipped in and out of consciousness as he continued to pound into her relentlessly. He often rattled on profanely about what whores and sluts all women were. He punched her a couple more times.

She was aware of him only in flashes, separated by lengthy periods of blackness. When she finally opened her eyes to find that he was gone, she felt no safer, no less afraid. She was leery of believing her eyes, thinking he was still there, that she simply could not see him.

But the pounding had stopped, and she wasn't being slugged in the face—or spat upon.

Finally, after a long silent time had passed, Vanessa groaned as she slowly worked herself up into a sitting position. She looked all around her and still did not see him. Her clothes were still stacked on the counter where she'd tossed them so long ago.

Pain throbbed between her legs. She reached down and touched herself, brought her hand up, and found blood on her fingertips.

She sat there awhile, thinking about what had just happened to her. At first, she focused on her pains, and a little self-pity crept into her thoughts; but it did not last long. All her thoughts were soon tinted the red of rage, of defiance.

I paid close attention, she thought as she got up. *I might be able to tell them something about this prick that no one else has yet. And I'm keeping his fucking spit so the cops can get some DNA from it!*

Once she was standing, she took some toilet tissue

from the roll, folded it up, and wiped the thick gob off her cheek. She placed the tissue on the counter by the sink. Then she slowly, stiffly, carefully began to put her clothes on before driving herself to the hospital to report the rape.

Andrea lay beneath Jimmy, reacting to each thrust with a jolt.

He'd come home even more agitated than he'd been before he'd left. He hadn't said a word to her until he finally said, "C'mon. To bed." She'd followed him, turning out the lights, and in the bedroom, he was already undressed and getting into bed. As soon as she slipped beneath the covers, he was on her.

She wanted so much to ask where he had gone, what he had done. But she knew better.

Jimmy got more and more frantic on top of her, grunting, panting. There had been no foreplay, no kissing or fondling. There never was, of course. He'd just gotten on top of her and gone at it, like always. He was more angry than usual as he pounded into her. He seemed furious, and as a result, his movements and sounds were savage. And now he was about to finish up. He made a low sound deep in his chest as he came, so stiff and rigid, as if he was afraid to let go, to cut loose, to let the orgasm take him over and make him wild. Sometimes she wondered if he even enjoyed sex—he never seemed to surrender himself to it, always remained in control. There was never any joy in him when they had sex. She had always thought sex should be joyful, playful, fun. Sometimes she wondered if Jimmy had even known how to play when he was a little boy.

He growled obscenities at her, spit in her face, and finally finished. He lay there for a moment, then rolled off of her, got up, and left the bedroom to go clean up.

Andrea would go in there after him, wash up, then come back to bed.

She thought of Jason. So far, he was the only man to have given her an orgasm.

When, she wondered, would she see him again?

22

HUNGER

Friday

Emily Crane embraced her husband and gave him a big kiss with a lot of tongue. He put a hand on her side, just above her hip, something that would normally make her feel very self-conscious because his hand rested on a roll of fat—but oddly, she didn't feel self-conscious at all. She felt strangely amorous.

"I'll see you tonight after work, okay?" she said. "And don't come home tired."

"Boy, you're really . . . frisky, aren't you?" Hugh said, smiling. "That was some pretty nice morning sex."

"I think it's because I've stopped taking the Valium. It knocked me out the last couple days or so. I feel like I just woke up from a long sleep. I feel good and horny."

Hugh smiled and nodded once, but there was no enthusiasm in his expression, nothing to indicate he looked forward to getting home that evening. He'd hardly returned her kiss at all.

"Everything okay?" Emily said, her smile gone.

"Sure. Fine. I'll see you tonight." He looked around for the kids. "Okay, let's go, kids." Donald and Annie followed him down the hall, then out the door.

Emily stood in the doorway between the hall and kitchen, wearing a burgundy robe and a pair of green *Shrek* slippers (it was one of her favorite movies), and a frown dug its way slowly into her face. She stood there a long time, frowning, thinking.

She happened to think that things had been wonderful. Didn't he feel the same way? Was it really that different for him because she was fat? Was it possible she'd been the only one enjoying herself?

If she'd known she would feel this good, she would've stopped taking the Valium sooner. She'd taken the Valium as directed, but it had dragged her down into the oily-black depths of a drug-induced sleep. Awake, it had made her feel lethargic.

She had dreamed when she slept—murky dreams, like several colors of paint being smeared together, and the only thing that ever made any sense was . . . a house.

There was a horrible scraping sound just outside—loud and gritty and irritating.

This was the first time, since truly waking up, that she'd thought of that house in her dreams. It was a big house, old and once beautiful, now broken down and decrepit, its paneless windows locked in a stare as dead as that of empty eye sockets.

That scraping sound again.

Emily stopped and headed back to the front door, muttering, "What the hell *is* that?"

She opened the front door and stepped out on the porch. Across the street, Mr. Shamblin was raking his leaves. It was January, and he was *finally* raking the soggy leaves all over his front lawn.

But why is it so loud? Emily thought, wincing. It was hurting her ears every time he dragged that metal-pronged rake over the ground.

She went back inside and closed the door and hurried

down the hall, trying to put some distance between herself and Mr. Shamblin's rake.

A shroud of depression suddenly fell over her, so totally and completely and smoothly that she hardly noticed the change. Her slippers shuffled on the floor as she went into the dining room, where the remains of breakfast were on the table. Emily was still hungry.

With Donald and Annie gone, that left only Jeannie. She sat at her little plastic red-and-yellow table beside the big oval oak table Emily had inherited from her grandmother. Jeannie was playing with her napkin, putting it on her head, then thrusting her butter knife through the air like a pirate's sword. Jeannie was very fond of the *Pirates of the Caribbean* movies.

Emily sat down at the table. Her plate was empty, but there were still pancakes left on the others, as well as a short stack on the platter in the center of the table. The platter also held what was left of the scrambled eggs and sausage links. Emily picked up her fork and speared the pancakes off the other plates. She poured some maple syrup over them and began to eat. Guilt crept into her thoughts, as well as familiar feelings of self-loathing that came with overeating, but she quickly shoved them back out again. She picked up the platter and scooped the rest of the eggs and sausage onto her plate. She knew the pancakes would fill her up before she got far. She was hungry, though, not just eating to be eating. Her hunger was gnawing at her now, even as she ate. The eggs disappeared, then the pancakes, the sausages. The plate was empty.

Emily frowned, because the pancakes had not filled her up. She was still hungry. Not for pancakes, really, but that was all she had at the moment. She speared the rest of the pancakes on the tray and plopped them onto her plate. She drenched them in raspberry syrup this time.

The house. It bothered her because there was something familiar about it. It appeared so clearly in her mind that it almost took on the feeling of a vision. She'd seen it before. But where? It was off some familiar road—she'd passed by it before, she was certain, but she'd never stopped to look at it closely. Yes, it was a house she frequently drove by. On the nights of her T.O.P.S. meetings, yes, she passed it going out of town and coming back.

There's that damned sound, she thought, *raking and raking, when will he stop?*

Emily opened her eyes and continued eating the pancakes as she mentally drove along the route she took every Tuesday night, and then the name dropped into her head with a mental *plunk*, like a stone dropped in a still pond . . .

The Laramie house, she thought.

That old eyesore remained standing only because it was on property owned by the Laramie family, and they weren't selling. People in Big Rock complained often. Years ago, when Emily was a girl, it had been a popular hangout for drug addicts looking for a place to get high undisturbed—until the Sheriff's Department disturbed them all the way to jail. The deputies monitored the place until they felt they'd chased off the undesirables, who then moved to the woods behind the park, where they'd always been in the first place.

Why am I thinking about the Laramie house? she wondered as she ate. She could not get the crystal-clear image of the house out of her mind. Broken windows with shards of glass like fangs, the porch with a sagging cover, the junglelike yard with wild vines and unpruned fruit trees, the crippled fence that leaned far inward toward the house, the wide-open gate, all those broken chunks of gray concrete walkway, the wooden porch steps, a couple of them broken—

I've never seen the house this close up, she thought. She stopped chewing, closed her eyes beneath her lined brow. She'd never done anything more than drive by the house, which stood back off Perryman Road. She'd never been close enough to see the broken concrete path—

Maybe there were pictures in the paper and I—no, no, that's not it.

—or the broken wooden steps, so how could she remember them?

You're not remembering, a voice whispered.

Emily jerked in her chair, gasping as she dropped her fork. The sound of the fork clattering loudly against her plate made her jerk again. Jeannie squealed, and Emily, who had nearly forgotten she was there, jerked and gasped again.

"Oh, God, baby," Emily said.

Jeannie babbled something.

"Yes, honey, you go ahead and drink your juice," Emily said, forcing a smile onto her face. She returned her attention to the remains of the pancakes.

The house would not go away. It remained glowing in her mind. Almost as if—

As if—

—it were being—

—projected into my mind—

—by some other source.

Emily threw her fork down and it made a racket when it hit the plate.

"That's just . . . *bullshit,*" she whispered to herself with teeth clenched tightly.

And yet, the pristine, clearer-than-life image of the Laramie house off Perryman Road remained . . . and remained . . .

When the pancakes were gone, Emily belched. But she was not satisfied. That undying hunger was still there, chewing on the inside walls of her stomach like a chittering red-eyed rodent. She closed her eyes—

That house, that damned house, there's that house again.

—and focused her attention on what she was feeling.

There was something she needed, something that would end this feeling in her gut and finally satisfy her.

Emily left the table and went to the refrigerator. On the way there, she was overcome with dizziness and nearly fell over. She propped an arm against the lip of the counter. The room tilted and spun drunkenly and she turned to face the sink, so put both hands on the edge of the counter. It passed about twenty seconds after it had started. Growling sounds gurgled in her stomach. She was more hungry now than she had been just a few minutes before—just before the dizzy spell.

Gordo, their gray short-haired tabby cat wandered into the kitchen, stopped, and stared up at her. The cat meowed once, then slowly backed away. Gordo turned around suddenly and hurried out.

Emily took a step back, testing herself. The dizziness was gone, but she moved cautiously, just in case. She went to the refrigerator, opened it, scanned its shelves.

She found half a submarine sandwich wrapped in plastic. She clawed the wrapper off and took a bite of the sandwich. Not only was it not what she needed, it was soggy and not very good. She tossed the sandwich across the room and into the garbage can at the end of the counter.

Back to the refrigerator, searching the shelves.

Leftover scalloped potatoes, chicken-and-mushroom casserole, cherry pie, pudding cups, some apples, a head of lettuce, a package of sliced dry salami—and hamburger. Her eyes kept going back to the package of raw hamburger. She'd bought it to make some chilimac. But now it just sat in its package, looking red on its little styrofoam tray, blood puddled around it. Her eyes returned to it again and again. Each time she looked at it, she felt a sudden relief inside her, a sense of satisfaction, but just a sense—not enough to satisfy that burning hunger.

It was almost as if she were hungry for—

No, she thought, *that's silly.*

She closed the refrigerator and opened the cupboards. Breakfast cereal, peanut butter, spices and seasonings, a package of Chips Ahoy cookies, Doritos. Nothing there.

Emily started to go back into the dining room to clear the table, but stopped in the center of the kitchen as her stomach made more sounds. She turned and went back to the refrigerator—

The Laramie house stood in the center of her forehead, broken and decayed like an old rotting corpse.

—thinking that maybe a chocolate pudding would help.

But it wasn't the chocolate pudding she looked for when she opened the refrigerator—her eyes went straight to the raw, red, bloody hamburger. Her eyebrows bunched together as she stared at it there on the top shelf, ready to cook up. Except she did not think about cooking it—she was quite taken by its color, the lovely red speckles with flecks of white fat.

She tucked her lower lip between her teeth and chewed on it as she reached slowly into the refrigerator and closed her hand on the edge of the package. She took it from the shelf, stepped back, let the refrigerator door swing closed on its own, took the hamburger to the sink.

Emily could smell it. She had never smelled raw hamburger before, but she could smell it now. It was tightly wrapped in plastic wrap, but she smelled it as if it were out of the package and right under her nose. A nice, salty, slightly coppery smell. Meat. Raw meat. And blood.

The next thing she knew, her nails were clawing at the wrap on the bottom of the package until it peeled away.

Jeannie began to cry, but it was a strangely distant sound.

Then, as if something had been edited from her life,

she went from tearing at the package to shoving clumps of the raw hamburger into her mouth, slurping the blood up from the bottom of the styrofoam tray. Suddenly she knew that *this* was *it*, the thing she so desperately wanted; this was what she'd craved, what she'd *needed*.

Well . . . almost. Not quite, but *almost*.

Emily shoved more into her mouth, and more, and her cheeks bulged, and she smelled and tasted the blood, and suddenly, as if waking up from a faint, she realized she was eating raw hamburger, that she had blood in her throat, and she bent at the waist and spat it into the sink, gagged, and a moment later, she vomited. She turned on the water and used her hand to scoop some from the faucet to her face. She grabbed a glass from the cupboard, filled it with water, and took some into her mouth. She swirled it around then spat it into the sink.

But that was it, a new voice said inside her. *You know it was—it was what you wanted, what you needed.*

"No," she said, shaking her head. "Uh-uh."

What's happening to me? Emily thought.

The image of the old house flared up brilliantly in her mind, so big and clear that she winced. The image dimmed, became a little hazy, and slowly, Emily's face relaxed.

Jeannie continued to cry, letting out long, piercing wails.

Dizziness washed over Emily and she swayed, quickly grabbing the edge of the counter to hold herself up. Hunger grumbled in her stomach, hunger that just a moment ago she had managed to satisfy. For the littlest while.

"I'm coming, Jeannie." She went through the kitchen, walking slowly, in fear of another dizzy spell, and into the dining room. At Jeannie's low plastic table, Emily bent down and picked her up.

Emily talked reassuringly to Jeannie as she walked her back into the kitchen, cooing to her, singing a little. Then after awhile, Emily fell silent and stopped walking around.

Jeannie's crying had stopped.

She was so warm against Emily . . . warmth that flowed through her, that gave her life . . . so plump with . . . with . . .

baby fat-baby fat-baby fat

. . . so warm . . . so small and easy to—

No! No, God, no!

—eat.

Emily quickly put her little girl down on the floor, and as she did that, she got a glimpse of her own hands, so dark, as if wearing gloves, fingers longer than usual. She stood up straight and held her hands out to look at them—

Oh, God, is that hair?

—and she screamed.

Her scream made Jeannie scream; then the little girl began to cry again, lifting her little arms up to Emily, asking without words to be held.

Another wave of dizziness overcame Emily and she fell to the floor. She quickly sat up and held out her hands again.

They were fine now. Chubby fingers, well-tended nails.

Just a moment ago, she could've sworn they'd been covered with brown hair.

What's wrong with me, Emily wondered. *Something is, that's for sure.*

She got up and went to the phone, picked it up and punched in Glory Hanrahan's number. She lived just a few houses down. She took care of infants and toddlers all day. Emily planned to call her and ask if she would take Jeannie for awhile. Then she would call her old

friend Terri March, who had two kids the same age as
Donald and Annie. She would ask Terri to please pick the
kids up at school along with her own and take them
home with her for awhile.

She wanted to be alone while she decided what to do.

She did not want her children near her until after
Hugh was home.

Emily was confused and sick and uncertain, but
mostly she was afraid. For them.

23

LAB WORK

Hurley walked into the Blind Dog Bar & Grill and went into the "grill" part of the establishment. He liked it because it was a dimly-lit place with a lot of polished dark wood, and the head of a moose mounted on the wall in the back. The moose, named Monty, wore big red sunglasses and an "I (heart) Big Rock" cap. The clock over the order window read 3:47. This was the first time since breakfast at home that he'd had a chance to stop and eat.

George sat in one of the booths in the back, beneath Monty, with a cup of coffee. His black leather briefcase stood beside the booth. George smiled and nodded.

"Hey," Hurley said.

"Hello, Sheriff."

"You wanted to see me?" Hurley said.

George nodded. "I recently received a call from the lab in Eureka. Paperwork's on its way to your office."

"And?"

"*Canis lupus.*"

"Whatzis whozit?"

"*Canis lupus*, Arlin—that's what the lab came up with. That little tuft of downy fur came from a wolf."

"A *wolf?*"

"Hi, Sheriff."

Hurley looked up at the middle-aged waitress, Jessie. She was thin and looked worn and tired, but she had a big smile.

"Hello, Jessie," he said. "What kind of soup you got?"

"Potato. And it's delicious. The cook tops it off with just a pinch of red pepper."

"I'll have a bowl of that. And coffee."

"You got it." And she was off.

"A *wolf?*" Hurley said again, leaning forward.

"Yeah, I found it hard to believe, too. For one thing, in order for a wolf to do the kind of damage that was done to those two bodies, it would have to be—" He leaned toward Hurley and lowered his voice. "—a *big* fuckin' wolf. For another thing, they couldn't classify it. It's not any species of wolf they could find listed anywhere."

"What does that mean?"

"I'm not sure. But I'm wondering—I know I said for certain that it *wasn't* an animal, but I looked up wolves on the Internet. None of them get big enough to do what was done to those bodies. The claws marks on the victims were spread apart like the fingers on a big human hand. The fangs had to be pretty damned large to do what they did. I can't think of *anything* that gets big enough to do what was done to those bodies. Aside from a bear. A bear could do that."

"But the fur didn't come from a bear," Hurley said.

"That's right. It came from a wolf."

Jessie came with Hurley's coffee mug in one hand and the pot in the other. She put the mug on the table and filled it, then refilled George's mug. "Be right back with your soup," she said as she left.

"Wait, I don't see how they can say it's a wolf if the species doesn't exist," Hurley said, shaking his head. "That means it must be something *else*, right?"

"Let me finish. I'm wondering if maybe the fur could come from something the killer was wearing."

"What, you think it was a person now?"

"I'm not sure. That's the thing. A wolf makes no sense, but neither does a person. *Nothing* makes sense."

Jessie returned with Hurley's soup, a slice of garlic toast, and a basket of crackers. "You'll like this, Sheriff," she said.

"Thanks, Jessie."

She smiled, then left them alone.

Hurley said, "So, we're back to, uh . . . nothing."

George shrugged. "I just calls 'em like I sees 'em, boss."

Hurley sighed. "I got a fucking serial rapist going around—he struck again last night, by the way—and I got an I don't *know* what going around slicing people up."

"Sucks to be you."

"People are going to start to catch on that something's up," Hurley said. "I'm going to get questions from the press—what am I saying, I'm *already* getting questions from the press. Dooley called from the *Herald*. Said, 'What's going on, Arlin? Do we have some kind of psycho on the loose?' I laughed and joked around a little, then told him that when I knew something, I'd let him know. But one more body shows up like that and they're going to be circling me like vultures over a slaughterhouse. Not just the papers, either, but every television station within a hundred miles, maybe those hyperactive cable networks if my luck is *really* bad."

He tasted his soup, but suddenly he wasn't very hungry anymore. A few minutes ago, his stomach had been growling—but that was before he'd started thinking about his situation. The soup was good, he just didn't feel like eating it anymore.

Frowning, Hurley said, "What am I doing here?"

"Having a late lunch."

"I'm not hungry. And I've got things to do. Maybe I should make some calls, see if there've been any circuses or animal shows in any of the surrounding areas. Does Eureka have a zoo?"

"I don't know."

"Maybe some big animal got loose. A bear. I figured it'd be a bear the lab came up with, something like that."

"Well, a bear could easily do that much damage, like I said. I talked to a couple people, though, and there hasn't been a bear sighting near town in decades. But if it were a bear, that would be bear fur, don't you think?"

"I'm not going to rule it out. Look, I've got to get back to the station. I don't feel right sitting here now. Too much going on." Hurley scooted out of the booth.

"See you later," George called.

Still frowning, Hurley said, "Yeah," as he left the restaurant and got into his SUV. He drove back to the station wearing a deep frown.

24

SCREAMS AND BLOODSHED

Hugh was tired when he got home from work. He'd shown houses all day in the rain to a couple of newly-weds from Los Angeles looking for a nice place to raise their kids. It was all they talked about all day, the kids they were going to have. The kids themselves couldn't have been more annoying than their eager parents-to-be. And *nothing* was good enough. No matter how much they liked a house initially, it just wasn't right for them. By the end of the day, he was sick of them both, and he was happy to go home.

He parked in the garage, took the three steps up to the door of the laundry room. He went inside, and passed through into the kitchen.

Immediately, he sensed that something was wrong. The house was dead silent. He stood in the kitchen and listened, and heard nothing.

"Hello?" he called as he took off his coat. He started across the kitchen, but stopped when something caught his eye in the two-basin sink. He frowned down at the clumps of raw hamburger in the bottom of the left basin. Some of it looked as if it had been vomited up. The rest of it looked like it had just come from the package, which was on the counter beside the sink—a white styrofoam tray with just a little blood pooled in one corner, the plastic cover tossed aside. Blood speckled the counter.

He walked into the living room and went to the small foyer, where he hung his coat in the closet. "Emily? Kids?"

"Up here!" Emily's voice cried from upstairs.

Hugh went up the stairs and started down the hall. The overhead lights were on and something red caught his attention. There was a smear of what appeared to be blood on the bathroom door. He frowned as he reached out for the doorknob to open it.

"Hugh?" Emily called from the master bedroom down the hall.

He turned to her voice, his hand two inches from the doorknob. He'd assumed she was in the bathroom because the door was not normally shut unless it was occupied. When he heard her, he continued on down the hall.

"Whose blood is on the bathroom door?" he said as he entered the bedroom.

The covers of their bed had been pulled back, and Emily lay naked and waiting, hands locked behind her head. She smiled as she said, "The kids are gone."

But there was something different about her, about the way she spoke—too fast, too urgently. Her eyes were wide with too much white showing, her smile too big.

"Fuck me, Hugh," she said.

He tried to smile. "Look, honey, I'm tired right now. All I want to do is—"

"No, really, fuck me, please. I *need* it."

"Emily, I'm trying to tell you, I had a bad day and I—"

She bounded off the bed and rushed at him. She clutched at the lapels of his suit coat and spoke through clenched teeth as tears trickled down her cheeks. "No, no, you don't understand, you *have* to, Hugh, I need it,

I'm serious, I *have* to *have* it, right *now*." As she spoke, she tore at his tie, ripped the buttons off his shirt, then pushed his coat over his shoulders and down his arms until it dropped to the floor. She jerked his tie from under his shirt collar and tossed it aside.

Hugh was alarmed. At first, judging by the savage look on her face, he'd thought she was attacking him in anger. Now she was stripping him. He decided to go along with her to keep her calm. But the truth was, he was worried about her. This was not typical behavior for her. Something was wrong. She seemed ... *manic*. But he went along as she unfastened his belt, then opened his pants. She dropped to one knee and took him into her mouth while he tried to kick off his shoes and remove his pants, and he nearly fell over. She stood again, grabbed his hips, and swung him around hard, throwing him onto the bed.

"Emily!" he said with irritation. He tried to peel off his socks, but was unable to.

She was on him a second later. He'd gotten hard in her mouth, so she went straight to it. Emily mounted him and began writhing and bucking on him, growling. She was actually *growling*. He frowned up at her when he noticed a faint stain around her mouth, a red smear.

"Have you been eating berries?" he said.

"Shut up and *fuck me!*" she growled as she bent forward and dug her nails into his chest.

"Hey, *ouch*, dammit!" he said.

He looked down at her hands to see if she'd broken the skin and saw something that did not look right. Emily had painted her nails black. No, those were not her nails—they were coming directly out of her fingertips. They were *claws*—curved, sharp, black claws. And there was ... *hair* on the backs of her hands. She sat up again.

Hugh looked up at her and gasped. A fine layer of brown fur covered her body.

Emily cried out in pain as sounds began to come from her body, awful sounds that made Hugh forget what they were doing—the horrible crunch of cartilage, the snap of bones cracking as her face and body changed before him, skin undulating, humping up and then smoothing out, stretching in places. Even though she kept crying out in pain—her voice got thicker and deeper—she continued to move frantically up and down on him as the lower half of her face jutted out. She kept moving on him even though his erection quickly dissolved—they were no longer having sex, but she did not seem to notice. Her mouth, now a snout, opened to reveal long, narrow fangs.

It was no longer Emily—it was something else, something horrible.

Hugh's eyes were opened to their limit and he released a series of staccato cries as he gawked up at her. He suddenly felt cold, and more frightened than he could ever remember being in his life.

She came forward again and placed large hairy clawed hands on his chest, hunching over him with much more size and muscle than she'd had just a moment ago, and those claws sliced into his skin. Blood bubbled up around them.

Hugh screamed, a high, shrill, ululating sound. He screamed again and again, kicked his legs and flailed his arms, but the creature weighed him down, kept him on the bed. The thing Emily had become leaned forward and closed its mouth on Hugh's shoulder. The fangs broke the skin—he felt the *pop-pop-pop-pop* of each fang breaking through his flesh—tore through muscle tissue, and scraped against bone as his scream went on and on. It tore a chunk of flesh and muscle from his shoulder and sat up again. It made wet smacking sounds as its long snout chewed noisily on the blood-dripping meat.

His screams became increasingly ragged and hoarse as they formed words, "It's eating me! *It's eating meee!*" over and over again.

The thing finished eating the piece of him, and came down for more, still making humping motions against his shriveled penis.

Hugh's screams—*"It's eating me! It's eating meee!"*—garbled into silence as the thing closed its snout over his mouth and began to eat his face.

Doris Whitacker dozed in her chair at the window, as she usually did after dinner. Tonight, she'd had a Healthy Choice frozen dinner—beef tips portabello, mashed potatoes and gravy, green beans, and an apple crisp for dessert. It had been delicious and filling, and she'd dozed off while watching a rerun of *Everybody Loves Raymond.*

Something woke her with a start. Something like . . . a scream? She blinked several times and looked at the television, thinking the sound had come from there. A cheerful tampon commercial was running. Doris frowned.

She heard the sound again. She muted the television with the remote and turned to her window.

It was a loud, high, hoarse scream, a *man's* scream. It came from across the street. Doris listened closely, leaning forward in her chair. It seemed to be coming from the Crane house. It sounded again and again and again—an ice-cold ululating wail filled with terror and pain. And . . . it spoke. Doris gasped a little as she heard the screaming voice declare something—three words over and over—then it was cut off mid-scream and followed by a dreadful silence. She'd been unable to understand what the screaming voice had said, she knew only that it had spoken.

A chill settled deep in Doris's bones, making them ache.

Something was happening over there, something terrible.

Doris reached for the phone to call the police.

Jason Sutherland sat at the narrow bar that was the only thing separating his tiny kitchen from his small living room. He drank from a bottle of Heineken as he watched an old horror movie on cable, *Mr. Sardonicus*. He stared at it, not really seeing it.

He thought, instead, about Andrea.

Jason had gone straight over there after work. He'd even left work a little early, unable to wait any longer, wanting so much to be with her. He'd gone to her door, rang the bell, and she'd opened it up smiling. She wore tight blue jeans and a red sweatshirt. She stepped back and let him in.

As soon as the front door was closed, they'd embraced and kissed.

"Come have a glass of wine with me," she'd said as she led him to the couch. "We need to talk." Two wineglasses stood on the coffee table by an open wine bottle.

Andrea poured, then sat next to him on the couch.

Frowning, Jason said, "I don't know if I like the sound of that."

"Of what?"

"Of us needing to talk. Is that bad?"

"Well, Jason . . . look." She stared at her glass of wine as she spoke. "I'm married. I have children. I can't . . . I mean, I shouldn't be . . . it's just not right for me to . . ." She lifted her head and turned to him. "Do you know what I'm trying to say?"

"I think so."

"We really shouldn't be . . . you know."

"Yeah. And?"

"And . . . and . . ."

They'd put down their drinks without tasting them and

embraced, pressing their mouths together. They'd quickly undressed each other until naked, and they'd made hungry love there on the couch. Whatever pangs of conscience had been bothering Andrea were forgotten amid moans and thrusts and lusty kisses.

Jason smiled at the memory as he sat at the bar in his apartment.

He heard something outside. He muted the television, then listened, frowning. He dropped off the bar stool and hurried to his bedroom in the front of the apartment. He went to the window on the left that looked out on Andrea's house. He heard the sound again, and realized it was coming from behind him. He hurried to the window across the room that looked out at the Cranes' house. It came from there.

Jason slid the window aside and touched his nose to the screen.

A man was screaming in the Crane house. Mr. Crane? He was screaming in agony—and then he spoke as he screamed.

"It's eating me! It's eating me! *It's eating meee! It's ea—*"
It stopped abruptly.

A bone-deep chill went through him, starting in his scalp, which tingled with gooseflesh, then cascading down his entire body.

There were children over there. Jason thought a moment, trying to remember how many kids the Cranes had—was it two? No, three—they had the little one, and the two older kids.

"Oh, God," he whispered when he thought of those kids being over there right now, whatever was going on. Somebody over there was in trouble.

Jason turned and jogged back through his apartment to the stairs. The stairwell was in the floor at the back. To help insulate the apartment, Jason had hung a large rug he'd found at a flea market over the opening. It was over six feet long and featured a giant picture of a leopard on a rock, surrounded by a colorful jungle. It was old and worn, but it suited his purpose. It was the perfect length and heaviness to cover that opening which otherwise would freeze him out in the winter.

He flung the rug off the opening and hurried down the stairs into the garage. He went up the steps to the door that led to the kitchen.

"Have you eaten?" Mom said.

He could smell something good cooking. "I'm not hungry yet, Mom."

"You *will* eat, though, right?" She leaned against the counter, her vodka tonic in one hand, cigarette in the other. "I'd hate to think of you starving up there."

"Mom, look at me. There's little chance of me starving. Where's Dad?"

"In the living room watching TV."

Jason hurried into the living room and found his dad stretched out in his recliner, sipping his scotch and soda.

"Dad, somebody's screaming over at the Cranes' house," Jason said.

Dad turned to him and frowned. "What? Screaming?"

"Yes, I think someone's being hurt."

"That's their business," Dad said, turning his eyes back to the television.

"Dad, I think maybe someone's—"

"Look." He frowned up at Jason. "It's none of your business. Don't get involved, okay? Just leave it alone. You want to call the police, do it anonymously. You do *not* want to get involved, trust me." He turned to the television again.

Jason turned and left the living room, angry. He should have known. His father was a diehard isolationist. "Don't get involved" was one of the creeds of his life. His father, Arthur Sutherland, Jr., was so uninvolved, he didn't even vote. He was Jason's father, and Jason loved him, but sometimes he was disgusted by him, too.

He went back out to the garage and stood at the bottom of the stairs, considering going up to his apartment and calling the police. But maybe it was nothing—maybe he hadn't heard what he thought he'd heard. He decided to step outside and listen. He crossed the garage to the door that led outside, and stepped out into the cold darkness. He wore a heavy sweater over a long-sleeved shirt, but it was still cold. He walked along the side of the garage on wet grass. It was drizzling—the very air seemed wet.

Jason froze when he heard a bizarre sound. It came from the west, toward the ocean. It was a high, plaintive howl.

Ar-ar-arrROOOOO!

It sounded twice.

Jason's scrotum shriveled, and gooseflesh crawled across his back like tiny insects. The sound had gone straight to the marrow of his bones.

The sound came again, but this time it was from the east, and closer.

Wolves? he thought as a shudder passed through him. *There are no wolves around here . . . are there? Dogs . . . it must be dogs.*

He stood there for awhile and listened, but the howls did not come again. He walked along the fence that stood between their driveway and the Cranes' driveway. At the end of the fence stood their mailbox. Jason walked between the end of the fence and the mailbox and then, hesitantly, up the Cranes' driveway, around the car, onto the walk that ran along the picture window in the front of the house, to the front door. He rang the doorbell.

He heard something in the house. A jumble of sounds. He turned his left ear toward the door and listened closer. Movement. And something else . . . something ugly. Growling.

Growling? he thought. He tried to remember if they had a dog. He knew they had a cat, but he couldn't remember the Cranes ever having a dog. That certainly wasn't a *cat* growling. Not a house cat, anyway—maybe a *big* cat, a tiger or a lion, something from the Discovery Channel, but not a house cat. He heard no more screams—

It's eating me! It's eating meee!

—or any other sounds of distress, but he felt no better. Something was definitely wrong in there.

"Hello? Anybody home?"

What a stupid thing to say, he thought.

"Hello? It's Jason Sutherland. From next door."

Wishing he'd brought a flashlight, he went to the front window. The drapes were wide open, and he could see into the living room. He cupped a hand to each side of his face and leaned in close, until his nose was touching the glass. He saw the couch, the chairs, the TV, the books and knickknacks on the shelves. The new hardcover Michael Connelly book was on the end table by the couch; the newspaper lay open on the floor beside one of the chairs.

Sudden movement to the left made him gasp. So fast, it was a blur at first, then it stood before him, up close— one moment it wasn't there, and the next it was.

The feral silver eyes held Jason's wide brown ones. He could not move, could not breathe, because he was seeing something that paralyzed him with fear, something he could not understand at first. Something that could not exist.

It was tall and broad, narrow-waisted, with knees that bent backward, the enormous body covered with brown fur. Jutting from the face was a long snout filled with fangs, with a black nose, and black lips that pulled back over the fangs.

Jason's mouth hung open until he said, "Oh, my God."

Very little of Emily Crane was left inside the large creature that stood at the window, and what was there slept. The creature's thoughts were very simple—it thought in images and feelings rather than words.

Its hunger had been satisfied for the moment. Now it had another need—it needed to go to the house that stood vividly in its mind. It was drawn to it, pressed on by a raw sense of urgency. From Emily's buried memory, the creature extracted the route to the house.

It stood at the window. There was someone outside, standing in its way. The creature barely gave the figure outside a thought before lifting its arms.

Jason saw a flash of claws as the creature brought its arms down hard and he jumped backward as the glass webbed for an instant, then crumbled with a resonant shattering. Through that cascade of broken glass, the thing leaped out of the living room, slammed into Jason, and knocked him backward.

Jason's back slammed to the ground, and all the air was expelled from his lungs as the thing weighed him down heavily. The creature had come down on him like a falling tree, and its harsh, gamey odor enveloped him.

Blurred flashes of claws and fangs rained down on Jason, along with a storm of searing, slicing pain.

25

THE CRIME SCENE

Jason's warm blood dribbled into his eyes, temporarily blinding him, as the fangs sank into the upper part of his left arm. He cried out in agony as they ground into his muscle. Before it could tear out a chunk of his arm, a voice called out sharply.

Startled, the creature pulled its fangs back out of Jason's flesh and lifted its head, blood dripping from its snout and fangs, and looked in the direction of the voice, toward the road.

A gunshot exploded and Jason happened to open one eye in time to see the top half of the creature's head disappear. The body collapsed backward, off him.

Jason crawled backward on his back, moving like a giant crab, until he was far enough away from the thing—no matter how dead it seemed—to get to his feet.

Once he was standing, he realized the thing on the lawn did not seem dead at all—it convulsed and flopped in the glow of the porch light, and something else . . . it was changing. The whole thing was altering before his eyes. One moment it was covered with brown fur, the next the fur was much shorter and skin was visible, and the next it was hairless skin, a fat, shifting belly, heavy breasts that plopped back and forth, a tuft of dark hair peeking out between the tops of the broad, heavy thighs—he thought, *Jesus God is that Mrs. Crane?*—and then it was that thing again, hairy and distorted, and all the while, he could hear those awful sounds—cartilage cracking and bones breaking again and again. But other than that, the thing made no sound, because the top half of its head was gone. It made no sense—how could it still be moving, jerking and flopping around like that?

"It'll die soon."

Jason used his right hand to wipe the blood from his eyes. The slashes on his face burned, and his left arm was paralyzed by pain—numb from the elbow down, but above that, nothing but agonizing pain. His bloody face was a mask of agony—eyes squinting, lips peeled back over his teeth, making a low groaning sound.

But he had heard the voice. He turned.

A tall man in a long black coat and old-fashioned hat, face shrouded in shadow, stood on the sidewalk in front of the house, a cane in his left hand, a shotgun in his right with the barrel pointed at the ground. His words were clipped, very precise. His voice was rough, like gravel being ground up. He turned to a dark car parked in the wrong direction behind him at the curb, its driver's side door hanging open. The man bent forward and put the shotgun in the backseat, then closed the door.

As the man turned back to Jason, his face was caught in the dull glow of the porch light. His right eye was covered by a black patch strapped to his head, and his face was horribly scarred and puckered. Shadow and light played over the long scars, making them look deeper than they really were, no doubt. He walked onto the lawn and approached Jason.

"Are you badly hurt?" the man said.

Jason opened his mouth to reply, then fainted.

As he pulled up in front of Doris's house, Hurley saw the figure standing in the yard across the street waving at him. The man waved one arm back and forth, high over his head.

Hurley flicked on his searchlight, manipulated the toggle until the light shone directly on that yard, on the tall man in the black coat and hat—

"Oh, boy," Hurley said.

—and on what appeared to be two bodies on the lawn. He realized that it was Emily Crane's address.

He'd been on his way home when Cherine in Dispatch relayed Doris's call. He'd agreed to take it, figuring it was another nuisance call. He'd been fully prepared to read Doris the riot act this time.

Maybe I should arrest her, he'd thought. *Scare her a little. Maybe then she'd think twice before calling.*

His eyes on those two dark figures on the lawn, Hurley grabbed the mike and said, "Trooper one in need of a bus and backup." He gave his location. "I've got what appear to be two bodies, a broken window, a strange man standing in the yard waving me over—something's cooking. Let's hurry up with that backup, people, I don't know what, but something's up over here."

He got out of the SUV, flashlight in hand, shut the door, and hurried across the street. He reached down and zipped up his green jacket—it was damned cold. His breath appeared before him, then was swept away by a bone-chilling breeze as he rushed forward.

"Sheriff Arlin Hurley," he said to the tall man.

"This young man is need of medical attention," the man said, leaning on a black cane with a silver handle.

Hurley eyed the man cautiously. "What happened here?" he said. He looked down at the young man on the lawn, his face bloody. He seemed to be passing in and out of consciousness. Hurley crouched down beside him and said, "I'm Sheriff Hurley. An ambulance is on the way."

"Thuh-thanks," the boy said, his voice hoarse.

"It should be here any minute, so don't worry, you're going to be fine," Hurley said, standing again. He hoped he was right, for the boy's sake.

He walked over to the other body. It was moving, writhing painfully.

"He was attacked," the man said as he came to Hurley's side. "The young man, I mean. He was attacked by that," he said as he pointed down at the thing before them with his cane.

As Hurley stood over the body, his mouth slowly opened. He stared dumbly down at the thing on the lawn. His eyes narrowed a little as he tried to figure out what he was seeing.

It did not help.

Hurley hunkered down beside the thing on the ground because it was making sounds. He listened, wondering if it was trying to speak, but it only made sickening gurgling sounds. That was not surprising considering the fact that most of its head was gone.

He could make out a woman's body, overweight, pale—about Emily's size, build, and color—but covered with hideous sores that seemed to grow larger before his eyes, all of them red and swollen and running. Blisters rose and popped as he watched, as if the body were bubbling like a witch's cauldron.

Emily? he thought. What remained of the face left no doubt in his mind: It was his receptionist.

The rest of the body was covered with patches of brown hair that came and went. One hand had five fingers with normal-looking nails and a wedding ring, while the other was buried in fur, and sported long, curved fingers that

came to deadly points—claws with bits of red tissue cling-
ing to them.

"It will die soon," the man said. "It's harmless now."

Hurley stood and said, "What the hell *is* it?"

"The answer to that question is quite lengthy, and one
that you probably will not like." Although his voice was
craggy, he spoke with a crisp East Coast accent, upper
crust. Even with that broken voice, he spoke as if he had
marbles in his mouth. There was no contempt or haugh-
tiness in his manner of speaking, but Hurley recognized
that the possibility for it was there—it was just that kind
of accent.

"Well, I—wait." Hurley turned to fully face the man.

He wore an eye patch and his face was badly scarred.

"Who are you?" Hurley said.

The man inclined his head cordially and said, "Daniel
Fargo is the name. And you, Sheriff—Harley, did you say?"

"Hurley, Arlin Hurley."

"You, Sheriff Hurley, are precisely the man I need to
talk to. But for now, I think we should concentrate on getting this young man some help. He's bleeding."

"An ambulance is on the way. Why are you here, Mr.
Fargo?" Hurley said.

"I got here only a few minutes before you. I have a police scanner in my car and I heard the call. I happened to
be very close by, so I thought I would check to see if this
was . . . well, if it happened to be what I was looking for.
And it was. That's why I'm still here. Do you know the
people who live at this house, Sheriff?"

"I do. And if you don't mind, I'm going to check on
them now."

Hurley walked carefully but unsuccessfully around the
pieces of glass—they crunched beneath his feet. He
stepped through the picture window—most of the pane
was gone, with only a few jagged shards jutting from the
edges—and into the living room.

"Hello? Hugh?" No answer. Hurley had a heavy, ominous feeling about what he was likely to find in the house.

"Hugh? It's Arlin, Hugh. You around?" His voice fell into empty rooms.

He went into the kitchen and found lumps of raw hamburger in the sink. On his way back out of the kitchen, he noticed three large drops of blood on the tile, just before the threshold. He bent down to get a closer look, to make sure it was blood. Just beyond the threshold, two shiny black boots appeared, with a cane next to the left one.

Hurley snapped upright and said, "Mr. Fargo, if you don't mind, this is a crime scene, and you are—"

"Has there been any raw meat left out in the kitchen?"

Hurley cocked his jaw to the right as he examined Fargo's face in the better light.

How could he know that?

Four long pale-pink scars dragged across his face from the left temple down across his nose, where one had dug deep and broken the nose, and down across the right cheek to the jaw. Others criss-crossed them, but the first four were the deepest. His upper lip had been restored, but not very well—it appeared crooked on his face. Fargo had grown a thick but well-trimmed mustache the color of iron just above it, improving the lip's appearance somewhat. Deep creases cut into his forehead above the black patch that covered his right eye. Bushy iron-gray brows arched sharply over his eyes.

Hurley put a hand on his hip. "Now what makes you ask that, Mr. Fargo?"

"Experience. A steak, maybe? Left out on the counter? Half-eaten?"

"Look, I don't know who you are, but you're in the middle of my crime scene. Have you already been in this house?"

"I have not."

"What are you, then, a psychic? You're gonna tell me what happened here? So you'll get on TV and—"

"I am most certainly not a psychic, Sheriff Hurley. Once upon a time, I was an English professor. At Yale. But that was a lifetime ago. Now, I spend my time and money finding and solving the very problem you find yourself facing right now, Sheriff Hurley. You've already had a couple of nasty killings. Eviscerated, half-eaten. What has the lab come up with, Sheriff? Are they as baffled as you are? Or have they come up with something solid but confusing? Like . . . a wolf?" He spoke the last two words quietly.

"Who the hell *are* you?" Hurley whispered.

"I'm being honest with you, Sheriff. My name is Daniel Allen Fargo. Would you like to see my driver's license?"

"As a matter of fact, I would."

"Fine. Just don't be alarmed—I'm only reaching for my wallet." Fargo slipped his right hand under his coat, came out with a long, slender, expensive-looking wine-colored leather wallet. He hooked his cane on his right elbow so he could slip his license out of the wallet and hand it to Hurley.

It was a Connecticut license, current, with an unmistakable photograph of Fargo.

"You said you have a police scanner in your car?" Hurley said, handing the license back. "Why?"

"For this very reason. I have tracked someone here to your town, someone I've been following for a long time now."

"Look, I don't have time for this, okay? But I need to know—how did you know about the raw meat?"

"The way I have it figured is this: The woman who is now dying on the front lawn was having urges and hungers she did not understand. Raw meat came closer than anything else to satisfying that hunger—but still, not quite. Is there a pet in the house?"

"A pet?"

"A dog, a cat?"

"Oh, I don't know if—wait, she's got a picture of a cat on her desk at work. Yeah, she has a cat."

"You will find its remains somewhere in the house."

"She has a family—a husband, three kids."

Fargo said nothing for a long moment, just stared down at the floor. Finally he lifted his head and said, "Then I do not envy you your job tonight, Sheriff Hurley."

Holy shit, Hurley thought. *Why can't anything just be easy?*

"Okay, look, Mr. Fargo, I want you to go outside to—you drove here, right?"

"Of course."

"Go get in your vehicle and stay there till I come out. Understand? Do not leave. I want to talk to you, but I can't right now, I've got other things to do."

"Sheriff?" Deputy Kopechne called.

"Yeah, I'll be right there," Hurley replied. To Fargo, he said, "Stay there until I come back out, and if the media shows up, don't you *dare* talk to them, understand? If you do, so help me God, I'll throw you in jail. Now, please, get out of here." He ushered Fargo back up the hall to the front of the house.

Kopechne stood in the center of the living room. There were other deputies out on the lawn.

"Now, what are you going to do, Mr. Fargo?" Hurley said as he took Fargo to the door.

"Stay in my car until you come back out, and I'm not to speak to the media."

"Very good. Don't forget it. Now," he said, opening the door, "out you go."

Hurley followed Fargo out the door and onto the lawn. As Fargo went on toward the street, Hurley went to Deputy Eddings's side and said quietly, "See that man with the hat?"

"Yes."

"Follow him to his car and tell him I told you to take his car keys. Then I want you to stand by that car and wait for me to come out and relieve you. He's not to talk to anyone. Understood?"

"No problem," Eddings said, and he was off.

Hurley went to the side of the strange Emily-creature on the lawn. Now it only twitched occasionally. The sores on its body had worsened. He reached down and lifted the left hand, looked at the wedding ring—he remembered Emily saying that Hugh had spent a fortune on the rock it sported, more than he could afford at the time.

Hurley went back into the house, closed the door, and turned to Kopechne. "My God, a few minutes ago, I was on my way home. To a nice dinner with my wife. Now I'm dealing with that thing on the lawn—did you *see* that?"

"What the hell *is* that?" Kopechne said, his eyes suddenly wide. He tossed Hurley a pair of latex gloves, and Hurley tucked the flashlight under his arm and put them on. Kopechne did the same.

"Well, it *was* Emily Crane."

"You kidding?" Kopechne said.

"Apparently, that guy out there knows what it is. He seems to know more about all of this than I do. But it looked to me like Emily. What's left of her, anyway. Come on, let's go upstairs. I'm dreading it, but we have to."

Hurley led the way. Every step up took him closer to the hallway up there and a possible bloodbath. He saw it in his head on the way up—blood sprayed on the walls, four bodies on the floor—one big, three small—like something out of a Tarantino movie. He did that often—the reality, no matter how awful, could not compete with his imagination, so no matter what awaited him, it wasn't as bad as what he saw in his head on the way there. But that could still be pretty fucking bad.

The hallway was empty. No blood on the walls, no bodies on the floor.

The floor creaked and popped beneath them as they made their way slowly along.

"Sheriff," Kopechne said.

Hurley stopped and turned around. Kopechne pointed at a closed door. There was a smear of blood on the creamy paint job.

He took in a deep breath through his nose, lips pressed together hard. He unsnapped his holster, drew his gun. Kopechne did the same.

They flanked the door, and Hurley reached out, turned the doorknob, and shoved the door open.

Silence. No movement, no sign of life at all.

But it wasn't *just* silence. It was a particular kind of silence that Hurley had heard before in his work—a silence heavier, thicker than normal, the kind of silence that wound around your neck and squeezed your throat closed. This silence was the sound of death.

Hurley stepped into the doorway, the grip of the gun resting in the palm of his left hand.

The bathroom was empty. But Hurley's eyes were immediately drawn to something in all that pale-blue and white—a splash of blood on the outer side of the bathtub at the other end of the room. The shower curtain had been drawn the length of the tub.

Hurley wondered what awaited him behind that curtain.

There was more blood on the floor at the base of the tub, some on the edge, a smear on the curtain.

Hurley did not want to look in that tub. But it was his job.

He led the way into the bathroom, past the towels on their racks, the cupboards, no doubt filled with more towels and washcloths. There were a couple of toys in one of the sinks and a big blue fish on the toilet lid.

Hurley slowly pulled the shower curtain back. It made a metallic hissing sound as it slid open.

He saw part of it to the left, under the faucet and shower. There were two more pieces at the other end of the tub. It had been a gray short-haired tabby. Now it was in three pieces.

Is there a pet in the house?

Dammit, Hurley thought. *Who the hell* is *that guy and how the hell does he know what he knows?*

There wasn't much left of the cat's entrails. They were . . . gone.

Raw meat came closer than anything else to satisfying that hunger—but still, not quite, Fargo had said.

"Fuck," Hurley said as he turned away from the bathtub, stepped around Kopechne, and left the bathroom quickly. He took a hard right just outside the door and continued down the hall, opening doors as he went along.

The children's bedrooms were empty—the girls' room with its many stuffed elephants and its collection of dolls, and the boy's room with its dinosaurs and sports posters.

The master bedroom, he decided, was at the end, and sure enough, there it was, and what he found came very close to what he'd seen in his head.

The telephone trilled throughout the house.

Hurley looked at the phone on the nightstand, let it ring a couple of times, then went over and picked it up.

"Hello?"

"Who's this?" a woman said.

"This is Sheriff Arlin Hurley. Are you a relative or friend of the Cranes?"

"Oh, my God. What's happened?"

"Who is this?"

The woman's voice began to fracture with panic. "I-I'm Emily's friend, Terri. I have her children over here. What's *happened*?"

"Uh . . . tell you what, Miss—?"

"March, Terri March. And it's Mrs."

"Mrs. March, I'm going to come over to your house as soon as possible, and we'll talk. Give me your address." He quickly pulled out his pad and pen and wrote down the address. "I'll be there as soon as I can get away from here."

"You're not going to tell me what's happened?"

"I'd rather discuss it in person."

"But what about Emily?"

"Look, Mrs. March, are you home alone?"

"My husband's here with me, and I have Emily's kids." She lowered her voice. "For God's *sake*, what's *happened* to her?"

"To be honest, Mrs. March, we're not quite sure yet. But I'll know more when I come to see you, and I'll tell you everything. I have to go now. I'll see you soon."

He turned the phone off and put it back on the night-stand, where it would never be answered again.

On the way back down the stairs, Hurley said, "Kopechne, I'm putting you in charge. Make sure *nobody* comes in this house except Forensics and the coroner. Call Eureka and get CSU over here to investigate this crime scene." His voice was still a little shaky from what he'd seen in the master bedroom. What was left of Hugh Crane was scattered all over the king-size bed, some of it dangling from the headboard, the lamp shade. Naked bloody ribs sticking up from the stripped-open torso. He took a deep breath and added, "Although that didn't look like something a criminal would do. It . . . it looked like something an animal would do." At the bottom of the stairs, Hurley stopped and turned to Kopechne. "Chase away any media. Tell them all I'll talk to them when I know more. Just hold everything together, know what I'm saying?"

"Yep."

Hurley slapped him on the shoulder, then took off the latex gloves and handed them to Kopechne. "Thanks. I've got other things to do."

He left the house. The ambulance was there and the young man who'd been unconscious on the lawn was gone. The horrific thing on the grass now lay completely still. Hurley headed for Fargo's car.

One of the EMTs spotted Hurley crossing the lawn and hurried over to his side. "Sheriff, I, uh, I've gotta ask," he said, walking along with Hurley, "that, uh, that body, that, uh, *thing* over there on the lawn—"

When he said nothing for a moment, Hurley said, "Yeah, what about it?"

"What the fuck *is* that?"

"It's a fucking patient, what does it look like? You're to take it to the hospital with you."

"I'm afraid to *touch* it!"

Hurley stopped on the sidewalk and faced the young man. He was small and wiry. "Look, I think it's dead. It's not going to hurt you in its current condition. And don't you take universal precautions?" he said, gesturing at the latex gloves the young man wore.

"But I've never seen anything like—"

"Goddammit, do I have to get somebody else over here to do your job? Don't you have a partner over there? Get *him* to do it! But don't bother *me* with it; I've got more problems than I can handle and I don't need—"

"Hey, hey," the guy said, arms raised in surrender. "Just asking, okay? Just asking."

Hurley wanted to pound his fist through a wall. He wanted to take a hammer to something breakable. He clenched and unclenched his fists as he crossed the street to the dark Mercedes he'd seen Fargo get into.

Fargo's window descended as Hurley approached.

"I'd like you to come to my office, Mr. Fargo," Hurley said. "It's very important that we talk."

"Must we go to your office?" Fargo said.

"What do you mean?"

"I have not eaten since breakfast, Sheriff, and I'm quite hungry. I'd be happy to buy dinner for both of us if you will only recommend a restaurant."

Deputy Eddings got out of the car on the other side.

Hurley leaned a hand on the top edge of the car, elbow locked. He ran his other hand down over his face. He pushed away from the car, reached into his jacket pocket and removed his cell phone. He flipped it open, punched a couple of buttons, and put it to his ear.

"Hi, sweetheart," he said. "I'm afraid I'm not going to make dinner tonight. It's unavoidable. . . . Well, this is a bad time. I'm gonna have to go. Okay? Bye-bye." He closed the phone and dropped it back in his pocket. He looked down at Fargo and said, "You like Chinese food?"

26

FARGO'S STORY

Mrs. Lee greeted Hurley with her usual warmth when he entered the Jade Garden with Fargo in tow at nine minutes past seven that evening.

"Sheriff, how nice to see you again," Mrs. Lee said. "You have a companion?"

"Yes, Mrs. Lee, this is Mr. Fargo. He and I would like a booth in the back."

"Certainly, of course, come this way."

Hurley had driven over in the SUV while Fargo had followed him in his Mercedes. It had begun to rain again, and Hurley had driven carefully so as not to lose Fargo in the night.

Mrs. Lee led them to a booth where the men removed their hats and coats, tossed them onto the benches ahead of them, and seated themselves.

Mrs. Lee brought them a pot of hot tea and two jade-green menus. Plates were already on the table, along with chopsticks wrapped in red linen napkins.

"I already know what I want," Hurley said. He turned to Fargo and said, "I'll order for both of us to save time."

Fargo scanned the menu briefly but chose to submit to Hurley's play to take control. "Go ahead, Sheriff," he said.

Hurley ordered. Mrs. Lee jotted the order down and gave them a little bow before leaving the table.

"Now," Hurley said, leaning forward a bit with arms folded on the table. "I want you to start talking. You mentioned a wolf. What do wolves have to do with what's happening in this town?"

"I'm right, aren't I? Did the lab find something—blood? Hair? Saliva?"

Hurley debated with himself over how much to tell Fargo. He still had no idea who this man was, from where he'd come.

"First, you tell me something," Hurley said. "You said you came here looking for someone. Who? And why?"

"I was searching for a man named Irving Taggart. Know the name?"

Frowning, Hurley shook his head. He turned the small teacup right-side-up and poured some steaming tea into it.

"I believe he's your missing John Doe," Fargo said.

Hurley thought about that a moment. *Do I have a missing John Doe?* Then he remembered the empty table in the morgue and thought, *Oh, yes, of course I do.* It was the John Doe who'd attacked Emily Crane on the road—the one she'd allegedly killed with the corkscrew—the one who'd walked out of the morgue, not behaving very dead.

Fargo said, "I have been reading the local paper, watching the local news broadcasts in my motel room since arriving. Which was not long ago. I've kept up. I know what is going on in your town, Sheriff Hurley. I know what the problem is, and I can help you to keep it from getting worse."

"Worse?"

"Yes, worse. Sheriff Hurley, you have an infestation of werewolves."

Hurley stared at him for a long time, his face blank. He

had no idea how to respond. Clearly, he was dining with a lunatic.

"Mr. Fargo," Hurley said, and then he left it hanging there. He bowed his head a moment, thinking, wondering how to approach this. His shoulders sagged as he sighed heavily. "I thought you knew something. Something helpful. I really did. For a moment there, I let my hopes get high."

"I *do* know something. I'm telling you. Your town has an infestation of werewolves that will soon become a full-blown outbreak if it is not contained immediately. Taggart is the source of this infestation, which means he will be able to communicate telepathically with the others—his descendants, so to speak. This telepathic contact will strengthen them, give them drive, purpose. Once he has successfully linked them all together and starts giving them commands—believe me, Sheriff, you *have* to keep that from happening, because once that happens . . . well, it's all over for Big Rock. Then the next town. And the next. You have to stop them *here*, Sheriff Hurley. While you still can."

"And how do you, uh—" An abrupt, breathy chuckle escaped Hurley. "—how do you propose I do that?"

"Find Irving Taggart. Learn who he's infected, then—"

"*Infected?*"

"Oh, yes, infected. Then we find those people, and learn who *they* have infected." With a shrug, Fargo added, "And, of course, we'll have to kill them all."

Hurley's mouth fell open. He frowned as he leaned even farther forward, his eyes wide. "*Kill* them?"

Fargo nodded. "They are no longer the people they once were, Sheriff Hurley. They are no longer human. If they are not killed, they will continue to kill people and eat them, as well as rape and spread the virus."

"Virus?"

"It is a virus, yes."

Hurley squinted at him. "A *virus*? Should you be talking to me, or the CDC?"

"Lupus venereus, it's called," Fargo said. "Well . . . that's what *I* call it. And I'm the one who funded the research that discovered it, and paid the scientists who worked on it, and coordinated the construction of the small lab where all this was done."

Mrs. Lee returned with their food on a tray. "Here you are, gentlemen," she said as she put the three dishes on the table. "Enjoy." She smiled as she turned and walked away.

"*What's* a virus?" Hurley said as if Mrs. Lee had not been there.

"The lycanthropy. It's rare, and we can thank God for that, but it does indeed exist. And it is *quite* contagious."

Hurley leaned back on the padded seat and began to dish up his dinner. "Look, Mr. Fargo, I don't think you're going to help by hanging around and insisting we have an outbreak of contagious werewolves in Big Rock." He tried to speak with a level voice, but it quavered a little. Crackpots infuriated him. Alien abductees, Bigfoot hunters, conspiracy theorists, Scientologists, UFO "experts"—they all annoyed the hell out of him. They were such a waste of . . . *thought*, of brain power.

Fargo smiled under his thick mustache. "I think you know I'm right. You are simply too afraid to admit it. You grasp for other answers, don't you? Other explanations. But none work. This one, however, does. And it scares the hell out of you, as it should. I am not crazy, Sheriff Hurley. Am I behaving like a mentally disturbed person? No. Maybe you have been trying to *tell* yourself I'm crazy, but you know better. Don't you, Sheriff Hurley? You know something very strange is going on in your town, don't you? The killings, the eviscerations. You can feel it in your *gut* that something is very wrong. Have you heard any odd sounds? Howling, perhaps? What about that thing on the lawn in front of the house tonight, Sheriff? You *saw* it. Half human, half wolf. You saw her in midtransformation. She was shot with shells loaded with silver buckshot. That's why she died. Were-wolves have a—"

"*Shot?*" Hurley said, his eyes widening. "Who shot her?"

Fargo stared at him levelly with one good eye, his food untouched; but he said nothing.

"You say she was shot, yes?" Hurley said.

"With silver buckshot. Werewolves have a violent, trau-matic allergic reaction to silver that is *always* fatal, even if it takes a little time to kill them. It disables them imme-diately and makes them—"

"I need real solutions, Fargo," Hurley said as he ate. "Not legends, not superstitions. And certainly not stories of a werewolf virus. And now, you tell me you've *killed* someone. Mr. Fargo, I'm the sheriff, I can't just sit here and—"

"What did you find in that house, Sheriff? How many had she killed? The entire family?"

Lips parted, Hurley stared at the man. He suddenly felt cold. An inner chill passed through him.

"Whoever you found, whatever was left—the remains were partially *eaten*, weren't they?"

After a moment, Fargo nodded once, then began to eat. "Who shot her, Fargo? You?"

He ignored the question. "You'll find more. Quickly. It's already happened to one of your deputies. It will start hap-pening all over town. Then it will spread beyond this town. Your bullets will not stop these creatures. Your weapons are useless without silver ammunition. You are helpless. With-out me, anyway. That is why I've come. To help you fight this, to save lives. You *need* me, Sheriff."

They ate together in silence for awhile. Fargo was the first to speak.

"What do *you* think is happening in your town, Sheriff Hurley?" he said.

"I think I've got a psycho on my hands. No, *two*. A couple of real freaks—one who rapes, one who kills."

"You think a *person* did all that damage to those victims?"

Hurley rolled his eyes and sighed. "Fargo, you *must* know how crazy your story is."

"Yes, I do know. Of *course* I do. But I also know what I've seen and touched and—See these scars on my face?"

Hurley nodded.

"I did not get them in a barroom brawl, I can assure you. I got them on Thanksgiving Day, sixteen years ago. I lost the eye later. Just a year and a half ago, to be precise. Would you like to hear about it?"

Hurley shrugged. "Frankly, I'd rather hear that than more stories about werewolves."

Fargo smiled and chuckled a little. He ate a short while longer, then took the napkin from his lap and dabbed his mouth as he leaned back in the seat. He pushed the plate away, tossed the napkin onto it; then he began to tell his story. . . .

It was to be a quiet Thanksgiving. Just my wife Debra and myself, and our daughter Rose and her husband of one year, Jeffrey. Rose was quite pregnant with their first child. She was seven months along. She was a small woman, quite petite, like her mother, making her enormous belly look almost as big as she was. She was so happy. You hear people talk of pregnant women having a glow—well, she did, she truly did. I don't think the smile ever left her face the whole day. Until . . . until it happened.

I married into money, Sheriff Hurley. That was not my reason for marrying Debra, it had nothing to do with it. But that did not change the fact that my wife was very rich when I married her. I fell in love with her, not her money, and I remained in love with her until her death. You see, her father had invented a particular kind of glue that revolutionized the production of envelopes and stamps and other adhesive products. He and Debra's mother had died years before, and being the only child, she had inherited their entire fortune. We lived very well in our mansion in New Haven, and our Thanksgiving dinner was cooked and served by servants. We had everything we needed and wanted. And yet, all that was taken away that day, in a matter of minutes.

They walked right in through our front door. I have no idea how they got past the front gate, which was kept locked, but they did. They came into the house as if they lived there, as if they owned the place. Two men and a woman. They wore filthy clothes that hung on them in tatters. They smelled like . . . like animals, a foul, gamey smell. They were laughing as they made their way into the dining room.

It was our custom to eat our Thanksgiving dinner early, so we could go for a walk afterward and work it off, or something. It was simply too heavy a meal to eat late. So we ate around five. It was just getting dark outside.

When I heard them, I frowned because I knew no one else was expected. I looked at Debra, puzzled, and she said, "I wonder who that could be." Maynard, our butler, cried out somewhere in the house and I heard him fall to the floor. I quickly pushed my chair back and stood. As I turned to go see what was happening, they entered the dining room, and after that, everything was chaos.

The woman was tall and big-boned, with long red hair. The men were both dark. Their ages—probably somewhere in their twenties. First, they attacked our dinner table. They threw plates against the wall, played catch with the ham, threw food all over my family.

"Get security!" I shouted.

They simply laughed. One of the men pulled Rose's chair back away from the table and hooked his arms under hers, dragging her from her chair. Rose screamed and Jeffrey and I immediately went to her aid, but the other man grabbed us both and pulled us back. I jerked from his grasp and turned around to face him, to punch him right in the face. But I froze.

He opened his mouth to reveal large fangs. And then, with ... popping and ... and crunching sounds, his face ... it *elongated*. The lower half of his face jutted outward. His nose became two twitching, glistening black nostrils at the end of a snout.

Debra and Rose kept screaming.

The man's face darkened, and I realized that was because he was very rapidly growing hair all over it. His height suddenly increased, right before my eyes. The tattered clothes that once hung off his body in loose strips were now tight because his body had thickened and become quite muscular.

The screams were awful. Now, along with Debra and Rose, the maid, Mrs. Blevins, screamed, too, and there were more screams coming from the other servants.

The man slapped my face. That was what it felt like at first, a simple but very hard slap. And then my slapped face began to bleed, and blood ran into my eyes and mouth. He slapped me again and again, all the while his thin, black lips grinning around all those sharp teeth. All I knew was that I was in terrible pain and bleeding badly. But I had to do something, I *had* to. Something irritating seemed to be attached to my face—several small hanging objects clung to my cheeks and forehead, dangling annoyingly. I did not realize at the time that it was torn skin dangling from my skull.

I do not remember much from that point onward. Mostly flashes of things. Blood splattering the walls. The sight of my wife's throat torn out and gushing and spurting blood. My daughter's clothes torn, her bare pregnant belly sliced open. I remember seeing them play catch with the bloody infant; then they took it apart and ate it, all three of them, sharing it among themselves.

I do not remember much. But I remember *that*.

I remember enough. More than enough.

And who was causing all this bloodshed? Was it two strange men and a strange woman? No, not anymore. They were no longer human. They were three monsters. Three tall, hairy, fanged, clawed *monsters*.

I woke up in a hospital, raving about werewolves. They drugged me, I went under, and slept for a few more days. When I came to again, I knew better than to tell the truth. If I did, they would most likely put me away. Instead, I described the two men and one woman who initially came into the house. They had me look at some mug shots, and I identified all three of them. Common criminals.

But that was down the line a ways. First, I had a few operations on my face. They did their best, but . . . it was too far gone ever to be made normal again.

I sold my house, I liquidated everything. I led a relatively humble life as I did a lot of reading on the Internet about werewolves. I became very familiar with the legend, but I found that it had little to do with the truth. I set up a lab and hired scientists, all of whom signed nondisclosure agreements. I set them to work on the problem.

I have hunted down and killed the woman, and one of the men.

The remaining man who killed my family is Irving Taggart. And he is here, in Big Rock.

Hurley had stopped eating halfway through Fargo's story, and now stared at him across the table. The inner chill that had hit him earlier had grown worse.

"I'm very sorry about your family," Hurley said quietly. "I intend to find Irving Taggart, and when I do, I'll do my best to see to it that he's charged with that along with everything else."

Fargo chuckled as he closed his eye and slowly turned his head back and forth. "You will not be catching him, Sheriff Hurley." He opened his eye. "That is not to say you aren't *good* enough to catch him. If he were just another human being, I have every confidence that you would, indeed, bring him to justice. But he is not. He is a very dangerous animal now, Sheriff Hurley. And he leads a growing pack of other very dangerous animals. He must be tracked down and killed like an animal, or he will continue to kill and eat people, to spread his monstrous virus, and to create more animals like himself. That is what I have been doing for the last fifteen years—tracking werewolves wherever I can find them. Fortunately for us, in my trek across the country, I have not encountered many. That means they have not yet settled in, they haven't really dug in their heels. Not yet. But they could, and it could begin right here in Big Rock."

"But, Mr. Fargo, I can't just—"

"Irving Taggart raped and infected Emily Crane when she broke down beside the road," Fargo said. "We know that much. Emily Crane then—I'm guessing, now—killed and ate her family. Am I right about that, Sheriff?"

Hurley hesitated a moment, then said, "Her, um . . . her husband. Her children weren't home."

Fargo said, "Did you find the remains of a pet? A dog, or a cat?"

Hurley lowered his eyes and stared at his walnut shrimp. He did not want to admit that he had found the cat. He still had not decided yet whether or not that detail would be released to the press.

"You did," Fargo said, his deep voice low. "Was it a cat, as you thought?"

Hurley gave the slightest of nods.

"Yes. It fits the pattern. Emily Crane was infected, and a couple days later, she was overwhelmed by a hunger for bloody raw meat. She was most likely given sedatives after the attack, and they slowed down the process, which is why it took a bit longer than usual. Typically, it happens within twenty-four hours. The raw steak or hamburger, or whatever it was she ate, did not satisfy her, because it was not warm and alive. She wanted fresh meat. Hot, pumping blood. She found it in her cat. Then her husband. My guess is that she insisted they have sex first, because that is part of what she craved, as well. Physical contact, orgasm, release—these are the other things for which the werewolf hungers. A very savage release, because it was very likely at that point that she began to eat her husband."

"Uh, look, you've already ruined my dinner." Hurley sat back and pushed his plate away.

"I am sorry, but this is not a time to be delicate. You have a virus to contain, Sheriff."

"If I *believe* you."

"Oh, no, not at all. You have a virus to contain whether you believe me or not." He smiled. "It is simply a matter of whether or not you decide to do something about it before more and more people contract it, and spread it."

Crushed ice coursed through Hurley's veins.

What if he's right? he wondered. As unlikely as it seemed, that thing on the lawn in front of the Cranes' house gave some support to what Fargo said. Hurley had looked at it, listened to it dying. It *had* been Emily Crane—and it *had* been half . . . something else.

But what? he thought. Was it true? Could such a thing be possible?

Hurley said, "What are you going to do if I don't believe you? If I ignore you, tell you to go away?"

"I will continue to do what it is I do. I will track Irving Taggart down and kill him before he can rape any more women and spread the virus. I will do my best to hunt down the others and kill them, as well. That will be easier once Taggart is dead. As I said, he links with them telepathically and has a good deal of control over them. Once he's dead, they will be weakened and confused. I will endeavor to make up for what you will not be doing. But I am just one man. You have an entire force at your command. With all that manpower, with the two of us working together, I think we could shut this virus down quickly. But it will take resolve, Sheriff. And great determination."

"Resolve and determination? To go around killing people because we *think* they're actually *werewolves*? That takes *resolve*? I'll tell you what it takes, Fargo. It takes a fucking psycho to do that. You want me to go through town and wipe some people out, just do some wholesale slaughter. You want me to—"

"I want you to *stop* them, Sheriff, before they over*take* this town, and then the next town, and the next. Before the infection spreads and becomes a nationwide plague."

Hurley closed his eyes a moment, rolled them once behind his eyelids, and said, "And how does such an infection spread?" he said, asking for it.

"Haven't I told you yet?" Fargo said. "I thought I had. Well . . . it spreads insidiously and quickly, Sheriff Hurley, because people, in the end, have learned nothing. It spreads easily because people have become complacent and not only fail, but *refuse* to take the precautions that only a couple decades ago were so—"

"Look, could you spare me the lecture?"

Fargo nodded once. "I'm sorry. The myth has it that it's passed through the bite. Not so, not at all. Besides, if one of those things starts biting you, it's going to *eat* you, so a virus is the least of your problems. No, this is more clever, more subtle. It is passed by way of the werewolf's other hunger, its other savage need." He arched a torn eyebrow over his good eye and smiled, although his disfigurement made his smile rather grotesque. "It is sexually transmitted, Sheriff Hurley."

Hurley froze. His lungs became blocks of ice in his chest.

Something about those words . . . the idea of some horrible virus that was sexually transmitted . . . something new and unknown that turned people into bloodthirsty monsters . . . it chilled him to the marrow of his bones.

Then Hurley remembered who he was listening to—Daniel Fargo: werewolf hunter.

Hurley stood and tossed his napkin onto the table. He leaned in and grabbed his jacket, put it on, and said, "I don't want to see you around during this investigation. During *any* investigation. Is that clear? If you show up, I'll arrest you for interfering, and anything else I can think of, and I will put you in *jail*. Is that understood, Mr. Fargo?"

"Clearly you are unable to admit to me what you've already—"

"Don't tell me what I'm thinking, either, dammit! I hate that. It pisses me off, and I'm already pissed. What you're asking me to do—I'm tempted to arrest you right now. In fact—" He quickly produced a pad and pen. "Where are you staying in town?"

"The Beachcomber Motor Lodge. Would you like to see my driver's license again?"

"Please."

Fargo removed his wallet, slid the license out, and handed it to the sheriff. Hurley copied down the relevant information from the license and handed it back. Fargo put it away again.

Hurley put the pad and pen away, then stabbed a finger at Fargo. "Don't leave town. You'll be hearing from me regarding the investigation into Emily Crane's death. In the meantime, stay away from me and my deputies. If you show up in the course of this investigation, or any others, my deputies will be instructed to arrest you on sight, just for showing up."

"Actually, I don't believe you can do that," Fargo said, frowning.

Hurley bent forward at the waist and said, "Well, it

doesn't *matter* whether you believe it or not, you *will* be arrested." He turned and took broad steps to the front of the restaurant. Mrs. Lee was at the register. "I'm in a rush, Mrs. Lee. You have my card number, just charge it, with the usual tip. And could you please have those leftovers packed up and sent over to the station for me?"

Always smiling, she nodded. "Of course, Sheriff, I'll have my son drive them over right away."

"Thanks, Mrs. Lee. Give my best to your family."

He left the restaurant and walked into the damp cold of the parking lot outside. The sea smell on the air came with a chilling bite. He wanted to slam a door, or put his fist through something. He hated it when people thought they knew what he was thinking, as if he were so predictable he could be read like a newspaper comic strip. And he hated crackpots who interfered with investigations.

Hurley took a few deep breaths, let them out slowly. Then he unlocked the door of the SUV, and got in.

Werewolves, he thought, and that icy chill fell over him again, a chill that had nothing to do with the weather. It reached him in places the winter weather could not.

He thought of that hideous thing on the Cranes' lawn—the big, lolling breasts, the fat belly. Emily Crane.

Werewolves, he thought again.

This time, he turned on the heater, and turned it up high.

27

JASON'S STORY

Hurley stared at the boy for awhile, holding his cap in his right hand, his right wrist held before him with his left hand. He did not want to believe he'd really heard what he thought the boy had just said.

He pulled the green, vinyl-upholstered chair in the corner over to the bedside. The pale blue curtain had been drawn all the way around the Emergency Room bed, so they were alone, just Hurley and Jason Sutherland. Hurley sat down in the chair. He suddenly felt tired, and his knees felt weak. He sat on the front edge of the chair, both hands holding his cap between his spread knees.

"A, uh . . . a *wolf*, you said?" Hurley asked, his voice hoarse. He cleared his throat.

The wounds on Jason's face and arm had been cleaned, stitches had been administered, and bandages applied. The white bandages covered his forehead and right cheek, and his upper left arm was wrapped in pristine white, as well. His dark hair sprouted in all directions, with strands of sparkling white in it.

When Hurley first had entered the room and pulled the curtain around the bed, Jason had been smiling. He'd said he felt surprisingly good, and that the doctor said his wounds weren't as deep as they'd first thought, and would probably heal well. He'd been in good spirits, a little goofy from the painkiller. Until Hurley asked for a detailed account of everything he remembered. Then the young man's mood had darkened.

"That's right," Jason said. "A wolf."

"There was a wolf . . . *inside* the Crane house?"

"That's right. It stood right there in front of me in the living room. It was a wolf, but at the same time . . . it wasn't any kind of wolf I've ever seen before. It was . . . *huge*. Bigger than any person I'd ever seen. I don't know how tall, maybe—"

"How *tall?*" Hurley said. "You mean it was standing? Upright?"

"Yes. That's what I mean, it wasn't any kind of wolf I've ever seen before. And then it came right for me, straight through the front window. Just swiped the glass with its claws and the window shattered."

"The wolf did this."

"Yes. It came at me, and I—hey, you don't think I know this sounds crazy?"

Hurley shrugged. "I didn't say anything."

"Yes you did. With your tone, your eyes. You're thinking I'm crazy, or something. But I'm not going to make something up just because it might sound better. I don't know what *else* to tell you, other than what really happened."

Hurley dropped his head, stared at his cap—tiny beads of moisture clung to the plastic that covered it. He felt a little sick to his stomach. He closed his eyes a moment and took a deep breath.

I've got one witness so far, Hurley thought, *but what do you want to bet there will be more. They'll start pouring in anytime now, won't they? People will be calling in were-wolf reports. Sightings, attacks, sightings of attacks. And it all lands in my lap.*

It was ridiculous, of course, the whole thing—*werewolves*, for God's sake. But what worried Hurley was that the idea was starting to make some kind of sense.

"You don't believe me, do you?" Jason said. "What do you think did this to my face? What do you think bit my arm? In the Emergency Room, the doctor knew right away that I'd been bitten by some kind of dog, or something. I told him a wolf, and he said, 'It must've been a *big* wolf,' because the bite mark was so big. *He* believed me—why can't you?"

Hurley lifted his head, stood again. "What makes you think I don't believe you? I haven't said a word. Tell me, Jason, what did it look like? In detail."

Jason shrugged, then winced in pain, groaned quietly. "It was covered with hair. With *fur*. Brown fur. All over its body and face, on its hands, or paws ... I'm not sure what to call them, but they're long, longer than hands, and they've got curved black claws coming out of each finger. That's what cut up my face."

"It wasn't the glass that cut you?"

Jason shook his head. "No, not at all. I jumped out of the way when the window broke. That thing, it dove for me. It came through the glass, then just kept coming through the air, as if it had jumped—like a kangaroo, or something. And it was on me, clawing me. I really don't remember much more than that."

The rail was up on the side of Jason's bed, and Hurley put his left hand on it as he said, "Jason, please don't be insulted by this next question, because I have to ask it. Give it a moment's thought, just *think* about it a little before you answer. Okay?"

"All right."

"Is there any chance at all—and I want you to give this some serious thought—is there any chance you hallucinated after being knocked unconscious?"

Jason slowly turned his head from side to side. "No—this was *before* I lost consciousness. I was wide awake when I saw that thing on the other side of that window. And when it came through at me."

Jason began to tremble in his bed.

"You okay, Jason?" Hurley asked. "You want me to call a nurse?"

"No, no. Just . . . the shivers. It'll pass. It happens when I think about it."

"About what?"

"The werewolf," Jason said, a little frustrated.

"It's a werewolf, now."

"No, it was *always* a werewolf."

"Then why did you keep saying 'wolf'?"

"Because that's what it is, dammit, a wolf. But it's a *werewolf*, whether you believe it or not, whether you think I'm—"

"Calm down, Jason." Hurley looked at the foot of the bed and saw another white blanket folded up there, unused. He reached down and pulled the extra blanket up over Jason, who continued to shiver. "Just calm down and try not to upset yourself. Take a few deep breaths." Hurley spoke to him slowly and softly.

Jason closed his eyes and gradually stopped shivering as he breathed deeply.

"Is your hair normally white in places?" Hurley asked.

Jason opened his eyes. "No. The doctor told me about that. I guess some of my hair turned white. I'm not surprised. I've never been so scared in my life. I didn't know it was possible to be that scared and live." He began to shiver again.

"You just calm down, now, Jason," Hurley said. "You feeling okay? I mean, that bite, something like that can be—"

"I'm okay," Jason said. His voice quavered, hands clutching the edge of the blanket.

"Are your parents here?"

"They left earlier. They would've stayed if they hadn't needed a drink so bad." The trembling worsened.

"You're *sure* you're okay?"

"I . . . I'm scared, Sheriff." Jason's trembling voice dropped to a whisper as he spoke. Still whispering, he said, "Scared shitless. Because of what's going to happen to me now."

"Happen? What's going to happen?"

Jason's eye was wide and desperate with fear as he stared at Hurley. "I've been bitten. I know what happens when they bite you."

"When who bites you?"

"*Werewolves!* Haven't you been *listening*?"

That again, Hurley thought. "Look, Jason, listen to me. About this, um, werewolf. I'm sure you *thought* you saw—"

"Don't patronize me!" Jason shouted, sitting up in his bed.

"Calm down, now, Jason."

Jason's eyes closed and he groaned in pain. He slowly sank back down on the bed. He lay there a moment, and slowly, his trembling calmed. When his eyes opened again and turned to Hurley, a tear fell from one and trickled down his cheek.

"I'm going to turn into one now," Jason whispered.

What had Fargo said? Something about the myth being false—that victims bitten by werewolves don't become werewolves?

That's right, Hurley thought. *He said it's sexually transmitted.* A mild shudder passed through him at the thought. When he spoke, Hurley realized his own words sounded weak, false.

"Jason, that's not possible. People don't turn *into* things. They just don't. They never have, and they never will. We're all human, Jason, you, me, all of us. We don't turn into things. And werewolves, Jason—"

. . . you have an infestation of werewolves . . .

"Look, Jason, I'm not doubting what you saw, okay? But let's face it—they don't exist. Even you admitted the idea sounded crazy. You're upset right now—you've been badly hurt and frightened. But you know—if not now, you will realize it later—you know as well as I do that they don't exist, Jason."

. . . infestation of werewolves . . .

Hurley gave the boy a big smile. "Well, you get better, Jason. If you need anything, I want you to feel free to call me, okay?"

"Yeah." He looked pale, with a little too much white showing in his eyes.

"You sure you're okay, Jason?" Hurley said. "You want me to call someone?"

He did not respond for some time. Then he simply said, "No."

Hurley said, "You take care."

He left the room, then the hospital. He got into his vehicle and just sat there awhile, hands on the wheel. His breath clouded in the air in front of his face. It was coming too fast. He took a couple of deep breaths.

Sheriff Hurley, you have an infestation of werewolves, Fargo had said with disarming confidence. *An infestation of werewolves.*

Hurley slowly turned his head back and forth, refusing to believe it—but unable to reject the theory, unable to let go of it. After seeing that thing on the Cranes' lawn . . . after hearing what Jason had said . . . he wasn't sure what he knew, or what to believe.

He still had to go see Emily Crane's friend Terri March before going home. He decided to drive back to the station first and see if anything else had come in. When he got there, he found that everything was quiet.

Hurley went to the desk sergeant, Tony Naccarato, and

said, "Tony, anything unusual happens tonight, anything at all, I want you to call me, understand?"

"You got it, Sheriff."

Hurley felt a pang of sadness when he thought of Emily Crane's children.

"And Tony," he said, "get Child Protective Services on the line for me. They've gotta have someone on call tonight. I've got a situation I need to hand off to them."

Jason found himself enjoying the painkiller he'd been given as he waited on the bed in the Emergency Room for his parents to come back and take him home. The doctor had come to see him right after the sheriff left and said he wanted to see him again in a couple of days.

As good as the painkiller made him feel, he could not shake his fear.

A werewolf, he thought groggily.

And if *that* were true, then it also had to be true that, on the next full moon the bite he had received would turn him into the very thing that had bitten him. Jason had seen all the old movies; he knew the story.

As bad as his fear was, it was not enough to make him forget Andrea Norton. He wondered how she was, if Jimmy were beating her up tonight. He wanted to call her, but he would have to wait until tomorrow when Jimmy was at work. Just to see her, to hold her hand—it was like an addiction, the kind of urge that comes from needing an addictive substance, the feeling of being hooked. At least, that was how he'd always imagined it to be—he'd never been hooked on anything before. He wanted to smell her, to feel her lips on his. He wondered if she knew yet that he was in the hospital, that he'd been hurt. She must have known something was going on when she saw all those Sheriff's cars and the ambulance. But what could she do? With Jimmy around, she couldn't call Jason, or even go to his house and ask about him. Like him, she had to wait until tomorrow.

Then he wondered if he should call her at all, if seeing her, if simply being *around* her might be putting her in danger. In the movies, the werewolf always tried to kill the person it loved the most. If the worst happened, if it did change him, he did not want to hurt Andrea. He would not be able to live with himself if he did anything to hurt Andrea.

The painkiller gave him a floating sensation. The television on the articulating arm over his bed played cartoons.

Jason closed his eyes and drifted in and out of sleep, and when he slept, he dreamed shadowy black-and-white nightmares of wolfmen stalking through misty graveyards.

28

MAKING OUT AT THE JAGS

Bobby killed the engine and left the radio playing.

Suzie sighed, then turned to him and smiled a little.

It had begun to rain again on their way up the hill, and now the rain made a steady roar on the roof of the car—a Toyota from somewhere back in the eighties. Water poured down the windshield, distorting the bushes that stood in the beams of the headlights, which Bobby had left on. They were alone there, the only car parked in the clearing beside Seaview Avenue.

"I figured it was fun last time," Bobby said, "so why not again?"

He reached over and stroked her hair—it was brown with recently-added blond highlights, and Suzie had to admit, it looked pretty damned good and touchable. But . . .

She laughed a little as Bobby's fingertips ran along the edge of her ear. Typically, she did not like anyone touching her ear—it sent unpleasant chills down her back and gave her the creeps. But even though she winced and laughingly pressed his hand between her shoulder and head to keep the fingers from moving over her ear, she decided to say nothing. She knew what she *wanted* to say, but was unsure of what she *should* say.

Suzie Camber was on her second date with Bobby Stanley. And it was the second time he'd brought her up to the Jags. That was what the locals called the place, anyway. It was a popular make-out spot for young people, a clearing at the edge of a rocky decline so sharp it was almost a cliff that overlooked a rocky section of the coast where waves crashed dramatically against large jagged rocks below. Suzie had not been there since high school. She was pretty sure that the high school students were the *only* ones who came to the Jags . . . besides Bobby.

They had gone to high school together, Suzie and Bobby, but that seemed so long ago. It had been only seven years, but it *felt* like a long time ago. Sometimes it felt like something that had happened to someone else. After high school, Suzie had gone to Humboldt with no idea what she wanted to study. She stayed for a semester, long enough to learn that college was not for her. Not then, anyway. She had been tired of school—exhausted, to be honest. Maybe she'd try college again a little later, but she wanted some time to herself for awhile. Neither of her parents had gone to college, and they'd had no great, burning desire for her to go. She'd had a few boring jobs over the space of a year and a half, but then she'd gotten a job at the Hot Topic store in the Northgate Mall—it gave her a chance to wear some of her leather clothes, which were encouraged among Hot Topic employees, in keeping with the chain's bad boy/girl image. Best of all, it was a job she liked. All her friends came by Hot Topic at least once a day, friends she'd made since high school, new friends. She'd been at Hot Topic ever since. She loved the job and had been made assistant manager a couple of years ago.

It was there that she'd seen Bobby again, after having lost track of him for awhile. He'd gone to live with his father in a suburb of San Francisco and was now back in

Big Rock. Bobby looked exactly the same as he had in high school. He was tall and lanky, his dark-blond hair a little shaggy, and that mustache he was *still* working on was still pretty thin. He even wore the same kind of clothes—they were the *same* clothes, for all she knew—jeans and T-shirts, and in colder weather, jeans and sweatshirts. At first, she'd found it kind of cute, the fact that he'd been preserved in a perfect state of . . . of high school.

The first date had been a trip down Memory Lane. He'd taken her to Carousel Pizza, where everyone used to hang out when they were in high school, each group to its own table. She hadn't been there since she'd been graduated. Carousel still had a large game room filled with video games and pinball machines, and while they waited for their pizza, Bobby had gotten a fistful of quarters, given her half of them, and they'd gone into the game room and played video games and pinball. Suzie wasn't much of a video game player, but she'd laughed a lot that evening while trying to play them with Bobby.

After eating, he'd driven her up to the Jags, and they'd made out for awhile. He ended up working his hand successfully between her legs, and he'd gotten her off that way—he'd done quite a good job, too. Then, to be fair, she gave him a hand job.

Then he'd asked her out again a week later. Back in high school, she'd always found Bobby to be a sort of diamond in the rough—cute, but possibly adorable with the right kind of overhaul. They'd traveled in different crowds, though. Suzie had been a rather popular cheerleader, while Bobby had run with a group of pranksters who'd been more interested in the next kegger than in cheerleaders, who might as well have been on another planet. Back then, it would have been socially impossible for them to date—that was one of the elements of high school she'd hated. But that was all behind them now, and they were adults, free to do as they pleased. She was curious to get beyond their past, to get to know him better. She realized they'd spent their first date talking mostly about her—she wanted to know more about him. And besides, he still had that cute-but-possibly-adorable quality about him. So she'd said yes.

Where had he taken her? Carousel Pizza. But this time, Suzie had noticed something she'd missed before—the man behind the counter had said, "Hey, Bobby, how's it going?" The man knew him. A group of guys seated around a table in the back had called out his name, almost in unison, and Bobby had gone back there to talk to them for a few minutes. Bobby was a *regular.* Did he *still* hang out at Carousel all the time, as he had back in high school?

Then he'd brought her back up here to the Jags.

And here we are, she thought, a bit sardonically, as she pulled his hand away from her ear and held it in both of hers. She thought a moment before speaking, licked her lips, and was about to say what she wanted to say, when he pressed his mouth over hers and pulled her to him in a kind of lopsided embrace.

Suzie had to admit, he was a good kisser. But after two dates in a row to Carousel, she'd begun to wonder if he still lived with his parents. Did he have a job? Had he changed at *all* since high school?

When was the last time he was up here with a girl? she wondered as she returned his kiss. It was difficult not to—he really *was* a good kisser. She thought, *Maybe that's why he only talked about me last time we went out.*

So they kissed for awhile, shifting this way and that, until they were more comfortable, but never pulling their lips apart.

Anyone who kisses this well, she thought distractedly, *has got to have some experience—surely Bobby's been with plenty of women since high school.*

Suzie did not want to hurt Bobby's feelings. Back in high school, Suzie somehow had gotten a reputation for being mean. But she was *not*, as she'd insisted back then and maintained today, and not being a mean person, she had no intention of saying anything that would insult or offend Bobby. But good kissing aside, she saw no future in this relationship.

She finally pulled away gently.

Bobby backed off then, too, breathing heavily. He sat back in his seat a moment, then chuckled and said, "Kinda hot in here, huh?"

All the windows had fogged up. Bobby rolled his window down halfway.

Suzie smiled and took in a breath to speak, when a rapid movement caught her eye just beyond Bobby, through the opening in the window.

The movement stopped.

Suzie held that breath. Her smile melted away as she realized she was looking at a single silver eye, with only an empty socket on the left. It peered into the car through the narrow opening.

She screamed a fraction of an instant before the window beside Bobby shattered into tiny safety-glass pieces and an enormous, hairy hand reached in. Black claws dragged through the flesh of Bobby's face. Bobby screamed.

Two hairy, clawed hands reached in then and closed on Bobby's head. They tore Bobby out of the car through the empty window and dropped him to the ground.

And all the while, Suzie screamed, her voice tearing at her throat. She pressed her back to the door, trying to get as far away from the thing as possible.

The thing dragged Bobby, struggling and screaming, away from the car by the head.

Rain pounded on the roof of the car, nearly drowning Bobby's screams outside.

Suzie's screams finally stopped and crumbled in a fit of sobs.

The creature's arms flailed and its claws slashed. That was all she could see in the dark—the violent movements. She could hear two things besides the rain on the roof: Bobby's screams, and something else . . . a growling, wet and animalistic.

Bobby's screams became a hoarse gurgle, and then he fell silent.

Suzie stared wide-eyed out the window, frozen in place, paralyzed. It was when she saw the creature ripping at Bobby viciously and heard the sound of wet tissue being torn away from bone that she snapped out of it and took a good look at her situation.

Suzie leaned forward in the seat and reached down between her feet for her purse. Hands shaking, she brought the purse to her lap. She plunged her right hand in and groped around for her cell phone. She removed it from her purse and it slipped from her hand. The phone bounced back and forth between her shaking hands for a moment, like a slippery bar of soap in the shower, then disappeared in the darkness beneath the steering wheel.

"Shit, oh shit, oh *shit*," she chanted as she dove under the wheel for the phone. Her right hand groped back and forth over the floorboard for the cell phone, but found nothing but leaves and mud. Instead of swearing, she released a long, high moan that went on and on as she searched for the cell phone. She tried to reach beneath the seat, but stopped when the car moved.

Suzie stopped moaning and struggled back up to a sitting position in her seat just in time to glimpse a naked man—

A naked man a naked man oh Jesus something else what's next a naked man what do I do what do I do—

—rounding the front corner of the car on her side. The fog on the windows was gone and she saw him coming straight for her door, his erection bobbing with each step.

The creature that had attacked Bobby was nowhere to be seen.

She had not locked the door.

Suzie let out a sharp cry as she twisted around to her right, reached over and—

—the naked man pulled the door open.

"Nooo!" Suzie screamed.

There was something wrong with the man—heavy patches of hair grew over parts of his body, his thighs, his chest and sides, his upper arms. He was smeared with something dark and wet. He was bearded, but there was something besides his beard, something about his face—in the center, it jutted outward into the snout of an animal. And his left eye was missing.

Her screams grew worse, until he punched her in the face.

Suzie was immediately silenced and knocked backward into the car. She lost conciousness for a few seconds. When she half-opened her eyes, the world tilted and spun and she felt blood trickle down into her throat, tasted its salty, coppery taste, and had a coughing fit. She could feel her nose and left eye swelling.

She was not sure where she was, but she was very cold. And someone was pawing at her. Her nostrils filled with the harsh, musky scent of an animal. She heard her clothes rip, felt someone roughly spread her legs.

Suzie opened her eyes the rest of the way and looked at the round, white object glowing in the center of the ceiling over her head. A light. Then she recognized it as a dome light in a car, and everything came back.

She lifted her head as he shoved into her. Suzie arched her body and screamed louder than she had so far that night.

He grunted and growled and slobbered on her.

Suzie stopped screaming. Her body went limp and jolted again and again as he pounded into her.

For Suzie, everything went away—what was being done to her, the cold, the horrible thing that had just happened to Bobby—it all dissolved in her mind, along with the rest of her awareness. Her eyes remained open, but she saw nothing.

Brandi Powell was beside herself with excitement. She was on her first date with Deke Quimby, and even though it was the middle of winter, cold and raining furiously, Deke was driving her up the hill to the Jags!

The rain fell hard and Deke had turned the windshield wipers all the way up. They swept furiously back and forth, but were still unable to keep the windshield clear.

Brandi knew this date was because of the Christmas party over at Charlotte Parver's house the night before Christmas Eve. Everybody had been drinking, and the smell of some strong marijuana had been skunklike in the air—Brandi had had a little of both. Deke had been there, too, loudly enjoying himself with his friends.

Deke Quimby was probably the best looking guy at Big Rock's Dwight D. Eisenhower High School. He was athletic, but he wasn't a jock. He was very intelligent— amazingly so to Brandi, who had to struggle in school—but not weird, like so many really smart students. Everyone liked him so much that he was president of the senior class.

At the Christmas party, Deke had ended up slumped next to her on the couch, so drunk he was semiconscious. His head lolled against her shoulder, and she left it there for the longest time, just sat perfectly still so he wouldn't wake up. When he did open his eyes, he sat up straight, yawned, lifted his arms high over his head and stretched them. Then he turned to Brandi, took her in his arms, and kissed her.

It was the biggest shock of her life. It was also the nicest. They'd sat there and kissed for a long time. Then, he'd stood, smiled down at her, and he'd said, "Merry Christmas." He'd left the party after that, leaving Brandi weak on the couch.

It had been all she'd thought about ever since. Until one evening, her cell phone rang, and it was Deke, asking her out to a movie. She thought he hadn't even known her name, but there he was on the phone, asking her out.

Brandi never had trouble getting dates. She was a curvaceous, pouty-lipped blonde with large brown bedroom eyes. But she did not get guys in the same stratosphere as Deke Quimby. Few girls did. For one thing, he'd been dating Amber Mitchell for the longest time. But that had ended at the beginning of his senior year.

Deke pulled off Seaview and onto the clearing that made up the Jags, and the headlights of his Acura swept over the tree trunks and bushes and—

"Oh, my God," Brandi said.

"What happened here?" Deke said as he brought the car to a stop, its headlights still on the other car.

The passenger's side door was open, and two pale, bare, female legs hung out, the knees bent, the rest of the body lying on its back in the car.

"Stay here," Deke said.

"Wait!" Brandi said.

"What?"

For one thing, Brandi sure as hell did *not* want her evening at the Jags with Deke Quimby to be ruined, but the chances of that were starting to look really good.

"Well," she said, "we could always go someplace else."

Deke frowned. "Are you kidding? Maybe she's sick, or hurt. I'll be right back."

Damn, she thought, mentally kicking herself for saying

the wrong thing. Now he probably thought she was some kind of cold, heartless monster.

She sat in the car, engine idling, heater running. There was soft, easy music on the CD player—she didn't know what it was, but it was nice, and she liked it. She watched as Deke went over to the other car, an old Toyota. Brandi recognized it because her older sister Cheri used to have one when Brandi was little. Deke wore a very nice sheerling-lined jacket with a hood, which he pulled up over his head. At the other car, he braced himself with one hand against the edge of the roof and leaned in through the open door. The car's headlights were still on, but Brandi didn't think the engine was running.

Something caught her eye. Movement beyond the Toyota.

Something rose up on the other side of the Toyota, something dark and very tall. Something *big*. It walked along the car to the front, then stepped into the headlight beams.

Brandi screamed when she saw it. She tried to get to the steering wheel, but her seatbelt was on and held her back. She struggled with it, unfastened it, then leaned over and pounded on the horn. She gave three bursts, then one long, sustained honk.

The thing came to this side of the Toyota and started toward Deke. Only the open car door stood between Deke and the large creature.

Deke pulled himself out of the Toyota, then stood and turned to her.

Brandi stopped screaming, but kept honking, even though it did no good.

Deke seemed to hear something behind him and spun around. The creature shoved the door closed, knocking Deke backward. The door slammed on the two bare legs, then swung back open again. The enormous creature was on Deke before he had his bearings. Brandi heard his screams as the thing lifted him up off the ground and buried its long, doglike snout into his throat.

Deke's scream did not last long—it collapsed into a harsh gargle, then stopped. He went limp in the creature's grasp. It threw him onto the muddy ground, then went to his body, got down, and began tearing at Deke.

"Oh, Jesus, help me, please, Jesus, God, Mary—" Brandi got her cell phone from her purse, turned it on, and punched in nine-one-one.

"Nine-one-one, what is your emergency?" the woman on the phone said.

Brandi babbled as her left hand crawled up the side of her face like a spider, then entangled its fingers in her hair, swept back through the hair until the fingers were free, then started over again.

The operator said, "Please calm down, miss—what is your emergency?"

"I-I-I—wait, wait," Brandi said as she watched the thing tear Deke apart and eat him—it was actually *eating him*. It took gobs of glistening things from inside him and closed its fangs on them, chewing. Jiggling tissue dangled from its snout as it chewed. But what would it do when it was finished?

Brandi found the master lock and locked all the doors. Then she put the phone to her ear again and said, "I'm at the Juh-Jags, the Jags up above town, above Big Rock, do you know—"

"Yes, I know where the Jags are."

"My date is being killed by a big monster, and it's already killed somebody else I think, and I-I'm in the car, alone, I'm *alone*, and it's eating him, Jesus help me, *it's eating him*!"

"*Who* is attacking your date?"

"No, no, it's not a person, it's this huge thing, this huge hairy *thing*, and it's—"

Brandi's throat closed as she watched the thing stand.

It towered over the Toyota. It turned slightly, until it faced her.

It began to come her way.

Brandi screamed, then said, "It's coming, it's coming this way, it's coming over here, to the car, it's, it's—"

Brandi dropped the cell phone and scrambled over the gearshift and the center console—

The thing reached the car and Brandi screamed as it slammed both hands down on the windshield and dragged its claws across the glass with a gnawing, sickening squealing sound, leaving behind eight white trails almost all the way across the glass.

—into the driver's seat. She could not reach the pedals and had to search for the handle that allowed her to move the seat forward—

The thing roared and pounded on the top of the car.

—and when she found it, she pulled it hard. The seat jerked forward, she sat up straight, put the gearshift in reverse, and slammed on the accelerator.

From the floorboard in front of the passenger's seat came the insectlike voice of the nine-one-one operator.

The creature turned then and walked back over to Deke's limp body. It hunkered down beside him and continued to eat.

Brandi let the car idle, put it back in park, and decided to wait for the police. She cried and sobbed and prayed as the thing ate pieces of Deke. Then it lifted its head and made a sound that made Brandi scream.

The thing eating Deke howled.

29

A CALL FROM GEORGE

Ella had made lasagna for dinner that night and offered to warm it up for Hurley when he got home.

"I already ate, sweetie," he said. "But thanks."

"Are you home for the night?" Ella asked.

"There's no telling," Hurley said. "That's the plan, but with everything that's been happening lately, there's not much that would surprise me."

He took a cup of coffee from the kitchen into the living room and turned on CNN—the local news was already over. Hurley wondered how long it would be before the national press got interested in Big Rock and its . . . what? Killer wolfman?

Hurley dozed in his recliner and passed in and out of a dream that was red with blood. In the dream, a constant trilling echoed from some other place, on and on. When it finally stopped, he was shaken. He opened his eyes and sat up, startled.

Ella was bent toward him with the phone in one hand. "A call for you. The deputy coroner."

"George?" Hurley said into the phone.

"I hope I'm not interrupting anything," George said.

Hurley yawned. "No. I was dozing in front of the TV. What's up?"

George Purdy sighed. "Could you come up to the hospital, Sheriff?"

"Sure. But why?"

"I need to talk to you about this, uh . . . this *thing* you sent me. ASAP."

"I'll be there in a few minutes."

Hurley turned the phone off and handed it back to Ella, who stood beside his chair.

"Don't you have deputies to do things for you?" Ella said, with a bit of a whine in her voice. But it was a pleasant whine, because he knew it was for him.

"I have deputies to do the things that deputies do," he said as he stood. "But I'm the only one who can do the things sheriffs do." He gave her a hug and a kiss, then went upstairs to dress warmly.

It was raining hard outside and Hurley drove the SUV through the downpour. Lightning flashed over the mountains in the distance.

He drove by the Laramie house. The chill he felt as he passed it annoyed him, but he couldn't help it. It hunkered there in the dark like some great troll, waiting for something tasty to happen by. As he drove, Hurley refused to look at the house. But he could not shake the feeling that it was watching him.

The hospital was a great lake of light atop Hospital Hill overlooking the town. Spears of light glowed down between the trees, illuminating the mist that hovered around the hill. Hurley parked in the Emergency Room lot. He went in through the ER entrance. In the basement, he rounded a few corners in the deserted corridor and came to the morgue. He pushed through one of the double, porthole doors.

"That you, Sheriff?" George called.

"None other."

Hurley turned to the right as George, bending down,

closed one of the drawers in the wall. He stood up and turned to Hurley smiling.

"What can I do for you, George?" Hurley said.

"You can tell me what the hell's on that table over there," George said, pointing.

Hurley looked in the direction of George's finger and his eyes fell on the stainless-steel table on which lay the twisted, hairy, pink-fleshed thing he'd found on the lawn in front of the Crane house.

The two men went to the table.

"I'd hoped *you* could do that," Hurley said, frowning down at the thing.

No, it was not really a thing. There was clearly a naked, heavyset woman in there. Her breasts were visible, although her shoulders and upper arms were covered with a coat of dark-brown fur, and were quite muscular, her back hunched. The white hillock of her hairless belly was pocked with moist open sores. The brown fur covered what was left of her face, and her mouth and nose appeared somewhat distorted—they appeared to be stretched outward from the face, but rounded—and yet, with all that, he could make out some of Emily Crane's features: her cheeks, her ears. Her wide-open mouth revealed teeth that came to sharp points.

Hurley had seen her on the lawn in the glow of the porch light. Seeing her now under the harsh lights of the morgue, in sickening detail, made Hurley's bowels feel loose.

Sheriff Hurley, you have an infestation of werewolves.

"Dear Jesus," Hurley breathed.

"You recognize her?"

"I'm afraid I do."

"Who is—*what* is she?"

"Just like I thought. It's the receptionist down at the station—Emily Crane. She was found in front of her house."

George stood on the opposite side of the table from Hurley. He put both hands on the guttered edge of the table and clutched it with white knuckles, as he leaned forward. "You're telling me this . . . this *thing* is a woman you know?" George said.

She died midtransformation.

Hurley nodded awhile, looking at the mess on the table, then said, "Yes."

Her forearms were hairless. Her fingernails had been replaced by long, curved, black claws that grew out of her fingertips. Her fat, white, cottage-cheese thighs were bare, but her lower legs were heavily furred and ended not in feet but in long hairy paws with black claws.

Raising his voice a little, George said, "Then would you mind telling me what the hell *happened* to her? I mean, God, Arlin, look at her! She's half . . . something *else*. Her knees, Arlin—they bend the—are you *looking* at them? They bend the wrong fucking *way*! And those aren't human feet—those are the feet of an animal! A dog, or a, a wolf, or *some*thing. And her teeth—look at her teeth, for God's sake! I don't like cutting something open unless I know what it is, so that's why I called you up here, Sheriff, because I want to know what the hell this is!"

Hurley looked across the table at George. The man's face was pale and intense. Unspilled tears glistened in his eyes and his lips trembled ever so slightly.

"This thing isn't human," George whispered. "It's not . . . *right*. What does it look like to you, Sheriff? Huh? Because it looks a hell of a lot to *me* like this woman was in the process of . . ." He merely breathed the rest of his words: ". . . of becoming something . . . else when she died."

. . . werewolves.

Hurley looked down at the Emily-thing again and slowly shook his head. "I can't explain it, George," he whispered. "But I'm very interested in knowing as much as I can about it. So why don't you do your best with it?"

George looked down at the remains with a look of consternation on his face. "Do my best?"

"Just approach it like any other autopsy, but take twice the usual number of photographs and make very careful notes, because I want to know every single detail of what you find."

She was shot with shells loaded with silver buckshot.

Looking down at the Emily-thing again, George said, "I just have one question, and I'm going to ask you not to laugh. I mean, I don't know what the hell this is, what I'm dealing with, it could be . . . anything. And because of that, I have to ask you, Arlin . . . are you . . . *sure* . . . it's dead?"

Werewolves have an allergic reaction to silver that is always fatal, even if it takes a little time to kill them.

Hurley could not get Daniel Fargo's voice out of his head. It spoke there again and again, echoing to the point of irritation, its words drilling themselves into his mind with the niggling whine of a mosquito flying around his ear.

"Yes," Hurley said, "I think he killed it."

"Who killed it?"

"I'm not positive, but I now suspect it was a man named Daniel Fargo. A man I need to see again. Right away."

Hurley turned away from the thing on the table and headed back for the door.

"Where are you going?" George said.

"To see if I can find him." He stopped and turned back to George. "Do me a favor. Don't let *anyone* see that thing, and don't talk to anyone about it, okay? *Especially* the press."

"Yeah, sure."

Hurley turned to leave, but George stopped him.

"Sheriff, tell me. What the hell's going on in this town?"

Hurley frowned. "You want to know the truth? I'm not

exactly sure. But I think . . . I *think* we've got an infestation of werewolves."

George's mouth opened to say something, but nothing came out.

Hurley was pushing through the door when his cell phone vibrated in his pocket. He stood in the open doorway as he took out his phone, and flipped it open.

"Hurley."

"I thought you might like to know, Sheriff," Sergeant Tony Naccarato said.

"Know what, Tony?"

"There's been a murder and a rape. Two murders, to be exact. Up on the Jags. Deputies are there now, but seeing it's another one, I thought I'd call you, like you said."

Hurley winced and cursed under his breath. "The Jags, you say? The make-out spot?"

"The one and only."

"Thanks for calling, Tony. I'm on my way."

As Hurley closed his phone, he said, "Son of a bitch."

"Bad news?" George said.

"Two more killings. And another rape. In the same place."

"The same place? How'd *that* happen?"

Hurley shook his head. "I'm almost afraid to find out."

"I guess I'll see you there," George said as Hurley left.

30

DEATH AT THE JAGS

The rain, which had been starting and stopping all day, had stopped once again as Hurley drove the winding, narrow road that led up the hill to the Jags. Through the pines, he caught glimpses of the pulsing glow of red and blue emergency lights up ahead. He made the final turn at the top of the hill and found two cruisers, two ambulances, and a couple of television news vans that had set up their lights. Two reporters stood in front of cameras talking into their microphones several yards to the side of the scene. He recognized both of them—Shana Myers from Channel 4 and Mike Wills from Channel 7.

"Oh, shit," Hurley said as he parked.

As Hurley got out, he could hear a woman crying somewhere and looked around until he saw the girl sitting in the back of one of the cruisers with the door open wide. He looked over at the other cruiser and saw the same thing—a young woman sitting in the backseat with the door open, but she was not crying, just sitting and staring, while a female deputy hunkered down, talking to her. He walked over to Deputy Kopechne.

"What's the story, Kopechne?"

"Two bodies, both found over there—" Kopechne pointed. "—one on each side of that car. We found a girl in each car."

"How bad are they?" Hurley asked.

"The one who's crying wasn't hurt at all, she's just really upset. But the other one says she was raped, and she's pretty beaten up."

"Who made the call?" Hurley said.

"The girl who's crying."

"Okay. I'll talk to her first. What about the bodies?"

"Oh, jeez, they're a mess. Just like the guy over on Magnolia, only worse, if that's possible."

"And the reporters?"

"I personally told them to back the hell off till you got here. They're all yours."

Hurley sighed as he turned and saw both of them coming his way, the man from Channel 7 and the woman from Channel 4.

"Hold 'em off," Hurley said.

He turned away and walked over to the car that held the crying young woman, whose sobs were strong enough to shake the cruiser's frame just a little. The sheriff hunkered down in the V formed by the open car door, and smiled at the girl, a teenager.

"Excuse me, Miss, but I'm Sheriff Hurley," he said quietly. "What's your name?"

"Brandi. Brandi Powell."

"I know this is a bad time, Brandi, but I need you to answer some questions. Would that be all right?"

She took in a deep, shaky breath and fought to hold back her sobs. After a moment, she took a small package of tissues from her purse, removed one, and blew her nose. Then she turned to him, her eyes puffy, her pretty face red and glistening with tears.

"Why did you call the police, Brandi?" Hurley said.

She told him, and as he listened, he felt a sick kind of sensation in his gut—the way the old elevator in the courthouse used to make him feel when it dropped a little too suddenly.

"It was . . . a monster," she said, her whispered voice hoarse from crying so much. "It was on the other side of that car; then it stood up, and . . . and . . . it was horrible. I-I didn't know such a thing *existed*, I mean, it was huge, and then it came around the car and . . . and it got him."

"Got who?"

"Deke. My date. I go to school with him. Or . . . I *went* to school with him." She sniffled and seemed about to start crying again.

"Could you describe it for me? This monster?" Hurley said, hoping to get her mind off crying before she started.

The features of her face pulled tightly inward toward the center as she thought about it. Then: "It looked like some kind of giant . . . deformed—"

Wolf, Hurley thought.

"—dog, or wolf, or something. It . . . it made this sound, that thing, that monster."

"What sound?"

"It howled."

A chill that was becoming very familiar moved through Hurley's bowels. He stood and said, "You sit tight, now, Brandi, and one of the EMTs will be with you soon."

"But I'm not hurt. I'm waiting for my parents. I called them. I can't drive."

"Oh. Okay. I'll probably have to talk to you some more later, but not right now."

The coroner's van pulled up as Hurley walked away from the cruiser. George Purdy got out carrying a flashlight and went over to talk to Deputy Kopechne. When George saw the sheriff, he waved and immediately headed toward Hurley.

"Well," George said. "Sounds like you've got a real hungry beast out there somewhere. Speaking of beasts . . . were you serious about what you said earlier? About what's doing this?"

"Afraid so," Hurley said with a nod. "I checked to see if anything escaped from an animal show in the area, or a zoo, or something."

"And?"

"Nope."

As they talked, they walked over to the nearest of the two bodies.

"Look, Arlin, this is going to get out. You've got two reporters here tonight, but next time, there will be more, I guarantee you. They're going to start coming in from out of town, because you know what this looks like, don't you? Until you admit publicly that this was done by a . . . an animal, or . . . *whatever*, people are going to think you've got a serial killer. Listen, Arlin, you've got to tell them the truth."

"You mean tell them what I told you?" Hurley said. "They'd lock me up."

"Don't be so sure. Coming from you, people might believe it." George got down on one knee and, using the flashlight, looked over the body on the ground.

"Let's say they did," Hurley said. "People would be afraid to leave their houses. Hunting parties would be organized and a bunch of drunks will probably end up shooting each *other*."

"Then tell them it's an animal," George said distractedly.

"How's it going to sound if I can't tell them what *kind* of animal?"

"It'll sound like you don't know yet, that's all."

Hurley silently thought about it, weighed the pros against the cons.

George said, "It took its time with this guy."

"What do you mean?"

"I mean it was in no hurry. It ate a lot more than it has in the past. This one was cleaned out." He looked up at Hurley. "Of course, that's assuming it's the same one. Has it occurred to you there might be more?"

Hurley sighed as he rubbed the back of his neck. He chose to ignore the question for the moment. He turned around and saw Kopechne holding back the two reporters. Their cameras were right behind them, a bright light mounted on each. Hurley walked over to them.

Shana Myers and Mike Wills immediately turned their attention away from Kopechne and began firing questions at Hurley.

"Look, I'm kind of busy right now," he said to them, "but I'll answer a couple of questions."

They both spoke at once.

"Just one at a time, okay?" Hurley said. "Shana."

"This has happened twice in one night," she said. "Is there a serial killer in Big Rock, Sheriff Hurley?" Then she turned the microphone toward him.

"We believe that the recent killings have been done by a, uh—" He cleared his throat. "—a wild animal," Hurley said. "All the forensic evidence points to that."

"What kind of animal?" Mike asked.

"Uh . . . we're not quite sure yet."

"What are you doing about it?" Shana said.

"Everything we can." Hurley thought fast as he tried to sound confident about a situation in which he had no confidence whatsoever. "We, uh, just came to the conclusion that it was a wild animal, and now we'll be organizing hunting parties and doing everything we possibly can to find it and stop it. Now, if you don't mind, I'm busy. Once we've got all the information we can gather about these killings, I'll hold a press conference and tell you everything I know. For now, though, I've got to go."

He turned away from them and went back to George.

"You're sure this is just like the others?" Hurley asked.

George nodded. "I'd bet my next paycheck on it. What do you plan to do next?"

Hurley shrugged. "Like I told the reporters, we'll have to organize hunting parties, find this thing, and kill it."

"Using silver bullets?"

"You know your werewolf mythology," Hurley said flatly.

George frowned. "You're really serious, aren't you?"

Hurley gave him a heavy-lidded look. "Do I look like I'm kidding around to you?"

George shrugged. "Sucks to be you."

Hurley sighed. "Right now it does, yep."

Headlights flashed over them and Hurley turned around to see who was driving up. He recognized Daniel Fargo's Mercedes.

Fargo parked the car and got out. He looked around until he found Hurley, then started walking toward him.

"Who's this guy?" George asked.

"Somebody I need to see." Hurley left George and met Fargo halfway.

"Took me awhile to find this place," Fargo said with a smile.

"Thought I said I didn't want to see you around any investigations," Hurley said, but also with a smile.

"That was before this happened. Twice in one night. You need me, Sheriff. I think by now, you know that." He stepped closer and lowered his voice. "This is going to happen again and again. It will rapidly escalate as the number of werewolves in the area increases, to the point where you'll be dealing with more and more killings every night. Then? It will get *worse*. And there will be more and more people with the virus, people who will have to be killed."

"You think I'm going to go around killing people because I think they have—"

"You won't have a choice."

They said nothing for a moment. Fargo looked all around, then turned to Hurley again.

"Tell me something, Sheriff," Fargo said. "Were either of those young women raped tonight?"

"The one over there at the ambulance," Hurley said, pointing briefly.

"Then the way I see it, those two dead men I heard about on the police scanner are not your problems, Sheriff Hurley. *She* is. Because in the next twenty-four hours or so, she will be transformed into the very thing that killed those two men, and everyone before them. And she will kill and eat more people, and create more like herself, and it will go on and on, until this town is *overrun* by werewolves, and they use it as a base camp, from where they will expand their hunting grounds, outward from the town like a spider's web. Until another town falls. And another, and another."

It took Hurley awhile before he opened his mouth to speak; then he shrugged as he whispered, "What do I do?"

Fargo nodded and smiled. "I'm glad you've finally asked that question. Now we can work together."

31

FINDING FARGO

Jason sat in the backseat of his parents' car, his parents in the front seat, Dad at the wheel.

While he was in the Emergency Room, Jason had managed to shove aside his fear of being transformed into a werewolf. Once he saw the looks he was getting from the nurses and doctor whenever he said he'd been attacked by a werewolf, he'd stopped talking about it. He'd decided to keep it to himself for the time being. But now, no matter how hard he tried to push those thoughts away, they festered inside him, throbbing with fear and tension and unbearable suspense. How long would it take? What if the moon doesn't really have to be full and it could happen at any time? He hadn't thought of *that* possibility before. But now, out under the black night sky, surrounded by darkness, those thoughts returned in force.

A werewolf, he thought. He replayed the memory over and over again in his mind, and with his mind's eye he carefully inspected the tall, hairy, fanged creature his memory conjured. How could it be anything else? Wolves did not walk upright—not *normal* wolves. They were four-legged creatures, and they did *not* use their front legs as arms. But this was a wolf that *did* walk on two legs, and *did* use its front legs as arms, and at the ends of those front legs were long, narrow, hairy hands with sharp black claws that grew from the ends of the fingers. *A werewolf,* he thought again.

Jason remembered the man who had come along and killed the werewolf. It seemed he'd come from nowhere, appearing like a guardian angel—tall, in that long coat and that old-fashioned hat, with that horribly scarred face.

He knows, Jason thought. *He knows what they are and how to kill them. I* have *to find that guy.*

Jason realized his father was talking to him and snapped himself out of his thoughts.

"What was that?" Jason said.

"I *said,* what were you doing over at the Cranes' house earlier tonight?" Dad said.

"Well . . . I told you," Jason said, his voice weak. "I heard a man screaming over there. Screaming, 'It's eating me! It's eating me!' I was worried about them."

"Didn't I tell you not to get involved?" Dad said. "*Didn't* I?"

"The screams were horrible. I should've just called the police." Jason frowned and whispered to himself, "Why didn't I just call the police?"

"You don't. Get. Involved, Jason," Dad said. "How many times have I told you that? Just mind your own business, and your life will be much less complicated."

Jason's mother turned around as much as her seatbelt would allow and tried to look at him. "Jason, honey, you still haven't told us exactly what happened. You said some kind of *wolf* attacked you? I must've misunderstood you, that *can't* be right."

Staring at the back of his mother's seat, Jason thought of all those fangs and claws, and the gamey odor that had come off the creature as it had descended on him.

When Jason said nothing, his mother went on. "What was it, Jason? How did you get hurt?"

Still, he said nothing.

"Jason, *please*," Mom said. "Tell us what happened."

"I . . . I don't want to talk about it anymore. Okay? Please? Can we just drop it for awhile?"

Mom frowned as she craned her neck around and looked at him. "Okay, sweetheart, if you'd rather not right now. That's fine." She turned and faced front again.

Jason slumped down in the backseat, wishing he could sink into the seat and disappear and get away from everything, especially his new knowledge—the knowledge that there really were werewolves out there.

What else, then? he wondered. *What else is out there?*

He wanted only one thing at that moment, and had ever since he'd fully regained consciousness earlier. He wanted to see Andrea, to hold her and be held by her.

"I think you should sleep in the house tonight, Jason," Mom said. "In your old room."

"Why?"

"So you'll be close by if you . . . I don't know, if you start feeling pain, or something."

"The doctor gave me some Vicodin. I'll be fine, Mom. I wouldn't be able to sleep in my old room. I'm too used to sleeping in the apartment now. Don't worry, Mom, I'll be fine, and if I'm not, I'll come down and wake you."

"Will you?" she said. "You promise?"

"Promise."

Normally, he would be annoyed and would remind his mother of his age, but not tonight. It felt good that she was concerned. He appreciated it deeply tonight, with the taste of his own blood still in his mouth.

Andrea. Just thinking about her made him feel better. But it wasn't enough. He wanted to see her.

When they got to the house, Dad parked in the driveway and Mom quickly got out and came to Jason's door before he could open it. She pulled it open and said, "Can you get out of the car all right?"

"Yeah, I'm okay, Mom, I'm fine. I just want to go up and take some Vicodin."

"Has the shot worn off already?"

He got out of the car and winced. "My arm hurts, is all."

"I know—I'll make you some hot chocolate and bring it to you."

Half of Jason's mouth curled up into a partial smile. She so desperately wanted to be needed by him, and he hated to disappoint her.

"That sounds good, Mom," he said they came to the front door. "With marshmallows."

"Oh, of course, honey."

Dad stepped around them, keys in hand, and unlocked the door, then led them inside. Lights had been left on in the house.

Jason followed his mother to the left and into the kitchen. She went to the counter, while he went through the laundry room, and out the door, into the garage. He went upstairs to his apartment.

He would wait for his mother to come up to the apartment with his hot chocolate. Then she would go back down and into the house, and she and Dad would go to bed. It would not take them long to fall asleep. It never did. They were fast, deep sleepers, due mostly to their fondness for evening cocktails. Jason had been taking advantage of his parents' deep sleep since he was a little kid, and he planned to do it again that night. He was hungry, so he would make himself a chicken sandwich. He would eat slowly, giving his parents plenty of time to drift off to sleep. Then he would go quietly down the stairs and get into his car and drive to the Sheriff's office. He remembered the sheriff and that man in the hat talking to each other. Maybe the sheriff or someone in the building could tell him who the man was and where to find him.

He knew there was no point in going to bed, because he knew he would be unable to sleep.

Jason was not sure if he would ever sleep again.

Half an hour later, Jason went out to his car, which was always parked at the curb directly in front of the house. Before getting in, he looked over at Andrea's house. There was a light in the living room glowing dimly beyond the closed drapes. He got in, drove away from his house, left his neighborhood, and went to the sheriff's station in the middle of town.

Rain had been replaced by a thick, chilling fog that gave the lights in town heavy, shimmering halos. The red, green, and amber traffic lights were softened, as if seen through a thick, gauzy filter.

Big Rock closed up early. It was around ten thirty when Jason drove into town, and everything was dark except the 7-Eleven, the sheriff's station, the Winchell's Donuts, and the Chevron with it's little mini-mart over by the freeway on-ramp.

Jason pulled into the empty parking lot and parked directly in front of the two-story building next to a cluster of handicap spaces. He got out and went up the narrow white walkway to the glass doors in front. He went inside.

The station was brightly lit and smelled of strong coffee. There was a bench against the wall on each side of Jason as he walked in; then the room opened up and there was a counter straight ahead. Beyond the counter, through the bulletproof window, was a room filled with desks and tables. The station was quiet, with a couple sheriff's deputies sitting at desks, a couple more standing and talking, drinking from white Styrofoam cups. A telephone trilled somewhere, and Jason could hear fingers clattering over a keyboard. There were a couple more benches against the walls on this side of the counter, and sitting in one of them reading a paperback book was the man Jason had last seen in the Cranes' front yard, the man with the badly scarred face. He still wore his long black coat and old-fashioned hat as he read, apparently oblivious to his surroundings.

Jason walked over to the bench and stood facing the man, who remained unaware of his presence.

Jason cleared his throat and said, "Um, excuse me."

The man lifted his head and his right eyebrow rose above the black patch. "I beg your pardon, were you speaking to me?"

Jason froze for a moment. Seeing the man's face in such good light was startling—the scars were even worse than they'd appeared outside in the dark earlier that night. "Uh, y-yes. My name is Jason Sutherland. I met you earlier tonight in my neighbor's front yard."

"Ah, yes, the young man with the injuries. How *are* you?"

"I'm okay. Not as bad as I'd thought, with all that blood."

"Yes, you were a bloody mess. I am glad to see you up and about. Sit down, Jason," the man said, patting the empty half of the bench.

Jason perched himself on the edge of the bench.

"My name is Daniel Fargo," the man said. "I'm here waiting for Sheriff Hurley. What brings you to the Sheriff's office?"

"Well, to tell the truth, I came here hoping to find *you*."

"Me? Whatever for?"

"Because you knew how to kill it. You knew what it was." He leaned a little closer to Fargo and lowered his voice. "It was a werewolf, wasn't it? An honest-to-God werewolf. I saw it and I don't know what else it could be. So please, tell me . . . what do you know about that thing?"

A red cardboard bookmark laid on the bench beside Fargo. He picked it up and gently placed it between the pages of the old dog-eared copy of an Irwin Shaw novel he was reading, then closed the book and set it down on the bench. He crossed one knee over the other and folded his hands together as he looked closely at Jason.

"Most of the time, when I want to convince someone they are dealing with an infestation of werewolves, I'm lucky if I get them simply to consider the possibility. Most never believe me, even when it looks them in the face. You, on the other hand, Jason, have just come to me and said the very thing it is so hard to convince most people of when I'm trying my very best. I commend you. You have an open mind."

"Open mind nothing. I *saw* it. It knocked the crap out of me. If you hadn't been there, that thing would've eaten me, wouldn't it?"

Fargo considered his answer a moment, then nodded once and said, "That was foremost on the creature's mind, I'm afraid, yes."

"Where do they come from? What can we do to stop them, to kill them?"

"I intend to talk to Sheriff Hurley about this very thing when he returns," Fargo said. "Why don't you sit in on that conversation. That way, I won't have to repeat it all."

"Okay. But there's one thing you have to tell me now. That thing bit me." He lightly touched his hand to his upper arm. "Does that mean that I'm going to . . ." It sounded so ridiculous, so silly, that Jason could not bring himself to say it out loud.

"Does that mean you will turn into a werewolf?" Fargo said, his head dipping forward as he smiled slightly.

"Exactly," Jason said with an enthusiastic nod.

"No. You have nothing to worry about there. In fact, you might as well toss out everything you think you know about werewolves. Most of the myths are just that— myths. They have little to do with the facts. It is true that werewolves have a fatal allergy to silver, but that is where the similarity ends. However, I'll save that for my conversation with the sheriff."

Jason's right leg bounced up and down and he shifted his position on the bench several times. He was immensely relieved that he would not be turning into a werewolf anytime soon, but at the same time, he was jittery, nervous, and he could not wait to hear what Fargo had to say.

32

FARGO AND JASON

Saturday

When Hurley arrived, Fargo urged the sheriff to include Jason in their meeting. Hurley agreed to this but reserved the right to jettison Jason from the office in the event confidential material was discussed. Hurley led them down the corridor to his office. He directed them to sit in the two metal-framed chairs that faced his desk as he went around and took his seat. Once they were settled, Hurley leaned forward and nodded at Jason. "Well, Jason, the way it looks, Emily Crane was . . . well, Fargo, how do you say it?"

"She was a werewolf, that's how you say it," Fargo said.

Hurley closed his eyes as he nodded. "I still can't bring myself to say it out loud."

"I know what you mean, Sheriff," Fargo said. "It takes some getting used to."

"Anyway," Hurley said, "Emily killed and ate a great deal of her husband. She also ate her cat. You were right, Fargo. There was raw hamburger in the kitchen sink, too."

Jason's eyes widened. "You mean, that . . . that was Mrs. Crane?"

Hurley watched the nervous young man as he shifted

in his chair and plucked at his shirt under his open jacket, pulling it away from his belly so it wouldn't cling to his round shape, trying so hard to hide the fact that he was overweight.

"Yes, it was. A little while ago, her sister had to identify what was left of her. There was a birthmark . . . which allowed her sister to make the ID. We covered up the parts of her that were, uh . . . that weren't . . . human. I figured her sister didn't need that on top of what had already happened. She can learn about that later." Hurley leaned back in his chair. "Okay. Let's hear everything you have to tell me, Fargo. This time, I'm listening."

"We might have waited too long, Sheriff," Fargo said. "It may be too late."

"Wait. What do you mean, *'too long'*? This all just happened. You just came—"

"It spreads fast, Sheriff. Between now and the last time I talked with you, they've had time to spread the virus some more."

"Virus?" Jason said.

Fargo turned to Jason and filled him in on the fact that the lycanthropy was spread through a sexually-transmitted virus. "Have you had sex with someone who might be a werewolf?"

Jason frowned, thought a moment, then said, "No. No, I haven't."

"See that you don't. A condom will prevent picking up the virus, but it won't protect you when she turns and starts to eat you. Lycanthropy turns a person into an animal with only two things on its mind—sex and food." He turned to Hurley. "The lycanthrope craves sex and can never get enough. It is a half-human creature, but without any human inhibitions. When it wants something, it takes it. It is a savage, ravenous animal that will stop at nothing to get what it wants. If you stand in its way, it will either severely injure you or kill you. You can shoot it, but its body will only spit those bullets right back out. It can regenerate with great speed. Stab it, and the wound closes itself and heals quickly. Kill it, and it will come back, given a little time to heal. That is why your John Doe disappeared, Sheriff Hurley. He got up and walked away, and he has been satisfying his hungers and spreading the virus ever since. It has no doubt found a comfortable and safe place to sleep during the day, and the others are drawn to that place, that den. The werewolf is, of course, nocturnal. The nights have not been safe in Big Rock since he arrived, and they will not be safe until he and everyone he has infected are dead."

"And you're convinced that John Doe is this man you've been hunting?" Hurley said.

"Irving Taggart," Fargo said.

"What about the werewolves themselves?" Jason said. "How much of the myth is true?"

"As I said earlier, you can dismiss the myth, for the most part. For example, the full moon has nothing to do with the werewolf's transformation. A lycanthrope can transform himself anytime he pleases, day or night, although they usually leave it up to their emotions to do it. A lycanthrope will turn if under stress, or angry—any intense emotional state—or if its hunger grows strong enough. So, in that sense, the lycanthrope is not *entirely* in control of its transformations. Especially the newer ones. Over time, they learn to control and manipulate their bodies' abilities. The older they are, the more in control they are. They can live forever, as long as they are not burned to death, and as long as silver is not introduced into their systems."

Jason absorbed the information, eyes wide, lips parted.

"Have I answered all your questions, Jason?" Fargo said.

He frowned, trying to come up with more questions. "I guess so," he said with doubt.

"Would you mind leaving us, then, please?"

"Oh, yeah." Jason stood. "Thanks for letting me sit in on this, Sheriff."

"Jason," Hurley said, "I'm going to have to insist that you tell no one about what we've discussed here tonight. That includes members of your family. You need to keep this entirely to yourself, do you understand?"

"Uh . . . yeah, sure," Jason said with a nod. "My family wouldn't believe me, anyway." Jason went to the door, opened it, turned to Fargo, and said, "Are you going to be around, Mr. Fargo?"

"Oh, yes. I'm not leaving town until Irving Taggart is killed or he leaves town first."

Jason nodded, then pulled the door closed as he left the office.

Hurley studied Fargo sitting across the desk. He questioned the wisdom of telling Jason Sutherland everything, of telling *anyone* everything, before they had a plan of attack.

That seemed to register on Hurley's face, because Fargo shrugged one shoulder and said, "He knew before he ever came to me. He knew right away it was a werewolf that attacked him. And he won't be the only one. What about the two young women at the Jags tonight? Did either of them say anything about a wolf?"

Hurley pursed his lips a moment, thinking. Then: "Yes, one of them did. The one who was talking. I'm going to the hospital later to see the girl who was raped."

Fargo spoke just above a whisper: "She has to die, Sheriff."

Hurley chewed on his lower lip. "In my line of work, we only punish people *after* they've done something wrong, not because we *think* they will. The idea of killing her because she was raped by that thing . . . it goes against everything I believe in."

Fargo stood and stepped up to Hurley's desk, pressed his hands flat to the desktop and leaned forward on elbow-locked arms. "Sheriff Hurley, you need to inform your deputies and arm them with silver. I have scores of silver knives in my car. A simple knife could save their lives in a confrontation with one of the werewolves, and it would *end* the life of the werewolf."

Hurley knew he had no choice, he would have to explain things to his deputies, even pull more deputies in from outlying stations—as many as possible would be required to hunt the things down.

"That's how we kill it," Hurley said. "How do we *find* it?"

"You get a call about an attack, you take *all* your deputies to the scene, and get there as soon as possible. If the thing isn't still there, we spread out and hunt for it. This is all I've been doing for years now. It's all I know these days. I've never had a Sheriff's Department at my disposal before, though, and that will make a great deal of difference. The problem will be the den, if we can find it. We won't know how many of the creatures are in there till we get there, so we'll need all the men you can get together. Newly infected werewolves will be drawn to the original werewolf—in this case, Irving Taggart. So there could be . . . well, however many will fit into the den. The bigger the den, the bigger the risk."

"We need to be armed with silver bullets," Hurley said. He sighed. "But how long will it take us to come up with that many silver bullets?"

Fargo smiled. "Not to worry, Sheriff. I have all the silver bullets you'll need."

33

A HOSPITAL VISIT

Suzie Camber's thoughts were just beginning to take shape again. For the first time since she had witnessed Bobby Stanley's brutal murder at the hands of—of what? What was it? And how long ago? She wasn't sure. Time seemed to have slipped away from her and no longer meant anything—she could have been lying in that Emergency Room bed for a few minutes or all night, she was unable to tell.

She burned and throbbed between her legs. It felt like something had torn her up down there. It was the only place on her body where she could feel anything. She was numb everywhere else, it seemed.

I was raped, she thought for the dozenth time.

The word filled her with dread, because sooner or later, her father would find out. She knew how he would react. He would tell her she brought it on herself with the clothes she wore, the people she hung out with, the way she behaved in public—flirting and joking around, not the way a lady should behave. She dreaded having to sit and listen to him lecture her, quote the Bible to her, tell her about the hellfire that surely awaited her.

Bobby was dead. She'd watched as that . . . what *was* it? She'd never seen anything like it in her life, not even on the Discovery Channel or Animal Planet, where you saw just about every animal thing there was on the globe. Whatever it was, it had done horrible things to Bobby . . . things that would haunt her for the rest of her life.

And then it had been gone, and that man . . . that half-naked one-eyed man with torn clothes dangling from his body in strips . . . that man had raped her.

There were clothes on that monster, too, she thought. *Dangling from it in strips, human clothes on that . . . that animal thing. The same clothes that were on the man who raped me.*

It made her head hurt. It was impossible. Surely her imagination had intervened and she'd only *thought* she'd seen the same tattered clothes on both man and monster.

"How are you feeling, sweetheart?" Mom asked. Daddy had not come to the hospital, leaving Mom to come alone. Suzie was grateful for that, even though it was only a delay of the inevitable.

Suzie turned her eyes to Mom without moving her head. She wanted to respond . . . but how? What would she say, do?

Suzie closed her eyes. She was unsure of how long they remained closed. She opened them when an unfamiliar voice said, "Mrs. Camber?"

A nurse was peering in through the part in the curtain.

"Yes?" Mom said.

"You have a phone call. You can take it on that phone on the wall over there."

"All right, thank you." The nurse disappeared and Mom turned to Suzie again. "I'll be right back, sweetheart. It's probably your father. Be right back, now, okay?"

Mom left the small enclosure, and Suzie was alone. She closed her eyes again.

Suzie preferred the warm darkness of the backs of her eyelids. She felt safe there, alone, unworried. Just floating in the blackness.

A sound. The rustling of the curtain. Had Mom returned already? Then the rustling of something else, some other material. Clothing?

Suzie opened her eyes. Slowly, her eyes grew larger as she looked up at the horrible scars on the man's face. They were darkened by the shadow of his broad-brimmed hat. He was all dark in a long black coat, dark clothes under it, a black eyepatch. The only thing that was not dark about him was the knife he held, with its long, slender, glinting silver blade. He was ugly as the devil. Maybe he *was* the devil, come to punish her for her sins. He quickly pulled the blanket and sheet down to uncover her chest.

Suzie could not move, and she found as she opened her mouth and tried to speak that she had no voice.

The pointed tip of the blade pressed between two of her ribs just to the left of her sternum.

Suzie's last thought as he·slid the silver blade into her was, *Maybe Daddy's right after all. . . .*

When Edith Camber put the receiver to her ear, she heard a dial tone. She frowned as she put the receiver back on its hook, then turned and looked around the crowded, bustling Emergency Room. Had someone hung up on the call? Edith was confused—who would call her here and then hang up before she got to the phone?

She turned and made her way through the Emergency Room, moved the curtain aside so she could return to Suzie's bedside. Edith said, "I don't understand, the line was—"

Suzie's eyes were closed. She was asleep. She looked so peaceful with the blanket and sheet tucked up to her neck, her arms limp at her sides. Edith smiled gently as she sat down in a metal-framed chair beside the bed.

Edith found herself thinking about what had been

done to her little girl. Tears burned her eyes. She prayed the police would catch her rapist and he would go to jail for a long time.

But for now, she was happy to see that Suzie had found a little peace in sleep.

34

NIGHT HUNGER

Andrea Norton awoke suddenly and with a gasp. She lay there staring into the darkness for awhile, tense and tingling. She rolled and tossed, trying to find a comfortable spot, but she could not relax enough to go back to sleep. An image remained in her mind, an image from her sleep. A dream . . . but then, not quite a dream. Something else. Something vivid and strange.

She turned and watched Jimmy sleep. He snored loudly. He'd come home early from work that day saying he didn't feel well. That was about *all* he'd said to her. He'd paced the house, drinking one beer after another—and yet he did not seem to get drunk. Instead, he'd become increasingly manic until he'd finally left the house. He'd come back late that night, just as she was on her way to bed. He'd looked as if he'd been in a barroom brawl. His clothes had been torn, and he'd had what looked like a smear of blood around his mouth. His eyes had been unusually wide, and yet he was clearly exhausted. Surprised, Andrea had taken in a breath to ask him what had happened, but those wide eyes had turned to her and narrowed. She'd kept quiet and gone to bed. Jimmy had stayed up awhile, finally coming to bed reeking of beer. She could still smell it now as he snored louder than usual.

She got out of bed and put on her heavy blue-and-gray robe and a pair of sneakers. She went to the kitchen, opened a cupboard, reached back behind the coffee mugs on the bottom shelf, and retrieved her hidden pack of Winstons and a Bic lighter. She stuffed them into the right pocket of her robe, then made a cup of tea.

All day long, she'd been unable to think of anything but Jason. But now, something else bothered her. In her sleep, she'd seen a house. But it was far more real than any dream. There was something very important about the house, but she was not sure what. It stirred in her a feeling of urgency and need, a pulling sensation, as if the house were drawing her in, dragging her mind toward its front door. The house was familiar, but she was unable to identify it. She had seen the house before, but couldn't remember where or when. Upon waking from that dream, she felt a strange hunger. She went to the refrigerator and looked for something to appease that hunger, but nothing appealed to her, nothing was right. She was hungry for . . . something.

Andrea closed the refrigerator and paced the kitchen, chewing on a thumbnail. She thought of Jason. No one had ever made love to her the way he had. No one had ever treated her that way, touched her that way. Certainly not Jimmy, and there had been only one guy before Jimmy. Of course, she'd never told Jimmy that—as far as Jimmy was concerned, he was her one and only.

Once her tea was ready, she took it with her to the front of the house and went out the front door. It was foggy and cold outside, but her robe was heavy. She sat down on the top step of the front porch, set her tea down beside her, and lit a cigarette. She so seldom smoked that when she did, the nicotine hit her hard and made her dizzy after that first puff. It felt good, that brief buzz, but it was gone almost before it started. Once again, she was feeling the strange anxiety that had dragged her from her sleep, thinking of that big dark house, trying to ignore the hunger clawing in her stomach, aching in her very bones.

She took another puff on the cigarette. If Jimmy knew she smoked, he would dole out some serious punishment. But he did not know. It was one of the few things Andrea had that was all her own, her little secret.

But as enjoyable as it was, she would give it up in an instant if only she could spend some time alone with Jason.

While Andrea thought of Jason, he was driving home from the sheriff's station and thinking of her, just as intensely, just as hungrily. He glanced at the dashboard clock—it was twelve forty-three in the morning, long before he'd have any chance of seeing Andrea. He had planned to see her that day, but when he'd gotten home from work, Jimmy had already come home, for some reason. So he had not been able to see Andrea at all that day.

He'd already decided to call in sick the following morning. His injuries were reason enough to miss a day. Besides, he was having Andrea withdrawal. He knew that Jimmy worked on Saturdays, so Andrea would be alone with her little girls that day. Thoughts of her chewed on his mind with tiny razorlike teeth.

He turned onto his street and looked ahead at his house. He pulled his gaze back just a bit when he thought he'd seen a shadowy figure on the porch in front of Andrea's house. He slowed down, and as he passed, he saw that Andrea was sitting on the top step. The burning red eye of a cigarette flared, then died down again.

Jason's heart suddenly pounded in his throat. He pulled over and parked at the curb in front of his house, got out of the car, and ran to her.

She was up off the porch and hurrying across the lawn, the cigarette between two fingers, trailing strings of smoke.

Andrea gasped as she got closer. "Your face! My God what happened to—not here, not here," she whispered as they closed the space between them. She tossed the cigarette away.

Jason smiled even though it hurt his injured face to do so. He grabbed her hand and quickly led her over to his house and into the garage.

"Let's go up to my apartment," Jason said.

He led the way up the stairs, pushed the rug away, and entered his apartment. She was right behind him. The second she was in, he threw an arm around her waist and pulled her to him hard. Andrea made a small sound in her throat as their lips met and Jason sucked her tongue into his mouth. As they kissed, he moved his hands all over her, at the same time leading her clumsily toward the bed.

She finally pulled away. "I can't be gone long, I don't know when he'll wake up."

Jason pulled back a little. "Really? Is there a chance he'll wake up and find you gone?"

She thought about it a moment, then smiled. "To be honest, he's pretty much down for the night. He's a very heavy sleeper, and he drank a *lot* of beer tonight."

"Just playing hard to get, huh?"

"What happened to your face?"

"Long story. I'll tell you later."

"All those bandages and—oh my God, your *hair!*"

"Yeah, that's funny, isn't it?"

"Funny? Jason, you have a streaks of *white* through your hair."

"It got scared white. That's what happened."

"Scared?" She looked at him with wide eyes. "Jason, what *happened?*"

He put his hands to the sides of her face and said, "Later, I promise."

"Oh. Okay."

Still holding her face, Jason kissed her.

Andrea undid the knot her belt was tied in, and it dropped to her sides.

"I'm pretty sure I've got time for this," she whispered. "If he wakes up, I'll just tell him I went for a walk."

Andrea pulled the sides of the robe back, revealing her pale breasts and the pink nipples that were already hard and standing erect. She let the robe slide down into a heap around her sneakers.

Jason sucked in a little gasp, unable to contain his reaction. He moved forward and kissed her again, softer this time, as he slowly ran his hands over her smooth, silky skin, pressing his erection against her.

"Do it now," she whispered against his lips. "Now. I don't want to wait anymore."

As Jason quickly removed his clothes, Andrea sat on the edge of the bed and took off her sneakers. Then she fell back on the bed and slid a hand between her legs, squeezing her pubis hard as she waited for Jason.

Once he was naked, he practically dove onto the bed.

"Now, now," Andrea whispered as Jason lay between her legs and entered her. She cried out once, a sharp, abrupt sound, but she smiled as she did it.

They did not hold back. She bucked beneath him as he pounded into her and every now and then laughed with delight. Andrea rolled them over so she was on top, and she rode him wildly. Jason was lost in the sensations, drowning in Andrea.

Her panting became loud grunting. The grunting became a low, guttural growl.

With a sharp cry, Andrea rolled off Jason.

It took him a moment to fully realize that she was no longer on top of him—he had to rise from the depths of sensation that had overcome him. He opened his eyes, and she was gone.

"Andrea?"

He sat up and looked around. She was no longer in the dark bedroom.

Jason swung his legs off the bed and staggered out of

the bedroom. He got little more than a glimpse of Andrea's head as it disappeared down the stairs, leaving the rug tossed aside.

He quickly put on his pants, then hurried after her, down the stairs, out of the garage.

Andrea was gone.

Jason went back inside and paced in his small living room. He ran a hand back through his hair several times. What had happened? What had gone wrong? Had he done something wrong? Had she become suddenly overwhelmed with guilt?

He realized she'd taken her robe and sneakers with her.

He stayed up for a while longer, deeply disturbed by Andrea's sudden exit. Finally, he surrendered to the fact that he would be unable to find out what had gone wrong until in the morning, and undressed and went to bed.

It took a little while, but he finally drifted off to sleep.

And in his sleep, he saw crystal-clear images of a big, dark house. . . .

Andrea had run naked from Jason's apartment and out into the bone-deep chill of the foggy night. She was running, but she was aware of that movement only dimly, as if her consciousness were being sucked into some deep, remote recess of her mind—her environment faded and became distant, as if she were looking through the wrong end of a telescope. She did not feel the cold, though she had left her robe in a heap on her front porch and run through the night. She was kept warm by something else, something like clothes but not clothes, because she was naked—and yet something covered her body.

The hunger had become a keening wail inside her. She'd crossed the street and gone between two houses to the wooded area beyond. When she pushed bushes out of the way, she saw her hands and what they had be-

come, but oddly it did not bother her. Everything felt . . .
right. Good. Except for the hunger. It chewed on her guts.

Then, the pain began, pain that was in her but somehow removed from her. She fell to the ground as her
bones began to break and cartilage bent and twisted.
She heard the crunching of the bones in her face, tasted
blood when she felt something cut through her gums in
her mouth. It tasted good. It seemed to take forever, but
at the same time, it seemed to be over in a moment, and
it was all from a murky distance, almost as if it were happening to someone else.

And then she felt . . . free.

She thought in pictures and feelings, not words.

She pushed on through the fog-shrouded woods, burning with hunger, until she came to the side of a dark
road. To her right, the road disappeared around a corner.
The fog glowed with oncoming lights that grew brighter
and brighter as the car approached the corner.

She stepped out into the road, headed for the other side.

The car came around the corner.

She stopped for just a moment, turned toward the
lights, lifted an arm to shield her eyes, then rushed forward across the road.

The car's brakes screamed as it swerved to a long,
squealing stop. The car had a bar of lights across the roof
that suddenly lit up in blue and red as the driver's side
door opened and a uniformed man got out.

She watched from the darkness at the side of the road.
She did not think *policeman*—she simply watched and
took in images, sounds, sensations.

The man walked away from the car and moved toward
the side of the road toward her. He held something in his
hand that lit up. The car's headlights behind him were
haloed by the fog.

She smelled his warmth, his flesh, and her hunger
swelled.

She did not wait. She bounded forward, the hunger throbbing inside her, and moved into the deputy's light.

He screamed as he staggered backward, a high shriek that fell flat as it was absorbed by the thick fog.

She was on him so fast, it surprised even her. She had to tear through his clothes to get to what she now knew would satisfy her burning hunger.

It was so good . . . so hot and wet . . . as good as the sex she'd been having with Jason when she'd run out. This was why she'd run away from Jason, to keep from doing this to him. But she did not think that . . . she simply understood it.

She made thick wet sounds as she finally satisfied her hunger. . . .

She moved through the woods again, going in a very specific direction, with a definite destination. She ran across deserted, foggy roads, ran along a creek that took her beneath a bridge, passed through a field of cows that erupted in panicked groans and grunts as they hurried away from her.

When she reached her destination, she was overwhelmed by a feeling of triumph.

The house stood before her. She moved toward it, up on the broken porch. She dove through a paneless window into the smelly, musty dark.

Once inside, her silver eyes scanned the darkness, and they saw that she was not alone. There was an other . . . an important other . . . and there were others like her with that important other. Many others.

She was no longer alone.

She felt safe at last, as if she was home, as if nothing could hurt her now.

She was precisely where she was supposed to be.

35

PREPARATIONS

Before joining the assembly of deputies in the briefing room shortly after nine on Saturday morning, Hurley led Fargo into his office.

"Sit down," Hurley said as he he closed the door. He went to his desk and propped his hips against the front edge.

Holding his hat in one hand and his cane in the other, Fargo sat on the padded chair before the desk and looked up at the sheriff. When Hurley said nothing for awhile and simply stared down at Fargo with a hard look on his face, Fargo said, "What is it, Sheriff?"

"A girl was murdered last night," Hurley said. He spoke very quietly, making Fargo lean slightly forward to hear him.

"Well . . . I'm sorry to—"

"The girl who was raped at the Jags last night. The girl I pointed out to you."

A silence fell between them and stretched on just long enough to make Fargo shift his position uncomfortably in the chair.

"Did you kill Suzie Camber because she was raped by one of your werewolves?" Hurley finally said.

Fargo sniffed and leaned back in the chair, made

himself comfortable. "Sheriff, these are not *my* were-wolves. These werewolves belong to your *town*, and I predict that, starting tonight, you're going to be so over-run by them that a single dead girl—who was about to *become* one of those werewolves—will be the least of your worries. As for last night—I was in my motel room."

"Okay. Let me tell *you* something," Hurley said, speaking very quietly again, his voice steady and sharp. "I don't care *how* many werewolves come out of the woodwork, a murder is a murder, and as long as I'm kicking, I'm going to find out who committed this one. If it was you, you're going away for a long time. The rest of your life, most likely."

"But Sheriff, there's—"

"Do you understand me, Fargo?"

Fargo held Hurley's one-eyed stare, but said nothing.

"Just don't plan on leaving town for awhile. If you do, I'll have my deputies hunt you down and bring you back."

Hurley pushed away from the desk and went to the door, opened it.

"Come on," he said. "They're waiting."

The deputies gathered in the briefing room stared blankly at Daniel Fargo as he stood behind the narrow, pale, pinewood pulpit at the front of the room. A heavy silence had fallen over the group, interrupted only by an occasional sniff or throat-clearing cough. Some of the deputies exchanged glances in the silence.

"Don't worry, you heard me right," Fargo said. "I said *werewolves*."

The briefing room was not very large, and it was a big crowd, with every folding metal chair occupied and deputies standing two or three deep along the walls all around the room. Deputies had been pulled in from other stations. Those not wearing uniforms worked later shifts but were called in to hear what Fargo had to say, because they would be dealing with the werewolves that night.

Hurley sat in a metal folding chair behind Fargo, one ankle resting on a knee, trying to look neutral, trying to keep his anxiety off his face. His deputies could not be allowed to see that. This was going to mess some of them up. Some might even refuse to believe. He needed to be firm and resolute, to keep his fears to himself.

Fargo discussed the only two ways one could kill a werewolf. "Silver and fire. You will be provided with the weapons necessary to combat these creatures, and tonight, we will go out on a massive hunt. We will rush to the first call that comes in that sounds like it might be one of these creatures at work. The nights to come are going to be especially dangerous, and for you, especially strange and nightmarish. Tonight will be bad enough— tomorrow night, as the virus continues to spread, there will be *more* of them. By the third night, you should have acclimated yourself to hunting and killing werewolves. Of course, if we haven't done away with them by then, it will most likely be too late. It takes a little getting used to, this business of slaying a monster you've always believed to be a fantasy. But I guarantee that if you can hold yourself together, you will be sufficiently armed against these lycanthropes. Once you start killing them, you'll regain your footing and feel a rush of self-confidence. Trust me . . . killing these things is *very* satisfying, and you *will* enjoy it."

As Fargo went on, explaining everything about the werewolves, his voice grew distant to Hurley, who was wading waist-deep in his thoughts. He thought of Ella. He had grown so comfortable in his marriage that he had never entertained the possibility that Ella had been unfaithful to him, or perhaps was *being* unfaithful to him then, without his knowledge. After all, she was still an attractive woman and could easily become involved with another man if she were so inclined. But was she?

I bet she wouldn't even tell me if she were raped. Hurley thought, and chips of ice slid down his spinal cord, spreading a chill through every nerve in his body.

She wouldn't—she'd be afraid of shaming him, of making trouble, of causing a fuss, afraid of a thousand things that had to do with *him*, never thinking of herself. She was made of iron, his Ella; she would stand up even to rape, and she would do it alone if she possibly could. It sounded crazy, but then, Ella was a little crazy. He was, too—that was why he'd become a cop. But Ella was a little crazy when it came to *him*—she would do anything, make any sacrifice, to make his life better, smoother, easier. Sometimes when he thought about it, he felt like crying, like he would never be able to repay her for that, never deserve everything she did for him and was to him. But she didn't expect repayment—his happiness was her repayment, she'd told him that herself. Sometimes, he wondered what he'd done to deserve her.

At the moment, though, he felt a slowly growing fear. It gradually tightened like a noose around his neck, squeezing off his air, crushing his windpipe. He frantically thought back over the last week, wondering if Ella had behaved differently, if there were any signs, no matter how small, that something was wrong. He could think of none.

C'mon, he thought, *the likelihood that Ella has been raped in the last couple days or is having an affair . . .*

It was absurd when he thought about it. And yet that absurdity did not calm his fears, which knew no absurdities, only frightening possibilities. His fear knew that if Ella were ever to be raped and not tell him about it, or if she ever were unfaithful to him, it would be *now*, when the danger was the greatest. That was the kind of luck he had. But as hard as he tried, he could think of nothing that might be a telltale sign that something bad had happened to her, that there was someone else, and even Ella wasn't good enough to keep something like a rape from seeping out of her at the seams, he was sure. Hurley was certain he would see something, would know something was wrong.

He closed his eyes and rubbed them hard with thumb and forefinger. These killings, these *things*—he still had a hard time using the word "werewolf," even in the privacy of his own mind.

Hurley stood as Fargo went on speaking. He went to the small office in the rear of the room, closed the door, and took his cell phone from his pocket. Ella answered on the second ring.

"Hey, honey," he said. "How are you?"

"I'm good. How about you?"

"Well, it's been a hell of a day. I'm going to be home late again. Probably very late. Look, do me a favor, okay?"

"Are you going to tell me to stay inside after dark again?" she said with a smile in her voice. "Sweetie, you only have to tell me once, really."

"Sorry. I worry. That maybe you'll forget, or you won't really take me seriously."

"Will you *finally* explain when you get home tonight?"

"Yes, I will. I promise. You're not going to believe it, but I'll tell you everything. Why should *I* be the only one having nightmares?"

"It's that bad?"

He laughed a cold laugh bled dry of humor. "Oh, this is a whopper. Look, I've got to go, honey. I don't know when I'll be home."

"That's okay. I'll make a little something for dinner and keep it for you in case you make it."

"Okay."

"Arlin, tell me the truth. Is this really bad?"

"Yes. It's bad. I'll explain it all when I come home. I . . . you, um . . . I just . . ."

"What is it?"

He felt a rush of throat-clenching love for her, felt it

swell in his chest until he could not breathe. He wanted to go home right then, to take her in his arms, and tell her again and again how much he loved her. He wanted to stay there and never leave, to protect her, to keep watch over her.

"I love you," he whispered.

"I love you, too, sweetie." He could hear the smile in her voice.

He put the phone back in his pocket. When Hurley opened the door and stepped out of the office, Fargo was talking about the werewolves' reaction to silver.

"Believe me, once you have an encounter with one of these things," Fargo said as Hurley went back up to the front and took his chair again, "you'll be happy to see it die a slow, painful death."

Hurley felt cramps in his gut as he thought about Fargo's words. He imagined werewolves jumping out of every shadow in the night, pouncing on their victims, ripping out throats, going for all the soft spots first, biting and tearing with sharp fangs, slicing flesh with their claws. It was the closest he'd ever come to a waking nightmare, and it made him jerk suddenly in his chair.

"Once a person catches the virus," Fargo went on, "it takes twenty-four to seventy-two hours for the change to take place. That process can be slowed down by certain drugs, certain diseases, and depending on the person's system, but it cannot be stopped. That person *will* change. And kill and eat others. There is no vaccine for the virus yet, although I have a team of scientists working on it in a small facility I have on the East Coast." He paused a moment, then looked back and forth over the crowd of deputies and said, "Any questions?"

The deputies stared at him with varying looks of disbelief. Finally, one hand went up, a young male deputy with a crew cut.

Fargo pointed at him and said, "Yes?"

The deputy said, "If they don't actually change in front of you, how can we tell if a person is a . . . a, uh . . ."

"A werewolf?"

The deputy nodded.

"It's not easy," Fargo said, "unless you know the person well. There are definite changes in a person with the virus, but they're subtle. They become more energetic. They talk a little faster, move a little faster, and seem more nervous than usual, almost manic. And they are extremely horny. The virus amps up the libido, because that is how it spreads. Let's say you have a significant other who has had sex with someone carrying the virus. *You* would notice the subtle changes—the nervousness, the increased sexual activity—but it is doubtful that others would. If you don't know the person, then it's extremely difficult to tell if he or she is a lycanthrope. But it's not totally impossible. Once you learn for certain that someone *is* a lycanthrope, you must kill that person in one of the ways I mentioned earlier. That person is no longer him- or herself, no longer human, and must be killed. I should ask now—has anyone noticed these changes in someone you know well?" When there was no response, Fargo smiled and said, "Well, that's good. All right. Before sundown tonight, we'll have silver bullets for all of you. There are plenty to go around. I've got 9mm and .40 caliber and .45 ACP. For you old-timers who just can't give up your revolvers, I've even got .357 magnums." He turned to Hurley and said, "Anything you want to add, Sheriff?"

Hurley stood and went to Fargo's side. He looked out over all the shocked faces that stared at him with eyes perhaps a little too wide.

"Does anyone have any questions for Mr. Fargo?" Hurley said. "Now is the time to ask whatever's on your mind—there won't be any time for it tonight." He waited, but no one raised a hand or spoke up. "Anything you want to ask is fine. Don't worry about sounding stupid—

when it comes to this subject, we're *all* stupid, okay? We are, after all, talking about *werewolves* here."

A black female deputy sitting near the center of the room in her street clothes slowly lifted her right hand.

"Deputy Mindy Cross," Hurley said, and she stood. "What is your question?"

"Okay, uh, my question is . . . are you *shittin'* me? *Werewolves?* While we're at it, let's check our cemeteries for zombies. Or, maybe they's a vampire workin' down at the blood bank."

Nervous laughter rose loud and long from the crowd of deputies. It was a release of tension more than a reaction to something funny, because the laughter was too big for Deputy Cross's little joke.

Hurley let them laugh. He smiled and nodded until it finally died down. He turned to Fargo and nodded slightly. Fargo went to a chair behind Hurley and sat down. Hurley clutched the edges of the pulpit and leaned forward slightly, passing his eyes over the group. "If you don't believe Mr. Fargo, you can believe *me*. I've found victims of these things, I've seen what they can do. Some of you have, too. All of you are painfully aware that we've lost two deputies in the last few days." He raised his voice a little as he said, "What you may *not* know is that both of these fine men were *ripped apart* and *eaten*. They were *eviscerated*. They were opened up and their internal organs were *eaten*."

Hurley paused a moment to let that sink in, watching as some of the deputies became slack-jawed and a little pale.

"I am not interested in losing any more good men and women to these things," he said. "*That* is why we're having this frank discussion this morning. I've finally got enough evidence to share with you, enough details to give you, to provide you with the tools you need to do your job and save this community. And it's not just *this* community. You heard what Mr. Fargo said—these things will increase in number and broaden their hunt to other towns, and eventually other states, until they're *everywhere*. And *you* . . . are our only hope."

He dropped his arms to his sides and stood up straighter, took in a deep breath and let it out slowly.

"Every eyewitness reports the same thing—a creature like a wolf, but one that stands upright like a man, only bigger than most men. The forensic evidence has been the same on every case—wolf DNA at the crime scenes. I *wish* this were a joke. But it's not."

He stopped talking for a moment and passed his gaze back and forth over the deputies.

"I'm seeing some pretty blank faces out there," Hurley said with a firm, no-nonsense tone. "Wrap your brains around this fast, people, because you're going to meet some of these things up close tonight, if we're lucky, so you'd better be *ready* for it." He looked over the deputies again, then said, "Okay, I'm seeing some fear in those eyes. That's more like it. You've got plenty to be afraid of, believe me. That fear, combined with your training, will save you tonight, and in the nights to come. I know you've all got families and loved ones at home, and I want you to be able to go home to them when it's time, safe and sound." He nodded once and said, "Okay. Some of you on duty right now will be working a partial shift tonight so we can cover this town in search of these things. Are there any other questions?"

More hands went up, and Hurley pointed them out one at a time. Together, he and Fargo answered their questions. By nightfall, he hoped to have pumped the deputies up enough so that the fear he saw in their eyes was backed by a steely eagerness.

But Hurley knew that, before any of them were ready, night would fall.

36

SATURDAY BLUES

Vanessa Peterman felt lonely. She had not left her apartment since getting back from the hospital early Friday morning. *That* had been a unpleasant ordeal, going to the hospital and saying she'd been raped. Now she knew why rape victims so often said that being put into the system after being raped was like being raped again. She had not slept since then, either, aside from occasionally nodding off and then jerking awake a moment later. When she *did* manage to drift off for awhile, her sleep was filled with vivid images of a large old house, dark and foreboding, but important . . . somehow urgently important. She needed very badly to go there, although she did not know why. She did not need to go there at this moment, not right now. But soon.

Along with her feelings of loneliness, Vanessa felt a hunger that was steadily growing stronger, a hunger for something she could not quite identify. And she felt an odd tension, too—a dark, heavy feeling that something wasn't right, that something bad was happening somewhere, or was about to happen. It was that strange sinking feeling that made her turn to a bottle of wine for comfort. She sat on her couch with a bottle of red wine and a glass on the end table beside her. There was a little wine left in the bottle, and the glass was only half-full. With her eyes clenched shut and her lips peeled back over grinding teeth, she pressed one hand to her head and dug the nails into the scalp beneath her auburn hair.

What's wrong with me? she thought.

Vanessa just wanted to shut everything off—the loud and clashing thoughts in her head, the twisting and writhing feelings in her gut. She just wanted it all to stop so she could think straight, or maybe take a nap. She had been spending a lot of time on that couch watching television. The channels and the shows were a blur over the hours that had passed. When she wasn't on the couch, she was in the bathtub or shower, bathing, scrubbing, making the water scalding hot, again and again.

More than anything during the dead time that had passed, Vanessa wondered about Hugh Crane. He filled her thoughts, even when they were bleary ones. Why hadn't she heard from him? He *always* called. Sometimes she got a little tired of his calls because they came so often, but she'd never uttered a word of complaint because she found them so cute and they made her feel so . . . cared for. Although she was tired of being alone, she was not sure she'd want to see Hugh right now, but she would love to hear his voice on the phone, talk to him a little. It was eighteen minutes after noon on Saturday—she wondered if he was out working. She had resisted the urge to call him on his cell phone. She had done that only a couple of times in the past—it was just too risky for her to call him. Hugh had told her there was always a chance he'd set his cell phone down somewhere in the house, a call would come in, and Emily would get to it before he could. Also, Hugh was a bad liar and preferred not to have to lie to Emily about who'd just called on his cell phone, because she would *know* he was lying, and she would want to know why.

"Fuck it," Vanessa said, her voice thick, the two words vaguely sliding into each other.

She got up slowly and moved lethargically away from the couch. She shuffled through the house, looking for the phone. She found it in the kitchen on the round breakfast table. She picked it up and took it back to the living room with her, flopped back into her spot on the end of the couch, and punched in Hugh's cell phone number. As she waited for the low purrs of the phone ringing at the other end, she took the cigarettes from the table, shook one out, and lit it.

Someone answered on the third ring. But it wasn't Hugh. It was a strange male voice.

"Hello?"

Vanessa said nothing for a moment. Lines cut into her forehead.

"Hello?" the man said again. "Uh, this is Hugh Crane's phone."

Vanessa's frown deepened. "Is . . . is Hugh there?"

"Who's this?"

"Is *Hugh* there?" she said again, suddenly sounding more urgent. A bad feeling sank deep into her stomach. "Who's *this*?"

"This is Deputy Mark Russell."

"Deputy? What's . . . um . . . where's Hugh?"

"I'm sorry, but Mr. Crane has, uh . . . he's passed away."

Vanessa shot to her feet without even realizing it. She dropped the phone and it thunked to the brown-and-tan-mottled carpet. The cigarette dropped from her lips and tapped onto the coffee table. She stood there with her mouth wide open and stared at nothing, eyes huge, her only movement for a long time the opening and closing of her hands into fists.

She felt nothing for what seemed a long, silent, fist-clenching time—then it all moved in fast and hard. The fact that Hugh was dead crashed into her like fierce stormy waves crashing against a rocky cliff.

Vanessa lost all control of herself. It was just too much,

one thing too many, and suddenly her thoughts were bright and clear and she was no longer drunk.

She moved through the apartment like the winds of a hurricane and managed to cause almost as much damage. She broke everything she could get her hands on, everything that would break. The apartment became filled with the sounds of breaking glass and silverware clanging to the kitchen floor. Back in the living room, she clutched the pot of one of her hanging philodendrons with both hands, jerked it hard and broke the hook that had held it, then lifted it high about her head and threw it downward hard onto the coffee table. The terra-cotta pot exploded, the glass top of the coffee table shattered.

Knuckles rattled on the frame of the screen door outside the apartment's front door. Someone pressed the annoying buzzer again and again. Then, more knocking.

Vanessa stopped.

Her breathing was accompanied by something she had no memory of ever doing before—each rapid exhalation was a growl. She wondered how long she'd been doing *that*. She looked around at all the destruction. At all the mess. But she was not thinking clearly, and the mess did not register in her mind as something she'd created.

"Vanessa? *Vanessa!*" It was Shirley Kidderman, a widow in her fifties who lived next door to Vanessa there on the second level of Willow Park Apartments. "Vanessa, are you all right in there?"

Vanessa realized she was not standing as she'd first thought—she squatted on the floor, knees up on each side, hands dangling between them.

What am I doing down here? she wondered.

From outside the door: "Vanessa! If you don't answer, I'm calling the police!"

Panting and growling . . .

Police? Vanessa thought. *No, no, I don't want the*

*police . . . do I? Definitely not. But . . . why not? I . . . I
don't know. I just don't want them involved.*

She felt as if she were waking from a deep, muddy
sleep. She stood up straight, stretched her arms above
her head, then avoided the broken glass on the floor as
best she could all the way to the door.

"Shuh—*Shirley*?" Vanessa called, her voice hoarse
from all her screaming.

"Are you okay in there, honey?"

Vanessa unlocked the door, pulled it open, then unlocked the screen door. Shirley pulled it open, and
Vanessa stood back so she could come in.

"Honey, you look like hell," Shirley said. "Is
everything—"

Then she saw the living room, all the destruction.

"Oh, my . . . God," Shirley said, her mouth dropping
open helplessly for a moment. Slowly, she turned to
Vanessa. "I think you should lie down, Nessa." She closed
the door, put an arm across Vanessa's shoulder, and carefully steered her through the broken glass to the the hall,
and down the hall to the bedroom. Shirley took her to
the bed, and they sat down on the edge. "I want you to
get undressed, and put on your nightie, or whatever it is
you sleep in—"

"Naked."

"Fine, then take off your clothes and—why are you
breathing like that, Nessa?"

Vanessa stopped breathing as her head jerked around
to look at Shirley, frowning, blinking. "Like what? Breathing like what?"

"Well," Shirley smiled, "it *sounded* like you were . . ."
She laughed once. "Like you were *growling*, honey."

"Growling."

"Yes."

"I . . . I . . . I'm sorry."

"You're not having trouble breathing, are you?" Shirley

frowned and cocked her head. "Should I take you to the hospital?"

"No, I . . . I can breathe just fine. He . . . he's dead."

"Who's dead?"

"Hugh." Vanessa had told Shirley all about Hugh—she told Shirley almost everything.

"Dead? How? What happened?"

"I don't know. I just called his cell phone, and someone . . . told me . . . that he's dead." Vanessa stood and clumsily undressed as Shirley pulled the bedcovers back.

Shirley stepped back and said, "You just take a nap, now, okay? You've been drinking, haven't you, hon?"

"Oh, yeah. For quite awhile, now. I think . . . my hair is numb." She turned naked to Shirley and smiled and laughed hoarsely.

But in spite of that smile, Shirley flinched a little, because suddenly, Vanessa just did not look herself, did not look quite right. Something—Shirley wasn't sure what, but *something*—about her face was different. Her hair? No, no. Her . . . her *eyebrows*. Yes. Had they always been *that* thick? Shirley did not think so. And was Vanessa developing a . . . *mustache*?

"You going for a new look, Nessa?" Shirley said.

"Uh . . . what?" she said as she got into bed.

"Oh, nothing." Once Vanessa was lying on her back in bed, Shirley swept the covers up and over her. "Now, you get some sleep, and I'll see what I can do with that mess out there."

Vanessa's hair was spread about her face on the pillow when she raised her head and said, "Oh, Shirley, you don't have to—"

"Don't tell me what I don't have to do. Now, sleep." Shirley crossed the room and turned off the overhead light. The blinds were closed. The room became dark.

Shirley frowned as she backed out of the bedroom door, deeply concerned for her friend.

Vanessa turned onto her right side and watched Shirley leave the bedroom—and she was asleep by the time Shirley pulled the door closed.

Jason was glad he'd decided to stay home from work that day.

He'd slept in, *way* in. He'd finally risen at . . . at—his eyes were so bleary when he sat up that he could not read the green numbers on the digital clock on his nightstand. It looked like something after noon. Was it *that* late? Why had he slept so long?

Jason went into the bathroom wearing only his boxers, and emptied his full bladder. When he was done, he went to the sink and washed his hands. He saw his face in the mirror—the bandages on his cheek and forehead had not gotten through the night in very good shape. They had peeled nearly all the way off.

Something . . . wasn't right.

He frowned at his reflection in the medicine-cabinet mirror over the sink, leaned in close. The cuts beneath those hanging bandages did not look the same. He reached up and took the bandages all the way off, and gasped.

The stitches in his forehead were still there, all four of them—but the wound they'd held together was gone. All the wounds on his face were gone.

Jason began tugging at the bandage on his upper left arm. He unraveled it as quickly as he could with his right hand—and the bite on his arm was gone. It was not *better*—it was *gone*.

"Holy shit," Jason breathed at himself in the mirror. He touched his face, the places where that creature's claws had broken the skin four times in a couple of drags across his face.

He went back into his bedroom and sat on the edge of the bed. He sat there for a long time, frowning, thinking

about his healed wounds. Finally, he stood with a sigh
and put on a robe, slipped his feet into black slippers,
and left his bedroom.

Mom had left a note on his refrigerator while he'd
slept.

Jason dear,
I want you to sleep as long as you can, so I'm not going
to disturb you. When you get up, let me know and I'll
fix you breakfast. Or lunch. Whatever you want.

The last thing Jason wanted was for her to see that he'd
healed overnight. She would go crazy. He wondered
what she would do. Probably call the pastor of her
church and insist there'd been a miracle.

He would put the bandages back on before leaving his
apartment so he would not have to explain his healed
wounds—because he could not explain them.

But as it turned out, he did not leave the apartment.

Jason's feet felt like blocks of lead and his arms were
filled with heavy sand as he went to the bar and, with effort, hiked himself up on one of the stools. He took a banana from the basket of fruit on the bar and peeled it, ate
it slowly, lips smacking as he chewed with his mouth
open, something he did not typically do—even his jaw
felt heavy.

He thought of his dreams—only one dream, really, over
and over again. Something about a house, that damned
house, so familiar—

It's the Laramie house, isn't it? he kept thinking.

—and yet so unreal, big and towering, a small jungle
growing up around it, the wind-blown winter branches
clawing at the old walls and squealing over what little
glass remained in the windows. The house pulled at him
in his dreams with a malignant strength.

Jason stood and staggered over to the window that

provided a view of Andrea's house and yard. Jimmy was home, his pickup in the driveway. Jason sighed as he thought about his time with Andrea much earlier that morning. Why had Andrea run off like that? What had gone wrong? Guilt made his chest feel full. He went back to his bed—this time, he flopped onto it, then turned onto his right side.

Jason was hungry. But it was a strange hunger. He was thinking about his hunger as he drifted off to sleep.

Andrea sat at the kitchen table with Jenny, each with a coloring book open before them, coloring the pictures. In the living room, some game blared loudly on the television as Jimmy watched it and made his way through a case of Budweiser. The baby was sleeping. Andrea was tired, her eyes heavy with gray half-moons beneath her eyes.

Jimmy had been behaving oddly all day. He seemed tired, and yet there was something oddly energetic about his behavior, something quick and jumpy. He did not speak to her, and behaved as if she wasn't there at all. That was typical of him—but it was the *only* typical thing about him that day. Otherwise, he did not seem himself at all. But Andrea found that she did not care. She was too preoccupied with her own thoughts.

She had only a foggy memory of the night before . . . of going to the house, of being with . . . others. She'd wanted to stay, but she felt a strong need to come back here, to take care of her children. But the need to stay there had been *powerful*.

It was really real, she thought. *All of it. I was there . . . with them . . . the others.*

"Look, Mommy," Jenny said, "I colored a green hippot . . . hippoto . . . Mommy, how do you say that word again?"

Andrea stared down at the book open before her, coloring in a picture of a giraffe. She worked absently on all the greenery surrounding the giraffe, and the tree from which it was eating—but she wasn't seeing it. Her staring eyes weren't seeing much of anything. She was lost deep inside her own mind.

"Mommy? What's this called?"

Still, Andrea did not answer. She was too busy studying the dark picture in her mind. It was a picture of that shadowy gray house and the others she'd seen there. She'd felt a strong sense of belonging with them, a *rightness* that had made leaving difficult.

The only other thing she was capable of thinking about was her hunger.

"Mommy? *Mom*my!" Jenny reached over, closed her little hand on the sleeve of Andrea's blue sweatshirt, and tugged a few times.

Finally, Andrea's whole body jolted in her chair and she looked down at her little girl. She cleared her throat, then said, a bit shakily, "Whuh-what, honey?" She frowned as she smacked her lips. There was an odd metallic taste in her mouth.

"This thing, Mommy, this animal," Jenny said. "What's it called again?"

"It's a hippopotamus. But you can call it a hippo."

"Thank you, Mommy." Jenny vigorously returned to her coloring, eyes intense, the tip of her tongue glistening in the corner of her mouth, lips pressed tightly together.

Andrea did not go on coloring. Instead, she stared down at the partially colored picture as she fell back into herself like someone falling down a deep well.

The house, and the others in it, would not leave her mind.

The hunger, which she'd experienced and satisfied earlier, gnawed at her. She remembered *how* she'd satisfied it. At first, she was horrified, but that passed quickly. Then she thought of the hot, wet gratification of feeding. Her tongue passed slowly over her lips.

She tried to think of Jason—of their times together, of the way he treated her, touched her, loved her—but her mind was held firmly in the memory of feeding.

What must Jason think of her, leaving him so suddenly like that? She knew it was for his own good . . . but how could she explain that to him? She would have to, though, sooner or later.

Andrea heard voices. Jenny's. And Jimmy's. Saying something to her. Was Jimmy . . . *shouting*?

A hand slapped her face.

Andrea was jerked from her dark thoughts and she realized there was something in her mouth, something waxy.

"The hell you *doing*, eating that thing?" Jimmy said.

It took a moment, but Andrea finally realized that she had been chewing up the green crayon in her hand. She spit the chewed-up pieces into her left palm.

Jimmy had not meant to slap her face—he'd slapped the crayon from her mouth. But that did not make her face sting any less.

"Fix me something," Jimmy said. "Fix me a . . . I don't know, a-a . . . a sandwich, maybe. And some chips, what kinda chips we got?"

Frowning and looking troubled, Andrea stood and went to the trash can, dropped the chewed-up crayon pieces into the garbage. "We don't have any chips," she said.

"What? Why not?"

"You ate them."

"Then why didn't you get *more*?"

"Because I just *haven't* yet. *Okay*?" Her words were clipped and cold—not the way she normally spoke to Jimmy.

His eyes widened with disbelief. "You getting funny with me?" he said. His eyes showed a lot of white, and he did not stop moving—he jittered and fidgeted, never holding still. He slapped her again, this time fully intending to hit her face. He slapped her so hard, she almost fell over. She turned to him, eyes glaring, and her lips pulled back as she prepared to say something, to *shout* something, but at the last second, she stopped.

What am I doing? she thought. *He'll beat me unconscious.*

"You gonna talk back to me?" he said. "Huh? You talking *back* to me now?"

"Nuh-no," she said, her voice quiet and soft again, meek. "No."

"Go get some chips."

"I . . . well, Jimmy, I . . ." *I what?* she thought. "I really don't think I should drive because I've got a, um, a really bad headache."

"Headache's not gonna kill you. Go down to the 7-Eleven on the corner. Get me some Doritos. The cool ranch flavor."

Andrea did not feel like driving—she wasn't sure she was *capable* of driving the way she felt; her hands trembled and her insides seemed to jiggle like Jell-O—but she did not see that she had much choice.

"Can I go, Mommy?" Jenny said.

"No, honey," Andrea said. "No, you stay here."

Jimmy got another beer and returned to his chair in the living room, to his game.

Anger surged through Andrea. She turned away from Jenny so the little girl would not see it on her face, the anger and hatred she suddenly felt for her husband. This was not typical of her—she usually felt cowed after he hit her or shouted at her. But at that moment, she burned with rage. She wanted to grab him and claw him and bite him and—Andrea took a deep, steadying breath. She leaned her hip against the counter and waited for it to pass, breathed it out of herself, tried to let go of it.

A few minutes later, her feet dragging and her mind

twisted with distraction, Andrea left the house to get Jimmy's chips. But as she drove, she was filled with a nauseating certainty that something very bad was going to happen soon.

37

THE CALM BEFORE THE STORM

Rain no longer fell from the corpse-gray sky, and the biting wind died down to nothing. A funereal stillness fell over Big Rock, heavy and ominous.

That Saturday morning and afternoon were as uneventful as the overcast, windless weather.

Below the Jags, foaming waves raged against the rocks and filled the air with undulating mist.

The two movie theaters in Big Rock did not do their usual booming weekend business, and even the mall wasn't very busy, with more space than usual in its sprawling parking lot. Most people stayed inside because of the cold weather and watched games or movies. That was what they told themselves, that it was because of the cold weather. The day simply felt . . . *off* somehow, as if it were not Saturday, but some other day, some day not marked on the calendar.

Twice the normal number of deputies prepared to go on patrol that night. Daniel Fargo provided them all with countless silver ammunition for their pistols, revolvers, and shotguns. Many of the deputies wore strange expressions on their faces that afternoon—no matter how Fargo put it, or how much Hurley reinforced it, they all had a hard time with the fact that, come that night, they would be on the lookout for *werewolves*.

As the day wore on, a thick fog moved in from the sea. It moved slowly, easing in and curling around buildings, oozing up streets, swirling around traffic lights and creating eerie halos.

Annie Culver was working dispatch, and 911 calls were at a minimum all day—a heart attack, a few car accidents, things like that, but not much for a weekend. At the end of Annie's shift, Shelly Blair relieved her and was told that it was slow. Shelly was glad to hear it—her three children had run her ragged all day, and she welcomed a slow shift.

But it was not to be.

As the day ended, something other than the darkness of night fell over Big Rock.

38

Incident at Willow Park Apartments

Shirley Kidderman had done her best with the mess in Vanessa Peterman's apartment, but she could not work miracles. She'd managed to sweep up the broken glass and vacuum up the tiny bits, as well as the dirt on the living room floor from the shattered potted plant. It had taken all afternoon, and the day was dying outside. Shirley's joints ached—they always ached a little these days, but the pain was worse now, having done so much bending over and sweeping and vacuuming.

Vanessa was still asleep in her bedroom. Shirley felt awful for the poor girl—she knew she cared for her married boyfriend a lot, and his death had hit her hard.

When she was finished cleaning, Shirley went into the kitchen, looked in the refrigerator for something cold to drink, and poured herself a glass of grape juice. She was drinking it when the piercing, horrible scream ripped through the silence from Vanessa's bedroom and so startled Shirley that she dropped the glass. It shattered on the floor and splashed grape juice over the tiles.

Shirley frowned down at the new mess and muttered, "Oh, of all the—"

The scream came again, and it did not stop. Shirley hurried through the apartment, down the hall, and stopped outside the closed bedroom door. Her eyes grew and her mouth fell open as she listened to the horrible sounds coming from inside—popping and crunching sounds, shattering glass, and screams, horrible screams.

"Van . . . Vanessa?" she said, her voice weak. She put her hand on the doorknob.

The screams changed, became deeper, rougher. They turned into animallike growling sounds.

Shirley started to turn the knob as she said, "Vanessa, are you—"

Something slammed into the door on the other side, and a splintered crack appeared down the center. Shirley was so startled, she cried out, then blurted, "My *Gawd!*" as she backed away from the door. "Vanessa? *Vanessa!*"

The door was pulled open.

Shirley slowly tilted her head back to look up at the creature, her mouth yawning, eyes open to their limit, arms out slightly at her sides with fingers splayed wide. Before Shirley could scream, her throat was slashed open so deeply that her head flopped all the way backward until it bounced between her shoulder blades. Before Shirley's body could collapse to the floor, the creature embraced her wavering torso and lowered its yawning, slobbering snout over the large opening in her neck to slurp at the ribbons of blood still pumping rhythmically from her torn throat.

The sun had just set, and the thick cloud cover blocked the light of the moon and stars. At the Willow Park apartment complex, bright lights around the central courtyard cast a glow through the misty night, illuminating the swimming pool.

Carrie Myers, a single mother of two, was about to take her children to McDonald's for dinner. She'd promised if they were good that day, they'd get Happy Meals for dinner, and they had done their best to be well-behaved all day long. Mickey was five and Danika, Dani for short, would be turning four next week. They came out of the upper-level apartment and Carrie finished putting on her coat, then turned around and locked the door behind them. She'd left the yellow antibug porch light on.

That was when she heard the sound. It was a horrible, inhuman scream that sent ice chips down Carrie's spine. Then she heard a growl, the kind of growl she would expect a large animal to make—loud and rumbling and frightening.

Carrie froze.

"Whassat, Mommy?" Dani asked.

The growl sounded again, and it was close. It seemed to be coming from the apartment two doors down. Carrie frowned, trying to remember who lived there. Shirley Kidderman lived right next door to Carrie, and on the other side was . . . some woman who usually kept to herself. Carrie could not remember her name. There'd been a lot of noise coming from there that morning—screaming and crashing and shattering. Carrie had looked out her door when she'd heard all that racket and saw Shirley going to the woman's apartment.

Farther down the walkway, at the bottom of the U formed by the apartment complex, a door opened up and Willard Borman stuck his head out. He wore a T-shirt, stretched taut over his sagging belly, baggy green pants, and blue slippers. He was a widower in his sixties who was always winking and making eyes at Carrie. He seemed harmless, but Carrie kept her distance. Willard frowned in the glow of his porch light; Carrie looked at him and shrugged.

"A animal," Mickey said. "Mommy, nobody's s'posed a have animals, huh?"

Carrie barely heard her son. She stood frozen in place with the house key still sticking out from her thumb and forefinger, wondering if they should go back inside.

The screaming and growling stopped. A heavy silence stretched on for awhile. Carrie started to move again, to head for the stairs with her children.

The door on the other side of Shirley Kidderman's apartment was pulled open.

Carrie stopped breathing, froze, and looked down the walk toward the apartment.

It had to duck to come through the doorway. It was enormous and hairy, with long, pointed ears and a narrow snout, and—

It turned and faced her and the children.

"Oh, Jesus!" Carrie said with a gasp. She turned and tried to put the key back in the lock to open the door so they could go back inside, but the key jittered and clicked clumsily against the doorknob and simply would *not* slide into the lock and—

The thing growled again as it came toward them.

Carrie screamed and grabbed her children, pushing them toward the stairs at the end of the walkway, saying, "Go, now, go go go!" She grabbed their wrists, one in each of Carrie's hands, and Dani was lifted up off the concrete as Carrie dragged Mickey along with them to the stairs. She hurried down the steps praying silently in her mind, *Please Jesus don't let us fall—what the hell* is *it?—don't let us fall don't don't don't—*

The thing put a long-fingered, clawed hand on the black metal railing and hiked its legs up and over the rail. It dropped from the upper level and landed in a squat on the concrete below, as easily as if it had jumped off a curb.

As Carrie screamed, Dani cried, and Mickey shouted, "Mommy Mommy Mommy!" They neared the bottom of the stairs.

All around the complex, doors opened and heads popped out, curtains were pulled aside, blinds were parted so eyes could see what all the commotion was.

A woman screamed from her doorway and someone else shouted, "Oh, my God!"

The creature went to the bottom of the stairs and started up.

"No!" Carrie screamed as she began to drag her children back up the stairs.

The creature was on them in two broad steps. With a backhanded swat, it knocked Carrie over the rail—she hit the concrete hard, and was dazed. Screaming, Mickey turned and tried to run up the steps. The creature swept Dani up and held her with both hands as it closed its snout on her chubby belly. The little girl made horrible gurgling sounds.

Carrie screamed gibberish as she struggled to her feet to fight the creature for her daughter, unaware that her head was bleeding.

The creature made wet snarling sounds as it ate Carrie's little girl.

Carrie threw herself at the beast, but it reached out and closed one hand on her face and twisted its wrist with a jerk. Carrie's neck snapped and she crumpled to the steps, dead.

The creature held Dani with both hands again, one at each end, as if she were an ear of corn, and buried its fangs into her bloody belly.

At the other end of the upper walkway, Willard Borman came out of his apartment with both arms spread, bent slightly at the waist, and beckoned for Mickey to come to him.

"Come on, boy, come on, hurry!"

Crying, Mickey ran to Willard, who grabbed his hand and pulled him through the open door of his apartment. Willard went in with the boy, but a moment later, he came out armed with a large pistol.

By then, the creature was back on the upper level. It

stopped to continue eating. Blood dribbled down from the small, still body that the creature held.

"Call nine-one-one!" someone shouted. The voice was nearly lost in the cacophony of screams and shouts that rose up from the complex as people watched the creature on the southern side of the upper level eat little Dani Myers.

Willard approached the creature, his pale face open with fear, and aimed the pistol. It fired with a loud crack once, twice, three times.

The creature tossed Dani's body over the rail and moved toward Willard.

Willard began to make a high, shrill sound as he fired the gun again and again.

The creature merely flinched with each shot as it closed in on him. It pulled back its right arm, then swung it in an arc, its claws slashing through Willard's thick neck. His severed head spun through the air, leaving a trail of spattering blood as it tumbled over the rail and dropped into the swimming pool below. Mists of red spread through the blue water. Willard's body fell backward, gun still aimed, and hit the concrete. It convulsed a few times before becoming still.

The creature turned to its right and faced the closest apartment window. Two faces peered through the glass, curtains pulled aside—a young man and woman gawked at the beast, horrified.

It pounded the windowpane, shattering the glass as it reached in and clutched the woman's shoulders. Without effort, it jerked the woman out the window, dragging her over the sharp shards of glass that stuck up from the bottom of the window frame.

The woman screamed and behind her, the man shouted in a high, tremulous voice, "No! No! No!"

More screams as the creature threw the woman over

the rail. Then, once again, the hulking beast hopped over the rail and dropped lightly into a crouch on the concrete below, just inches from the still body of the woman who had landed with a splat only a moment before. It went to her on all fours, tore at her clothes, and exposed her flesh. It clawed at her breasts with one hand, lifting her upper body off the concrete with the other so it could close its fangs on one of them, tearing and chewing on the breast and finally pulling it away, leaving behind a great black hole where the breast had been. It made satisfied grunting sounds as it ate.

The two bright lamps on each side of the courtyard threw flaring bars of light through the mist, casting long shadows over the concrete.

A young man with long blond hair, wearing jeans and a pale, baggy sweater left his ground-level apartment on the northern side of the complex and came around the corner of the fenced-in pool to the side where the creature was eating. He lifted something small in his right hand and held it out before his face. The red light blinking on the digital camera he held stopped, then it flashed a bright, electric white as he took a picture of the ravenous werewolf.

With the flash, the creature lifted its head from the bloody woman it was eating and roared furiously, blood dripping from its wet, matted snout. It dove over the woman's corpse and was directly in front of the photographer in a heartbeat.

The young man flashed another picture, then dropped his camera as he frantically stumbled backward, screaming, "No! Help! Jesus God somebody help me help—"

The young man fell over backward and the creature was on him.

In the distance, plaintively wailing sirens could be heard, first one, then another, and still more joining the chorus. The sirens grew louder as they drew closer and mixed with the screams that continued to sound all around the apartment complex.

The creature that had once been Vanessa Peterman paid the sirens no attention. It was too busy tearing into and eating the long-haired photographer.

Hurley's SUV had barely stopped moving when he shot out the door and ran toward the complex, his .38 in his right hand, loaded with silver bullets. Fargo exited the passenger side and hurried along with the Sheriff. He carried a shotgun.

A squadron of patrol cars converged behind him, their sirens dropping off in a staggered diminishment of sound. Some of the cars stopped so suddenly, their tires yelped against the wet pavement. Car doors pounded shut. Footsteps clattered over the pavement as deputies drew their sidearms, all loaded with silver bullets. Some carried .12 gauge shotguns holding shells loaded with silver buckshot.

The fog glowed around porch lights in the complex and curled ominously around the two lamps that cast pools of light in the courtyard.

The deputies spread out in the courtyard, some going to the remains of the dead bodies on the concrete.

People began to come out of their apartments on both levels, and some of them shouted at the deputies all at once, making their words indistinguishable.

"Whoa, whoa," Hurley shouted, holding up a hand. "You!" He pointed at a man standing just outside his apartment on the ground level. "Where is it? Where *is* it?"

"It went out back, behind this side," the man said, gesturing with one hand.

Hurley called to his deputies, "You guys—go around that side. The rest of you, come with me around this side."

Hurley led half his deputies around behind the southern side of the complex. They passed the row of carports and went beyond to the gravelly area that stretched from the parking area to the fence, their feet kicking through the weeds. Flashlight beams swept in all directions. They said nothing, just looked, hunted, all of them tense, anticipating the first sight of what they'd been told was a werewolf.

But it was not there.

They went around to the eastern end of the complex, the bottom of the *U*, and met up with the deputies who'd gone around the northern side of the building. The flashlight beams passed through the low mist, crossing like insubstantial swords.

They found nothing.

Hurley called all the deputies, who gathered around him.

"I want you all to go to the other side of this perimeter wall on both sides," he said, "and meet in the back. Ross, you and Jessup come with me back to the apartments and let's talk to the residents, find out what they saw. Lewis, call a couple of buses out here right away to tend to the wounded. Any of you see this thing, I want you to fill the fucker full of silver. Okay, get going."

The deputies dispersed as Ross and Jessup headed with Hurley back toward the courtyard. They were approaching some of the frightened-looking residents when they heard the screams of several men, closely followed by a keening roar.

Hurley turned and ran in the direction of the sound.

The screams continued as they neared, then quickly, one by one, they stopped.

The deputies followed Hurley to the gate and around the edge of the perimeter wall. They jogged along the wall, their flashlight beams bouncing ahead of them.

Other deputies came running from the other direction.

"Son of a bitch," Hurley said as he neared the bodies on the ground.

He stopped and looked down at them as the deputies

turned their flashlights on the corpses. The bodies of five deputies were on the ground, pieces of them scattered around a few feet away. A couple deputies groaned. One turned away and vomited.

Hurley and all the deputies turned and looked in all directions.

They saw nothing. But they heard something . . . in the near distance across the road in a wooded area.

A high, chilling howl.

39

DOMESTIC SQUABBLE

Jimmy Norton felt restless. And hungry. His hands trembled, and he could not hold still. A darkening gray pressed at the windows, the day dying outside. Jimmy would go out soon. He shivered in anticipation of it. He could not wait to go out again, to rape, to feed, to cut loose in ways he'd never before been able to do. Jimmy liked what he had become, enjoyed the power he felt, the strength, the . . . invincibility.

But he could not stop shaking as he paced the living room, back and forth in front of the television that gibbered on and on, ignored.

"Make me a drink," he said as Andrea came through the living room on her way to the kitchen. "Scotch and ice."

"Make it yourself," she said hoarsely. When she'd gotten back from the 7-Eleven, she'd taken the kids over to her sister's because she said she didn't feel well. When she'd returned, she'd taken her clothes off again and put the robe back on. She wore it still.

"What did you say?" Jimmy said, no longer pacing. He glared at Andrea.

She stopped and turned to him, frowning, her hair mussed, her arms folded tightly across her chest. "I *said* . . . make it your*self*. I don't feel well."

"Goddammit, I told you to get me a drink. So why don't you just—"

But she ignored him and walked on into the kitchen.

Anger burned red behind Jimmy's eyes. Andrea simply did not talk to him that way. He heard the crunch in his head of his teeth grinding together. Fists clenched, he stalked into the kitchen after her, moved up behind her fast, and grabbed her elbow, spun her around roughly. "You're gonna get me a drink or I'm gonna—"

"Get your fucking hands off me!" she shouted, jerking her elbow out of his grasp. She bent forward slightly at the waist and her hands curled into fists. "You want a drink you can just get it yourself. *Okay?*" She turned her back to him then and went to the refrigerator. She opened the door and bent forward, examining the shelves.

Jimmy froze in place for a moment. Anger flowed like acid through his veins. He felt the change coming on, felt it moving through him. He stumbled backward, out of the kitchen, as his body began to alter itself, as bones snapped and cartilage popped and hair grew and his shoulders and arms ripped through the plaid shirt he wore. A heavy coat of black hair grew over his entire face and body. His jeans became too short, the denim tore as his legs expanded, arms growing longer—

And he roared, the sound thick with his anger. He stood just outside the kitchen door, his breathing heavy and rumbling with a growl, saliva dribbling from his fanged snout, as unsettling sounds came from the kitchen.

More snapping and crunching . . .

He moved forward, ducked his head as he went through the doorway, back into the kitchen. He turned to face Andrea.

But she was not Andrea anymore. Her robe hung from her new, larger body in tatters. The overhead light shimmered in the dark, gold-streaked blond hair that now covered her. When she saw him, her thin black lips peeled back over long fangs.

He tensed, ready to lunge forward at her.

She moved first and pounced on him with a wet, slavering growl.

He released a long, surprised roar as her fangs sank into his neck, as her claws pierced the skin of his upper arms.

They flew backward together into the dining room and slammed into the table, knocking it on its side and sending chairs scattering.

Her fangs tore a chunk of flesh out of his neck and he shrieked in pain as he tore his claws across her front, ripping through her left breast, and down across her abdomen. She opened her snout wide and wailed in pain.

Doris Whitacker frowned and cocked her head, listening. She picked up the remote, muted the television, and continued to listen.

She heard it again—a horrible sound, like nothing she'd heard before. Her mouth opened as she heard it again and again. She was not even sure how she would describe it when she called the Sheriff's Department, which she planned to do.

It was nothing human, no—this was an animal sound, something savage and dangerous.

Doris listened more closely, eyes narrowed. She realized there were *two* sounds—they were very much alike, but there were definitely two.

She put a hand on each armrest and lifted herself out of her chair. She turned, walked through the living room, and went to the front door. She opened it and stepped up to the closed and locked screen door.

It was icy cold, and a gray fog moved in as darkness fell.

From across the street, glass shattered and something else was crushed noisily, followed by more crashing. The racket continued, accompanied by frightening growls and shrieks that made gooseflesh crawl across her shoulders and back. Doris touched four fingertips to her bottom lip as she frowned at the Norton house across the street. The sounds were coming from there, but they were unlike any of the other sounds she'd ever heard from that house. She'd heard shouting, she'd heard glass break—but nothing like this.

What's happening over there? she wondered. Earlier, she'd seen Andrea take the children somewhere and come back a little later without them. But had they come back? She feared for them if they were over there now.

Doris returned to her chair, sat down, and picked up the phone. She'd promised not to call nine hundred and eleven anymore, but this seemed urgent enough to justify it. She punched the three buttons, put the phone to her ear, and waited.

Jason wondered if he were dying.

He was curled up in bed, shivering—no, it was more of a shudder than a shiver, almost a *convulsion*. It wracked his bones, made his teeth clack together. And yet he was perspiring, making the sheets cling to his skin. Then there was the hunger. It gnawed at his insides like a horde of rats, but nothing satisfied it. And that house—

The Laramie house, the Laramie house . . .

—would not leave his mind. It tugged at him, confused his thoughts.

His mother had come up to check on him and he'd snapped at her to go away and leave him alone. That bothered him—he'd never spoken to either of his parents that way before—but it was not foremost in his mind at the moment. The thing that weighed most heavily on his mind was the question of what was happening to him.

Lying in bed, Jason's heart throbbed in his ears, and he could hear the thick rushing of blood through his veins. He'd turned on none of the lights in his apartment, and as the day died, shadows lengthened until it was completely dark.

No longer able to tolerate the clammy feeling of the wet sheets, Jason got out of bed. The apartment was cold, so he put on a sweatshirt, sweatpants, and slippers. He stumbled around turning on lights. In the bathroom, he looked at himself in the mirror over the sink.

His face looked narrower than usual, eyes sunken deep in their sockets, with dark half-circles beneath them, skin shiny with perspiration and the color of bone.

In the periphery of his consciousness, Jason heard something outside his bathroom window, something coming from Andrea's house—an animalistic growling, glass shattering, things crashing. But his attention was focused on his face in the mirror, on the hunger growling in his belly.

A metallic, silvery flash sparkled in his eyes. It startled him and he jerked back away from the mirror with a slight gasp.

Then he heard them again, those sounds from next door—growling, crashing, loud thumping. And something else—a growl that became a high shriek. In that shriek he recognized the voice.

"Andrea," he said, his voice dry and hoarse.

Jason hurried out of the bathroom, through the apartment only vaguely noticing that he moved smoothly, easily, rounding the edge of the bar, avoiding a chair, sweeping down the stairs to the garage. The shivering was gone suddenly. He felt strong and confident. But that was relegated to the back of his thoughts—he was focused on Andrea's safety.

As Jimmy and Andrea fought and struggled in the house, shreds of their tattered clothes dangled and flapped from their bodies. Their growls blended into a roar; the impact of their bodies against the walls and floor made the house tremble. Each bled from wounds inflicted by the other—blood spattered the floor and the broken pieces of furniture in the living room—but the wounds closed up rapidly. As they fought, more cuts and gashes were inflicted, more blood shed, but they did not last long.

They stumbled to a stop when something slammed heavily against the front door. Jimmy's ears twitched forward, Andrea's upper lip peeled back over glistening, blood-streaked fangs, and each turned to the door with a low, chest-deep growl.

Again, something thudded against the door so hard, the entire house quivered. A long, splintered crack appeared down the center of the door with a loud *crunch*. Along with the thud came another growl, vicious and gurgling with saliva. Another slam against the door, and another—the crack opened up.

Something punched through the crack—a long, muscular arm covered with light brown hair, and a hand with long, slender, black-clawed fingers curled into a fist.

With one more slam, the door exploded inward in a storm of wooden chunks, shards, and chips.

Jason burst into the living room with a menacing growl, head tilted forward, narrowed eyes glaring at Jimmy from below a head of wild, white-streaked hair. He stood there for just a moment, hardly long enough to get his bearings. Then, arms outstretched, he launched himself at Jimmy with a high, hateful roar.

At the same time, Andrea attacked Jimmy as well.

Although he struggled and slashed and snapped his fangs, Jimmy went down beneath their weight. Jason and Andrea were without mercy—their claws and fangs sliced through Jimmy's flesh repeatedly, cutting deeper, opening him wider. Jimmy's movements became stiff and slow, and his growls dissolved into throaty gurgles, but he continued to fight.

Somewhere in the distance outside, a siren wailed.

Hurley hit the brake, and his SUV squealed to a stop in front of Doris Whitacker's house. Cruisers pulled in fast behind him and clogged the street as they came to a stop, their red and blue lights throbbing.

"A familiar neighborhood," Fargo said, the shotgun between his knees, its barrel pointing at the floorboard.

Hurley looked at the computer screen attached to his console and rechecked the address; then his eyes fell on the appropriate house across the street. The front door was open and he could see erratic movement inside. He got out of the SUV and slammed his door, which was quickly followed by Fargo's on the other side. Then the doors of the cruisers slammed one after another, like muffled gunshots that echoed up and down the street, and footsteps clattered across the pavement as the deputies followed Hurley to the house.

Hurley heard the growling as soon as he was outside the SUV, and it grew louder as he drew closer to the house. The house sounded like a zoo gone wild inside. He stopped on the lawn and turned to the deputies, their weapons drawn.

"Surround the house," he said. "Be alert, and be prepared to open fire."

As the deputies began to fan out, something shot out of the open door. No, Hurley realized—it was *two* somethings. They were very big, and quite hairy.

Fargo did not hesitate. He fired his shotgun.

The creatures moved fast.

The deputies stopped in their tracks and spun around at the sound of gunfire. Some of them spotted the fleeing creatures. Guns were raised and fired, including Hurley's.

The creatures became two blurred shadows racing through the darkness.

"After them!" Hurley shouted, sweeping his hand at four nearby deputies, who fell into pursuit.

A moment later, the creatures were gone.

"Shit," Hurley said.

"Look," Fargo said, pointing as they moved closer to the house. "Another one."

Hurley realized that the door he'd thought was open was actually *gone*—it lay scattered in pieces around the floor inside. And there was something else on the floor, something large that writhed and bucked as it made sounds that were a cross between long groans and growls.

"Quickly," Fargo said as he picked up his pace, leaning on the cane as he limped over the wet grass.

The two men rushed up to the empty doorway. The creature on the floor was wounded, but not dead.

"It's recovering," Fargo said, lifting his shotgun as he stepped through the doorway, with Hurley behind him. Fargo stood over the creature and nearly touched the barrel to its head.

The shotgun exploded. So did the creature's head. Fargo lowered the gun to the creature's torn and bloody abdomen and fired again.

Hurley watched the creature as it jerked and convulsed on the floor. Then he looked at Fargo and said, "I'm gonna get some deputies in here and search the house."

"Don't worry, there are no more of them here," Fargo said. "If there were, we'd know."

"Just the same."

Hurley turned and left the house as Fargo stared down at the blistering, dying thing on the floor.

40

JASON AND ANDREA

As Jason and Andrea put the gunfire behind them, ran past the houses and into the misty, dripping woods beyond, the human beings they'd been earlier had only the vaguest, most remote sense of their surroundings. Their intellects had been overcome and deeply supressed by something more primitive, an animal instinct that was led by an acute, powerful sense of smell and sharp, crystal-clear hearing.

Jason was very aware of one thing, though—it was an image in his mind, vivid and hot: an old, dark, dilapidated house . . .

He heard everything around him, even those things at some distance. As they'd run away from the gunfire, he'd heard the bullets flying like tiny hummingbirds past his ears. There had been pursuing footsteps behind them, but they'd quickly faded as Jason and Andrea sprinted ahead. Now, he could smell the wet earth and wood all around him, the leaves, the weeds. Even more, he could smell Andrea next to him, her flesh, her fur, her—

Blood?

Suddenly, he realized she was falling behind him as he ran. He stopped and turned, a low, almost inaudible growl in his chest.

She'd fallen to the ground. Jason went to her side and hunkered down.

She was bleeding from her neck from a small hole. She began to shiver, then quake. As she released a sound that was in part a growl, and in part a high, frightened cry, she rolled over and arched her back, as if in the midst of a seizure.

Jason knelt beside her and whined. His supressed human consciousness stirred deep in his mind and words and feelings—

silver

pain

death

—began to float to the surface of his more primitive consciousness.

Andrea roared as her body began to jerk and quake, releasing thick popping sounds, and her flesh began to bubble in places like boiling water. Her fangs receded as her long muzzle seemed to melt away beneath bulging, pained eyes. Fingers shortened—

silver

bullets

silver bullets

—and sharp, black claws disappeared. Her gold-streaked blond fur began to thin out. The process went back and forth as blisters opened up on her flesh and blood and fluids dribbled from them. Her breathing became ragged and strained.

Andrea's eyes, now back to their normal soft brown, turned to Jason's and pleaded for help, for relief from pain, for protection from fear.

Jason felt himself begin to change as the words and feelings became clearer in his mind.

silver

bullet

kill

reaction
allergic reaction
silver bullet
God oh God oh God—
—silver bullets, that man said silver bullets would kill the werewolves and—
—what's happened to me how did I become this thing how how how this thing—
—they fired at us and a bullet hit her and now she's—

"Andrea!" he cried, his voice thick, heavy, and cracked, not quite his own yet as he continued to return to his former self.

Her cries grew louder, more desperate, more pained.

Jason saw his hand—a small patch of brown fur still on the back of it—reach down and clutch hers—an undulating, blistering, constantly changing thing—and hold tight.

It's killing her, he thought. *She's dying.*

He held her hand tightly between both of his, as if he could prevent it, keep her there with him, stop her death. His eyes stung with tears.

Andrea arched her back again as the fanged muzzle jutted from her face once more, then began to retreat again. Her head tilted back, mouth open, and she released a long, miserable howl.

"You hear that?" Hurley said to no one in particular as he stood on the front porch. Several deputies standing around the bottom of the front steps turned toward him, then some of them cocked their heads and listened.

The streetlights were dully reflected in glowing pools on the wet pavement, sparkling here and there on the shiny surfaces of puddles. Up and down the street, dogs barked. Somewhere, a cat shrieked.

Then the sound came again—high and sustained and quavering.

Gooseflesh passed over Hurley's shoulders and back in a sheet. The sound was separate from the barking dogs—separate and *different*. It had a richer quality than the sounds of the dogs . . . a *bigger* quality.

"A howl," one of the deputies said.

"Over that way," another said, pointing across the street.

"Deputy Kopechne, get the coroner out here."

"Right away, Sheriff," the deputy said, turning and walking away.

"You four, and you two," Hurley said, pointing deputies out as he skipped the steps and jumped down to the sidewalk below. "They haven't gone far. Come with me. Now."

He took his flashlight from his belt and turned it on as he ran across the lawn and into the street, which throbbed with the red-and-blue lights of the cruisers parked all along the sidewalks on both sides. The deputies ran with him, flicking on their flashlights, their footsteps machine-gunning over the wet pavement. They ran across Doris Whitacker's front lawn and down the left side of her house. At the rear of the backyard, they vaulted over a four-foot wooden fence and rushed across the short expanse of empty field beyond it, then into the woods.

Jason heard a distinctly canine whimpering and realized it was coming from him. On his knees, he rocked forward and back, clutching Andrea's hand as he watched her die.

She continued to change back and forth, blisters rising on her bubbling flesh, sores opening and running. She howled again, the sound cutting through the misty night.

"Andrea . . . Andrea . . ."

Jason repeated her name again and again as she grew worse, became more and more unrecognizable. He spoke her name softly, though he felt like screaming until his throat tore open, like tearing his hair out, clawing his own flesh, and gouging his eyes. Hot tears ran down his cheeks as he died inside.

Gradually, he became aware of other sounds, in the distance at first, but rapidly growing closer—rustling bushes, footsteps, quiet voices. Jason turned and looked back the way they had come, his eyes narrowing as he focused his hearing in that direction.

They're coming, he thought.

Behind those running sounds were others—two groups were rapidly heading toward him.

He looked down at Andrea again and fought to pull himself together. He leaned in close, until his face was almost touching hers. He placed his hand gently to her cheek, feeling the horrible, moist activity in her flesh.

"Andrea," he breathed, not knowing if she could hear him, if she was even aware of his presence. Her eyes looked through him as they narrowed in pain and agony. "Andrea, I . . . I love you. I love you."

Her body jerked violently under him once, twice, then stiffened. She made a choking sound in her throat.

The footsteps and the sounds of voices grew even closer. They would come through the mist soon, both groups, and they would see him. They would raise their guns and fire, and the silver bullets would pierce his flesh. Then he would become like Andrea . . . and eventually, he would die.

Jason stood slowly, his body changing again as he did so—the hair returning, the muzzle growing out of his face, teeth lengthening into fangs. When he looked down at Andrea, she was still lying rigidly on the ground, making awful gurgling sounds. He tore his eyes from her, forced himself to turn away.

As he ran into the woods, that old house was foremost in his mind once again. But vaguely, he was aware of the hot tears stinging his eyes.

The beam of Hurley's flashlight fell on the first group of deputies, then lowered to the body on the ground. It was still alive, but he immediately recognized the condition and knew it was dying.

Two of the deputies spoke almost simultaneously:

"Holy shit."

"Oh, my *God*."

Hurley hissed, "Shh!" He listened for a moment, but heard no movement around them, no sounds of something retreating quickly. "Well," he said, looking down at the bleeding, wheezing creature, "we got *one* of the two, anyway."

"Shouldn't we, uh . . . kill it?" a deputy asked, his voice unsteady.

"We already have," Hurley said. "It just takes a little while for them to die."

He looked ahead into the dark, dripping woods and wondered where the other one had gone.

41

IN THE HOUSE

The house rose up out of the night and grew quickly in size, filling Jason's field of vision—as if *it* were approaching *him* rather than the other way around.

As he'd headed for the house, led by an inner sense of direction that seemed to be coming from somewhere *outside* his head, Jason's belly had growled with hunger, and his heart still ached over the loss of Andrea. But as strong as these feelings were, his hunger and emotional pain could not overwhelm the need, burning like fire in the front of his mind, to make his way to the house. Something there drew him, reeled him in like a fish on a line.

The house stood before him, a blacker structure against the blackness of the night, with soft light glowing vaguely in some of the broken, glass-fanged windows. Jason stood cautiously across the street, staring at the house from the safety of a stand of Sitka spruce trees, eyes narrowed, his breath loud in his alert ears. He could feel the beating of his heart in his chest. Pulled toward the house by something he did not understand, he moved forward across a deep ditch running with water that was cold against his feet, then loped into the road and headed toward the house.

Light suddenly surrounded him and he turned to his left and raised his claws slightly, just as two glowing orbs rushed at him fast. A terrible screaming sound, vaguely familiar, cut through the night—

tires

brakes

—and the lights veered sharply to the right. For an instant, Jason caught a glimpse of two pale, horrified faces beyond the windshield—a man and a woman. The car thumped loudly as it hit the ditch, then slammed into the trunk of one of the spruce trees with a thunderous crunch. Upon impact, the car's lights blinked out and the passenger shot through the windshield like a missile, flying clear of the hood and disappearing into the dark.

Still standing in the road, Jason turned away from the wrecked car and almost immediately forgot about it as he focused his attention once again on the house. He crossed the road quickly, before any more lights came, and bounded over the broken-down old fence in front of the house. He stood on the broken walkway that led to the porch and stared at the house.

A voice spoke inside his head:

"You're heeere . . . come iiin . . . come iiin . . . come iiin . . . "

Jason lifted his leg past the broken front steps and moved up onto the porch. It creaked and crackled under his weight but held him as he went to the door. He stopped and stood there for a long moment, uncertain, mildly confused. The house seemed to be trying to embrace him, to take him in invisible arms and hold him closely, tightly.

He sensed something . . . an unfamiliar feeling, but one he recognized nonetheless. He sensed . . . *others*. Suddenly, he knew he was no longer alone. On the other side of the battered, cracked old door in front of him, there were others . . . like him . . . hungry . . . burning with lust . . . and there was something else . . . some*one* else . . . a strong presence that felt even stronger as it drew nearer to him, until—

The door was pulled open slowly. In the darkness beyond stood a tall, hulking figure.

Jason focused his eyes, released a low, warning growl without even realizing he was doing it. At the same time, he felt the tingling sensation of his fur shifting over his flesh, as if a breeze were passing over him. The figure stood perfectly still, and yet Jason felt as if it were moving closer to him, closing in suddenly, stepping into his space and crowding him.

A single silver eye stared back at him for awhile, then the shape stepped forward. It had halted its transformation around the halfway mark—it was a man covered with hair, with tall, pointed ears on each side of his head, and a mouthful of fangs but no snout. His left eye was gone and skin had mostly grown over the empty socket.

The man spoke in a low, rumbling voice, and as he spoke one word; the same word was echoed in Jason's head, as if the wolf-man were communicating with him in two ways at once:

"Jason."

"*Jaaason.*"

For an instant, a terrible fear rose up in Jason. He took a fraction of a step backward and almost turned and ran, but other eyes appeared in the darkness behind the hairy, one-eyed man. They glimmered and flashed as they stared directly into Jason's eyes—

—and suddenly, he felt welcomed, as if they had been waiting for him. For indeed they had, and now they were glad he'd arrived.

Just out of the reach of his mind's hearing, like voices that could barely be heard on a radio with bad reception, Jason heard the others, felt them, picked up the very edges of their thoughts as they reached out to him from behind their glistening eyes. At the same time, he heard them with his ears, as well—the low, not unpleasant growling sounds they made deep in their chests. The growls were almost voices, but still not quite human.

"Come—"

"—*iiin*—"

"—in," the man said. "You're—"

"—*hooome*—"

"—home now." He lifted his arm slowly, reached out a hand to Jason, its black claws like needles coming from the tips of his fingers.

Jason took in a deep breath, then released it tremulously. He stepped forward as the man and the others stepped back, and Jason entered the house.

Doris peered out her front window through her binoculars. Sheriff's Department cruisers were parked everywhere, most of them with their red-and-blue bars of light on top flashing, the colors bleeding all over the road and sidewalks and yards. Through the open doorway of the Norton house, she could see a body lying on the floor. It seemed to be moving slightly, but no one was nearby or helping out—all the police were outside.

Others in the neighborhood were coming out of their homes slowly, looking around, talking quietly to one another in their yards in the glow of their porch lights.

When she'd heard all the gunfire earlier, Doris had automatically reached for the phone to call the police. Then she'd realized they were already there—that *they* were the ones doing the shooting.

Movement caught her attention and she turned the binoculars a little to the right. She saw Sheriff Hurley crossing the street with a group of deputies, approaching the house.

More movement, again to the right—a news van from Channel 4.

Frowning, Doris muttered, "What's happening over there?"

When he saw the news van pull up and double-park beside a cruiser at the curb, Hurley groaned, "Oh, shit." It was bad enough that they were following him around from the scene of one killing to another, but he knew if they saw that thing on the floor in the house, he would never be able to keep things quiet. The reporters would start a panic in the town—in the whole county—and it would make his job a lot harder than it was already. Hurley turned to the deputies. "Get some tape and cordon off this entire yard, right now. Make sure *nobody* gets near that house, understand? And somebody go stand in that doorway—I don't want that body to be visible from out here. Get something and cover it up, while you're at it."

Several of them replied positively as Hurley broke away from them and went to the news van as its two doors opened.

Here we go, Hurley thought.

The first thing Jason noticed inside the house was the smell. It was, in part, dusty and moldy, but there was something else almost overpowering those odors—the heavily musky, gamey animal smells of the other figures that lurked in the murky darkness.

Candles burned in a few places, their glow shifting back and forth, giving the darkness a kind of secret animation, a flickering life that jittered over the figures around the room. Some stood, others sat or crouched, all in groups of two, three, or four, curiously sniffing each other. Some of them grunted as they rutted savagely on the floor, or on dusty old furniture, or against the walls. Still others stood and watched Jason as he came into the house.

Jason's hunger gnawed at his gut. But he realized that was not all he was feeling—he could feel the hunger of the others! Their urge to feed, their need to bite into warm flesh and feel and taste hot blood was as powerful as his. Combined, those hungers and urges formed a sort of vibration, an invisible aura that surrounded them all, a silent and unseen shower in which they eagerly bathed.

They were enjoying it. The anticipation of what was to come—the hunt for the right prey, the stalking of the prey, the attack and the kill, the explosive release of savage sex—seemed to be as powerful as the real thing. But then, Jason did not know—he had not yet fed.

The one-eyed man began to communicate with them silently, not with words, but feelings and pictures. He comforted, he reassured, he encouraged their hunger and their urge to hunt and kill and fuck—but all the while, he subtly impressed upon them his primacy, his leadership. He made sure they had no doubt about his alpha status.

He was like them, and yet different, because he was older, stronger, more practiced in the ways of the hunt, far more experienced in the kill. He emanated power and strength.

Jason feared the man—it was a fear he could not control or reason with, but one imbued with great respect for the creature that stood before him.

Something in the room changed. The air became charged. Suddenly, the other creatures in the room were all standing, shifting from foot to foot, making low, rumbling sounds.

Jason felt it, too. It came from the man—

Taggart

—who stood perfectly still among them—

Irving

—sending his thoughts and feelings out to all of them.

Taggart Irving Taggart Irving Taggart

The name entered Jason's mind from the outside, infiltrated his primitive thought processes.

Taggart was stirring their hunger like the boiling contents of a steaming pot, making it roil. He expressed to them the feeling of the kill, the sensation of their fangs popping through flesh, the taste of blood bubbling up into their mouths, and it was making them restless. Those engaged in sex stopped and pulled apart so they could pace as they kept their eyes on Taggart.

They breathed harder, faster, fidgeted nervously, all of them—even Jason. His heart thundered in his chest. He could feel the very blood rushing through his veins. He wanted to—no, he *needed* to feed, *had* to. But something held him there, looking at Taggart. Large invisible hands pressed his feet to the floor. Some distant part of Jason's mind understood that it was Taggart himself—he was not quite done with them yet.

Taggart worked them into a frenzy. The house hummed with their deep growls and chuffing snorts, their pacing footsteps, and the occasional snapping of their jaws.

Saliva dripped from Jason's snout as he closed his eyes and lost himself in the sensations Taggart was sending— warm, tender skin, hot, salty blood pumping into his mouth, the taste of the raw, wet flesh. As these sensations moved through him, he pictured only one face, one person. The person he held responsible for the death of Andrea. The leader of those men who had fired their guns and sent a bullet into her neck.

Sheriff Arlin Hurley.

A sharp sound interrupted Jason's reverie and that of all the others.

A voice crying out. Then, pounding.

"Hello? Help me! Please!"

The room fell silent and every head turned toward the front door.

"Hello? Is anyone there?"

Taggart turned his body around to face the door.

"I'm hurt! Somebody please help! We've had a wreck . . . across the street! My wife—" The voice was interrupted by sobs. "I think . . . my wife . . . is dead!"

The room filled with the sound of thick, heavy breathing.

Taggart went to the door, reached out and turned the knob, pulled it open.

A figure huddled low on the porch.

"Will you help me? Please, call an ambu—"

Taggart bent down, grabbed the man with both hands, and jerked him easily through the door into the house. He kicked the door shut and threw the man over the floor toward the others.

Jason smelled the blood. So did the others.

They all surged forward, but Taggart stopped them.

"Wait! New ones—"

"—*Neeewww*—"

"—first. You . . . and you . . . and—"

"—*yoooouuu*—"

"—you, come here."

Taggart gestured for Jason and the other new ones to come forward.

The others grumbled their protest.

As Jason neared the man—

"Wait! No! Wait, please, I'm hurt, I can't—what're you *doing*?"

—the smell of blood grew stronger. Jason's consciousness winked in and out of a bleary, foggy state of helplessness as he threw himself forward and pounced on the man along with the other new ones.

The man began to scream and fight weakly, but he was no match for them.

Jason felt his fangs pierce the man's skin, felt the blood well up in his mouth, tasted the warm, juicy, raw meat underneath.

The man's screams stopped with a gagging sound.

Jason consumed bites of the man, growling and grunting as he fed. But he did not eat much. He stopped when the face of Sheriff Arlin Hurley appeared behind his eyes again.

Jason lifted his head and looked around, his muzzle dripping with the man's blood. His eyes found Taggart in the flickering darkness.

Taggart slowly lifted his arms—

"Feeed! Feeeeed!"

—as he looked around at all of them.

There was a great, noisy rush as the creatures left the house. Some went out windows while others bottle-necked at the front door, but they left the house quickly, eagerly.

Hungrily.

And Jason went with them, bounding over the bloody, savaged corpse on the floor.

Once outside, he felt better—he had not realized how closed in and imprisoned he'd felt in the house. Now he was out in the open, in the night. He quickly put distance between himself and the house as he ran across the street and disappeared into the woods on the other side.

He ran back the way he had come with only two images vivid in his mind.

First, Andrea's face, smiling softly at him, her eyes warm, skin soft.

And second, the face of Sheriff Arlin Hurley, whom he looked forward to eating.

42

STALKING THE PREY

"Do me a favor and just go, okay?" Hurley said to Shana Myers.

She smiled and said, "Sorry, Sheriff, but I am doing my *job*, after all."

They stood in front of the double-parked news van, in the glow of its headlights, surrounded by pools of pulsing red and blue light. Deputies were about to finish putting yellow crime scene tape around the front yard and the house. A moment earlier, it had begun to sprinkle a little, and the drops glimmered in the van's headlights like tiny gems. Shana's cameraman stood in the van's open driver's side door, getting his equipment together.

"I realize that," Hurley said. "But at the moment, there's simply nothing to report."

She tossed her head back and laughed. "Sheriff, it looks like nearly every deputy you *have* is out here tonight. With all these deputies running around, how can there be nothing to report? Also, there've been reports of police activity and gunfire on this street. Is all this for just one wild animal?"

He did not respond, just turned his head and looked into the throbbing blue-and-red glow all around them.

"Is there more than one?" she said. "Just what *kind* of wild animal gets this sort of attention, Sheriff?"

Hurley sighed, then opened his mouth to reply, but he stopped when he saw George Purdy's van pull up and double-park in front of the house beside a cruiser. He turned to Shana again and said, "Look, stick around if you want, but I can't let you anywhere near that house, and I have no comment for now."

"But how can you—"

"I *told* you, I have nothing to say. I'll talk to you when I have something more to offer."

As he walked away, the van from Channel 7 drove up.

"Damn," Hurley muttered.

George killed the engine and lights; then he and his young male assistant got out. George came around the front of the van to meet Hurley while the assistant hung back and waited.

"What've you got?" George said as they stood close, his voice low.

"A couple more just like Emily Crane," Hurley said. "Same condition. A reaction to silver."

"You mean, silver *bullets*."

"Of course. One's in the house, the other's out in the woods across the street, on the other side of those houses. Go in the house first, cover that thing up, and get it out of here as soon as you can. Whatever you do, don't let these reporters get near it, understand? Don't even let them see it. Once you've got that one under wraps, you can take care of the one in the woods."

"Gotcha."

"C'mon," Hurley said as he went to the cordon and lifted it up. He and George ducked under it and headed across the yard.

"Sheriff!" called Mike Wills from Channel 7. "Could I have a word with you?"

Hurley did not even turn around. He turned his head

slightly and called over his shoulder, "No comment right now."

"You know what you're going to tell them yet?" George asked as they went up the porch steps.

Hurley laughed. "Are you kidding? I don't have any damned idea."

The smell of Ella Hurley's meat loaf cooking in the oven filled the house. It was a warm smell, rich with seasonings. Arlin loved her meat loaf. The recipe had been passed down from her grandmother to her mother, and then to her, and Ella had given it to her daughter. Along with its particular blend of seasonings, it included chili sauce instead of the usual ketchup, sliced mushrooms, and a spear of dill pickle buried in the center of the loaf.

Outside, it began to rain hard enough for Ella to hear the sound of the rainfall. It was a constant soft whisper that surrounded the house. She stood at the stove in a creamy cashmere sweater and colorful, flower print broomstick skirt.

It was twenty-four minutes after seven. Broccoli steamed and rice pilaf cooked on the stove. Ella did not even know if Arlin would be coming home in time for dinner. Even so, she'd decided to go ahead and cook. As good as it was fresh out of the oven, the meat loaf was even better later on cold sandwiches, and that was Arlin's favorite way to eat it. She would cook the meat loaf, have some for herself with the broccoli and rice pilaf. Then she would put it away in the refrigerator—he could have a sandwich when he got home, however late that might be.

As she took the broccoli off the burner, glass shattered somewhere in the house. Ella froze, her eyes suddenly wide.

Something thumped loudly in the house and Ella gasped. The breaking glass had been one thing—a branch or a thrown rock could've hit a window, or perhaps someone outside the house had broken something—but the thumping was *inside* the house.

Someone had come in.

Ella turned around and crossed the kitchen, went through the doorway to the hall, then stopped and listened.

Another sound, this one indistinguishable, so quiet and nearly inaudible that it made Ella wonder if she had heard it at all. But if she *had*—if there really *had* been a sound just then—it was unmistakably the sound of movement.

She headed down the hall toward the front of the house. As she passed the closed door of the downstairs bedroom, she heard what she thought was the floor creaking on the other side. She stumbled to a stop and jerked her head around to look at the closed bedroom door, lips parted, brow creased in a frown. Her right elbow was bent, her hand frozen at the level of her throat.

A heavy silence stretched out, interrupted only by the sound of the falling rain outside.

Ella was not quite sure what to do. If someone was in the bedroom, should she go to the phone and call Arlin, or should she simply get out of the house immediatley? Then again, what if the sounds she'd heard were not inside at all and she had merely allowed her imagination to run rampant? She would be mortified if she ran out of her house in a panic for nothing.

She stood there unmoving for what seemed a long time. After a good length of silence, with no sound at all, the tension began to ease out of her. She started to turn around to go back to the kitchen, started to think to herself that it had been her imagination after all, when the bedroom door was jerked open. Framed in the dark doorway was a hulking, silver-eyed beast.

A horrible animal growl filled the world. Ella screamed, but beneath the horrible growl, she could not hear her own voice. At the same time, she jolted her body back around and broke into a run for the front of the house.

Something clamped onto her hair and jerked her backward.

Ella screamed, but she did not panic. She threw herself forward with every ounce of strength she had.

Her scalp burned as hair was ripped out of her head by the roots. She gulped the pain down like acid reflux and kept running, until she got to the stairs. She spun to her right and took the staircase two steps at a time.

At no point did she look back, but she could hear the person—no, it was a *thing*—behind her in pursuit. It breathed heavily and made a moist, grumbling sound as it came after her. She picked up the smell of the creature—a heavy animal smell, gamey and musky—and somehow, that stirred more terror in her than anything else.

At the top of the stairs, Ella's toe hit the edge of the landing and she stumbled forward, almost fell, but waved her arms at her sides as she kept plunging forward, regained her balance, and did not stop.

The bathroom came first, to her right. She almost ducked in there, closed the door, and locked it, but a thought stopped her:

Telephone!

She had to call Arlin. He would either come himself, or send someone else immediately. The only phone upstairs was beyond the closed door of the master bedroom.

At the end of the hall.

Jason reached the edge of the woods. He was fully transformed, lost in his animal self, following his laserlike senses of smell and hearing. The heavy darkness of the

woods gently gave way to the soft glow that came from
the windows of houses along the street.

The sound of rain falling pattered all around him, but
Jason pushed that aside to listen for other smaller
sounds. He could smell the group of people gathered
around the Norton house some time before he could see
them. Jason hunkered down low, and as he hurried
through a backyard and along the side of a house, he in-
stinctively broke down the smells to those of individuals
in the group, one person at a time.

Jason stood at the corner of the house, pressed against
the wall and concealed in darkness. Droplets of water
clung to his fur, but he barely noticed the rainfall. His
shiny black nose twitched as he frantically sniffed at the
buffet of people in the street and on the sidewalks and in
the yard of the Norton house.

His interest, however, was in one person alone.

Jason's eyes passed over all the activity in the street
and in and around the yard of the Norton house, looking
for Sheriff Arlin Hurley.

There. Standing on the sidewalk talking to three
deputies. He seemed tense and preoccupied as he gestured with his arms, animated but at the same time a bit
stiff.

Jason continued to sniff until he found Hurley's scent.
He isolated it from the ocean of other smells, and locked
onto it.

Andrea's face rose up behind Jason's glaring eyes.
Something in his chest twisted until it ached and made
his throat constrict. He flinched and pushed the pain
away, made Andrea's face disappear. He turned his attention back to the sidewalk across the street and focused
again on Sheriff Hurley.

Jason's thin black lips twitched, then pulled back
slowly to reveal his glimmering fangs in what was almost

a savage smile. The quiet rumble in his chest was like two rocks being ground together.

He had found his prey.

Ella grabbed the doorknob and flung herself against the door as she turned it. In one smooth movement, she threw herself into the bedroom, slammed the door shut behind her, then spun around and locked it a fraction of a second before the creature slammed into it on the other side.

She was torn—should she push Arlin's dresser in front of the door or go to the phone first? She decided on the phone.

Ella ran to the nightstand on her side of the bed.

The thing slammed against the door again and again.

She took the phone from its base, turned it on, and hit the memory button for Arlin's cell phone. She put the phone to her ear and waited to hear the line at the other end purr.

The bedroom shuddered each time the creature in the hall slammed against the door.

Ella thought she heard the wooden door begin to crack.

Hurley found himself standing in the rain on the sidewalk, alone for a moment, and he took the chance to close his eyes. He took a deep breath, let it out slowly. He was surprised there had been no more calls since the one that had brought them here to this house. He expected more—he *knew* they were coming—and, of course, just because there hadn't been another call yet did not mean there weren't people out there getting hurt and killed. Raped. Eaten.

George and his assistant came out of the house carrying the covered body on a stretcher. They put the body in the van; then George approached Hurley.

"Where in the woods?" George said.

"I'll have someone show you," Hurley said. Pointing across the street, he said, "It's beyond those houses, just a little—"

In his pocket, he felt his cell phone vibrate at the same time that he heard it chirp.

Hurley cocked his head and took a moment to frown, although he had no idea why. Then he took the phone from his pocket and opened it.

Jason hunkered in the rain beside the house, watching, listening, smelling.

A high, mechanical, birdlike chirp cut through the night. Jason's pointed ears twitched and turned toward the sound—across the street. He watched as Hurley reached into his pocket, then put his right hand to his ear.

Jason waited.

A moment later, Hurley tensed up, bent forward slightly, and shouted something. He shouted a word again and again—

"Ella? Ella? *Ella!*"

—as he began to walk in a small circle.

Others turned toward him when they heard him shout.

Hurley took his hand away from his ear, returned it to his pocket. He turned to some of his deputies and barked orders, gesturing with his hand as he started toward his SUV at the curb.

Jason tensed, prepared to move.

Four deputies ran to two cruisers along with Hurley, who got into the SUV, slammed the door, and started the engine. The cruisers roared to life.

Still hunkered down, Jason moved away from the house, across the yard, and down to the sidewalk.

As Hurley and the cruisers pulled away from the curb, sirens wailing to life, Jason broke into a run. Forgetting the two cruisers, Jason focused entirely on Hurley's vehicle. Staying off to the side of the road in the dark, avoiding the glow of streetlights, Jason broke into a full run as he pursued the SUV. He moved with a speed and ease he'd never known before, blending in with the night.

The rain pebbled him, and the cold night air rushed over his face as he ran. Along with the hunger he hoped to satisfy soon, Jason felt exhilaration.

43

JASON AND HURLEY

The SUV came to a shrieking stop in front of Hurley's house. He shifted into park, killed the engine and siren, and jerked the key from the ignition before throwing the door open and lunging out.

Ella had been unable to say anything on the phone—she'd simply screamed his name again and again. In the background, Hurley heard a sound that had chilled his blood and made his intestines feel loose: growling.

Light glowed through the closed curtains of the windows. The Victorian house looked as pleasant and welcoming as all the other houses on the street.

The two cruisers stopped behind him in the road in front of the house. On the roofs of the cruisers and the SUV, spinning lights spilled red and blue in all directions. Two deputies got out of each car and followed Hurley, who ran across the yard to the front door.

"Ella!" he shouted, drawing his gun with his right hand, holding his keys in his left. He bounded past the three front porch steps without touching them. He did not bother trying the door—he knew it would be locked.

He slipped the key in, turned it, twisted the knob, then shoved the door open and ran inside.

Panting quietly, Jason huddled behind a crape myrtle across the street from Hurley's house. The rain cooled him after his run.

Somewhere in the distance, a high, piercing howl stabbed the night.

Down the street, a car started, its engine revving before it sped away.

The barking of dogs came from up and down the street.

Jason watched as Hurley entered the house, calling out repeatedly. The deputies rushed forward across the yard. Movement above caught Jason's attention, and he looked up.

A second-story window had been opened and a large, dark figure crawled out carefully and stepped over to the porch roof. Moving with stealth and grace, it went to the front edge and hunkered there, silent and motionless, watching the deputies as they neared the house.

Just before the two deputies in the center reached the porch, the figure on the porch roof dropped soundlessly through the night.

It spread its arms wide and landed on the two deputies, dropping them to the ground. The figure immediately began to slash and bite, attacking them viciously. The two men released high, shrill screams, firing their guns wildly. The guns popped sharply, like firecrackers going off in the night.

The other two deputies turned and headed toward their fallen comrades.

The figure was up in an instant and on one more of the deputies, swinging its arms furiously.

More screaming.

More gunfire.

Jason realized the figure—one of his own kind, large and powerful—had distracted the deputies completely. Staying low, he moved out from behind the crape myrtle and headed across the street.

Hurley dropped his keys as he entered the house. He called his wife's name again and again as he rushed through it, turning on lights where needed as he moved from room to room. He did not stop until he entered the downstairs bedroom. He stood just inside the doorway for a moment and stared across the room at the window that had been shattered. Shards of glass glimmered on the floor.

He spun around and ran down the hall, up the stairs, calling her name repeatedly.

He saw the battered and splintered door of the master bedroom hanging open at the end of the hall. He fell silent as he pushed himself to run even faster, his heart exploding repeatedly in his chest.

Ella lay on her back across the bed, arms stretched out at her sides. The pale blue bedspread was mussed. Her sweater was badly torn, her skirt hiked up around her waist. Her black panties lay crumpled on one of the pillows. Her legs, bleeding from harsh scratches, were spread wide. The patch of hair between them glimmered with fluids. Her breasts rose and fell slightly with each shallow breath.

The room reeked of sex, and something else—a stinging animal gaminess. Ella was alone.

"Oh, Jesus," Hurley cried as he lunged toward her. He put his gun on the bed as he knelt on the mattress and leaned forward over Ella, his hands on her shoulders. "Ella? Baby? Honey?"

Like her legs, her pale face had been scratched. She bled from a bite on the side of her neck. Her eyes were open to their limit, staring up at the ceiling. When Hurley spoke, she seemed not to hear him. She did not look at him, just stared blankly up at the ceiling, her mouth open.

He gently put his hand to the side of his wife's face as his vision pixelated with burning tears. His mouth opened wide. The room filled with a sound—a long, hoarse wail that went on and on.

Ella still did not look at him, did not make a sound.

Pain filled Hurley's chest as his heart broke. He realized gradually that the sustained sound in the room came from him. It rose up from his aching chest, an agonized wail, and tore through his throat, filling the room with his horror, his pain.

He cut the wail off abruptly, became silent.

Sounds came from outside—a jagged roar, a pain-filled scream, the cracking of gunfire—but to Hurley, they were a thousand miles away.

Once a person catches the virus, Fargo had said, *it takes twenty-four to seventy-two hours for the change to take place. That process can be slowed down . . . but it cannot be stopped. That person* will *change. And kill and eat others.*

Hurley clenched his eyes shut.

Once you learn for certain that someone is a lycanthrope, you must kill that person . . .

He ground his teeth together.

That person is no longer him- or herself, no longer human, and must be killed.

His burning throat constricted.

. . . must be killed . . .

Tears streamed down his cheeks.

. . . must be killed . . .

He tried to imagine Ella changing into . . . something else. Some kind of bloodthirsty animal. He could not. The image would not come.

That person will *change . . .*

It was impossible.

. . . must be killed . . .

Incomprehensible.

. . . will change . . .

Something cut sharply through his pain then, clearing the fog in his mind. Training, experience—whatever it was, it shifted his focus enough so that he registered the sounds coming from outside.

Hurley sat up and turned his head toward the window.

Through the open window, from below, he heard the sound of one of his deputies screaming in pain. He realized that a moment earlier he'd heard gunshots.

His eyes dropped down to the gun beside him on the bed. He reached over and picked it up. It felt heavier than before.

He looked at Ella again.

. . . will change . . .

He imagined her beautiful face melting away, becoming something else . . . something ugly and savage and inhuman.

. . . must be killed . . .

Hurley moved his hand very slowly until the bore of his gun lightly touched Ella's right temple.

. . . must be killed . . .

His face twisted into a mask of pain as he applied pressure to the trigger.

Another scream rose up from below.

With a soft cry, Hurley jerked the gun away from Ella's head. He tore his eyes from her face and turned once again to the open window.

He knew he had to act.

He got up and staggered to the doorway. He turned for a moment and looked back at Ella.

The only movement she made was that of breathing. Hurley's eyes were drawn again to the fluids that sparkled between her legs.

Tearing himself away from the bedroom was as difficult as tearing his own skin off with his bare fingers. He walked back down the hall, then jogged, then ran to the stairs, skipping steps as he went down.

The screams grew louder and there was more gunfire. A shrill, pained roar responded to the gunfire, then someone shouted, "I got it! I got it!"

At the bottom of the stairs, Hurley turned sharply to the right, then jolted to a halt, staring with wide, moist eyes.

The creature stood just inside the front door, glaring at him. It would've had to duck to come through the doorway. Its arms, muscular beneath all that light brown fur, were held out slightly at each side, long fingers curled inward, its head tilted forward.

For a moment, Hurley forgot everything—where he was, what he was doing there—as his eyes took in the werewolf standing before him. He kept thinking one word over and over in his mind:

Impossible. Impossible.

Outside, something released a long, miserable howl as men's voices shouted at one another. Hurley barely heard the sounds.

The thin black lips of the creature's muzzle curled back over glistening fangs and it made a deadly, menacing sound that nearly stopped Hurley's heart. Hatred burned like lava in its eyes. It bent slightly at the waist as its arms, bent at the elbows, moved farther outward on the sides, and Hurley knew it was tensing to pounce, to attack him.

In one instant, the creature was rooted to the floor, and in the next, it had launched itself into the air toward him.

Hurley remembered he was holding a gun. He jerked his arm up as the creature engulfed his field of vision, then he fired.

The werewolf slammed into him like a freight train and they both flew backward. Air exploded from Hurley's lungs as he landed hard on his back under the creature's weight.

The muzzle of the gun was pressed hard against the creature's body. Hurley fired again as the werewolf's jaws closed on his left shoulder, just above his collarbone. Hurley cried out in pain.

An instant later, the creature withdrew its fangs from his flesh and jerked its head back as it released a long shrieking sound. Its entire body convulsed once, twice, then it cried out again. It looked down at Hurley then, its head trembling, eyes wide, mouth yawning open. The hatred it had shown for Hurley a moment ago was replaced by confusion, then pain, and finally fear.

As he lay beneath the suddenly quaking creature, paralyzed with terror, pain burning in his shoulder, Hurley felt a surge of anger that almost overwhelmed his fear. He sensed a sudden weakness in the beast, and it pressed him on. Certain that this was the creature that had raped Ella, he opened his mouth and roared at the werewolf just as it had roared at him. At the same time, he struggled to push it off his body.

The werewolf rolled off Hurley, who immediately began to crawl backward on his back, gasping for breath, still clutching his gun. Beneath his jacket, he could feel the blood flowing from his wounded shoulder. It throbbed with pain that radiated down his left arm and into his back. He clumsily scrambled to his feet and aimed the gun at the werewolf.

On the floor at the foot of the stairs, the creature lay on its back, making agonized sounds as its body writhed and twisted.

One of the deputies stumbled in through the open front door and said, "Sheriff, we—" He stopped when he saw the convulsing beast on the floor. "Oh, shit." Then he turned his pale, shocked face to Hurley and said, "You're hurt."

Hurley, still trying to catch his breath, shook his head

and dismissed the deputy's remark with a wave of his hand. He took his eyes off the creature on the floor long enough to see that it was Deputy Scott Fredricks.

"We got one out front," Fredricks said. "It, uh—well, the others are hurt pretty bad. I think Hewitt might be dead. But we got it. It's on the lawn right now, and I think it's dying."

Hurley frowned at him. "Another? Of *these*?" he said, jerking his head toward the thing on the floor, which was groaning and gurgling.

"Yeah. It dropped down on us from above. I think it came out of an upstairs window."

Confused, Hurley cautiously stepped over to the werewolf on the floor. As he glared down at it, the creature's body began to shift and bubble, making horrible popping and tearing sounds. The fur coating its body retreated to reveal blistering, bleeding skin. The muzzle seemed to melt as the face became more human. The body was soft and fleshy, and as it regained its humanity, the face became more and more familiar.

Hurley gasped when he recognized the boy. "Juh . . . *Jason*?" he said.

Jason's horrified, miserable face turned to Hurley. He stared up at the sheriff with just enough recognition in his eyes for Hurley to know that he was right—it *was* Jason Sutherland, the boy who had been attacked by Emily Crane.

The color left Deputy Fredricks's face as he looked down at the changing creature. "You *know* this thing, Sheriff?" he said.

Hurley did not reply, just stared down at the boy.

Jason rocked back and forth, howling in pain and fear.

From the front yard, Hurley could hear another creature making the same sound.

Hurley dropped to one knee beside the undulating, transforming, and retransforming creature on the floor.

The eyes were clenched in pain as the fangs shortened, lengthened, then shortened again, blood dribbling from the disrupted gums. "Jason?" he said. Then, louder and sharper, "*Jason!*"

The eyes opened and looked up at Hurley through glimmering tears.

"Jason, did you attack my wife?"

"Nuh-nuh . . . nuh-nuh . . ." Frustrated with speech, Jason slowly shook his head back and forth.

Hurley fought to gather his thoughts. He knew this was some kind of opportunity, but after the events of the last few minutes—Ella's phone call, finding her in the bedroom upstairs, seeing her like that, knowing what had been done to her, then being attacked himself—his thoughts were scattered and bleary. He remembered Fargo saying something about a den . . . the need to find out where the werewolves gathered.

Fluids ran from Jason's glistening wounds as his bones and muscles snapped and bunched and released beneath his skin.

Hurley clenched his teeth and closed his eyes a moment, trying to push aside the severe pain in his wounded shoulder, the burning image of Ella's wounded eyes. When he opened his eyes again, he said, "Jason, where are they? The other werewolves, the alpha male—where *are* they?"

Jason's eyes lost their focus for a moment and seemed to look through Hurley, then rolled upward to reveal the whites.

"Jason!" Hurley shouted, leaning closer to him. "Where are the others?"

His eyes opened again as his face melted, reshaped, then reshaped again. "Luh . . . Luh . . ." His body stiffened and he cried out in pain. Still looking up at Hurley, he tried again: "Lara . . . *meeee!*" he cried.

Hurley frowned. "What?"

Voice trembling, words interrupted by grunts and cries of pain, Jason said, "Huh-huh-*house*! Luh-Luh-Lara-meeee-huh-*house*!"

It did not make sense at first. Hurley had to run it through his mind a few times. Then it clicked.

The Laramie house, he thought, his eyes widening with sudden understanding.

Hurley stood and holstered his weapon. He searched the floor until he found the keys he'd dropped earlier, then picked them up. He turned to Fredricks and grabbed his elbow, leading him out of the house.

"Your wife—" Fredricks started to say.

"How many are hurt?" Hurley said as he limped down the porch steps, wincing with pain. He saw a couple deputies lying on the lawn, and a third deputy was tending to one of them.

"We might've lost Hewitt," Fredricks said. "But Jackson and Boyd are still alive. They're hurt bad, but alive. That thing dropped down and—"

"Get a bus over here for them right away, Fredricks. Get a *couple* buses over here, one for my wife."

"Your wife? Is she—"

"She's upstairs. She's been . . . hurt. She needs help. So get a couple buses right away. Stay and hold things down here. I've got to go."

Hurley let go of the deputy's elbow and headed down the front walk.

"But what about these . . . *things*?" Fredricks said.

"Don't worry about them," Hurley called back. "They're dying." Moving as fast as he could given the pain he was in, Hurley went to the SUV and got in. He started the engine, then got on the radio and put out a call for everyone to head for the Laramie house.

He kept seeing Ella . . . her eyes . . . the deadly fluid glimmering between her legs. He forced himself to shove the hurtful images from his mind. For the time being, he had to struggle through the smothering pain that threatened to overwhelm him. He would have to fall apart later.

Pain consumed Jason.

It began deep inside, then worked itself out to the surface of his skin until it was no longer inside him—he was inside it.

A small voice somewhere far in the back of Jason's mind said, *How? How did this happen to me? To Andrea? How did we . . . become . . . these things?*

As the pain grew worse and surpassed anything he could have imagined, and even anything he was capable of properly registering in his mind, Andrea's face materialized. First she appeared in his mind, but then, in the shimmering refractions of his tears, her face wavered and glistened into being. She did not replace his agony, but for those final moments, she diverted his attention away from it somewhat, held his eyes, and even made his lips twitch a little into an attempted smile.

The vision of Andrea did not speak. She simply smiled at him.

In his pain and misery, Jason tried to say her name, but only made a gurgling, rasping sound. It was the last sound he made. But he was given some comfort by it, by Andrea's beautiful face, which was the last thing he ever saw—even if it was only in his mind's eye.

44

AT THE LARAMIE HOUSE

The black night shimmered with the rainfall that slashed through it. When Hurley got out of his SUV, the first thing he heard was a high, lingering howl in the distance. He stood in the rain and looked around.

Some cruisers had already arrived. Others were driving up and stopping. As he walked away from the SUV, Hurley saw Fargo approaching him under an umbrella.

"Even if this is the den, Sheriff," Fargo said, "chances are it's empty right now. They're out hunting and feeding. But tell me—what makes you think this *is* the den?"

"One of the werewolves told me." Hurley frowned up at the house and his chest became tight, his throat constricted slightly.

I'm going to have to go in *there,* he thought with dread.

Fargo stepped closer to him. "You . . . you *talked* to one of the werewolves?"

"Remember Jason Sutherland? The boy who came into my office with you?"

"Yes."

"Him. He came to my house. Tried to kill me. I shot him. While he was dying, he told me the den was here."

Fargo looked away a moment, his eyes narrowing. "That poor boy."

"Sheriff."

Hurley turned around to face Deputy Gwen Parma. She was tall and slender, her blond hair cut short beneath her rain-protected cap.

"What is it, Deputy?"

"There's a car across the street. Looks like a recent accident. It hit a tree. Someone went through the windshield, a woman. She's lying dead a few yards away."

"Okay. Why don't you take care of that while we deal with the house."

"It seems she was the passenger, though," Deputy Parma said. "We can't find the driver."

"Hm. All right, it's all yours, Parma."

She turned and walked away.

Hurley turned to Fargo again. "So, you're pretty sure they're not in there?"

"Not right now," Fargo said. "They're nocturnal, Sheriff. They're on the hunt. And when they're done hunting and feeding for the night, there's no guarantee they'll come back here. They have homes to go back to, human lives to return to during the day. The only assurance we have is that the alpha male will return here—*if* this is his den."

Hurley sighed. "Then we'll wait for him." He turned to Fargo and said, "I can't let you get involved in this."

"I'm not asking you," Fargo said. "I'm *insisting*."

"I've already endangered you enough tonight, Mr. Fargo. I'll have a deputy take you back to your car." He added firmly, "Whether you want to go or not. This isn't up to you. This is dangerous, and you're not a member of this department."

"Then deputize me."

Hurley chuckled. "This isn't a Western."

"Sheriff, this man helped kill my family. I've spent years searching for him. I've crossed the country to your little town to find him and—"

"And now you'll let *me* deal with him. You're the one

who came to me, remember? Now I'm going to do my job. We're going to handle this *my* way."

Fargo opened his mouth to speak again, but said nothing. His chin worked back and forth as rain pattered on his umbrella. He did not move.

"You have no idea what I've been through tonight, Mr. Fargo," Hurley said, his voice trembling slightly. "Don't push me. I'm not in the mood for it." He called Deputy Mark Selwyn over. "Take Mr. Fargo back to his car at the station. Then I want you to follow him back to his hotel. Once he's situated, you can come back here."

The deputy nodded, then turned to Fargo.

"I'll come back, Sheriff," Fargo said. "On my own."

"And I'll have you arrested." When Hurley spoke again, it was through clenched teeth. "Don't fuck with me, Fargo, not now, not tonight. I'm *serious*. Go back to your hotel. I'll call you when it's all over."

"What if you don't call? What if you can't?"

Hurley shrugged. "Then you'll know something went wrong. Go on, now. I'll talk to you later."

Reluctantly, Fargo followed the deputy through the rain to a cruiser.

Within the next minutes, Hurley instructed the team of deputies to surround the house and remain as concealed as possible. Only if the werewolves, or anyone else, approached were they to use their radios. Hurley contacted Shelly back at the station and instructed her to maintain radio silence until further notice—any incoming calls were to be handled by the team of deputies remaining at the station. He chose three deputies—Kopechne, Walt Lucas, and T. J. Sanford—to go inside the house with him.

He knew there was no way to hide all the cruisers parked in front of the house—upon arriving, he'd instructed his deputies to turn off all the roof lights and kill the engines and headlights, but the cars themselves were plainly visible. It bothered him, but there was nothing he could do about it now. He had to hope that any werewolves approaching the house would be confident and arrogant enough to see no threat in the presence of police.

Again, Hurley looked at the house. A heavy, slightly nauseating feeling of dread moved through his insides. Images and feelings from his boyhood experience with the house crept through his mind like thieves.

He clenched his teeth and pushed the thoughts away. He had no choice. He would have to go in.

As Deputy Selwyn drove away, Fargo's good eye stayed on the big run-down old house, at its black, empty windows. He turned his head to watch it through the rain as Selwyn drove by, then looked over his shoulder to peer through the metal mesh divider separating the front and back of the cruiser and out the back window as the house grew smaller in the distance.

He felt helpless. He had no evidence other than Hurley's assurance that the house was indeed the den of the alpha male. Hurley had a lot of deputies with him, but Fargo knew how little that mattered if the alpha male returned with the pack, or even merely a segment of the pack. He could not shake a feeling of urgency, a sense that he should do *something*—but Hurley would not allow it.

"What hotel you staying in?" the deputy said.

"It appears there *are* no hotels in Big Rock," Fargo said, distracted. "I'm staying at the Beachcomber Motor Lodge." Lost in his thoughts, Fargo barely heard the deputy's next question. Finally, he turned and said, "I'm sorry, what was that?"

"I said, is it nice?" Deputy Selwyn said.

Fargo nodded silently, and a moment later, he muttered, "Yes, sure."

As the deputy drove them back to the station, Fargo

chewed on his lower lip, frowning and worrying about Sheriff Hurley, the large team of deputies, and everyone in the town of Big Rock.

"Sheriff, look at this."

Hurley stepped up onto the creaky porch in front of the house and looked down at the spot where Deputy Kopechne was shining his flashlight. The porch roof had kept the wooden porch mostly dry, but there was a dark puddle in front of the door, surrounded by other dark spots. Hurley moved his flashlight and looked beyond the dark spots.

"Prints," Hurley said quietly. "In what appears to be blood."

"Prints?" Kopechne said, frowning. "You're sure?"

"Yep. Footprints. Not human, but definitely footprints. Everybody be careful—don't step in this blood."

Hurley moved around the blood and went to the front door ahead of the deputies. It had not been completely closed and stood open an inch or so. He thought of the last time he'd stood before the door. It had seemed so much bigger back then—Hurley had been only a boy, so everything was bigger then. Now, the door was old and rotting and not at all threatening. But it did not calm the anxiety he felt in his chest.

"I know nobody lives here," Kopechne said, "but, uh . . . what about a warrant, Sheriff?"

Hurley said, "Which judge do you think will most likely be willing to sign a warrant allowing us to come in here and search for werewolves?"

Kopechne nodded. "You've got a point."

"Don't worry," Hurley said, "I'll take full responsibility for this." He put the flashlight in his left hand and drew his gun. The deputies did the same. The beam of the sheriff's flashlight preceded them into the dark house.

Hurley expected to encounter the smell of mold and

decay that he remembered from his first visit to the house. Instead, he curled his nose at the same rank, gamey odor he'd smelled in his own bedroom earlier, where he'd found Ella.

Oh, Jesus, he thought, *Ella, poor Ella, what am I going to do with Ella, what am I going to—*

There was another smell in the house, also familiar— blood.

"Stinks in here," Sanford muttered.

Their feet crunched over grit and broken glass, and the wooden floor creaked and popped as they slowly moved forward and spread out. The constant whisper of rainfall came from outside. From somewhere in the house came the steady plinking of dripping water.

"Oh, shit," Lucas said, his voice breaking. "Sheriff."

Hurley turned and his flashlight beam fell on a lumpy, jagged hump that glistened with moisture on the floor. It took a moment to understand what he was seeing—the remains of a human being. Tattered clothes, ripped flesh, jagged fractured bones that jutted upward from the torn, broken mass, all surrounded by puddled and spattered blood. A foot away lay a roundish object in another puddle of blood—the victim's head, its mouth yawning open. The ravaging of the victim had taken place recently—the blood had just begun to grow thick and tacky.

The odor, the blood on the porch, now this, Hurley thought. *Jason was right—this is the den.*

Hurley moved deeper into the house, sweeping his light back and forth until it fell on the old rotted couch. He came to a stop and stared silently at it. It had collapsed in the middle. It was hidden beneath a thick layer of dust and cobwebs. There at the left end of the couch sat what remained of the figure that had haunted so many of his nightmares, that had stirred such terror in him as a boy. It hardly appeared to have been human now—a crumbling pile of old clothes and bones, its head having fallen into what once had been its lap.

"What the hell is *that*?" Lucas said.

Hurley stared at it silently for awhile, then sighed. "It's been here a long time. I've seen it before. Once, when I was a little boy and came in here on a dare. Probably a transient. Some bum who came in here for shelter a long time ago and died, maybe. I don't know." Seeing it now was somehow calming. The boogeyman was not so menacing after all—little more than a pile of sticks and the remains of rotted fabric. He turned away from it and faced his deputies. "Let's move through the house," he said quietly. "Kopechne, come upstairs with me. You guys look around down here. Be careful, and keep your eyes and ears open. Anything happens, don't hesitate to shout. Or shoot."

The stairs were rickety, and Hurley and Kopechne kept their flashlight beams on the steps ahead of them to avoid any that were broken. At the top were two hallways—one straight ahead, and a shorter one to the right. Hurley nodded his head to direct Kopechne to the right, while he went on ahead.

Other than the rainfall, the dripping, and the creaking floors, the house was silent.

The upstairs rooms held only a few dusty, rotten pieces of furniture. In one room there was a filthy mattress on the floor, some blood-stained bones that looked human, and fresh. Was this where Irving Taggart had been staying? Had he brought back some food from the hunt? Something to snack on? If so, Taggart was not in the house now. As Fargo had said, he was out hunting with the others, feeding.

That means people are dying, Hurley thought. *And I'm here doing nothing about it.*

He left the room and headed back toward the stairs. Kopechne appeared ahead of him and said, "This place is empty."

Hurley nodded. "Yeah, that's what I expected. They've—"

An agonized scream cut through the rainfall outside, followed by a gunshot. Then more screams, more gunfire.

For a moment, Hurley and Kopechne were paralyzed where they stood.

A deep, animal roar sounded out there, followed by another.

Then a howl.

The night outside erupted in a cacophony of screams and cries and gunfire.

Hurley threw himself forward and skipped steps on the way down the stairs. On the ground floor, Sanford and Lucas were already headed for the front door.

Outside, the sounds of pain and fear—and the menacing growls of the werewolves—came from every direction, all around the house. Hurley did not know where to go first.

No one had transmitted a warning on the radio—whatever had happened had happened suddenly, unexpectedly.

Hurley stumbled to a halt at the foot of the front porch steps.

Just beyond the cruisers parked at the edge of the road, touched by the glow of a streetlight a short distance to the right down the road, tall figures moved forward steadily—*very* tall, hulking, casting long shadows over the glimmering wet pavement. They came from the woods across the street.

Hurley raised his gun and fired once, twice, a third time—but the figures that had been there were gone in a heartbeat. They were no longer straight ahead of him, but coming in from the right and left.

The shrieks and cries of his deputies surrounded the house.

Hurley darted to the right, rushed around the corner of

the house, and nearly ran into a deputy kneeling on the ground. Hurley could not tell who it was at first—in the beam of his flashlight, the face was dark with blood, and a flap of skin dangled from the right cheek. Then the sheriff recognized Deputy Alan Stark.

"They're everywhere!" the deputy screamed. "We're surrounded! They came outta nowhere, they were—"

A shaggy arm swiped suddenly out of the darkness and curved claws struck Deputy Stark's neck. His head tumbled through the air, thumped to the ground, and the body dropped limply.

Hurley turned his flashlight on the creature and fired without hesitation. The werewolf flinched, then lunged toward him with a growl. Hurley fired again.

It staggered to a halt. Its silver eyes widened with shock and confusion. It made an ugly sound of pain, then staggered to one side and dropped to its knees, Hurley forgotten.

The sheriff moved on, but without destination or purpose.

Deputies fell and staggered all around him. Some fought and struggled in the grip of the large creatures, but were quickly silenced and killed with the snap of fanged jaws or the slice of a hairy, clawed hand.

Another werewolf stepped in front of him and Hurley fired once—followed by an empty click. The werewolf staggered backward with a whining cry and disappeared into the darkness.

Hurley tried to reload, but his hands shook and he dropped the gun.

There was movement everywhere, the sounds of running, of bodies lunging through bushes and tall weeds. They were accompanied by sounds of pain and death, and the savage cries of wild, ravenous animals.

He thought of the shotgun in his SUV. He quickly turned and ran toward the front of the house.

Hurley slammed so hard into something large and hairy that the impact knocked him backward, and he fell to the ground. His flashight slipped from his hand, spun through the air, and disappeared in a patch of ferns.

Cold rain fell on him where he lay. But the cold he'd been feeling suddenly grew worse, and cut through him to his marrow.

Something above him engulfed his field of vision.

The screams of the wounded and dying cut through the darkness all around.

A chilling howl rose up, then another, and another.

Something large descended on Hurley. It closed its hands on the front of his jacket and lifted him from the ground without effort. It pulled him close, his feet off the ground, until there was little more than an inch between the creature's face and Hurley's.

It had only one eye. The left eye socket was empty and shallow.

Its face hovered somewhere between that of a man and that of a wolf. The right eye studied him.

"This . . . is . . . *Fargo's* work," it said, its voice a rumbling threat. "*He* brought you here. Yes?" Its hot breath smelled of blood and rotting meat.

Hurley stared in silent horror and panic.

"*Yes?*" it prodded, shaking him slightly.

Slowly, Hurley nodded.

The sounds of death and chaos went on all around them, but Hurley's attention was focused with laser precision on the face before him.

"Where is he?" the creature asked.

Hurley's mouth was as dry as a desert rock. Thoughts swirled in his mind.

Several long seconds passed before the creature said, "Tell me."

Hurley could not muster a voice.

The creature's grip tightened on Hurley's jacket as it growled, "*Tell* me . . . and you'll live."

The three words worked their way up from Hurley's fear-strangled throat and croaked out of his dry mouth before he knew he was saying them: "Buh-Beachcomber Motor Luh-Lodge!"

A slow smile stretched over the hideous face, revealing lengthening fangs.

Oh, Ella, Hurley thought, the name sounding in his mind with a note of terrified, hopeless surrender.

As the creature spoke, its mouth and nose extended into a long, triangular muzzle that drained what little humanity remained in its features. It said, "I lied."

Fargo was pacing his motel room, leaning heavily on his cane, when the knock at the door came. More than two hours had passed, and Fargo's nerves had grown raw as he waited for the phone to ring.

The knock came again, harder this time.

"Fargo?" a muffled voice said.

Standing in the middle of the room, frowning at the door, Fargo said, "Who is it?"

The voice said something garbled and indistinguishable, but the word "sheriff" stood out from it all.

"Sheriff Hurley?" Fargo said urgently, hurrying to the door.

He pulled the chain, turned the deadbolt, and swept the door open.

Daniel Fargo had time before dying to do only one thing—with his unpatched left eye, he recognized Irving Taggart's face.

Days later . . .

The sleeping baby curled up in the bassinet in the empty, bare-walled living room began to cry.

The cry had a hollow sound in the unfurnished room. Cardboard boxes of all sizes were stacked everywhere over the hardwood floor.

Lucy hurried from the kitchen, bent down over the bassinet, and picked up her baby girl.

"Oh, is Mommy's baby all woke up now?" she said through a smile as she pulled little Carla Jean Ives to her chest. Lucy's red hair was pulled back from her fair, freckled face and tied in a ponytail with a string of green yarn. She wore a paint-stained gray sweatshirt, jeans, and an old pair of blue deck shoes. She bobbed Carla gently in her arms until the cries became gurgling murmurs.

Lucy carried the baby back into the kitchen, where she'd left her cell phone on the counter. She picked up the phone and put it to her ear again. "Carla's awake now, Mom, so I should probably go."

"Does Larry have anyone to help him?" Lucy's mother said.

"Nobody but Eddie and me."

"Well, I hate to think of you doing all that work alone, honey. Can't you call someone for help?"

"We just got here, Mom. We don't know anyone."

"Why didn't you hire movers?"

"We can't afford that right now."

"You should've *said* something! I would've been happy to pay for movers."

"Don't worry, Mom, we'll be fine, really."

"Is Larry going to be able to start the new job next week? I mean, if you don't have any help moving in—"

"Look, Mom, I need to feed Carla now, then I should go out and help Larry finish unloading the truck. We're going to be fine, I promise."

"Well . . . okay. You'll call me this evening?"

"Yes, as soon as Carla and Eddie are down for the night, I'll call you."

"All right. Give Larry my love."

After ending the conversation, Lucy turned the phone off and put it down on the counter again. She talked baby talk to Carla as she carried her over to the high chair and settled her in. Then she searched the grocery bags on the card table they'd set up in the kitchen and found a jar of baby food.

Pounding footsteps stomped into the house accompanied by the voices of two little boys making race-car noises. Nine-year-old Eddie came into the kitchen with a chubby blond boy and said, "Hey, Mom, this is our neighbor, Clay!"

Lucy smiled down at the boy and said, "Hello, Clay."

"He lives next door," Eddie said. "He's got a Nintendo Wii! Can I go over and play it with him?"

"Not right now, honey," Lucy said. "Daddy and I need you to help us as much as you can, okay? We need to unload that truck and get the stuff in the house in case it rains. We've got furniture all over the front yard."

"Can I help?" Clay said.

"Sure, if you'd like," Lucy said.

"But Dad doesn't need any help right now," Eddie said. "He's talking to the cop."

Lucy's smile fell away. "Cop?"

"Yeah, out on the front lawn."

Frowning, Lucy went to the window that looked out on the front yard. A Sheriff's Department SUV was parked at the curb in front of the house, and Larry stood beside a uniformed officer on the lawn, their backs to her. The officer held a cell phone to his left ear.

Lucy picked up the baby again and left the kitchen. She went through the living room and out the front door to the porch.

Fat gray clouds crowded the sky, but beams of sunlight broke through the narrow spaces in between. The air was cool and damp and carried a hint of the ocean's scent.

"Larry?" Lucy said.

He turned to her, smiled, then walked over to the porch. "Hey," he said, "our big girl's awake, huh?"

The officer continued to talk on the phone.

Quietly, Lucy said, "Is everything all right?"

"Oh, yeah, sure. He's the sheriff. He just happened to be driving by and he saw the truck and all the stuff on the lawn, so he stopped to welcome us to the neighborhood."

"Oh," she said, her eyebrows bobbing up. "Well, that was nice." She looked past Larry at the sheriff as he took the phone away from his ear, folded it closed, and dropped it into his pocket. He turned around and smiled up at her as he approached.

"You must be Lucy," he said amiably. "Nice to meet you. Welcome to Big Rock."

"Nice to meet you, too," she said, noticing the black patch over his left eye.

"I'm the sheriff of Pine County," he said. "Sheriff Irving Taggart.